Pot Shot

Pot Shot

LAURA PIPER LEE

NEW YORK

Cover design by Patrick Sullivan
Cover art by Vi-An Nguyen
Cover images by Shutterstock.com: Tony Oshlick (leaf), MOJI (vectors)

Union Square & Co.
Hachette Book Group
1290 Avenue of the Americas, New York, NY 10104
unionsquareandco.com
@unionsqandco

First Edition: May 2026

Union Square & Co. is an imprint of Grand Central Publishing, a division of Hachette Book Group, Inc. The Union Square & Co. name and logo are registered trademarks of Hachette Book Group, Inc.

Library of Congress Cataloging-in-Publication Data has been applied for.

ISBNs: 978-1-4549-6555-8 (trade paperback), 978-1-4549-6556-5 (ebook)

Printed in Canada

MRQ-L

10 9 8 7 6 5 4 3 2

For anyone who's ever felt
like they had to hide
the hurting parts of themselves
to be easier to love.

AUTHOR'S NOTE

Pot Shot is a fun, heartwarming romantic comedy, but please be aware that the story also contains discussions and depictions of chronic illness, Crohn's disease, Parkinson's disease, seizure disorders, cancer, disability, anxiety, depression, consensual sex scenes, and of course, cannabis use. This book does not contain medical advice. If you are interested in any of the topics discussed, please talk with a qualified healthcare provider to learn more.

CHAPTER ONE

NOMI

It's eleven p.m. the night before our Memorial Day beach trip, so you know what *that* means.

Pube chores.

Grimacing, I wrestle the electric razor free from its packaging. As a natural brunette, I have no choice. When I purchased the red, bandana-printed bikini, I didn't realize it'd look like a bearded bandit robbing the county bank down there. I've gotta take care of business.

Regrettably, business is *booming*.

I plug in the razor and hike a foot onto the bathroom counter. I saw this tip on a male makeover show, and if men can buzz their body hair away, why can't I? It's satisfying, removing whole stripes of hair at a time, and way less painful than waxing. *Genius*, I huff.

I traverse nooks and crannies with ease and pause for a quick tug of weed from my vape. It's a new strain I'm trying for work, and my head feels thick and syrupy. The body high's spreading, too, and a pleasant, giddy rush tingles in my lower belly.

Ahh. I make a mental note. *This is horny pot.*

I take another hit, admiring the line of my leg in the mirror's reflection, then release the vapor seductively in an exaggerated pucker.

Behold your Valedictorian, Sparrow Nook, New Jersey, for she has come *far*.

The clipper guard yanks a thick patch and I hiss, nearly losing my balance. I toss the offending plastic away. I need a closer shave, anyway, which will be good enough as long as nobody gets too close down there.

Fortunately/unfortunately, nobody ever does. Contrary to what my best friends Eve and Graham think, I don't *try* not to date. It comes very naturally. When I was younger, I was too sick to care. Now that my Crohn's disease is technically in remission, which means I only get sick once or twice a month instead of constant misery, I *still* don't care. Dating is hard, stressful, and involves too many restaurants and public bathrooms. It's easier to just…not, and focus on my health, friendships, and opening my dream business—a cannabis dispensary with lounge à la Amsterdam "coffeehouse." Great lighting, excellent vibes, and a place you can buy, partake, *and* socialize.

I sigh dreamily as I raze my bikini line down to the skin.

Once New Jersey legalized cannabis, it was like a spotlight clicked on and an aggressive stage manager whisper-yelled *"Showtime!"* before shoving me onstage. I'd been lost for so long, unsure of what to do with my life when illness consumed so much of it. But as soon as the legislation passed, I started researching how to open my own dispensary. I got a job at the first one in the area, worked up to manager, and I've been planning and saving ever since.

See? No time for love.

When the right hemisphere of my mons pubis is suitably bald, I eye the narrow strip of hair lining the inner sanctum.

You could leave it, Spinster Nomi whispers in my head. *Nobody will ever see it. <cackles>*

I take another tug of weed.

She's right, of course. Nobody has ventured this far since . . . when was that party where I made out with Lil Dom, Sparrow Nook's goofiest cop?

Ugh, she fake retches in my head. *I still can't believe you made out with Lil Dom!*

"I was lonely," I mutter aloud. "I liked his mustache."

See? You can't be trusted, she says. *Leave the inner bush as deterrent.*

I sigh. As much as I'd like to, it looks ridiculous. How can I respect *myself* with the Swedish Chef lurking in my panties? It's like a soul patch with too much soul. A metaphorical NO TRESPASSERS sign surrounded by weeds. I take another hit, lean into the one-legged lunge on my counter, and spread myself carefully—

My front door slams against the wall. I shriek as the bulky razor slips, colliding horrifically with flesh, then falls. My foot careens off the counter.

"Nomi!" Eve calls. "You've gotta try these! Nomi?"

I look down at the warm, slick coating of blood on my fingers and the shrieks graduate to screams. Eve throws the bathroom door open, and now she's screaming, too. Evangeline Ionides may present as a black cat lesbian, but she's the human equivalent of the pot-laced cinnamon rolls she makes every Christmas. Eve does not *do* strife; she cannot witness suffering. A softie of the highest order.

"Jesus, Nomi!" Eve gapes at my hunched body naked from the waist down. Blood drips between my fingers onto the tile, and she covers her eyes immediately. "Is that your period?! Why's it so heavy, oh my GOD!"

"*No,* you dweeb! I cut myself shaving!" I moan at the sharp stinging pain coming from just left of center, in folds town. "Hand me a towel!"

Eve fumbles one-handed around my bathroom, still covering her eyes, chanting *oh, God* until she finds a towel and throws it at me. It lands over my head. Everything goes dark.

"*Eve!*" I stumble into the wall. "*Fuck!* I'm the one with the injury—calm down!"

"How can I calm down?!" Eve screeches. "You want to have children one day!"

Her words are muffled by the towel still over my head. I can't let go of the—*area*—or else the world will end. My head feels strange and light.

"Call Dr. Appa—I think I need stitches." I stagger into her. "Please, Eve. Need you to be *calm*."

"Okay, okay, this is okay," Eve says far too loudly as she holds me up. "I'm gonna wrap your—"

"—area."

"—area," Eve agrees, "with this towel."

"Don't make me move my hands," I mewl. I'm the little Dutch boy with his finger in the dike, except this is taking all my fingers, and I'm theoretically straight.

Eve grabs the towel and wraps it around my lower half. It's big enough for the edges to meet but not fold over, so she holds them shut as we shuffle pathetically to her car.

"How did this happen?!"

"You! You happened! Your car's out front—I thought you were upstairs, asleep!" Eve and I share an old Craftsman bungalow split into two extremely non-regulation apartments that her Uncle Dimitri rents to us super cheap. The *reason* it's so cheap is that the only way to reach the upstairs apartment is by walking through the downstairs apartment to the one stairwell. This isn't the first time Eve's terrified me by barging in, but it's definitely the bloodiest.

"I was at Graham's because it's too hot to bake upstairs right now. We perfected the new recipe for the pot scones, by the way. The key was *pomegranate*—can you believe it? The tart sweet blends with the cannabis just right, and I was so excited, I couldn't wait to show you!" Eve, our future dispensary's ultra-talented baker, stops chattering to gag a little at my bloody leg, then guides me into the front seat and buckles me in. "Do you want one?"

"*No!*"

"You sure? You know how scones dry out. They won't keep for tomorrow—"

"Eve, drive!" I blink against the bleary weight of the drugs already in my system. "Wait, *can* you drive? Are you high right now?"

"No." She glances at my toweled lap and laughs nervously. "Not yet at least. Scones haven't hit."

"*Scones?* Plural?!"

"Experimentation requires sacrifice, Nomi!"

Eve speeds through the streets of Sparrow Nook, our quaint town located halfway between Philadelphia and the long, sandy strip of the Jersey Shore. So help me God, Eve better not get us pulled over for speeding. Lil Dom got dumped a month ago, and speeding tickets in Sparrow Nook have tripled since. There was an article about it in the paper and everything.

"Was it the big flap?" Eve's eyes flick from the road to me.

"Huh?"

"You know, the big flap. Every woman has one big flap."

"What? No, they don't."

"Hate to pull the lesbian card, but I've seen *quite* a few flaps, and—"

"*Eve!* Just park!"

Eve jerks into a spot in front of the old Strange Drugs Pharmacy. The COMING SOON: FOR LEASE sign in its window winks at me as Eve pulls me from the car. I moan, not wanting my dream location for our dispensary to see me like this. We waddle past it—me in front, Eve holding my towel from behind—one door down to the clinic run by Sparrow Nook's beloved Dr. Srinivasan, better known as Dr. Appa. Sparrow Nook doesn't have its own hospital or emergency room—you'd have to drive half an hour for that—but we do have Dr. Appa. During the day, he runs a family practice, and at night, he has on-call urgent-care hours.

And tonight, I need poor, elderly Dr. Appa to urgently care for my *area*.

"You called ahead, right?" I pant as Eve readjusts my towel.

"Yeah, Dr. Appa said the new guy's working tonight."

"*New* guy?" I wail, a wave of dizziness crashing over me. "I don't want a *new* guy! I want Dr. Appa!"

"NEW GUY!" Eve yells as soon as we're inside. "WE HAVE AN EMERGENCY!"

The reception area is empty and quiet except for the buzz of the fluorescent lights, the daytime staff long gone. It's creepy. Standing here, inconveniently high and half-naked beneath a towel in front of the kids' area with its disappointing wooden toys, feels *especially* wrong. Footsteps hurry from the back, and I blink as the new guy's face comes into focus. Dark, wavy hair parted on the side, the tips ending in springy little curls. A pair of gold-rimmed glasses shoved high on a long, straight nose. Behind them, big, blue eyes stare at me in disbelief.

No.

The broad-shouldered man in the white doctor coat freezes. His face turns pale and ashen, as if it's *his* vulva that's hemorrhaging. "Nomi… *Wyeth*?"

"*No!*" I try to step backward, but Eve's there, blocking my exit.

"Yes, that's her name!" Eve speaks loudly from behind my back. "Her big flap's bleeding out, doctor. I think she's confused." Eve, who clearly hasn't even *looked* at New Guy, corrals me toward him. I'm still clutching my area, too afraid to let up the pressure, and her shove knocks me off balance. I tip over, my face smooshing against the name embroidered in blue cursive over his chest pocket, confirming that, *yes*, my worst nightmare is happening *right now*.

Dr. Julian D'Angelo.

First my high school rival, briefly my . . . I don't *know* what, then my absolute nemesis and now, apparently, my *doctor*? What's he doing here? He lives in Philly—works in an ER there, last I heard. He hates Sparrow Nook!

Julian catches me by the elbows with a sharp intake of air as he clocks the blood running down my legs. The horrified recognition of who I am is replaced with professional medical urgency.

"What happened?"

Before I can stutter out *clearance rack electric razor*, Eve gasps, mentally a moment behind us.

"Julian D'Angelo?!" Her hands go distressingly slack, and then, I feel it: the cool kiss of air on my ass as Eve drops the towel. In the immortal words of Kate McKinnon, I'm now Porky-Pigging it in my cropped T-shirt and nothing else in front of Julian fucking D'Angelo.

Maybe I should just bleed out.

Julian eyes us. "Are you on *recreational drugs*?"

Eve blurts out "*No!*"—a juvenile reflex to Julian's big cop energy, though cannabis is fully legal. The obvious lie is undercut by my stupid T-shirt featuring a red-eyed Colonel Sanders holding a bucket of green buds labeled *THC*, which our eyes flick to simultaneously.

Julian's jaw clamps shut, and then he *picks me up* princess-style like I weigh nothing. In high school, Julian was a string bean of a guy—all height, spite, and sharp elbows. But *Dr. Julian D'Angelo* is—wow. Something *altogether* different. I stare up at the freshly shaven line of his jaw and try to process this stunning turn of events as my life force drains from my vulva.

Julian was the first person I met at Sparrow Nook High. I'd just moved to the sleepy, *almost-a-shore* town from Atlanta two weeks before my senior year. As a quiet, southern goth girl with a perfect GPA, the move up north felt tantamount to social annihilation. A feeling confirmed when I walked into the debate team's practice after school hoping to find my people and found Julian instead. He took one look at my dyed-black hair and skull-patterned fishnets, rolled his bespectacled blue eyes, and said: *Detention's down the hall.*

I've been pissed at him ever since.

Julian was completely obsessed with prestige and being the best. The best GPA, the best SAT scores, first place at every debate tournament—he won every single accolade.

Until I snatched *valedictorian* out of his maniacal hands. Which are now, coincidentally, about to inspect folds town.

"Tell me what happened," he orders.

"Pube chores!" Eve yells just as I say, "Shaving accident!"

I moan, more from mortification than pain at this point.

Julian enters Patient Room #2 and lowers me gently onto a white table-cot that I immediately ruin, then pulls out the stirrups for my feet. "LET GO OF YOUR VULVA," he commands at an insane volume, but I shake my head furiously.

"I can't, I can't!"

"*Yes,* you *can.*" The latex glove slaps his skin as he pulls it on. He glares at me as he approaches with an epic amount of gauze. "I have to look at your—"

"—area," I mewl.

Julian's face is redder than I've ever seen it. "*—vulva,*" he corrects, which is so much worse. Oh, God. Julian D'Angelo's going to see my *vulva.*

"Where's the injury?" he barks.

"She said somewhere left of center," Eve supplies from the doorway. "In folds town!"

Jesus, I said that *aloud*?

"Only family can be back here." His eyes narrow. "Are you *family*?"

Eve considers this. "I mean, not technically, but from a spiritual perspective—"

"Then *get out*!"

My eyes widen. Julian has the bedside manner of a German shepherd on meth. Eve winces at me apologetically, then runs for the waiting room.

He spins back to me. "On the count of three, you're going to let go, and I'm going to staunch the wound with this gauze. You will be *fine*. Ready?"

"No," I cry. "Call Dr. Appa! Make him come in!"

"Dr. Srinivasan is at home asleep, so you're stuck with me, Wyeth." Julian's blue eyes are as intense now as they were staring me down across our debate podiums. "One."

"No-no-no!"

"Two." He leans forward, like he's about to pounce.

I squinch up my entire face.

"THREE!"

And God help me, I do it. I let go. I squeal as Julian's broad palm comes down like a hammer against the entire area. There's at least an inch of gauze between us, but the firm pressure feels like such relief, I collapse backward, limp. When I open my eyes, Julian's poised between my parted legs. His face is nearly purple now.

He's breathing in, silently counting to four and out for a count of six.

"Are you—alright?" What is it with other people experiencing palpable distress over *my* bloody vu—area?

His eyes snap up to mine. "I'm *fine*. Once again, are you under the influence of recreational drugs?"

"No."

Yes. But I'm not telling him that.

I scowl at the wall. Guess legalization didn't shake Julian's historic scorn for cannabis.

His gaze flicks down to the gauze, then back to my face. He clears his throat. “The bleeding is under control now. I’m going to remove the gauze so I can inspect the wound.”

“No!” I slam my knees together on instinct, trapping his hand there. Julian’s expression is truly alarmed. “I-I’m scared,” I finally admit, my knees slacking open.

“I’ll be gentle,” he says, his voice low and strangely husky. It plucks something inside of me. Julian sucks a deep breath in and repositions his palm slightly, sending a wave of heat through my broken bits up to my belly.

Oh, NO! Spinster Nomi gasps. *The horny pot!*

Now I’m as red as Julian. I start to cover my face with my hands, but they’re coated with blood. There’s nowhere to hide in this hell I’ve entered. *Please don’t get wet. Please don’t get—*

“I’m peeling back the corner.” Julian removes the gauze. Another sharp breath in.

“Is it that bad?” I cry.

“No, but I need to—remove the blood—to examine the laceration.” His words come out thick, and he clears his throat as he dabs the area with saline-soaked gauze. His touch is surprisingly soothing, and I start the same breathing technique just to keep my head on straight about this.

Julian D’Angelo is cleaning my vulva.

Julian D’ANGELO is CLEANING my VULVA.

JULIAN D’ANG—

“Wyeth...” He bites both of his lips in, making direct, unblinking eye contact with, oh *hell*, folds town. “You need sutures.”

“No,” I whisper, even though part of me always knew this is how it would end. Not the stitches, exactly, but dying of embarrassment. You don’t get to thirty-three as a woman with Crohn’s disease, arguably the most embarrassing disease of all time, without coming close to expiring via mortification.

And now, my time has come.

"Slide forward."

I scoot toward the cot's edge, but my face twists in discomfort, and wordlessly, Julian places his large hands on either side of my hips and lifts. His skin is warm through the gloves, giving me goose bumps down the length of my legs as he tugs me forward, bringing me to the cot's edge.

I want to *die.* And also, have sex.

Julian lifts my left calf, *also* unshaven, until it's bent at the knee, placing my foot gingerly into one of the stirrups, then the other. My knees instinctively fall together, but he pulls them apart to step fully between my legs. The sight of stern, adult Julian hovering over me, his face taut with vicious concentration, sends a lightning bolt through my entire being.

Oh, Jesus. I'm *definitely* getting wet.

Julian lowers himself onto a stool between my stirrups until all I can see is his disembodied head floating between my legs. With one hand, he parts my flesh, giving him full access to my—

"Left labium," he says to no one, his voice strangely choked, "laceration approximately—three centimeters, presenting with mild damage to the—soft tissue."

He sounds like a doctor on an ER show, but there's no nurse standing by to hand him instruments. Meanwhile I've entered some Zen, dissociative state as the guy who once petitioned the Sparrow Nook Board of Education to revoke my valedictorian eligibility on the sole basis that my prior credits were earned in *Georgia*, and thus, inherently suspect, slathers a numbing cream across folds town. I turn and face the wall, squeezing my lips shut as Julian D'Angelo proceeds to stitch up my *labium.*

"All done." He peels off his gloves and tosses them in the trash, then bolts for the door. I stare at his fleeing back in disbelief.

"Wait!"

Julian freezes and, reluctantly, peers at me over his shoulder. "What?"

I blink, then gesture below. "What do I do about this?"

He frowns at my half-shaved bush, a study in contrasts. Finally, he coughs.

"It's a... vibe. I guess."

I blink. "I was referring to the fact I have no pants?"

Julian's eyes widen behind his gold frames, and the blush returns full force. "*Ah.*" He disappears and returns a moment later with scrubs, facing the door while I hobble into the soft pants one leg at a time. I feel the need to say something, to smooth over this moment with a laugh, with *anything* that would make it feel like what just happened won't embarrass me until the end of time.

"I can't believe Julian D'Asshole just sewed up my labium." I don't know why the old nickname half the school called him comes back to me now, or why I thought using it would be a good idea. He always hated it, and by the look of his tightening shoulders, he still does. He swirls around to face me, all pretenses of professional courtesy gone.

"Well, *I* can't believe I had to deal with Nomi Wyeth's mangled genitalia because of"—his eyes flash as he air quotes—"*pube chores.*" He shakes his head, disgusted. "Congratulations, Wyeth. You've ruined lasagna forever."

My mouth drops open. Did he just compare my vulva to, to, *lasagna*?! Fury floods my entire body.

"Whatever, Julian, you've *always* wanted to see my vulva, and you know it!" I storm into the hallway, holding up the too-big scrubs by the waistband.

"Keep the laceration clean and dry!" He sticks his head into the hallway to yell after me. "And I did *not* want to see your vulva!"

CHAPTER TWO

JULIAN

I *did* want to see her vulva.

I lope back and forth in my office like a wild animal penned in a cage, which is what this combination-Pizza-Hut-Taco-Bell-Family-Practice-Urgent-Care-Clinic feels like right now. I take off my glasses and fling them on the desk, then release a guttural groan at the ceiling. Nomi Wyeth was stretched out half naked before me, fulfilling every one of my formative sexual fantasies—save for the stage two laceration on her outer labia, I'm not a *total* freak—and what did I do?

I said the shape of her remaining pubic hair was a *vibe*.

I run my palms down my face and groan again.

I should resign. Ridiculous commentary aside, I . . . felt things when treating her, and that's unacceptable. The doctor-patient relationship is built on trust that depends on my professional detachment from normally exciting body parts, and yet, there was *nothing* detached about pressing my palm against Nomi's soft, warm cunt. My eyes flutter back in my head, dick stiffening for the second time tonight.

I bark out a sharp laugh of despair. The only way I could be more of a disgrace would be rubbing one out in my office while the memory of my last patient and, coincidentally, the only woman who's ever driven me insane, is still fresh.

I slam down in my chair. After a minute of cradling my throbbing skull, I call Eric's emergency line. The phone rings five times before a groggy voice answers:

"Dr. Sampson speaking, what is your emergency?"

"Eric," I croak. "I have to resign from the medical profession."

There's some muffled cursing while Eric adjusts the phone. "Julian, it's after midnight. What, and I say this with love, the *fuck* is wrong with you?"

"I got a semi-erection while suturing a stage two laceration on my high school crush's vulva."

Eric curses again, this time directly into the receiver. "Okay. That's bad. What happened?"

I regale the entire saga, from the moment Nomi showed up to the unfortunate lasagna comment. "I even considered masturbating in my office," I confess wearily. "But I called you instead."

Eric exhales. "There are things you don't have to tell me. Many things, in fact."

"You're my advisor," I counter.

"I was," Eric agrees. "Years ago. When you were in medical school. Now I'm just some guy you call in the middle of the night instead of whacking off."

"Eric, could you not make this about you? I'm in crisis." I lay my forehead flat against the desk and prop the cell phone against my ear. "How does one resign from the medical profession?"

"You're not resigning. You didn't *do* anything inappropriate. Well, except for the lasagna comment."

I whimper.

"—and ultimately, nothing inappropriate occurred," Eric concludes. "You are a human. These things happen."

"Has it ever happened to you?" I sit up straighter.

Eric snorts. "I'm an orthopedic surgeon that specializes in feet. I've never gotten an erection while performing a bunionectomy."

"What about a semi?"

"What do *you* think?"

"That I'm a reprobate." I slump back down. "I'm so disappointed in myself. First Philly Gen, and now this. I can't even make it in a goddamn family practice."

"This is a new position for you. You just left one of the biggest hospitals in the country, where you had specialized colleagues that handled all the gynecological emergencies that came in, right?"

I pause, not wanting to be made to feel better but also unable to argue with my advisor. "Well, yes."

"Ergo, you don't have experience with vulvas."

"Yes, I do," I spout indignantly. Maybe not a lot of *repeat* experience because, according to the last woman I slept with, my looks only go so far in overcoming my personality.

"With *treating* vulvas," Eric amends, the smile in his voice audible. "And this wasn't some random stranger, which would be very concerning. This was a special person from your past."

"She's not special," I spit out. "She's a stoner who carved my heart out with a blunt."

"That's... not how those work. Alright, Julian. I've got to keep this line clear for actual patients with actual emergencies. You gonna be okay?"

"No! You haven't given me advice yet!"

"Sure I have. Let's do a recap: First, don't quit the medical profession. You're an incredible doctor with subpar social skills. You got away with that in the ER until you didn't, which is how you've landed here. You've got six months to improve your atrocious bedside manner before Philly Gen will consider taking you back. This family practice position will force you to level up, and you need to take it seriously."

I groan.

"Second, don't masturbate in your office, and don't call me instead, either."

"But you're my advisor!"

"Not in the job description. Third, you need to apologize to Ms. Stoner."

"Are you sure avoiding her for the rest of my life isn't a viable alternative to," I take a deep breath, "*apologizing*"?

"It isn't, because after you apologize, you're going to ask her out. And if she offers you a puff, by God, take it. I've never met a man who could benefit more from smoking weed than you."

"I can't believe you just said that."

"Believe it, Dr. D'Angelo. That is your chief advisor's medical opinion."

"Yes, sir." Funny how fast that flies out of my mouth, all these years later. "But I *resent it*, sir."

I don't remember exactly when Dr. Sampson became *Eric*, perhaps during residency? But he said at our first advisory meeting during orientation week in medical school that if I had a question, I could always come to him.

He's openly regretted that a few dozen times since.

After we disconnect, I spend the rest of the shift in a mortified haze with occasional breaks of activity. Ms. Petrillo's grandson with a high temperature and a bad case of the flu. Billy Clark's broken thumb. Nothing to top Nomi's mangled labia, though. God, I feel terrible, betrayed by my body in a moment when a patient needed me to be professional. Worse, there's nothing to break me out of the loop of shame and frustration I keep cycling through. Nobody could ruin lasagna, it's *impossible*! Seeing Nomi after so many years—still beautiful, still feisty in that hot-blooded way of hers, still in Sparrow Nook doing nothing with her life? It's maddening, and this idle night shift is making it worse. Time passed relentlessly in the Philly Gen ER, every heartbeat bringing a new disaster to triage. I didn't have time for this ridiculous introspection. But by morning, I've reconciled with what must be done:

I'll apologize to Nomi Wyeth.

Even though she stole my valedictorian title *and* my heart only to throw it all away smoking weed with that terror Eve Ionides, I'll do it. I'll apologize to the first girl I ever kissed. The first person to break my heart. And because the universe hates me, the first vulva I've ever stitched up.

What a night.

"Good morning, Julian." Dr. Srinivasan putters into our shared office at seven thirty, newspaper under one arm, a large coffee in the other. "How did your shift go?"

I stand up and smooth the front of my coat, the memory of Nomi's pert ass momentarily parching my mouth. "Uneventful."

"Oh?" Dr. Srinivasan plops down in the rolling chair I just vacated and promptly adjusts the height, springing him up half a foot taller. "That is interesting, as I received a complaint about you to my cell phone."

The blood drains from my upper extremities and pools in my belly. Did Nomi spy the outline of my semi-erect penis? It's aggressively present when I'm at zero stimulation and outrageous when fully erect. A former girlfriend dubbed it a *protruder*, and I've been self-conscious of it ever since.

Or was it Eve Ionides? Did that mean little lesbian *see my penis*?!

"Calm down, Julian, you look like you're about to stroke out." Dr. Srinivasan gestures for me to sit, and I do, reluctantly. I've known him since I was little and coming in for my own yearly checkups. It's still an adjustment to think of him as my boss.

Dr. Srinivasan looks at me appraisingly, but he doesn't check the front of my pants, which is a good sign, I think. "Ms. Petrillo texted that you were very rude and implied her grandson contracted the flu from, and I quote, 'licking doorknobs.'"

I exhale, letting my back rest against the seat. "He's three years old. Aren't they all licking doorknobs at that age?"

"No, they're not tall enough. You also received a complaint from Mr. Donahue about his diabetic medication two days ago."

"What did I say to him?"

His eyebrow arches, disrupting the rows of forehead wrinkles like a stone thrown into a lake. "You called his insulin his cheesecake shots."

I arch my brow right back. "He eats a slice every morning, Dr. Srinivasan. For *breakfast*!"

Dr. Srinivasan sighs. "The last thing a patient wants is their doctor's scorn. It's your job to help, not to shame."

"Even when they're being stupid?"

"*Especially* when they're being stupid." Dr. Srinivasan chuckles. "Being a primary care physician in a town this size requires you to be more than right—it requires you to listen and be *likable.* Skills you must learn if you want Philly Gen to reinstate you."

I cross my arms. "My ER patients never complained I wasn't likable."

"Well, my patients aren't unconscious or bleeding out, Julian. You have to be nicer to these ones."

I scowl, aware that I'm sulking and unable to stop it. I should be kissing Dr. Srinivasan's feet for the opportunity to serve my probation here. After what happened at Philly Gen, I had to beg Dr. Riveras not to fire me on the spot. If it were up to the Corringtons, Philly's richest family, the hospital's biggest donor, and coincidentally, the sponsor for my fellowship, I'd never practice medicine again. But Dr. Riveras relented after I agreed to take a six-month leave of absence to *work on my nonexistent people skills* and *learn how to listen for fucking once* and *get my head out of my own ass.* The best way to do that, she decided, was by serving in the ultimate patient service capacity—as a primary care physician in a family practice out of the public eye long enough that the Corringtons forget what I did.

Which turned out to be nearly impossible. Dr. Riveras didn't report me to the state medical board for what happened, but word still traveled fast. I contacted every family practice within thirty miles of Philadelphia, but I was as employable as RFK, Jr. in a vaccine clinic. Nobody would have me because nobody wanted to cross the Corringtons.

Nobody except Dr. Srinivasan. And *only* because my mother called and asked him on my behalf. I cringe reflexively, gutted that my poor mom, who spent the last five years of my father's life rescuing him, had to rescue me, too—something I vowed she'd never need to do. When my father passed away and abandoned us for good, twelve-year-old Julian sat silently at his service, listening to all his friends and family laugh and cry over what a good time Anthony D'Angelo was. The life of the party. He could take more shots than a boxer and keep standing, as if that was something to be proud of. Nobody talked about *after* the big accident—how it left him hobbled and unsure, how he retreated from the real world into our garage and let Mom bear all the burdens of our family. But that's the Anthony D'Angelo that *I* knew, and I swore the day we buried him I'd be nothing like him. That I'd be the best. The best son, the best student, the best doctor, and one day, the best husband. The best father. The people I love would *always* know how much, because I'd take the best care of them.

But I never realized how alienating becoming the best would be. How the long hours studying pushed away friends, the longer hours working made dating impossible, and how my determination to succeed seemed to be a never-ending source of complaints from my family. It doesn't matter that I landed a competitive fellowship at one of the most prestigious hospitals in the country—here, I'm Little Julie Try-Hard and Julian D'Asshole, somehow the biggest joke in an entire family of jokes. The D'Angelos are to Sparrow Nook like pigeons are to New York City: *everywhere*, and typically fighting over pizza. It's impossible to go anywhere in town without running into one of my loser relatives, which is why yesterday I drove twenty minutes to the good grocery store. The last time I went to the local Acme, my Aunt Patty was the only cashier working. After tutting over each of my items, she informed the entire eighty-seven D'Angelos on the family text chain that I was buying orgasmic bananas. It was a typo, I *think*, but I've received unsolicited banana pics for a solid week. Is it any wonder that in Sparrow Nook, the D'Angelo name solicits an eyeroll and a pitying laugh? I've spent my whole life trying to set myself above and apart from the D'Angelos, to prove that I'm not like *any* of them. That, unlike them and my irresponsible, undependable heartbreak of a father, I am a force to be reckoned with and respected.

And yet, here I am, enduring the spectacle of my ridiculous family while I languish in this purgatory, forced to treat people who think diner cheesecake is a valid source of protein until December. There's nothing for it—I *have* to convince Dr. Riveras to reinstate me and get my career back on track to becoming the best, where I belong.

But to do that, I have to learn to be... *likable*?

How the hell am I going to do that?

CHAPTER THREE

NOMI

"Welcome to Xscape Your Brain: An Herbaceous Experience, this is your cannabis counselor, Nomi. How can I help you?" I press the headset to my ear to hear the crackly drive-through order, making me feel like a Secret Service agent receiving covert tactical information, or Britney Spears. Except in my case, the voice that burbles through the headphones is a fourteen-year-old trying to get around the legal buying age.

"Ah, yes," the child clears his throat, "I would like two pounds of *Mom-Mom's Hasherole*, please."

I glance at the drive-through camera screen and the pack of giggling ninth graders on Huffy bikes. "We don't sell by the pound, Tom D'Angelo. Or to kids, for that matter."

"I'm not—Tom," Tom squeals, then remembers to pitch his voice lower. "I'm Tom's older brother—*Desmond.* Are you . . . busy later?"

I sigh into the mouthpiece. "Vacate the drive-through now, or I'll contact your Aunt Veronica."

"RUN!" Tom screeches. Rubber tires squeal as the little doofuses scramble away. I shift on the drive-through window seat, uncomfortably aware of the pad I'm wearing in lieu of a bandage. Eve bought me the thickest maxi pads known to woman as penance for ruining my shore weekend. You can't dip a healing wound in the Atlantic Ocean.

Not off the Jersey Shore, at least.

I hate drive-through duty. Damon knows it, too. Whenever I irritate him, boom—the next shift I'm on the headset passing out cannabis packed in little boxes with arched handles and psychedelic letters proclaiming: *Happy Feels.*

Normally I'd never side with a giant corporation over a small business owner, but I sincerely hope McDonald's sues Damon's ass. Besides, he's not *that* small of a business owner. He's got three Xscape Your Brain: An Herbaceous Experience locations in the greater Jersey Shore area already, which equates to three crimes against humanity. With white lacquered surfaces and illuminated glass cases, XYB is sterile and echoey, made worse by the deafening electronic music Damon blares twenty-four seven. If you held a rave at a mall Clinique counter, this is what it would feel like. I hate it with every cell in my body.

But it's the only dispensary within driving distance, and the employee discounts are decent, so.

"That'll be two hundred and fifty dollars, please drive around." I lean through the opening, pass off the *Happy Feels*, and sigh.

"Customer service, Nomi." Damon dances toward me with a deeply serious expression he probably thinks is brooding and sexy.

It's not.

"Could you be less..." He flings a hand at me, hips still moving. "*—depressed*?"

"Sure, Damon." I plaster on a smile that makes him flinch out of beat. "Is this better?"

He rolls his eyes and tucks a lock of his limp, brown hair behind an ear. "You're never going to be promoted to manager with that attitude."

I'm already manager. Damon's just the power-hungry forty-something owner who comes by to dance and screw up my meticulous schedules so he can put me on drive-through duty. I blow out a breath. "Right. Thanks for the feedback, boss." That honorific usually mollifies him enough to return to the synth hell from whence he came, but for some reason, Damon's still pulsing in front of me.

"Why did you order a shipment of Orangutan Titties this month?"

Ah. That's why.

I straighten in my seat. "It's a great strain. The balance of terpenes and high THC content makes it particularly effective for chronic pain and severe anxiety. With Ms. Fleming's condition, I thought—"

"Ms. Fleming is *one* customer, Nomi. People want party pot! Buds N Roses. Donkey Bush. Cuntsicle." Damon narrows his eyes. "It's unacceptable to change our standing order to push your medicinal bummer weed."

"Orangutan Titties is a great time! It's euphoric and relaxing—not everyone wants to laugh for four hours straight and do donuts in the parking lot."

Damon arches an eyebrow, making his long face longer. "*Everyone* wants to laugh for four hours straight and do donuts in the parking lot, *Nomi.* That is the herbaceous experience we are selling. Not old people getting stoned and watching *Jeopardy!*"

My jaw clenches. That's mine and Graham's favorite pastime.

"But people need medicinal strains, too," I press, knowing I should shut up. Eve and I are one month out from opening our dispensary, and the money's gonna be so tight, I *need* this job to last until we do. But this is my biggest frustration with Damon. "A large portion of your customer base comes here because they want an alternative to harsh pharmaceutical remedies. They need our help."

Damon leans into my space close enough I can smell his condescension.

Or maybe that's just the Taco Bell he had for lunch.

"Then *help* your old, sad bastards with Cuntsicle."

The doorbell chimes, and in walks Mr. Gutierrez. He's slower these days and needs a cane, but his grin is as big as ever. "Nomi! How lucky you're here today!"

I smile back, shifting past Damon to meet Mr. Gutierrez at the counter. "As if you don't know my schedule by heart."

Mr. Gutierrez leans over the counter to yell above the music. "You're the only one here who knows what works!"

Damon scowls and dances toward the sound system. A second later, the volume increases.

After listening, or trying to, anyway, to Mr. Gutierrez's latest rash of symptoms—rigid shoulders and tremors down his right arm—I find the newest strain I ordered for him. High CBD, low THC, with promising research on its symptom management for Parkinson's disease. Helping people navigate the endless variety of strains to achieve what they're looking for—whether it's pain relief, something to quell nausea, or just a good time—is my favorite part of this job. It took me years to learn how to manage my Crohn's disease with medicinal cannabis when traditional western medicine failed me. After the second time I spontaneously developed an allergic reaction to the intense Crohn's medications my doctors kept prescribing, I decided no more. No more ridiculously expensive prescriptions, no more collateral damage to my kidneys, no more sitting for hours hooked to an IV pumping me full of chemicals my body keeps rejecting. My fancy GI specialists wouldn't listen to me, but Dr. Appa does, and together we've searched for a gentler way to live through my disease ever since.

I'm about to ring up Mr. Gutierrez when Damon clears his throat loudly from behind me. I breathe deeply before giving Mr. Gutierrez a tight customer service smile. "Mr. Gutierrez: Would you be interested in learning more about our bestselling strain, Cuntsicle?"

Mr. Gutierrez's brows pinch together, confused. "*Whatsicle*, dear?"

I cannot *wait* to get out of here.

My phone dings an hour later, the message bringing a surge of joy.

VERONICA D'ANGELO-BORK, REAL ESTATE AGENT

Miracle of miracles, I got the first showing for us! I had to pull MAJOR strings. Are you free in twenty minutes, babe?

I glance at the office and curse. Damon's still inside, his uncooked shrimp of a body hunched in my chair. *Fuck.* He's hooked up his Xbox.

VERONICA D'ANGELO-BORK, REAL ESTATE AGENT

Well???

I bite my lips in, then bang out an all-caps !!YES!! reply.

"Hey." I tap one of my junior cannabis counselors on the shoulder, a guy with shoulder-length dark hair, and motion for him to take over at the drive-through window. "Try to keep your back turned to the store, okay?"

The junior counselor salutes me, knowing the drill well. Despite Henry being six inches taller, thickly shouldered, and a twenty-five-year-old *man*, once the headsets come on, Damon can't tell us apart.

I inform the rest of the staff to tell Damon I'm in the bathroom if he asks, *with lady problems* if he presses, and then sneak out into the beautiful summer day.

After my escape from Xscape, I drive ten over the speed limit all the way downtown, Lil Dom be damned, and pull into the same spot Eve and I parked in during the vulval emergency. From instinct or trauma or whatever's possessed me into thinking about Julian and his palm all weekend,

I glance at Dr. Appa's clinic next door. What is Julian doing here? Surely he can't be moving back home—he detests Sparrow Nook and always has. But why is *he* the "new guy" working for Dr. Appa, then?

I forcibly dispel these questions and gaze upon the red brick building and its original name painted in beautiful, chipping cursive above the storefront. With large picture windows covered in yellowed newspaper, Strange Drugs Pharmacy is basically a mystery, and I am *dying* to see what's inside. It's been closed to the public for ages, but the newspaper did a retrospective on it a few years ago with pictures of its old-timey soda fountain, complete with shiny metal counters, red vinyl bar stools, and cozy booths for girls in tight sweaters and big skirts. When the city council announced its plans to lease the historic building, I *knew*. Strange Drugs would be the perfect location for my dispensary, and I'd do anything to get it.

Veronica's out front, tapping on her phone with a ferocious set of purple nails that could pick locks.

"Babe!" Veronica calls by way of greeting. She calls all her clients *babe*, probably to avoid forgetting names.

Veronica fixes her shark-black eyes on me and grips me by both shoulders. "Listen up. I had to buy Ms. Gruber *three* boxes of chocolates to get the first showing appointment to give us a chance in hell of leasing this spot. There is a lot of interest, babe. A *lot*. One potential tenant has been courting the city manager for *months* now."

"Do we have a chance?" I swallow, already feeling the disappointment of losing our dream spot clump in my throat.

"Of course we do. I didn't buy fifty dollars' worth of nougat for nothing! But you have to be prepared to move. None of your overanalytical anxious girl bullshit today, okay?" Her dagger-tipped nails press into my skin. "You want this place? You *take it*."

The pressure on my arms intensifies until I realize I'm supposed to nod, which I do vigorously.

God. Real estate agents are *terrifying.*

The listing agent arrives, which turns out to be Lexi Holmes, the hot, popular girl from my senior year at Sparrow Nook High. She's got shiny blonde hair, a raging personality disorder if you ask Eve, and even longer nails than Veronica, hers bejeweled. Veronica's eyes narrow as she takes them in.

"Right this way, *ma'am,*" Lexi simpers as she unlocks the front door and holds it open for Veronica. It's been two minutes, and Veronica's ready to cut a bitch.

I gasp as we enter, making Lexi titter. "It's something special, right? After the city council took ownership, they began years of restoration efforts. They put a lot of money into this place."

It shows. The original green-and-cream checkerboard floor tiles look new, the long counter painted the same meadow green, topped with a shiny metal cap. The chrome barstools with their wine-red vinyl seats pop, drawing the eye. The pièce de résistance, though, is the red neon sign hanging behind the counter against the white tiled walls. In large block letters, it states STRANGE DRUGS.

"Oh my God, does that still work?" I feel like I might stop breathing and keel over from pure joy.

"It's actually a re-creation, so it works perfectly." Lexi beams at us. "The idea was to fully restore the historic pharmacy and set up the town museum here, but then the old courthouse came open, and it was a better space for the city council's vision. That's why this beauty's on the market now!"

It's meant to be. For me to open my modern-day pharmacy in this historic one that prioritized both health *and* providing a space for customers to socialize, it's one hundred percent my destiny.

And thank God, my destiny's finally here. When I first got sick, it felt like some disinterested overlord pressed pause on my entire forward trajectory. Me and food always had a rocky relationship, but halfway through senior year, it went from *it's complicated* to *it's Crohn's disease.* After meals, it felt like I was walking around with a stomach full of loose knives, stabbing me over and over until the cramping would begin and I'd race for a bathroom where I'd moan and rock and wonder if, this time, I was actually dying. It got so bad, I'd refuse to eat for entire debate tournaments, subsisting off nibbles of protein bars and adrenaline for days at a time to avoid the next brutalizing attack. The doctors back in Georgia claimed it was the physical manifestation of my anxiety, but after we moved to Sparrow Nook, Mom took me to Dr. Appa, and he listened. After an hour of talking through every symptom, Dr. Appa suspected the true identity of my personal boogeyman. He referred me to a gastrointestinal specialist at Philadelphia General Hospital to confirm the diagnosis with testing, and my battle against Crohn's officially began.

It was a long time before my condition stabilized. After winter break my senior year, I didn't come back to school. Not right away, at least. They put me on Hospital-Homebound, which meant that a grizzled teacher came to my house once a week to drop off assignments and proctor my tests. I'd already snagged valedictorian, but it killed me giving up debate. Julian and I had just swept the state tourney and qualified for nationals, but after my doctors found out how I'd been coping with the intrinsic stress of tournaments, i.e., by developing disordered eating, debate was forbidden. I was so ashamed of what was wrong with me, I never told him why I quit. What would I have said? *Hi Julian, thanks for all the amazing kisses after we won first at state, btw I'll be spending the rest of my life in the bathroom because I have a diarrhea disease!*

No way. So, I hid from Julian and debate and the stressful life I left behind. It was easier that way, and when I finally did go back to school a few months later, Eve Ionides, the sardonic queer girl who perpetually wore beanies, punched me in the shoulder and asked if I wanted to sign up for Crew. The drama club was short a lighting operator for the spring production, and I said yes. Crew was easy, and drama kids were hilarious sluts, Eve the best of them all. Smoking up with her and laughing our asses off in the theater's balcony was a welcome relief after the intensity of debate and Julian and, surprisingly, a relief physically, too. Weed brought back my appetite. When a flare-up knocked me out, it was the only thing that eased the horrible pain.

The prescriptions emptying Mom's bank account couldn't do that.

Pot was how I got through life from that point on, which was terrifying since it was illegal then, but I couldn't give up the one solution I'd found. When Eve and I scraped up enough money to go to Amsterdam for spring break our senior year of college, the coffeehouse culture there showed us what life could be like in a legalized future, where cannabis was appreciated for all the good it can do. We wanted to bring that peaceful, harmonious vibe back home.

And now, we finally can.

I yank Veronica to the side.

"I want it," I growl. "Make it happen!"

"Are you sure?" Veronica stares me down. "The city council hasn't approved your license to operate the dispensary yet."

"It's in the bag," I reply with more confidence than is strictly warranted. "The final vote is next week."

"What if they don't give you the cigar bar exception to the no-smoking indoors ordinance?"

"The back lot then." I lick my dry lips. "It'll be the perfect smoking patio."

"They're asking five hundred over your upper limit."

I wince, but nod again.

Veronica's predator eyes flash with approval. "They'll want the down payment today—three months' rent. Can you handle that?"

I swallow, stomach bottoming out. While Eve's my partner, she's even broker than I am since part-time baking and self-publishing lesbian erotica isn't a fast ticket to the easy life. This part of our endeavor all comes down to me. I've been saving up for years, opting to drive my rattling Subaru into its grave, and living for cheap. The fact that a huge chunk of all those years of sacrifice is about to pour out of my bank account is both terrifying and exhilarating, because I've never bet on myself before. But Strange Drugs is undeniably perfect, and it's either move now or lose it.

"Let's make an offer."

"*I'll* make the offer. You stay quiet."

"Hi-ii! It's us again!" Veronica sweeps us both back to the soda fountain area, where Lexi sits at the counter waiting. "Okay, here's the deal: we want it, and you're going to lease it to my client at this rate per month with the price locked in for the entire five-year term." Veronica slips a piece of paper across the counter to the listing agent, whose eyes widen just so.

"And why would *my* client agree to that?" Lexi's tone has gone cool and professional.

"Because Sparrow Nook loves this place, and the city council has spent ridiculous amounts of taxpayer dollars to restore it. My client will keep the historic renovations in tip-top shape, so the town still has its historic pharmacy *and* a thriving new business." Veronica places a hand on one hip as she eyes the soda fountain skeptically. "How many other interested parties would be willing to leave up a neon sign screaming STRANGE DRUGS? From what I heard, your lead contender wants to open a *chain restaurant* in here." Veronica leans in for the kill. "This is a way for the city council to save face for spending all that taxpayer money and never delivering, and might I remind you, it's an election year. Heads will roll if you let an Applebee's come in and bulldoze this space."

"I'll—just call the city manager." Lexi scurries into the kitchen, and Veronica grins at me.

My eyebrows rise. "You are the scariest D'Angelo."

"You flatter me, babe." Veronica throws an arm around my shoulders. "But that's my mother."

"Speaking of scary D'Angelos, um, what's with your cousin coming back home?"

"Frankie?"

"No, Julian." I'm aware my cheeks are tinged pink, but I push forward anyways. "I... saw him the other day."

Veronica snorts. "That condescending d-bag moved back a few weeks ago after he fucked up his gig at Philly Gen. He's working at Dr. Appa's now."

I swallow, stress-sweat prickling beneath my shaggy bangs. Veronica's just confirming what I already saw with my own eyes, but it still raises my blood pressure.

Concerning since I can no longer go to my doctor about it.

Veronica, apex predator that she is, picks up on my discomfort immediately. "He's not back forever or anything. He's on probation, and Dr. Appa's letting him work off his time here. He'll move back to Philly as soon as his time is up." Veronica looks down her nose. "That doesn't change your mind, does it?"

"No." I cross my arms tightly. I've had my eye on this building for years—no surly phantom from my past can scare me off now just because he works next door. Even if he *did* just handle my labia professionally and I'll never look at lasagna again without feeling mortified. I'll figure out his exact schedule so I never see him. Easy.

Veronica makes a small, satisfied huff, and I side-eye her.

"What?"

"The pot-smoking valedictorian who stole Julian's thunder is opening up Sparrow Nook's first dispensary, and straight-laced, better-than-everybody Julian's gonna have to walk by it every day to serve his glorified community service hours." She smirks. "He's gonna lose his goddamn mind."

A small, nervous laugh escapes my mouth. I'll never forget the day he found me smoking up with Eve behind the theater after I came back to school. Julian went on this tirade about how I was ruining my life, how I'd never be anything and nobody'd ever want to be with a loser like me. Those words haunted me for years. He didn't know that pot was my lifeline back then, that it was saving me from the agony I experienced every time I tried to eat. And he couldn't know what I really heard in his horrible words was that *Crohn's* was ruining my life, that *it* would stand in my way of becoming anything, and that nobody would ever want to be with someone as sick and hopeless as me.

Even all these years later, those words still feel true.

Veronica's studying me closely, and I force a big, bright smile on my face. Julian may have written me off as a loser, but for the first time in ages, I'm finally winning. Judgmental, unfortunately gorgeous Julian can't take that away from me, especially not now that he's spinning out in his own shame spiral.

I clear my throat. "Do you know what he did? At Philly Gen?"

Veronica gives me a conspiratorial smile. "No. But for my favorite babe, I'll find out."

Lexi reappears with a big smile, and then I'm shaking hands, trembling with joy while Veronica patiently pats my shoulder as I review the paperwork that'll change my whole life. Soon there'll be no more Damon or Cuntsicle or waiting for my life to begin. Next week, I'll have my license to operate, and next month, we'll open our doors to Stranger Drugs officially. With Eve's edible bakery counter, my extensive knowledge of product and dispensary operations, and one thousand percent better vibes than XYB, Stranger Drugs will be a huge success. It even has office space for the nonprofit I'm cofounding to expunge the records of individuals convicted of marijuana-related offenses prior to state legalization. Being able to gift free office space and a dedicated portion of the dispensary's proceeds will finally get it off the ground, and the rush of knowing all the good we're about to do fills me up with a golden, shimmery happiness.

A golden, shimmery, *poor* happiness, but still. I can cash flow a few months' expenses, and investing in my dream is worth the uncertainty. If I have to work next door to a certain asshole doctor, at least I get to delight in running a successful dispensary and rubbing it in his intense face, proving once and for all that I, Nomi Wyeth, am both a pothead *and* a cunning businesswoman, and I *do* have a future being exactly who I am after all.

I cross the final *t* in *Wyeth* on the lease with a flourish.

Fuck you, Julian D'Angelo. I *win.*

CHAPTER FOUR

JULIAN

I glide into a spot in front of the clinic, parking my new Volvo hybrid behind an ancient Subaru, its bumper covered in stickers so faded, the words flicker in and out like ghosts. The few still legible include a witchy *Coexist*; two flying cartoon guys proclaiming *Flight of the Conchords*; and a big, fat marijuana leaf that says *I* 🔥 *New Jersey*, the only one that looks new.

Nomi.

My heart thrums in a wild, tachycardiac stress response to those old bumper stickers, their exact placement burned into my memory alongside every other detail about Nomi I hoarded our senior year. I got my first glimpse of the *new girl* when she showed up to the inaugural varsity debate team practice. Dressed all in black, her long, dark waves dyed the color of a moonlit night, she looked so—so *intimidating*—but when our eyes met, my mouth hanging slightly open, she smiled, soft and seeking.

And I stupidly told her she was in the wrong place. She had to be, I thought. Because someone that beautiful and interesting and completely fucking *cool* could not *also* be a varsity debate nerd like me. We weren't the same species of human. She was the one wearing calf-high lace-up boots, and I was the servant ready to lick them. That soft smile transformed into a scowl as she entered the room anyway and took her seat opposite me, but it returned when our coach enthusiastically welcomed her, already aware of her total domination in the southeast debate circuit and her strong performance nationally. By the end of practice, I was in total awe of her, and she hated me like everybody else did. But it didn't matter to my heart. Nomi Wyeth was an argument I couldn't win and a fight I was desperate to have. We battled every day after that—across the podium, over valedictorian, and later, when the arguing turned to frantic kisses in dark classrooms after practice, that felt like a battle, too.

And now fifteen years later, I'm back, and here we are, battling again, and I'm losing, again. All it would take is one call from Nomi, and all hope of returning to Philly Gen would be vanquished for good. I have to apologize, and I *have* to get it right.

But she's here, *now*? I'm not ready—I haven't perfected the speech I spent the weekend rewriting. I hit Eric's number, cursing when it goes straight to voicemail.

"Eric—just texted you my revised apology speech. Could you please review? Nomi's here, and—"

A beeping sound interrupts me from my car's speakers, and my mother's name appears on the center console. "Accept call from Mom?" the robot voice asks.

I hastily disconnect the call to answer the other, my heart now pounding in my chest. Maybe it's the way we lost Dad, or all the years I've spent in Emergency Medicine, but every time Mom calls, my sympathetic nervous system goes into full fight-or-flight mode, always expecting the worst. Mom knows this and usually texts before calling to say: I'm fine, everything's fine, gonna call you now, okay sweetie? Love you.

But she didn't text this time. The muscles in my throat constrict.

"Everything okay, Mom?" I half-bellow into the speakerphone. "Are you okay?"

"Yes, yes, sorry to scare you, sweetie, my texts aren't working. I'm spending the night at your Great Aunt Edna's house because she's not feeling well."

I exhale shakily. "Okay, thanks for letting me know."

"Also, Aunt Edna wants you to visit—you haven't been by yet. Fix that soon, okay, Julie? Now get to work, can't be late for Dr. Appa. Love you, bye." Mom hangs up, no response from me required.

I press my hand to my chest, willing the anxiety to recede into its cave until it emerges again and terrorizes me another day.

There is no emergency, everyone you love is okay. I breathe in and out, repeating the mantra in my head, eyes closed as I grip the steering wheel. I *almost* believe it.

The sound of nails rapping against the window tears me from my breathing exercise.

Fucking *hell.* My cousin Veronica's grinning on the other side of the glass, her eyes narrowed in fiendish glee. "*Julian!* We were just talking about you!"

Then I see her, standing in front of the old Strange Drugs Pharmacy. Nomi's bright-eyed and grinning, but not at me. She's staring down at a stack of papers in her hands. She looks up at Veronica's words, and my rapid pulse flounders, then slows in despair as her joyous expression vanishes upon seeing me, a reaction as familiar as the bumper stickers.

I launch out of the car.

"Veronica." The car door shuts behind me like a terse punctuation mark. I want to walk briskly past them, disappear into the clinic's comforting fluorescent lights, and lose myself in the medical service of others, the only time I ever feel worthy.

But *dammit*, I have orders, and running away isn't an option. My jaw clenches, as if trying to prevent the word, but I force it open. "Wyeth."

Well. That's a start.

She rolls her eyes.

"You two are neighbors now! Nomi just leased Strange Drugs, but I assured her you won't be around for long. Your probation from Philly

Gen's—what? Six months?" Veronica smiles as if airing my dirty laundry is the best part of her day.

"It's not probation; it's an intensive residency." My gaze flicks back reluctantly to Veronica as I grind out the carefully negotiated language Philly Gen's legal counsel prepared to save face in the event the hospital wants to reinstate me. I glance at Nomi. "You leased the old pharmacy?" The surprise is evident in my voice. "*Why?*"

Nomi clears her throat and, rather than answer me, turns to Veronica. "I've got to go, but when can I take possession?"

Veronica hands her a small ring of keys. "Technically the lease doesn't begin until July first, but since no one's using the space, they've agreed to let you move in early. But no business until after the city council meeting, okay?"

And it's back—that joyous look from earlier. It makes my heart sing, though I did nothing to earn it and have no right to savor it.

"Oh my God, Veronica, you're amazing!" Nomi grabs my evilest cousin and hugs her like she isn't a cobra wearing a human skin suit. "Thank you!"

Veronica smiles at her, actually *smiles*, and it doesn't feel nefarious at all.

So, it's just me that everyone hates. Got it.

Nomi's eyes flick to me then away just as fast as she hurries toward her car. It's probably twenty years old at this point, easy. How does she pass inspection? Is it safe for her to drive? The image of a badly burned woman pulled from the wreckage of her car coding beneath my hands last year rattles my brain like a thunderclap, momentarily robbing me of my breath. I forcibly shove the awful memory away when I realize my window of opportunity is about to pass me by.

"Wyeth—wait," I call to her back, which stiffens as she stops with her key in the door. She doesn't have automatic locks? That's *definitely* not safe in today's dark parking garages. My brain's already shuffling through former patients, looking for comparators, but her clipped voice cuts it off.

"What, Julian?" She may be annoyed, but I can't help relishing the way her lips still wrap around my name. The slight lilt of her southern accent, all that's left after fifteen years in New Jersey, curls around the vowels like vines on a gate. It used to drive me wild.

"I need to talk to you."

Veronica lifts one full eyebrow in my direction.

"About your—health."

Nomi's chin drops as she regards me with open disbelief. "No, you don't."

"*Yes*, I *do*," I snap reflexively, that old knee-jerk desire to argue with her rearing up. I try again. "Please?"

Her sigh is audible from seven feet away, but she re-locks her car and joins me on the curb. Now both of Veronica's eyebrows are arched high, and she huffs out a laugh. "Okay, you two. Have fun with that."

I clear my throat, then turn on my heel, hoping Nomi will follow but simultaneously terrified she won't until I hear the soft thuds of her boots behind me. I don't face her until we're standing in the office I share with Dr. Srinivasan and I've shut the door behind us. I considered a patient room at first, but I can't handle seeing Nomi Wyeth sprawled on a hospital bed ever again. Plus, this setting feels right for an apology, though now that we're *both* in here, the room feels too small, which is ridiculous. She's the size of a fairy. I flee to the other side of the desk and sit, cursing when the chair still positioned to Dr. Srinivasan's short height puts my knees nearly level with the desk. Nomi watches as I grope for the adjustment lever, then plummet to where I'm a foot off the floor.

Is there anything more awkward than adjusting an office chair in front of an audience?

Finally, I get it to a comfortable height, which involves a weird squatting maneuver over the chair that I'll ruminate on for *months*. I wipe my damp forehead as her pouty mouth quirks upward. She's still dressed in black, but instead of a ripped-up band T-shirt like high school, this one's form-fitting and simple, with short, capped sleeves that highlight the smooth lines of her arms, contrasting against the pale skin there. The same pale skin as her inner thighs, which I now inconveniently know. Also, this time she's wearing pants, so that's disappointing.

"Well? You wanted to discuss my health?"

My eyes dart back to her face, and I've stupidly forgotten why I summoned her back here. *To apologize*, Eric's voice says in my head, *and ask her out.*

"Right. Your health." I swivel toward the computer and bring up her chart to stall for a second. I'm not *really* going to ask her out because Eric told me to. Or because I got an ill-timed boner. Or even because the curves of her cheekbones and little slope of her nose, and God, the bow of her lips, the same soft, summer red of watermelon, all combine with her large, brown eyes to make the prettiest face I've ever seen. Even now, with her peeved, impatient expression, I'm overcome with the desire to simply stare at her. But I can't ask her out after I sewed up her labia three days ago—how creepy is that? Besides, based on that *ridiculous* Colonel Sanders shirt she was wearing, she's still a stoner.

So, maintain health pretense, apologize, no asking out. Case closed.

"How's the laceration healing? Have you been keeping it, um. Dry?" My eyes widen in alarm as I suddenly recall the shore trip she mentioned. "You didn't dip that thing in the Atlantic Ocean, did you? No pools?"

Thoughts of infected labia majora flash before my eyes, my heartbeat picking up in anxious concern.

"Maybe I should take a look—"

"No!" Nomi blurts out, hands raised. "I did not *'dip that thing'* in any bodies of pestilent water, and there will be no more *looks* because Dr. Appa is my doctor, not you."

The words shouldn't sting. I *do not* permit them to sting.

"His *name* is Dr. Srinivasan, Wyeth." I cock my head to the side. "You realize you're calling him Doctor Daddy, right?"

"Don't make it weird, Julian." Nomi heaves a sigh. "Now, is this extremely valuable use of my time over?"

"No." I quickly hammer an inquiry that pulls up her medical history to hide my flustered face behind the computer screen. I still have to apologize and not ask her out. My eyes flit aimlessly over what appears to be a decade-old MRI report of her abdomen and latch onto a set of words that I absolutely should *not say out loud*. And yet...

"Moderate stool burden?" I frown at the screen in surprise, then at her abdomen, as if it's got secrets. "You have a *moderate stool burden*?"

"Jesus, what are you looking at?!" Nomi turns scarlet, then lunges over the desk for the mouse and closes out all the windows. "Stay out of my medical records, you nosy bastard!"

She collapses back in her seat with an angry huff. "Now was there something you actually wanted to say, or did you bring me back here to violate HIPAA and embarrass me?"

"Actually, to violate HIPAA—"

The murderous look in her eyes stops me cold. I clear my throat. "Er, yes. I wanted to apologize for how I behaved before." Then, when she doesn't react, I add, "When I sutured your vulva?"

"Yes, *Julian*, I know when you're referring to." Nomi rakes her fingers into the hair at her temples. "*Jesus.*"

"I was very rude, and I shouldn't have mentioned lasagna." I adjust my glasses while Nomi closes her eyes, unwilling to look at me. "It's not even true—nobody could ruin lasagna. Anyway, I'm sorry. Seeing you after all these years just... caught me off guard. And I'm sorry. Again."

Surprisingly, I find that I *am* sorry. Sorry that she still has this hold over me, that she can still, after all this time, get the better of me. That even now, as I apologize and try to make things right between us, she hates me so much she won't even look at me.

Her eyes flip open, and in a forcibly calm voice, she says, "Thank you. I do not forgive you, though, because now *I'll* never be able to look at lasagna again. I appreciate you stitching up the right hole and everything, but I will be going now."

Ugh. I knew I should've avoided her until I die! For once, Eric was wrong—just because my sad, pathetic body is still attracted to Nomi's doesn't mean we should *date.* Preposterous. She is a stoner; I am a doctor. She breaks hearts, I fix them. I stand as she stands, then rush toward the door to open it for her, but she gets there first.

She pauses there. "I would appreciate never talking about this again."

"Duly noted." I trail after her down the hallway. "So, what are you opening next door, anyway?" I rush out, feeling strangely desperate to stretch the conversation. I don't know why; this has been one of the most awkward exchanges of my life.

She spins on her heels, looking up at me with manufactured patience. "Let's make something clear: we're not friends. We're not even acquaintances. You're somebody I used to know, and we had a *very* unfortunate run-in a few days ago, that's it. My business is exactly that—*my* business—and I want you and your judgmental attitude to stay the hell out of it."

And with that, she exits the clinic out into the jewel-skied evening, her curt, devastating words stirring up every one of my most antagonistic feelings.

"Call if there's any vaginal swelling!" I yell after her on the bustling sidewalk, satisfied when a few heads turn to stare. "Or strange, troublesome discharge!"

Now *that's* how you violate HIPAA.

It's a slow, emergency-free evening in Sparrow Nook with nothing to distract me from the unaccountable irritation I feel that Nomi's opening a mystery business next door. In the Strange Drugs pharmacy, too—what could it be? A gift shop? Seems unlike her, but it's been fifteen years. Maybe she's gotten into decorative tea towels. What do hot, formerly goth women in their thirties care about, anyway? Tarot readings? Supplements? Cats? Fuck if I know. But I'd be lying if I said I wasn't consumed with curiosity. The idea of her starting her own business feels like a glimpse of the fish-netted Nomi of yore that tortured me with her determination to beat me in everything. God, I miss that Nomi. If only she hadn't thrown it all away, we could've been . . . well.

We could've been everything. We were going to go to Yale together, and instead of endless studying alone, my life would've been endless studying *with Nomi*. Late nights and early mornings in the library *with Nomi*. Working and striving and accomplishing everything we dreamed of, together. The best with the best. It's hard to look at the woman who starred in all my teenage dreams of the illustrious future we'd share after she abruptly and with zero explanation dropped out of school, out of my life, and the life she was building for herself, too. It was even harder to see her half-naked wearing nothing but a red-eyed Colonel Sanders shirt, still stuck in the town I thought we'd escape together.

But maybe there's still some spark of that old Nomi left.

I quickly pull up the city council's dinky website—the next meeting is one week from today. Veronica said Nomi couldn't do any "business" before the next city council meeting, so she must be waiting on some kind of permission or licensure to be voted on next week.

With a satisfied grunt, I add the meeting to my calendar.

CHAPTER FIVE

NOMI

There's only one benefit to throwing a party, and it's that you should, in theory, know everyone there. No awkward introductions. No accidental run-ins with reviled exes. No small talk with strangers in the bathroom line. This one positive is so good, it's almost worth all the negatives, which count in the dozens—from feeling personally responsible for everyone's good time to the never-ending cleanup the next day.

And yet, when half the town shows up to your tiny house ready to get stoned, that one benefit flies out the window. It's only eight p.m., and I've already met more people than I can possibly remember, all thanks to Eve. A few days ago, we vaped enough Orangutan Titties to put down a small horse and were watching *Jeopardy!* with Graham since he's practicing to take the show's qualifying test when she abruptly sat up from my floor like a possessed puppet.

"We should have a party!"

"A *party*?" I frowned at her. She'd had even more Titties than I had. "But... we're in our thirties."

"Come on, Nomi. For one night, we can pretend otherwise! It'd be a fundraiser, with proceeds benefiting the dispensary. A... *pot luck*!"

"How would people bringing dishes to share help the dispensary?"

"Oh my God, Nomi, quit being so literal!" Eve grabbed me by the arms and pulled me off the couch; she's very strong when she's stoned. "I'll bake a full tasting menu for people to try, and we'll gather donations at the door to enter. We'll invite the whole town and get them to sign a—a letter of support or something. They'll make the case to the city council for us, Nomi. It's a win-win!"

And so, the Stranger Drugs Pot Luck was born. Word got around faster than we anticipated, and wider, too. There are hundreds of people here, milling about the tables on our bulb-lit front lawn, the mismatched menagerie of beach chairs in our backyard, and the air-conditioned tunnel of rooms between them. But plus side, the giant cannabis-leaf piñata I'm wearing slung over my body is already stuffed with donations, and Eve and Graham's are nearly full, too. After I deposit the proceeds from my full piñata into Eve's apartment, I resume my position on the front porch, welcoming guests, receiving donations, and keeping a hawk eye out for any council members. If they see the town's enthusiastic support for our venture tonight, that'd do more for us than next week's presentation ever could.

"Baaaaabe, looking hot!" Veronica D'Angelo-Bork calls as she sashays up our front walk like it's a red carpet, and I'm from *E! News* waiting to interview her. She appraises my yolky gold sundress and the length of leg exposed between its short hem and the tops of my favorite boots, a burnished bronze set of vintage Frye. "It's giving 1970s *Come Fuck Me* Bohemian Nashville."

I huff. "I was going for *Come Fund Me*, but close enough."

Veronica steps away to greet a client just as Gisella D'Angelo bustles up, an aging Italian beauty with a short, silver-streaked black bob and a huge smile, escorted by Dr. Appa, who's on her arm and looking quite dashing as well in his sporty plaid blazer and matching bow tie.

I wonder if Julian knows his mom is banging his boss.

"Nomi, sweetie! How are you?" Gisella leans in to kiss my cheek. "Feeling well?"

Gisella gets all the dirt on me thanks to her weekly coffee-and-antiquing dates with my mom. She's abundantly kind, though, and while I do not share my health with most people, Gisella's love and attention feels genuine and understanding in a way that never rankles.

"Yes, feeling great, thank you for coming. Great to see you, too, Dr. Appa."

"What you're doing for this community is laudable, Nomi." Dr. Appa gives me a warm, fatherly smile as he slips a hundred-dollar bill into my piñata. "Cannabis has many wonderful medicinal and recreational uses, and it has been unfairly vilified for decades just for being pleasurable."

"Hear, hear!" Gisella says.

I smile. "Someone should tell Julian that."

"Who can tell that boy anything?" Gisella rolls her eyes. "Where's Jenny, honey? I want to say hello."

"Mom's in the dining room with the baked goods," I grin. "Where else?"

Gisella and Dr. Appa stroll inside, greeting everyone as they go as the beloved town celebrities they are, and Veronica swoops back to my side, adjusting a lock of my long curtain bangs until she's satisfied. She may be intimidating, but she's the kind of dependable that'll never let you walk around with something in your teeth. Her eyes flicker beyond my shoulder, and she leans in to whisper, "Council Members Min and Shar coming in hot. Look alive, babe, and go *get that license*."

I spin on my boot heels. "Council-friends!" I use their preferred title, hold out my hand, and shake each of theirs as they walk up the front steps, commanding myself not to tremble. "Welcome, and thank you for coming."

"Look at this turnout." Shar, pronounced like *Cher*, nods appreciatively as her sharp eyes scan the crowds. The most pragmatic of the Council-friends, Shar owns a successful accounting practice and is primarily driven by increasing tax profits for the town. "Half of Sparrow Nook is here to support you."

"People use cannabis for many reasons—to have fun, relax, address chronic health conditions and pain—but the nearest dispensary is over half an hour away. If we had our own small, bespoke dispensary conveniently located on Main Street? As you can see," I gesture to the boisterous party, "people would be *thrilled.* Here, let me preview what Stranger Drugs will offer." I usher the Council-friends inside toward the sample display menu.

Min Lee whistles as she reads along. She owns the local Asian supermarket whose customer base expanded hundred-fold overnight thanks to the bestselling memoir *Crying in H Mart* by Michelle Zauner. As such, Min is extremely sensitive to aging hipster millennial needs, from translated explanations on the soy sauce aisle to their comfort cannabis. As she told me last week, "*stoned people are hungry people.*" Her vote is in the proverbial cotton tote bag, and I have her to thank for getting Shar here tonight.

"What a spread!" Min glances up and winks. "Good pricing, too. Are you planning on a rewards program for frequent buyers?"

"Absolutely. Clients will start earning gifts immediately. We want to develop a devoted customer base and encourage repeat business, which will help expand our offerings while providing a meaningful tax revenue stream to Sparrow Nook." I wink back, grateful for the alley-oop. "Our model is based on local, fresh product with a diversified menu designed to meet every cannabis user at their comfort level and need. I also have an extremely talented baker lined up whose edibles are so delicious, they're going to draw their own visitors to Sparrow Nook."

I wave my hand at the truly epic table spread Eve's created. We raided thrift stores yesterday for every vintage cake stand, platter, and bespoke ceramic surface in township lines, and the resulting effect is somewhere between my grandmother's china cabinet and the Mad Hatter's tea party. Each dish features some gorgeous dessert that will make you groan in pleasure then send you to space. From inspired classics like fudge-topped brownies marbled with cream cheese to Eve's trippier creations, like Fruity Pebbles treats melted together with green weed mallows, there's something for every palate. She even made a stack of her legendary high-protein, high-THC sativa granola bars that I eat whenever I need to clean my entire house in pure euphoria.

I grin at the Council-friends' starstruck expressions. "Care to sample anything?"

Min expertly retrieves a raspberry glazed donut from a dwindling platter with a pair of bakers' tongs she'll be too stoned to use in about half an hour.

Shar, with her arms folded, is still regarding me, though. "How will your model differ from the competition?"

I almost don't hear her. The music, a chill blend of unobtrusive but exceedingly hip songs curated by Graham for the party, changes abruptly to something with a seething, pulsing beat. I *hate* it. With effort, I wrench my eyes back to Shar's.

"Stranger Drugs will be a one-of-a-kind boutique experience that curates its offerings to meet our customers' needs while providing a pleasant, convivial atmosphere to socialize in." I have to struggle to be heard now. What was Graham thinking? "The closest dispensaries are all Xscape Your Brain locations. While XYB is a small chain, it's also heavily corporatized, preferring to source big-batch strains from mega growers and manufacturers instead of buying high-quality cannabis grown here in the Garden State. The product they carry is cheaper, sure, but it's lower quality, too—more variable in its stated percentages of THC to CBD, and often stale and less effective."

"You know a lot about the competition," Shar yells back. "Though it doesn't sound like much competition, does it?"

Smugness fills my petty, business-loving heart.

"I've worked at the South Harbor XYB location for the last five years as the chief cannabis counselor and manager." I smile conspiratorially, then lean over to shout, "and I can't *wait* to quit!"

"Too bad." A snide, nasal male voice rises above my head like a malodorous cloud of bad energy, and I whip around. Damon, in black vinyl pants and his *going-out* platforms, towers over me. His rubbery lips are gathered into a sneer. "Because you're *fired*!"

My breath catches, and I step back, bumping into Shar.

I spin around to face them, smiling and clapping my hands once. "I'm so sorry, Council-friends, please excuse me—I need to confer with this . . . uh, client. Enjoy the party!"

I grab Damon by his faded Moby T-shirt and drag him to the side. "What're *you* doing here?" It's a dumb question, but the sight of my horrible boss looming like a venomous centipede on two of its hundred legs is so jarring, so *nightmare-come-to-life*, my brain can't process the information.

"Reconnaissance, what else?" Damon crumples one of our green party flyers in his fist and takes a step forward. His vinyl pants squeal in protest. "You really thought you could open a dispensary in *my* state without me finding out?"

"I . . . yes?" I swallow. "It's a pretty big state."

"*Wrong*," Damon spits out. "Well, right. It is a big state, but you were wrong about *me*, finding out," he adds unnecessarily. "Because I *did*."

This is why I can't respect him.

"And *you're fired*!" he says again, watching my face gleefully like he's hoping I'll cry.

"Come on, Damon—let me finish the month. We've just started the inventory clean-out, and I still need to put in all the new orders. Half the staff is on vacation, for God's sake! You're screwing yourself over if you fire me right now. Please reconsider?" The cringe gripping me is so intense, it feels like Pilates. "Boss?"

"No." Damon's S-shaped spine straightens a few degrees as a tight, satisfied smirk dimples his face. "Little Miss Tummy-aches thinks she has what it takes to open a successful dispensary? There's no *sick leave* when you run your own business, Nomi. There's no one smarter, older, and more successful around to rescue you when you make your dumb decisions. And there's gonna be no job waiting for you at XYB when your girly joke of a dispensary fails to get its license next week!"

My brows draw together, and now I'm *pissed*. Pissed that Damon's shooting himself in the platformed boot to spite me, pissed that he's ruining my careful balancing act of a budget, and more than anything, pissed that he's standing here in *my* house, fouling up the vibes with his toxic presence. I'm going to have to sage the whole place!

"Stranger Drugs is *going to* happen."

He steps forward again, the vinyl lining his taint groaning and shrieking as if captive against its will. His lips curl in a malevolent smile.

"You sure about that?"

CHAPTER SIX

JULIAN

I should've known I wouldn't get to eat dinner. It's the full moon, and per that rock's capricious influence, minor emergencies trundle into the clinic all night. Broken arms, stitches, the gruesome removal of a rusty nail from Randy Thompson's foot—none of which quells the hunger pangs throbbing in my gut. When it slows down around nine p.m., I heat up a piece of sad, cheese-less veggie lasagna I made in a weird fit of Wyeth preoccupation. As I'm putting the first bite in my mouth, my phone buzzes on the table.

My eyes narrow. If it's the goddamn D'Angelo family text chain I've left and been aggressively re-added to three times, I'll harness this hanger to reply so obnoxiously they'll *finally* leave me alone.

DR. SRINIVASAN

Hello, Julian. I have polluted my body and impaired my judgment and thus require you to pick me up. We need a ride home.

DR. SRINIVASAN

It was not with cheesecake. 🤣

Then, a gif of Snoop Dogg with 8-bit sunglasses that slide down his nose, revealing marijuana leaves for eyes, appears.

Dr. Srinivasan's sending *gifs*? About *weed*?!

An address comes next. Where is he, a bar? No, the address is residential. And who is this "we"? Dr. Srinivasan is a confirmed bachelor and has never been married. I can only surmise from the gif and texts that Dr. Srinivasan has gone to a *party* and gotten intoxicated by *marijuana* with *friends*.

After several seconds of internal rage at being asked to do this and yet knowing I can't say no after the number of complaints I received this week, I bang out a quick affirmative that I'll be there soon. With a pang of frustrated longing, I shove my uneaten lasagna back into the fridge, turn the clinic's sign to CLOSED, and lock up.

It's a Friday night, and the June air feels heavy and liquid. When I get to my car, I throw off my doctor's coat, then groan at what I'm wearing. The flat-front navy chinos and linen button-down were fine for doctoring, but now I have to bust into some party to haul off Dr. Srinivasan looking like a yacht police-boy. I quickly undo the top two buttons, then roll up the sleeves to my forearms. To tuck, or untuck? Or that strange, mysterious compromise—the front tuck only?

I stand there frantically assessing my reflection in the window when hushed laughter makes me whip around. A mother and her two teenage daughters watch me from the sidewalk.

"Well?" I snap. "I'm going to a marijuana party. Should I leave this tucked in or out?"

"Out," the daughters say in unison, but the mother lifts her hand to her chin, pondering.

"Turn around."

Exasperated, I do as I'm told. When I finish revolving, her eyes twinkle. "In," she says. "*Definitely* in." She leads her daughters past me, then gives me a lascivious wink over her shoulder.

Unsettling, but I leave the shirt tucked in.

The closest parking spot is two blocks away, but it's soon evident where the party is based on the happy chatter emanating from the crowded lawn. My stomach squeezes in a sour twist all the way to my sternum, the uniquely high school feeling of *everyone's hanging out without me* still hurtful after all these years. You'd think I'd be used to it by now. I'm always so busy focusing on my work I don't see units of casual friendship forming until *wham*, there's a happy hour or a party or a weekend trip that everyone else enjoyed together without me. Even worse are the times I find out beforehand and am awkwardly invited last minute to join. Standing there, holding a beer I don't intend to drink, trying to make small talk with people politely waiting for me to leave before the real fun begins? *Ugh.*

I walk up the front path, squinting around the lawn. "Dr. Srinivasan?" I lean over to peer at a man sitting at a crowded table, but it's not him. I don't recognize anyone, in fact, until a man in a Hawaiian shirt narrows his eyes. "What're *you* doing here, Doc?"

I don't remember this patient, but he reminds me of the shady IT guy who steals the dinosaur embryos in *Jurassic Park*. Judging by his frosty reception, he's probably one of the twenty-two complainants Dr. Srinivasan has heard from this month. I straighten to my full height. "Looking for Dr. Srinivasan—have you seen him?"

"Who?" The word punches out of the man's mouth in that distinctly New Jersey way.

I clench my jaw. "Dr.... Appa."

"Oh. The *good* doctor. Yeah, he's around here somewhere. Check inside." The man sniffs. "Near the *cheesecake*."

Ah. Diabetic Mr. Donahue. A giant brownie sits in front of him, and I glance at it pointedly, ignoring the kick of petulant hunger it causes in my own empty stomach, before resuming my search. But Dr. Srinivasan isn't on the lawn, nor is he schmoozing with the unlikely mix of city council members and constituents on the front porch. I enter the house, looking for the so-called *good* doctor who got too high to drive himself home.

"Dr. Srinivasan?" I call through the crowded living room.

"Babe, *no*!" a familiar voice shouts, then the room bursts into laughter. Spine tingling, I turn slowly and see approximately ten percent of the town's D'Angelo population. Veronica's laughing so hard, she's dipped sideways into her sister Betty. Surrounding them are my cousins Frankie, Albert, Bianca, Gia, Adriana, and worst of all, the three *Ohs*: Marco, Aldo, and Ellio, who was named after a beloved frozen pizza brand. The *Ohs* and I used to play every day after school at Aunt Edna's until they discovered pomade and girls and later formed their own janitorial services company and I went to medical school.

Veronica lightly dabs the laughter-tears away when she sees me. "Julie!" She frowns and grins at the same time, incredulous. "What're you doing here?"

"Looking for Dr. Srinivasan." I grit my jaw, preparing for the usual onslaught of family ribbing and knowing I'm too hangry to handle it well. My cousins exchange loaded glances but say nothing. "He texted that he needs a ride."

Understanding washes over Veronica's bronzed face, and maybe a touch of *oh, shit*. After a second, she shoves a fishbowl full of cash at me. "Well, if you want to walk through the party, that'll be twenty dollars."

This party has a *cover charge*? I start to argue, but my cousins are waiting to make fun of me for doing just that, so I whip out my wallet and deposit a twenty in the bowl, then stalk off.

I check the dining room next, then the kitchen, the hall, even a closet. I clench my fists to my sides, frustrated that I can't find him and resentful to be surrounded by people having fun when I'm not and, more than anything, *hungry*. I work out too hard to weather calorie depletion this severe.

Worse, there's a smorgasbord of baked goods in the middle of the dining room, arrayed in tantalizing heaps of simple carbohydrates glazed with even simpler carbohydrates, with little artsy cards labeling each item. It seems to be an honest-to-goodness bake sale, which, weird. I hover in front of it, glowering at the bad decision I'm about to make to protect everyone here. They think I'm an asshole when fed? Ten more minutes of my plummeting blood sugar, and they'll call the cops. I start to reach for a big, fudge-topped brownie when a plate of fulsome granola bars catches my eye. They're the least tried item based on how tall the stack still is, but I can't understand why. They're thick and inviting, studded with raisins, pumpkin seeds, oats, and cashews with the sticky-sweet smell of fresh maple syrup lingering overhead. I squint at the card and read: *Hemp Hemp Hooray! Protein Bars* and exhale gratefully, reaching for one. Hemp seeds are a fantastic source of protein. There's a suggested donation of ten dollars each for the food items, which is extortion, but I'm too hungry to put up a fight.

My teeth sink into the gooey granola bar, and an involuntary grunt issues from my mouth. Buttery with a touch of sweetness, the right balance of crunch and chew, infused with something *tangy* that I can't place. It counters the sweet and salt perfectly. In three outrageous bites, I've finished the whole thing and feel immediately better. I happily plunk another ten-dollar bill in and eat a second one, which is even better than the first, somehow. There's little bits of coconut, and *ahh,* prunes? Is that the source of the delightful funky tang? Whoever made these is a genius.

My hand is reaching for a *third* when I stop suddenly—I'm supposed to be doing something. I frown a bit. What is it? There's a good, giddy feeling spooling through my whole body, making it hard to think. What am I *forgetting*? My pulse speeds up uncomfortably. It feels important. What is it?

"Heyooo, Julie. Didja find Dr. Appa yet?" My cousin Marco appears next to me.

"That's *it*!" I exhale heavily, then laugh as the mounting anxiety recedes within me like the tide. I pat Marco on the back, then lean in for a side hug, unaccountably grateful. "Thanks, man."

Marco turns a puzzled face toward me as the hug continues. "Eh. Don't mention it. Short guys are easy to lose in a party."

I nod slowly. The wisdom of this statement is *irrefutable*.

Marco taps his chin, eyes darting between a sticky bun and a green-cream cannoli, then waves them off. "Ah, I better not."

I point at the granola bars. "Those are the most delicious protein bars I've ever tasted. You've *got* to try one."

Marco raises one thick, black eyebrow at me. It's perfectly groomed, which started around the time he got his first serious girlfriend.

The thought plucks a note of melancholy in the center of my chest.

"I wish I had a girlfriend," I murmur at the protein bars.

"D'jeet one of those?" Marco nudges me to bring me out of the mists of sadness that have claimed me as one of their wraiths.

"Huh?" It takes a second to translate the Jersey dialect—d'jeet, meaning *did you eat*. I'm out of practice speaking my own language? How *sad*. Everything is so *sad*. I clutch a hand to my chest. "Oh. Yeah. Two, actually."

"*Two?*" Marco's chin drops as both his brows lift high into his hairline. He's got a great hairline, just like Uncle Rocco.

"You're probably never going bald," I muse.

Marco tips his head back and laughs so hard, it makes his chest rise up and down with each *har, har, har*. I watch it, mesmerized. It's the funniest thing I've ever seen. Now I'm laughing, staring down at my own chest. Am I doing it, too? I *am*!

Marco slings an arm around my shoulders, little chuckles still rippling through him, and corrals me toward the backyard. "Come on, Julie. I'll help you look for Dr. Appa."

"*Right!* Dr. Appa!" I grab three cookies to go.

The warm night air encases me like a pair of silky bike shorts, but all over my body. Like if I pulled a second pair over my head and stuck my arms through. I laugh, *loud*, feeling free and light and covered in silky bike shorts. Marco brings me over to a beer pong table, where the other two Ohs, Aldo and Ellio, are setting up to battle against mean, little Eve Ionides and Graham Keegan, who was positively merciless in Quiz Bowl but otherwise a nice guy. I step behind Marco for safety.

"Anyone seen Dr. Appa?" Marco asks on my behalf.

"Yeah, maybe ten minutes ago?" Graham says. "He's inside."

"He isn't, though!" I run my palms down my face. "He's too short. So *elusive*."

"Lemme take care of it." Marco gestures for my phone, quickly rattles off a text, then smiles to himself as a fast reply comes in. "Dr. Appa's meeting us here."

"*Thank you*." My eyes feel strangely wet. I had no clue Marco was this—this—

Nice.

"Don't mention it, buddy." He claps me on the shoulder. "We're gonna have a good time."

Marco joins his brothers on the opposite end of the table as Eve finishes filling the last red cup of the beer pyramid. Beeramid.

I snort, and Eve looks up at me like I'm deranged. "What's wrong with him?" she asks Marco.

"Beeramid!" I proffer, gesturing at the red cups.

Her eyes dart from me to Marco. "My question stands."

"He ate two of your protein bars." Marco grins.

"*You* made the protein bars?" My eyes widen. I take one of Eve's small, lesbian hands in both of my own and briefly consider proposing.

There'd be no sex, sure, but I would keep her rich in oats. "I had no idea you could make protein. You're *so* talented."

"*Two?!*" Eve exclaims up at me, just like Marco did.

"What? I paid for them." I swallow, insecurity rising within me viciously. "I hadn't eaten anything all day."

Eve blinks at me, then slowly retracts her genius baking fingers from my adoring grip. "This should be interesting."

"Eh, he'll be fine." Marco air-practices the arc of his shot. "We'll order some pizza if it gets too much."

Pizza...

Suddenly I've never wanted anything more.

"What is this?" Graham asks as Marco takes his place in the front of the Ohs' line-up. "We were two-on-two!"

Marco gestures. "Julie's standing right there, man."

I glance at Eve, who's eyeing me warily. "Should I play—"

What is this game called again? My brain feels like it's made of trampoline; everything I ask it to recall bounces right off. I squeeze my eyes shut.

"—with your... cups?"

"Ew, God, don't say it like that!" Eve recoils but moves out of the way to give me first turn. "Just get the ball into *their* cups. *Their cups*, Julian."

I grasp the ball between my fingers and swallow as I step up to the table. Eve and Graham have never liked me, and I'm certain that if I fuck this up, they never will. The one time I tried to play this in college, I didn't get a single ball in. I got so angry at the stiff-arm jokes and losing that I stormed off and refused to play ever again. But now, the mechanics of my body glide in an easy harmony as my shoulder externally rotates, the muscles adducting to accelerate the throw enough to propel it across the table. I'm as surprised as everyone else when the ball lands with a frothy, little *plink* into the Ohs' front cup.

"Okay, Julian!" Eve claps like a tiny, maniacal coach. "Do that again!"

I can't believe it, but the second throw lands, and the third one, too. Eve and Graham become increasingly belligerent with each sunken ball, jumping up and down behind me, whooping like hype guys in a parking lot fight. The Ohs, who I've spent my adult life desperately avoiding, are even *more* supportive, pumping their fists and chanting *Julie, Julie, Julie* with each of my wins before groaning good-naturedly and emptying another of their dwindling cups. Other voices join in the cheering, our table the center of a small, enthusiastic crowd. Graham retrieves the slick ball and hands it to me. My cousins haven't even had a turn yet. One cup remains.

"You can do it, son!" Eve squeezes my non-throwing arm with steely determination in her eyes.

This shot has become the most important goal in my life. Half the town is watching, and for once, they're rooting for *me*. There's no ill will, no rolling eyes, no *can you believe this guy* shakes of their heads. Even Mr. Donahue is hunched forward, palms braced against his thighs, spectating from the sidelines.

"I've got odds on a perfect game, perfect game—who's in?" A few hands reach over his shoulder to press cash into his.

I press the ball to my chest, touched. Mr. Donahue's... taking *bets*?

Sweat prickles down my neck as I lower my throwing arm and turn to address the crowd. "I just want to say, your support means everything."

Cheers boom around me. I am Rocky, entering the ring. Jon Bon Jovi spotted in the frozen aisle at Shop Rite. Guy Fieri's frosted tips just, like, all the time.

"When I first grasped this ball—"

Eve yanks my sleeve. "Just shoot. No speech."

"Right." I clear my throat. "I won't let you down!" I thrust my arm high into the air, feeling the rowdy cheering in my very bones.

I take my spot, aim, and—

plink.

The crowd goes *wild.*

"Aww, great job, sweetie!" I turn around as a soft hand pats my back, my heart lurching in my chest as the crowd disperses.

"Mom?"

Her face is loose and happy, and it breaks into a grin positively dripping with oxytocin. She is wearing a long, lime-green feather boa and a plastic top hat intended for St. Patrick's Day, except somebody has taped a weed leaf over its shamrock. Her eyes are bloodshot and dilated.

Beside her is Dr. Srinivasan, smiling proudly and housing a bag of Cheetos.

I blink at her, utterly dumbfounded, as she pulls me into a big, embarrassing hug, swaying side to side and refusing to let me go. The smell emanating from her clothing brings me back like a time machine to our old garage, where Dad languished day after day, doing absolutely nothing with his life and—and—

Smoking marijuana.

"Are you *high*?" I pull out of her arms forcefully, but she doesn't seem to clock my question or my rising anger.

"This is wonderfully open-minded of you, Julie. Supporting Nomi's dispensary at her Pot Luck like this." Mom beams dopily at me. "I'm so proud of you, sweetie."

Pot luck? Nomi? *Dispensary?!*

I can't process any of this because Mom's standing there, stoned out of her mind in her ridiculous weed hat, and *still,* her words pulse through me like a bigger, stronger heartbeat than my own.

I'm so proud of you, sweetie.

My eyes feel suspiciously heavy, like they might produce *tears* over this, which is outrageous and cannot be borne.

"I'm not here because I'm *open-minded,*" I spit it out like it's a dirty word. "I'm here to pick up Dr. Srinivasan."

Her grin falters, then collapses into the small, disappointed frown I know too well. Dr. Srinivasan places a calm hand on her shoulder. "I'm sorry, Gisella."

"I can't believe you, Mom!" I rake my fingers into my hair. "I can't believe you're *here*, doing *drugs*!" I point at Dr. Srinivasan. "With *him*!"

Before she can say another word, I turn and flee into the house, up the stairs within, through a door I slam shut behind me, and then, out the window.

Shit. I should've stopped with the door.

CHAPTER SEVEN

NOMI

Fuck. I flex my fingers into fists as I pace across my bedroom. That fucker *fired* me. And in front of Council-friends! Even if they forget the travesty they just witnessed, I needed my XYB job to help cover start-up costs. My savings was hit hard by the deposits required to lease the building, and now, I have a month's salary *less* to pay my bills; keep me fed, watered, and smoked up; *and* bankroll Stranger Drugs?

A darker, more troubling thought hits—what's going to happen to my health insurance? I haven't had a bad flare in a few years, but the last one resulted in a brief hospitalization that would've bankrupted me without my XYB insurance. COBRA benefits should be available, but at a jaw-dropping cost. I squeeze my eyes closed. Thank God for this party because whatever we've managed to raise is now critically important to keeping me afloat.

I pull my vape out of my dress's pocket and take three deep pulls, sighing as the calming chemicals hit my bloodstream. I'd vowed to stay clearheaded until I schmoozed with the Council-friends, but now that that ship's sailed, been attacked by pirates, and is lying broken in Davy Jones's Locker, I better head off this full-body panic attack before it sets in.

A knock rattles against my door. "Excuse me?"

I open it and find a random guy waiting outside. "Um, there's a man on your roof? He's freaking out. Thought you should know."

"*Great.*" I stomp past him toward the internal staircase. We must've forgotten to lock Eve's door, and now I have to go lure some stoned townie safely off my roof. What a fucking night.

I enter Eve's empty apartment. "Hello?" Directly across from the front door, the tall window is cranked open, its curtains dancing in the breeze. Eve keeps it up whenever she's baking to let out the heat, and since she was up here baking all day, I'm not surprised she left it open.

I *am* surprised to hear a man's raspy cry for help on the other side of it, though.

"Stay put, I'm coming!" Sighing heavily, I sit on the open sash, butt first, then swing my legs over and ease out onto the gentle pitch of the gabled roof. I straighten, still holding onto the window dormer for balance, then nearly fall off anyway.

No.

My head rears back with a violence. I blink, but the malevolent specter haunting my chimney remains.

"Julian?"

Broad shoulders encased beneath pale pink linen turn first. It *can't* be Julian, but then that Clark Kent jawline appears, like a road that dead ends in those slutty little glasses, and *Jesus,* it *is* him. The night's humid breeze has re-formed his neat, black waves into a soft starburst of dark curls. With his navy chinos, brown loafers, and striking blue eyes, Julian is Wall Street devastating. He is soap opera gorgeous. He is—

"STUCK ON THIS ROOF!" he bellows, hands desperately gripping the chimney like they're grinding on the dance floor.

"What are you doing on my *roof*?!"

"Being stuck," he wails.

I have so many questions. Infinity questions. Why is Julian here? Why is he on my roof? Why is he humping my chimney and wailing about it? My mouth opens and closes several times, but there's nothing for it—he's actually scared, his torso rising and falling so rapidly, I'm worried he'll faint.

Jesus. I have to rescue Julian D'Angelo.

Luckily it's a pretty straightforward rescue. Five easy steps, and I'm already at the chimney and offering my hand. Our roof isn't a big deal. If you can walk up a wheelchair ramp surrounded by handrails without losing your balance, then you can climb it. Still, Julian shudders in my grip. His eyes are so pale in the moonlight, they look almost clear. Like ice-melt. Shimmering, terrified ice-melt. But looking down at me, he seems to remember who I am, and a flash of that old Julian self-consciousness flares to life. He straightens as tall as he can, clutching the chimney with one hand and me with the other. "Okay, um. What's the plan? 911? Firefighters?"

"We're going to calmly walk four steps over there, to the flat part. See?"

"*Move?* You can't be serious! That's how people end up in my ER like sacks of broken twigs, Nomi! Goopy, squelching sacks of twigs!"

I wrinkle my nose. "Could you not get grossly poetic right now? I've done this hundreds of times. It's fine."

I tug him forward, but he shakes his head.

"I *can't.*"

"*Yes,* you *can.*" I say the words firmly, a near verbatim imitation of him the night he stitched me up. The icy, authoritative tone works, because he finally relinquishes his hold on the chimney to grab me with both hands. One wrenches around my arm, the other bracketing my hip hard enough he might leave a mark.

I silently curse the shiver it sends down my spine. He whimpers a little, and *oh, Jesus,* I like that, *too*!

Goddammit, Spinster Nomi mutters from deep within her knitting cave. *Someone vaped the HORNY POT AGAIN.*

I forcibly shake off the effects of Julian's proximity and lead him over the dry, wooden shingles to our destination. It takes a second, but he finally releases his grip on me so that I can ease down onto the roof and sit, tucking my dress's poplin skirt beneath me. I pat the space next to me, and he sinks in a sad, shaking heap of long man limbs, the whole party below us.

"Now. Why are you on my roof?"

Julian draws his legs up to his chest, folding his arms around them, and starts rocking. This trauma response is deeply on the nose. "I was angry," he begins.

"Okay."

"I stormed inside, then upstairs."

"In another person's house. Sure." My voice is wry.

He doesn't notice.

"And then I just...kept storming." His whole face wrinkles in confusion, as if his answer doesn't make sense to him, either. He removes his glasses and rubs his eyes with a balled-up fist before putting them back on. The gesture is so—coarse. So unexpectedly childlike. *Everything* about Julian seems off right now. "That chimney came out of *nowhere.*"

"Yeah." I cock my head at him, fully suspicious now. "They do that."

Julian nods glumly, like what I've said is the sad truth of it. He doesn't argue, or frown, or roll his eyes with exasperation, or anything.

What's *wrong* with him?

And more importantly, why is he here? Is he trying to sabotage the Pot Luck? Because if so, he's either doing a terrible job, or his machinations are so brilliant, they're undetectable. And Julian doesn't *do* terrible jobs. He's uniformly, infuriatingly proficient. At everything.

Something *pings* against the roof, an acorn maybe, tittering as it rolls over the edge.

Julian's head swivels around. "Was that a raccoon?"

"No, it's probably—"

"*Shhh!*" Julian scoots closer and presses a big palm over my mouth. The heat of him this close raises the hairs all over my body as his chest swells, hiding me in the shadow of his torso. His face is frozen, but his eyes dart all around. A distinct *titta-titta-titta* sound comes from behind us.

"I *knew* it," Julian says, his voice low and panicked. "You're in*fested*!"

I peel his palm off my mouth, disturbed to find that his other hand is pressed flat against my lower back in this strangely possessive, protective position, like he's ready to fight whatever's out here on my behalf, but he's probably going to die about it. "Julian—there are no raccoons. Look." I point to where the sound is coming from and the scrawny peach-colored kitten scratching its claws on the wooden shingles. "It's just Big Bird."

After a few, strained seconds, Julian slowly recedes from my personal space. I shouldn't be amused, but I am, all the anger and anxiety at being fired at my own party dissipating in the wake of Julian's ridiculousness. Big Bird must sense his need, too, because he hops gamely up into Julian's lap. Julian immediately curls him into his arms, tucking Big Bird's head beneath his chin.

"Why do you call him Big Bird when he's so wittle?" He presses a kiss into the kitten's head, which makes me laugh.

"Because the first thing he did when Eve brought him home was kill a big bird."

Julian coughs and rears back, revolted.

"You still haven't explained why you're *here*." I articulate each word, hoping they'll turn this ketchup bottle of an impostor upside down and shake him until the *real* Julian comes gushing out.

It earns me a quick, defensive cut of his eyes. "I didn't intentionally crash your marijuana party, if that's what you're implying. Dr. Srinivasan needed a ride home because he was intoxicated, but when I got here, I couldn't find him, which made me angry because I was starving, but then somehow, I was playing *beer pong*? Which is weird because I never play games, but I was *amazing*, Nomi, everyone was cheering, even your mean little lesbian—"

"Eve, cheering?" I blink. "You're sure it was *my* mean little lesbian?"

"Yes!" he insists. "She even called me son! Then my actual mother told me she was proud of me." He sighs, resting his chin on his chest dolefully as he strokes Big Bird's little kitten beard.

My head dips as I try to parse through this for any semblance of logical meaning. "And... that made you mad?"

"Very!" He looks at me with hurt indignation, as if I should know this already. "My mom was under the influence of cannabis, Nomi! Just like Dr. Srinivasan!"

"It is pretty weird seeing your parents high for the first time," I concede, feeling a little sorry for him despite myself. He looks so despondent, and there's something precious about a man cuddling a kitten, even a man and kitten as annoying as these two. "Not quite walking-in-on-sex level, but up there."

He squeezes his eyes shut. "She knows how I feel about marijuana, she saw what it did to Dad! Saw how it ruined his life, then my life. Then her life. And his life," he repeats, losing the thread.

My eyebrows rise. Even though Mom is close friends with Gisella, I still haven't heard the full story of her late husband and Julian's father. All I know is that he passed away when Julian was young, and that according to Gisella, Julian was never the same. He wouldn't talk about him when we were in high school, and I never prodded. Some people wear their grief like a sprung bear trap, and touching the area only makes it worse.

You try to talk to them, to let them know you can be a safe space for their feelings, but even that is unbearable, and they lash out at you, snarling, before hobbling off to seethe in pain alone. I didn't want Julian to push me away, so I never asked.

So why is he suddenly willing to talk about it now? Is he drunk?

"And now Mom's smoking it, too. Just like he did."

"Vaping it," I correct. I sold Gisella the newest Pax myself, but I don't tell Julian this. "Probably."

He runs his palms down his cheeks. "Ugh. My mom *vapes*." He twists to face me, his expression suddenly accusatory. "And you're opening a dispensary!"

I sigh heavily. I wondered when we'd get to this. "Yep."

"To dispense marijuana!"

"That is the plan."

"To my *mother*?!"

"I mean..." I start to explain it's not my role to prevent people's mothers from using cannabis, but all I can focus on are his eyes. Because behind those infuriatingly hot frames, his pale-blue irises contrast prettily against the telltale pink sclera of the recently stoned.

Oh, fuck. Is Julian high?

It suddenly all makes sense. The roof, the rambling, the kindness. He's *high* as *fuck*, and he *doesn't know*!

How did this happen? The party's purpose is no secret. There are signs everywhere asking for donations to support the dispensary. Does Julian not know what weed smells like? Tastes like? Did the table full of festively green, funky food with high price tags not tip him off?

"You ate something off the dining table, didn't you?"

"Why does *everyone* keep asking me that?" Julian exclaims. "I paid your outrageous suggested donations!"

"What did you eat, Julian?!"

Julian huffs. "This is fat shaming. You know that, right?"

"Okay, you are *not* using that term correctly, we'll talk about that later, but for right now, tell me what you ate!"

He starts to protest, but stops, his eyes cranking open. "Was the food poisoned?"

"Poisoned? No, you weirdo. But infused with Eve's famous cannabis budder? Yes."

Now Julian's head is rattling side to side, a pure, unadulterated rejection of the truth. "No! They were protein bars! They're good for you!"

"The Hemp Hemp Hooray bars?" My brows round into my bangs. They are one of the strongest edibles on the table, meant for our devoted fans of cross-country running while high. "How many did you have?"

Julian's visibly frightened now. "Two? I didn't know!"

"At ten dollars a pop?! You didn't think that was weird?"

"They were delicious!" he wails before nuzzling into Big Bird's fur, murdered birds forgotten. "I thought they were all natural! Fancy! Bespoke!"

A smile tugs at the corners of my mouth. Julian has always been so dramatic. As if to prove my point even more, his head jolts up, his eyes full blue moons of terror.

"*What about the cookies?*" he hoarses out in a perfect horror-movie whisper.

A laugh bubbles out, which I instantly regret. Julian's really scared, and that shouldn't be funny. It's not. It's just, has anyone ever uttered *those* words with *that* inflection in the history of humankind? I think not.

"Nomi! *What about the cookies?!*"

Another laugh escapes before I can clap a hand over my mouth. Julian looks utterly betrayed.

"I'm sorry," I choke out. "It's just—you keep saying that so seriously, but they're cookies, which are the least serious things ever, and—"

Julian takes me by both shoulders. "*WHAT ABOUT THE COOKIES!*"

"Yes!" I laugh out. "They contain five milligrams of THC each. Why, did you house those, too?" I wipe the tears leaking from my eyes as Julian's hands slowly slip down my arms, then fall off completely.

He nods once, tight. Terrified.

My eyebrows rise. "Oh. Shit. How many?"

"I don't remember," he moans.

"Okay." I force excess chill into my words, my demeanor, my vibe. Last thing Julian needs is to see me panic. "How much money did you put down on the table?"

"Fifty dollars."

"Oh, boy," I say softly. Fifty dollars' worth of edibles, eaten all at once, would be a one-way ticket to space for experienced users. And Julian's a total baby. Whatever he's feeling now is just the beginning.

I do not tell him this.

"You're going to be fine." I pat him on the shoulder lamely. "You need some food and water, and then sleep. You'll be back to normal in the morning."

"I'm not going to be *fine*! I can't get those brain cells back, Nomi! Oh, God, no wonder I've felt so good—I'm stoned! I'm addicted already, I can tell!" Julian shoves Big Bird at me, then bolts upright to his feet. "I've got to call my advisor! Or is he here?" Julian frowns for a second, then looks down at the party below. "ERIC?!" he screams at the lawn.

"Julian, whoa—wait a minute, let me help—"

"You did this on purpose, didn't you? You probably think it's hilarious!" Julian sways out of my reach, seemingly oblivious that we're on a roof, and takes a step back. "You stay away from me, Nomi Wyeth! You and your—your baked goods!"

"*Jesus*, hold on to something! Julian, *no*!" I reach for him, but he's already stumbling backward. A surge of horror floods my entire system as I watch his arms windmill by his sides for one terrible second before he falls, ass first, off my roof.

CHAPTER EIGHT

JULIAN

S*creams.*

"Was that Julian D'Asshole?"

I wake up slowly in Nomi's big, scratchy bush.

The irony. I *cackle.*

"Julie?! You okay, bro?" Marco hovers over me with a worried brow.

"Um. Maybe?" I squint my eyes, but there's only one of him. No neuro trauma, that's good. "Can you pull me out of here? I'm trapped—" A *giggle* escapes my mouth.

I've never giggled in my life. It happens *again.*

"—in Nomi's giant *bush.*"

Marco's face cracks into a luminous, relieved grin. "He's fine, everybody!" The party cheers as my cousins partition me into thirds, Marco grabbing me by the armpits, Aldo by the ankles, and Ellio stuck with my ass to lift me from the overgrown hedge that saved my life. I contract muscle by muscle, starting with my toes and working my way up, testing for injury as I've instructed a thousand different patients. When I squeeze my butt cheeks, Ellio curses and nearly drops me. I cackle again. Our ridiculous D'Angelo quartet collectively stumbles, bringing us all to the ground.

"I'm sorry for squeezing my butt cheeks, bro," I say as contritely as I can, which isn't very because I'm howling with laughter. "That probably felt really weird."

"Yeah, man." Ellio laughs uncomfortably. "Are you sure you're okay?"

"Oh, I ate fifty dollars and am becoming my father!" I explain, still howling. "I'm doomed!" I push up to sitting, and my arm twinges, then goes strangely numb. I check to make sure it's still there.

It is! I smile happily and hug it to my chest.

"You're gonna be fine, buddy." Marco eases up to standing, brushing the dirt off the knees of his Armani Exchange jeans. I bet he hated getting them dirty, but he did it, for me. Warmth radiates through my entire chest, but then *Nomi* appears, like a tiny golden fairy, and pushes through the crowd.

"Julian! Are you hurt?" She falls to her knees and runs her hands frantically down my arms, over my shoulders, up both sides of my neck. Each point of contact between her and me sends a pleasurable web of sensation jolting through my nervous system. "You're bleeding—you're all scratched up!"

"I fell off your roof." I smile into her eyes.

"Yes, you did," she says slowly, her worry morphing into something else. Is that her own small smile? "How are you feeling?" Her voice is so gentle, it feels like cool silk fluttering against hot skin. It brings me back to the front seat in her old Subaru, fifteen years ago, when she used that soft, quiet voice to tell me all her dreams. "Concentrate for me, okay? Does anything hurt?"

I try to do what Nomi asks. Why do my thoughts feel slippery and buoyant? Then, I remember—I was really mad about something. Really, *really* mad. What was it? I gaze into Nomi's face, searching, but what could I have possibly been angry about when she's here, looking at me, talking to me, *being with me*? There's no trace of her usual scorn or frustration, just wide-open concern and relief. Relief that I'm okay. That I made it out of her bush alive.

A laugh rumbles in my chest.

"What is it?" Worry rises on her face.

I shrug, then give her my most playboy smile. "Oh, I just keep ending up in your bush."

Her eyes widen, and then she bursts out a single, shocked laugh. "I cannot *believe* you just said that."

I waggle my eyebrows, unable to stop performing for her smile, her approval, her *laugh*. It fills me up, makes me as buoyant as my thoughts. Her happiness feels like food lifted to my starving mouth, and I'm suddenly convinced that if she'd let me, I'd sing for this supper of smiles every night.

Also, I'm *starving*. The hunger's come back with a vengeance.

Nomi helps me to my feet. "Come on, let's get you cleaned up."

"Okay, but can there also be food?"

Nomi laughs again as she escorts me through the back door, but it peters out into a sigh as she takes in my broad shoulders, incredible pectorals, and tight, thick torso. "You eat so much pizza, don't you."

"*So* much," I agree as a lazy, punch-drunk grin spreads across my face. I fish out a hundred-dollar bill and crumple it into her hand. "Buy this many, please. A pepperoni one. And banana peppers. And one with sausage. And a veggie one, for balance. And—"

"Are there any pizzas you *don't* want? That might be easier."

"—AND," I continue, diplomatically ignoring her ridiculous question, "cinnamon rolls."

"Julian. Pizza Palace will not have cinnamon rolls."

"Oh, ye of wittle faith!"

"That is the second time tonight you said *wittle*, and I just want you to know, I will *not* be forgetting it." Nomi quickly orders from her phone, her tongue darting across her lower lip in concentration. I can't stop staring at it.

She hesitates, then leads me into what must be her bedroom. "I'll get the first-aid kit. You stay here."

My eyes drink it all in. I saw her high school bedroom once—covered in band posters, everything in shades of witchy black and lavender. But this room is a dark, emerald green, the color of a winter forest. The curtains are velvet, the mirrors trimmed in brass. The wooden furniture gleams like copper, antique but restored.

It's so . . . mature.

"Wow," I mumble as I sit on the bed, my eyes snagging on the nightstand. "That's a *huge* vibrator."

"*What?!*" Nomi screeches from the attached bathroom. I lean over, possessed by the need to hold it.

"Oh man, this joker's a plug-in? This must have some serious horses power." In my hand, it feels like an old-timey microphone. A gigantic one. I tap it and wink at myself in the mirror. "Is this thing on?"

Nomi appears suddenly, her arms full of medical supplies.

"Put that down!"

" 'Cause I'm your ladaaaaaay!" I belt out, pointing to her as she drops the supplies and lunges at me. "And you are my maaaa*yaaah-yaaah*-an."

"Why are you singing Céline Dion?!"

"It's our song, don't you remember? It played when we first held hands." I wrestle the vibrator away like a toy I'm refusing to share, which, I guess it is. "Whenever you REAAACH for meeeee," I wheeze out, laughing as Nomi climbs over me, grabbing at it wildly, starting to laugh now, too. "I'll do all that I caaaaaa*yaaah-yaaaah*-an!"

I finally manage to find the on switch, and it *roars* to life just as Nomi sends me sprawling onto my back, fully atop me, breasts smushed against my chest, her hand clasped around mine which is clasped around the teeth-rattling *behemoth* she uses to pleasure herself. The thought rings like a bell through my entire body, stiffening my dick in a delicious rush. My laughter turns to groans beneath her, my body thoroughly confused as to what's happening right now.

Just then, steps pause outside Nomi's open bedroom door. "Hey, cuz? We're heading out, you need a—HEYOOO!" Marco's eyebrows meet his gelled-back bangs as he sees me on my back, Nomi straddling my lap, and the giant vibrator buzzing in our joined grip. His hands shoot into the air. "Excuse me! Did *not* mean to disturb youse!"

"Marco!" Nomi shrieks, still fumbling to turn off the vibrator. "It's not what it looks like!"

"PLEASE! As you were!" Marco flashes me a huge wink and closes the door, through which I can hear his muffled announcement: "The hostess has retired for the evening. Let no man, woman, or nonbinary individual disturb this room!"

Fuck, Marco is cool. How did I not realize this before?

My eyes return to Nomi's, and I see the happy confusion I'm feeling staring back at me.

"You remember?" she asks breathlessly. "The song that played when we first held hands?" Her cheeks are flushed a pretty pink from our wrestling, and her bottom lip, so pouty and full, is partially hidden where she's biting it in. The flush carries down her neck, across her collarbone, down the tops of her round breasts brimming the low neckline of her dress.

"I remember everything." My confession leads to a sharp intake of her breath. Both of her hands are clasped around my one, over my head, and my one free arm longs to caress the arch of her back, dig my fingers into her hip, and grind her against me. My arm actually flops a bit at my side, like it wants to but can't.

Concerning, really. I'd be more worried, but shooting stars explode at every point of contact between us, and I'm too dazzled by the sensation to think of anything else.

She shifts against me to steal her vibrator back, but the movement puts the apex of her thighs directly against the massive erection throbbing beneath these summer-weight chinos. Her eyes flutter shut, and forget it, I was practically flaccid before compared to the column of rock slotted against her now.

"Oh, God, I'm *Stonehenge*," I murmur, dazed with excruciating pleasure. "The balance beam, and you're my gymnast."

Nomi blinks dreamily down at me. "What?"

"Can I kiss you?" I let go of the vibrator to run my good hand down the side of her face, fingers dipping into her long waves. "Please, Nomi? Oh, God, *please*?" I'm begging, and I don't even care, I've never wanted anything more. I murmur *please* over and over again as her beautiful, confused face draws closer, giving us both time to avert this kiss before it happens. I'm still begging when her full mouth drops lightly onto mine, and a seismic shift upends my entire world. Land torn apart, then crushed together anew, all the continents of who I am reborn under one new flag, ruled by a new empire—*Nomi*.

My fingers find the back of her head, the curve of her neck, and the kiss opens up, deepens, expands until it's all consuming, open ocean, no land in sight. The feel of her small body lying on top of mine is the most comprehensive pressure I've ever experienced, calming me, grounding me, the spiraling tentacles of my ever-reaching anxiety receding into my body quick and vicious, like one of those stressful tape measures handy types use. The soft wet of her mouth sliding against mine makes my cock ache and strain, and she's begun to rock gently against it. I groan into her, pulling her tightly into me, and a sigh of pleasure escapes her lips before we crush together again. Our mingled breath fogs the lenses of my glasses, but I can't stop staring at her face as it slides through expressions of longing and pleasure, like I'm watching her get off behind the steamed glass of a shower.

Oh, *God*, Nomi in a fucking *shower*?? My good hand slides from her head down the arch of her spine, resting in the curve there, until she grabs my hand and drags it lower, under her dress, and presses it against her ass. I grip her, feeling madness at the information my fingers send to my brain, the rounded wedge of flesh between panty and leg visible in my mind as I anchor her to me, turning her gentle rocking into a rough, grinding punishment that I'll crave now for the rest of my life.

"*Nomi*," I moan, my voice cracking, loud enough that everything stops.

Nomi's eyes open. She blinks down at me and gasps, seeming to remember *it's a' me, Julian!* cue Mario Bros music. In one heartbreaking instant, she scrambles up my torso, grabs the vibrator, and rolls off, leaving us both panting on our backs, lying side by side. The whole interlude felt like hours, but in reality, was probably less than a minute. Only one minute of kissing her—that's all I get? I want to *cry*.

Oh, shit. I can see my hard-on without lifting my head.

My eyes shift to her just as her eyes shift to *me*, down there, then sees *me* seeing *her* see *it*.

"Oh my God." She covers her face with both hands. "What were we thinking?!"

"That that was amazing?" I roll onto my side, staring at her in bleary-eyed wonder. "That that felt better than anything I've ever experienced?"

Nomi shoots up to sitting. "It's the pot's fault. Some kinds make people horny, that's all."

"It does?"

"Yes. Does your body feel, um—" she pauses to swallow, "extra sensitive to touch right now?"

I nod vigorously.

"Well, that's why," she says, her voice strangely high-pitched. "Nothing to do with us or our feelings whatsoever." She pulls her dress's hem down, then lurches to standing, grabbing all the hastily dropped first-aid supplies and depositing them on the bed. Then, she throws a towel at me, a T-shirt, and after a beat of digging around her drawers, a pair of sweatpants, too. "You should shower to clean off all those cuts, then you can put those on, we'll eat, and I'll call you a Lyft home."

I feel strangely evicted from our kiss, hurt in a way I can't explain. "It was just the pot?" I repeat, frowning as I try to process this. "But it felt so real."

Nomi, hearing the hurt in my voice, sits back down and awkwardly pats my leg. "Yeah. But it's okay. Sometimes cannabis makes you chase pleasure, that's all. I promise you, tomorrow you'll realize what a crazy idea kissing each other is, and you'll understand." Her eyes dart toward my massive erection, then back to mine as she quickly withdraws her hand. "Trust me, okay? You are very, *very* stoned right now, and I've been smoking, too."

"Okay." I yawn, my eyes feeling delightfully heavy, if sad. Since starting work at the ER, sleep has become a utilitarian act, devoid of any pleasure. Two hours here, five hours there. Maybe a full eight on a rare weekend off. My body is trained to fall asleep the second my eyes close, then wake up from a period of dreamless black, like a battery dinging when recharged. But right now, I feel like a cat languidly lying in a puddle of sunlight, eyes squeezed closed in little satisfied diagonals. I stretch luxuriously across Nomi's down comforter.

"Yell if you need anything." She eyes me suspiciously, then shuts the door, which is so weird because she immediately starts knocking on it again. "Julian? Are you decent?"

I blink at the door as she slowly opens it. She sighs, exasperated for some reason. "You didn't shower yet?"

"You just left."

"Twenty-five minutes ago."

"Impossible," I murmur as she marches inside, forces me up and out of her bed and into the bathroom. I sniff the air like a bloodhound. "The pizza's here!" Also like a bloodhound, I feel like howling about it.

"You can't have any until you shower."

"Aww, Nomi—please? Please, I'm *so hungry*." I hear myself whining like a small, dejected child. A truly pathetic, starving child. To *Nomi Wyeth*. First for kissing, and now for pizza. And yet, I continue to do it without an iota of shame as she unbuttons my tattered shirt swiftly and throws it in her hamper. I can't stop thinking about the pizza, about Nomi holding it to her mouth, biting it, cheese stretching—

Oh damn. The boner's back.

"*Jesus*, Julian!" She throws her hand over her eyes.

"I think it's from the pizza!" I wail. "A slice will make it go away!"

And that's how I end up naked eating pizza in Nomi Wyeth's shower, her hand holding a slice beyond the curtain to my face while I dutifully wash all my cuts.

It may have taken a lot of negotiation to get me into the shower, but it takes almost as much to get me out. I like arguing with Nomi too much—always have. Ultimately, I use up all her hot water before I'm willing to leave the haven of girl-smelling steam I've created from using all her products. But the cold water hits me like a slap in the balls, and shrieking, I finally step back out and wrap myself in the giant fluffy towel she left for me. I huddle within its luxe terrycloth embrace, smiling dazedly as I exit the bathroom like a lavender-scented Sith Lord fresh from the spa.

Nomi glances up from her floor, where she's sitting cross-legged with a plate of pizza, and laughs.

"Why are you doing that thing with your face?" She makes a swirly gesture at her own mouth. "That . . . smiling thing."

"It's just, everything's so *nice* here." I nuzzle in the towel. "Your comforter, your towels, this bed." I heave myself onto it in a running jump, then groan happily. "It's like a hotel made of you. I'd never leave if home was this nice."

Nomi shrugs. "Creature comforts are how I get by."

"What do you mean?"

"I . . . don't get out much," she finishes suddenly, as though she almost said something else but changed her mind. "Home needs to be special when you spend so much time in it."

Nomi dabs Neosporin on the long scratches on my back I can't reach, which I *try* not to get a boner about. I cannot develop a Pavlovian boner response to the smell of antibiotic ointments in my profession. Then, when I get stuck because of my bum arm, she helps pull her fresh T-shirt over my head. It's super soft, like everything in her world, and fits me skintight. She sucks a breath in when she sees my left arm.

"Julian . . . is your arm supposed to be that color?"

I glance down at the angry purple streak painting my forearm. "Hmm," I muse, noting how big it's grown since I took the shower. "Nope."

Nomi winces. "Should we call Dr. Appa?"

"That stoner?" I snort. "Nah. It's fine."

It's definitely not fine. But it doesn't really hurt and also . . . I just don't *care*? My head feels thick and pleasant, my stomach ravenous, and my entire body, inexplicably, the shade of *pink*. And all that matters right now is *being here* and *eating pizza* and *mmm*. Nestled next to Nomi on her couch, housing my sixth slice, and talking animatedly about every random thing that pops into my brain feels like life on an alien planet and yet simultaneously, like an inevitability my entire life has been moving toward. I feel *good*. I feel *happy*. And, judging by the way Nomi's laughing against my side, not at *all* disgusted with my company, she feels the same way, too.

My God, Eric was *right*.

That intelligent bastard was a hundred percent right, I *should* ask Nomi out! The kiss alone is proof there's something magical between us, and stoned or not, this has been the best night of my life.

"Julian?" Nomi pokes me in the side. "You okay?" She's been watching me closely, taking care of me through my drug-fueled stupor, and when she ribs me, it feels playful and kind.

Is this what dating Nomi would be like? Nights on her plush couch, watching TV with the volume low so we can talk over it, eating pizza and laughing and—and—

Getting high?

The thought punches me straight in the stomach.

"I can't," I blurt out.

Nomi frowns. "Can't what?" And *fuck*, even her frown is beautiful. The gentle furrow between her brows, her sharp, inquisitive eyes, the quiet demand she places on the universe to explain itself because she has a right to know. She looks at me like she wants to understand me, and dammit if it doesn't make me feel like the most important man in the world.

But I can't throw everything away to sit on this couch, even if Nomi's sitting beside me on it.

"I can't—eat any more pizza," I finish lamely, which is a lie, but I force myself to abandon the slice. When was the last time I let myself have pizza? An eight-pack of abs ago?

She assesses me a few seconds longer, then glances at the clock on the wall, one of those cat types with the swinging tail and moving eyes. "It's really late. Whatever you're still feeling, you'll sleep it off by morning. Drink this." She hands me a tall glass of water and watches me gulp it down, then disappears. My heart pangs at the cold spot at my side, where a few seconds ago, her warm body had been. When she returns, it's with another glass of water, a big, fluffy pillow, and the softest blanket I've ever felt. I nuzzle it against my face, breathing in the smell of Nomi's laundry detergent, and exhale, feeling magically better.

"I'm in there if you need anything." She points at her bedroom door. She must sense the angst building in my chest at her leaving because she adds, kindly, "You'll be okay, Julian. I promise. And... thanks."

"For what?"

"For cheering me up. I—was having a pretty rough night, until you came along."

"You're welcome," I sigh happily as I snuggle under the blanket, smelling of her. "I'll come anytime you want."

She rolls her eyes and looks at me, bemused, as if she *also* cannot believe that I'm sprawled out on her couch. She turns off the lamp, the last source of light in the living room, and leaves, her bedroom door snicking softly shut behind her.

I can't *wait* to see her again.

Something is *profoundly* wrong with my mouth.

My tongue creaks in protest as I rip it from my palate, glued there by the vestiges of my dried-up saliva. It feels too big, coated in sandpaper, and when it finally wrenches free, it makes a sound like Velcro. Moving it triggers my gag reflex, and I shoot up from the couch, *whose couch am I on*, and grab at the glass on the coffee table.

Fuck, it's empty! I stumble-run for the hall bathroom, filling the glass from the tap then gulping it down. I finish, breathless, then blink until my tear ducts release some moisture into my bloodshot sclera.

The image in the mirror is blurred at the edges, *where the fuck are my glasses*, and utterly unrecognizable. My hair is a mop of bedhead, completely flat on one side, a bouffant on the other. My respectable clothes are gone, cruelly replaced by a pair of silky pink sweatpants that cling to every crevice and end at midcalf. Likewise, the tiny T-shirt someone has dressed me in ends in a bare midriff. I peel it up to read the words screaming in hot pink: Kiss & Tale, A Romance Bookshop, Collingswood, NJ.

The *fuck* is going on?

My whole body aches, and for some reason, my left arm is tender, painful, and three times the size of my right, a real-life Popeye situation. A streak of red is painted across my mouth, and squinting, I scrape a bit of it off and smell.

Is that *oregano*?! I stand up straight, then gasp at the mound blooming beneath the T-shirt. I poke at it in disbelief, only for it to spring back.

Pizza belly! I have *pizza belly*!

"Julian?" An instant later, Nomi Wyeth appears in the doorway, and I shriek, yanking down the tiny T-shirt to cover my bloated abdomen.

"Oh, sorry!" she yips, then turns awkwardly to give me privacy.

Memories of the night bumble back with all the grace of a middle-aged man doing Pilates. Disturbing. Wrong. Painful to endure. These are *Nomi Wyeth's* clothes. I—spent the night here. Nothing happened, except for—*oh, God*—when I stole her vibrator?! The feel of her straddling my lap courses through me, *that* memory crystal clear, as well as the massive boner that resulted. And the kiss...

My eyes flutter shut remembering the kiss. The slide of her soft pout against my bottom lip, the feel of her ass in my hand. How I *begged*.

Oh, God. I think I'm going to die.

"Is everything okay?" she asks without turning around. "Are you, um. Still stoned?"

Stoned... that's *right*—that's what happened to me! I ate those protein bars, and then I—the memories get fuzzier after that. They have the hazy quality of a dream where nothing you said or did makes any sense, and yet it happened anyway, and despite everything seeming incredibly stupid now, when it happened there was a vibe, a good one.

Everyone liked me. Everyone was cheering for *me*. My cousins, Eve, people I didn't even know.

Did that really happen?

"You got me stoned..." I blink.

Nomi snorts. "You got yourself stoned by raiding the edibles table at our Pot Luck fundraiser."

"Pot Luck fundraiser?"

"Last night was a fundraiser for my dispensary. Do you remember anything?"

"Yeah, that you got me stoned, then made me fall off your roof!" I glare down at my Popeye arm, remembering now how it wouldn't work last night. "And then you *straddled me*!"

"Whoa!" Nomi turns around, all concern for my privacy lost in flushed indignation. "None of that is my fault! You fell off because you started freaking out, like you're doing right now by the way, and then *you* started playing with *my vibrator*! I had to get it back!" She crosses her arms over her chest.

"I wasn't playing with it!"

"What else do you call singing into it like a microphone?" Nomi's eyes narrow. "Singing *Céline Dion*. How am I supposed to use it after witnessing *that*?"

A tight, blistering panic has taken over my chest, pushing out my organs. Who needs oxygen? Raw mortification fuels me now.

What else did I do last night?

When I try to remember details, what floats up is just Nomi. Nomi on my lap. Nomi's hand peeking through the shower curtain, holding a slice of pizza for me to eat so I'd shower. Nomi on the couch, her shoulder shaking next to mine as she laughed.

"I didn't ask you out, did I?" I demand.

Nomi rears back like I pushed her. "No, why would you think that?"

"Oh, I don't know, perhaps because I woke up after being drugged dressed like a femme Ken doll in your house?! Anything could've happened!" I throw my arms in the air, then immediately groan as my left arm explodes in agony. "And I think you broke my arm!"

Nomi shakes her head, disgusted. "Well. The spell's broken. You're back to yourself now." She sniffs, her eyes strangely wet. "You should leave."

I stomp past her, cradling my destroyed left appendage, and snatch my glasses and phone from the coffee table.

My messages app sports a bone-chilling *178* red flag. Has someone died?!

I unlock my phone and nearly vomit.

The D'Angelo family text chain is popping off before my eyes. Pictures of me come in, one after another. Me with the perfect beer pong throw. Me pumping my fist like I won the Olympic gold. Me chest-bumping midair with Ellio. Interspersed between the picture texts are a hodgepodge of emojis—laughing faces, skulls, praise hands.

Julian got stoned?!

OMG, tell us everything!

He was the life of the party!

I heard he sang Céline Dion to Nomi! Like right in her face.

Noooo ☠☠☠

Titanic WAS his favorite movie in kindergarten, tho.

Well, I heard he fell off the roof!

No! 😮 That's a sin.

He did!!

Four pictures of me teetering, falling, then sprawled across the hedge, then grinning up from the ground hit the text chain in quick succession.

He's fine, tho.

He was great. Marco pipes in. Then he hooked up with Nomi Wyeth! 😎

Yes!!! Julie could use a good rogering!! That gem was from Mom.

A flood of good jobs! come in next, along with baby emojis and wedding bells.

OMG COULD YOU PLEASE STOP TALKING ABOUT ME, MY GOD!!!!!! I hammer out the text one-handed, order a Lyft because I can't drive right now, then shove the phone away. When I look up, Nomi's leaning against the doorframe, arms crossed tightly over her chest. A look of profound disappointment hangs on her face.

You did that, my brain whispers. *You bastard, you're making her sad!*

"Thanks for ruining my reputation!" I burst out. "The whole town's talking about what a fool I am!"

"Whatever, Julian." She hands me a stack of my freshly washed clothes from last night. How dare she, honestly!

The spell is broken alright. It felt so good last night, when everyone was rooting for me for once. I should've known it wasn't real. People don't smile at *me*. My cousins don't hang out with *me*. And when Nomi Wyeth tilts her pretty chin up to meet my gaze, it isn't to kiss *me*.

Not the real me, at least.

God, I feel ridiculous. Dumber than I've ever felt. The cringe is soul-deep, wringing every last bit of me out in mortified disgust.

"Marijuana is dangerous—it almost killed me last night!" I levy a finger at Nomi. "Your dispensary is going to hurt people! It's going to turn this whole town into a den of even bigger losers than it already is."

Nomi's face burns bright red with her own growing anger. "You're such an asshole! Do you even hear yourself? Cannabis didn't almost kill you last night, but your ignorant, knee-jerk reaction to it could have!"

I can't believe I almost asked her out. There's no world where Doctor Julian D'Angelo falls in love with *street* pharmacist Nomi Wyeth.

Whatever, I was intoxicated with the devil's lettuce.

And now, the whole town knows it. What if Dr. Riveras finds out? The thought makes my heart hammer in my chest. I've got to do what Dr. Riveras said: keep my head down and *stay clean*. I've got to control this narrative.

Dr. Julian D'Angelo doesn't do drugs and sing Céline Dion.

Dr. Julian D'Angelo *fights* drugs, *fights* dispensaries that prey upon poor people's paychecks. Dr. Julian D'Angelo *is a hero*.

"You better prepare for the fight of your life, Nomi Wyeth, because this is war."

I shoulder past Nomi, who's back to hating me again, just like always. Fine by me. If she only likes me when I stoop to her level, then she better get used to hating me because I'll never do it again.

When my Lyft arrives, thankfully driven by nobody I went to high school with, I Google the name until I find the email address I'm looking for.

Council Member Tonuto,

As a threshold matter, I refuse to use the term "Council-friend." It is ridiculous.

I am an esteemed member of the healthcare community in Sparrow Nook, and as such, I must state my utter contempt and disapproval for the proposed cannabis dispensary and lounge the council is set to vote upon at the upcoming meeting. Not only is this den of iniquity slated to open in the historic Strange Drugs Pharmacy building, which is directly next door to my FAMILY CLINIC, where there are CHILDREN present (at times), it is also a danger to Sparrow Nook's already dwindling intellectual capabilities. We cannot afford any more rank idiots in this small town; we are filled to capacity. I urge you to vote against Ms. Wyeth's outrageous business endeavor (truly, has anything appropriate ever happened in a so-called "lounge"?) and amend the agenda to allow a public debate immediately following Ms. Wyeth's presentation next week. I will then educate the council about the evils of marijuana and expose Ms. Wyeth as the wolf in sheep's clothing that she is.

Sincerely,
Dr. Julian D'Angelo, BS (Hons), MS, MD, ABEM
Board Certified Emergency Medicine Physician
Lead Physician, Philadelphia General Hospital, Level 1
Trauma Center (Currently on Research Sabbatical)
Physician in Residence, Dr. Srinivasan's Family Care and
Urgent Clinic
Chief Resident, Yale University EM Residency Program
PoCUS, AIME, ATLS, ACLS, PALS, ALSO Certified

CHAPTER NINE

NOMI

"Nomi, honey? You in there?"

Mom knocks on my stall like it's my office door, which it kind of is. I found a quiet bathroom on the second floor of City Hall and camped out here with my flash cards rather than slowly go insane waiting in the audience. This is my way. It's when I'm stuck in public that the painful spasms usually begin, so starting with the bathroom is like reverse psychology for my colon. It sounds crazy until you learn the gut has so many neurons, it's considered the second brain and, terrifyingly, can operate independently of your real brain.

So yes. I *do* negotiate with terrorists.

"Yep. Is it time?" I tap my flash cards against my thighs.

"We're one agenda item away from the presentation," Eve says, her combat boots visible next to Mom's sensible clogs. "How are you feeling?"

My abdomen feels like I'm being squeezed by King Kong. "Good, fine, okay." After a second, I add, "Excellent."

"Lots of choices there," Eve says gamely, though nerves simmer in her tone, too. "Ready to come out?"

I release a deep breath. I feel like a big, smelly dog balking on its leash before going into the groomer's. Instead of being held down while some college student named Bucky clips my nails, though, I have to stand up in front of the auditorium in a sleek black skirt suit Mom convinced me to wear. And then, I have to be convincing. I have to be fantastic. I have to persuade three out of five council members to approve a cannabis dispensary on Main Street in our picture-perfect downtown.

I unlock the door and smooth my suit.

Eve's eyebrows lift. "Wow."

"Is it bad?" I spin to look at my ass in the mirror, as if *it's* to blame. "I feel like I'm in corporate cosplay."

"No way. This—" Eve gestures to the entirety of me, "—is amazing. I'm listening to you. I'm doing what you say. Have you seen yourself in those shoulder pads? *Major* top energy."

"Yeah?" I ask in a small voice.

"You look great, honey." Mom smiles, her pride evident. Is this what she wishes I looked like all the time? The stable, well-employed office worker Nomi instead of the chronically ill stoner who hates waistbands?

We walk toward the auditorium's side entrance. The clacking of my heels against the speckled, faux-terrazzo floors clashes with the beat of my pounding heart, which I both hear *and* feel in my ears.

"So . . . there's something you should know." Eve clears her throat.

My terrorist colon spasms against the tight skirt. "*What?*"

"They added a public debate on the dispensary prior to the vote," Eve says in a rush. "Julian's signed up to speak."

I stop dead in the hallway. "*What?!*"

"This doesn't change anything," Mom says with forced calm. "Give your presentation, and when he gets up to speak about the medical impacts, you'll refute them with the most recent studies and can even share your own story."

"I'm not discussing my health problems in public, Mom."

"Don't you think explaining how cannabis has positively affected your own quality of life would be compelling? Tax profits are great, but a personal connection touches the heart." Mom takes my hand, swinging it lightly between us. "I know you don't like sharing about your Crohn's disease, but if there ever was a time to show both sides of the cannabis debate—how it could help the town financially *and* change people's lives at an individual level—it's now."

My skin burns red at the words *your Crohn's disease*, this life sentence I can never commute. I glance at Eve, but she's averted her eyes. It's such a double-edged sword to have a disease that's invisible to others ninety percent of the time but horribly, degradingly on display the rest. On one hand, you're grateful that your pain is private, that you can lock yourself away in your bathroom and emerge later pretending that you're fine. But then, when the pain becomes too much, when you retreat too often, stay away too long, when you lose weight, then your hair, and even your smile no longer feels accessible... then people start asking questions.

Why aren't you eating?

Where have you been?

Going home already?

And you're desperate to have that privacy back to shield you from them, and them from the truth, while the other part of you wants to stamp your foot and cry, *I've been sick this whole time! I've been hurting this whole time!* Feeling so angry that nobody really knows you because your humiliating, debilitating pain has become the sum total of *who you are*.

That's what it feels like during a flare, and until I got my disease somewhat under control, what it felt like all the time. Eventually, the healthy days gave me the strength to claw back some of my identity held hostage by the pain, but the fear of active disease returning is always there. Trying too hard, living too much, or letting go of my privacy all feel like strategic failures in this never-ending war I've been conscripted into. I've put my neck out enough as it is.

I blink away the tears welling in my eyes, embarrassed yet again (*always embarrassed*), and huff out a weak laugh. "Nobody wants to hear about my diarrhea."

"Well, maybe not in detail, honey, but how cannabis kept you out of the hospital and, over time, put you into remission? Yes, I think they would."

Eve squeezes my arm. "We need to go in."

"Good luck, baby," Mom says, resigned. "You'll do great."

"Thanks, Mom." I blow out a big breath. The municipal guard checks my visitor badge, nods, and opens the door for us. The presentation before mine by Mr. Wilson Phillips, whose name *nobody* thinks is as funny as I do, is concluding.

"And that's why I hope youse will vote to investigate Sammy's Steaks, so-called Best Cheesesteaks This Side of the Delaware, for misleadin' advertising. They don't even use provolone!" With that, Wilson Phillips saunters away, leaving a trail of mic feedback and a scandalized audience.

The crowd murmurs as Sammy DiFiore, owner of Sammy's Steaks, makes his way to the podium next. "First of all, Cooper Sharp, or GTFO, am I right?"

The whispering intensifies, the crowd divided on this cheese take.

"Second, half the businesses in this town claim to be the best this side of the Delaware. There's nothing wrong with pride in your business, and today's complaint by Mr. *Phillips*," Sammy eyes each member of the council, "is another example of the unfair disparagement of my steak shop."

Council-friend Mike Tonuto, a car dealership magnate, conservative, and Italian man who cherishes his .1 percent Irish heritage for all of March, leans over the desk, his thick, pale lips nearly kissing the tiny microphone head. "Exactly what are you inferring, Mr. DiFiore?"

"You *know* what I'm inferring, Mr. *Tonuto*." Sammy narrows his eyes. "I've been audited, investigated by the zoning commission, and inspected three times this year by the health department." He glances at the audience. "All glowing scores, mind you. Your steaks are in safe, clean hands at Sammy's. But the city council's unfair treatment of my shop must stop! I pay my taxes on time, I'm a good citizen of this town, and I'm sick of being targeted like this."

The Council-friends exchange wary glances, and Chair-friend Chester bangs his gavel. "The city council will vote on whether to investigate claims of misleading advertising at Sammy's Steaks at the next meeting. This item is closed." He bangs the gavel again, which he's upgraded recently. "Next up, Ms. Wyeth and," he squints at the agenda, "the Stranger Drugs dispensary?"

I stand, and Julian's cruel, ice-queen eyes home in on me. A smirk twists his full lips into something fantastically obnoxious. This *fool* wants to debate *me*? Doesn't he remember how I blew his sterling record out of the water? Hot, competitive energy surges up from my core. His eyes register the change in mine, and his smirk turns gleeful.

My palm flexes, Mr. Darcy about to slap a bitch.

"*I will annihilate you*," I mouth the words to him in exaggerated, bared-teeth fashion as I walk to the front. *Annihilate* isn't the easiest word to mouth, but after a confused pause, he registers my meaning.

The red tip of his tongue presses archly against his upper lip as he feigns consideration of my threat. After a second, the expression resolves into an insolent smile.

"We'll see, Shoulder Pads."

I take my place at the podium, ready to *destroy* this jerk. The audiovisual tech loads my presentation, now visible on a large screen where both the council and audience can see it.

I take a deep, steadying breath, wishing I'd vaped the new strain I got for anxiety rather than broach this straight-brained. Public speaking never scared me growing up—I was great at it, a nationally ranked speaker in debate. But once Crohn's kicked in and every stressful event triggered a painful attack, I developed a fear response to the public presentations I used to dominate. Now, microphones equal pain. Attention equals embarrassment. Putting myself out there at all equals quality time with the nearest toilet.

But I can do this. I've practiced. I'm prepared. And dammit, it's terrifying, but I want this. If my dispensary's future isn't inspiration enough, now I want to defeat Julian D'Angelo, too.

I straighten my shoulders to their full, padded glory. "Good afternoon, council members and citizens of—"

"Council-*friends*," Chair-friend Chester corrects into his mic. "We're all friends in lovely Sparrow Nook, New Jersey," he recites, sounding anything but friendly.

"Oh, ho, that we are!" I present a single finger-gun at Chester, then die a little on the inside. He's a swing voter, oscillating wildly between the liberal left and conservative right with *zero* warning, but I'm hoping he's a stoner at heart. How else can you explain a gun-toting gay conspiracy theorist who wrote in Missy Elliott for president, is obsessed with the Revolutionary War, and only shops at Tractor Supply?

Weed. I *pray* that it's weed.

Then, there's Council-friend Min Lee, second only to Julian for the highest person at our Pot Luck due to all the donuts she consumed. She will vote yes. She's tight with Council-friend Shar, a profit-driven accountant, but I couldn't get a read on Shar at the Pot Luck. I did learn she's obsessed with Beyoncé's country album, though. I *feel* this means a yes.

Next to Shar is Council-friend Vlad. He owns the tile-and-flooring store and can often be found steaming his hairy chest at his wife's Russian banya. He has amazing pores and will vote however Mike Tonuto votes.

Last in the line-up is Tonuto. He speaks too fast, calls everyone *dear*, and works in his dealership's latest sales event at every meeting. He's either losing his hearing or strategically deaf to women's voices—he never seems to hear a word I'm saying. He is profits-driven like Shar, so . . . maybe?

One definite yes and four maybes. I need *two* of those maybes to get the local license approved.

I clear my throat, wincing at the mic's feedback. My gut feels like a balloon that wants to pop, but I ignore it *and* the pervasive sense that Julian's laughing at me. Mom beams at me from where she sits beside Gisella, a duo of supportive mom energy in the audience. Eve catches my eye next, standing past the screen. She mouths *major top energy*, then gestures for me to hurry up.

"As I was saying, thank you for having me here today. I'm Nomi Wyeth, and I'm here to win your approval to open the first cannabis dispensary and lounge in downtown Sparrow Nook!"

"Wait, what'd she say?" Wilson Phillips glances up from his phone where he sits next to Sammy, like they're *not* nemeses.

"This lady's gonna sell weed downtown." Sammy eyes me and sniffs approvingly. "Looks classy, too."

"She's not," Julian says behind a fake cough.

My eyes narrow, and I'm ready to knock Julian to the floor and press my heel into the sensitive flesh of his neck. Perhaps I should be thankful because, thanks to Julian and his rage-inducing smirk, my nerves disappear, completely consumed by our old, competitive rivalry, and the presentation goes flawlessly. Whenever I feel my energy slip, all it takes is a glance at Julian's mounting dismay and the pouty set to his mouth, and I'm back. The Council-friends are little deer eating from my palm, asking interested questions between slides about tax revenues, job creation, and the nonprofit Stranger Drugs will fund to expunge marijuana-related offenses from people's criminal records.

Of the Council, Tonuto looks the least engaged, almost comically unimpressed as slide after slide shows all the positive benefits a dispensary will have. It's a show, I'm certain of it, but that's not surprising. Mike Tonuto is clickbait personified, always withholding, always performing, obnoxiously demanding your attention. Perhaps he's just annoyed that all eyes are on someone else for once, but still. I wish I could read his mind. Him and Vlad vote as a block, usually conservative, always money driven. Without Tonuto and Vlad, I desperately need Chester, who just asked me whether I'd sell acid when the psychedelic revolution reshapes America.

"If that happens, sir—"

"*When* that happens."

"When that happens, Chair, you'll be the first person I consult with." This was apparently the right answer, as Chester nods and bangs his gavel approvingly. Because I'm feeling saucy, I give him the finger-guns again. Two, this time.

When the presentation concludes, the audience breaks into real applause. I look out and see customers who regularly drive all the way to XYB for strains to treat their multiple sclerosis and chronic pain. I also see Gareth, a long-haired Jesus of a man, whooping unabashedly. He loves Cuntsicle and getting high and, more than anything, laughing. Cannabis is for anyone old enough to legally partake, whether it's for a good time or to make what time you still have good. I feel like a hero, providing this comfort to Sparrow Nook. Not some underemployed, now *un*employed loser who barely made it through college because her body betrayed her every chance it got. A hero.

Their hero.

I also see my ex-boss Damon, arms sullenly folded over his Iron Maiden T-shirt. I swallow, but he's already hurt me the only way he can, and I'm still standing.

"Thank you, dear. That was very sweet." Council-friend Tonuto thumps the desk twice, and the tech pulls up a second podium opposite mine.

"We will now hear from the public on the proposed dispensary," Chairfriend Chester announces. Ms. Wyeth, you may respond to any questions or comments posed to you, if you wish. First up is Dr. Julian D'Angelo."

Julian is wearing his white doctor's coat, a stethoscope draped around his neck, and a condescending smile as he steps behind the podium. One arm of his coat is empty, his left arm in a sling nestled against his chest. I don't feel sorry for him, though. Per Gisella, it's not even broken. His chin dips, his ice-blue eyes searing as he stares me down, and if there weren't a hundred people watching, I'd have sworn he was about to stride over, grab my chin, and tell me off between hot, vicious kisses.

Which, thanks to the Pot Luck and my *profoundly* bad decisions, I can imagine easily.

I blink, forcing the idea back to the pit of my most embarrassing fantasies, right alongside sex with a masked Batman and that hot old guy who dresses like Santa. What's wrong with me? Julian's the worst.

"Thank you, Council. I'm here because I am a *doctor*."

I already want to punch him.

"And as a *doctor*, I have serious concerns with Ms. Wyeth's dingy pot parlor, which will be an eyesore on our wholesome downtown and will plunge Sparrow Nook into a downward spiral of lost potential, poor health outcomes, and unnatural, unproductive *leisure time*, which is antithetical to New Jersey's strong, capitalist economy." Julian utters *leisure time* like it's something you'd find on the other side of a gas station glory hole.

I can't stop myself from groaning aloud.

"Something to say, Ms. Wyeth?" Min asks.

"Everything Dr. D'Angelo just said is false, and moreover, insulting to Sparrow Nook. My dispensary will be located in the old Strange Drugs pharmacy, which city council renovated beautifully, and we will provide the same meaningful blend of treatment, joy, and space for the community to gather that the original pharmacy provided for seventy years." I lean over my podium. "Furthermore, Sparrow Nook has always prided itself on being a respite from the never-ending rat race, and our ability to relax and enjoy life does *not* take away from our ability to take care of business nine to five."

A swell of *yeah!* and *that's right!* lifts from the audience, as well as one tentative *work/life balance!*

"Ms. Wyeth, it'd be cute how naive you are about this addictive, federally illegal drug if it weren't so dangerous for our town." Julian sniffs. "Marijuana use negatively impacts IQ, memory, and motivation. I ask you, Council—can Sparrow Nook afford to lose more intelligence?"

"Doctor, the only thing lacking intelligence here is your opening argument. The most recent longitudinal studies have shown *no* causal link between cannabis and lowered IQ, unlike alcohol and tobacco, which we enjoy in moderation and are still *generally* intelligent," I add, nodding around the room to generate agreement. "As for motivational impacts, a recent study shows the exact opposite—in states where recreational cannabis is permitted, older individuals remain in the workforce longer due to an improved quality of life and less pain and stress." I turn to the council. "I've included both studies in the appendix submitted with my application, among others you'll find helpful."

Council-friend Shar eyes me appreciatively before activating her mic. "Improving our town's quality of life and longevity in the workforce at the same time is very compelling, Ms. Wyeth. At no cost to the city council, too."

Julian's nostrils flare. The apex of his outrageous cheekbones is stained a salmon pink of indignation.

We love to see it.

"Secondly," Julian growls into his mic. "Marijuana is a known gateway drug to harder, more dangerous substance use."

I roll my eyes because *of course* Julian would spew Reagan-era drug propaganda. "That argument is fundamentally flawed because it draws an imaginary line between Drugs with a capital *D* and everything else. Marijuana isn't some metaphorical door to the 'Kingdom of Drugs' unless *you* decide it is. And if you really care about the sequence of use, we could just as easily say alcohol is the real gateway drug—studies show that alcohol use precedes experimentation with cannabis and everything else."

"But that presumes all alcohol users go on to try marijuana, which isn't true!" Julian sputters.

"*Exactly*—which is the same problem with saying cannabis is a gateway to harder drugs! Maybe most cocaine users have tried cannabis, but studies show that most cannabis users never try anything harder. The fact is, if someone is predisposed to trying harder drugs, they're going to do it whether cannabis is readily available or not."

Julian blinks at me, his mouth opening and closing like a fish stranded on land. The audience has been watching us argue like a Williams sisters match, their heads whipping back and forth between our podiums. The air in the room has a distinct *oh, shiiiit* vibe.

"Marijuana takes people you love away from you," Julian blurts. "It makes them less than who they were before, it distracts them from their responsibilities to their families, their lives, and their friends, and worse, it convinces them that's okay! To be less than. To hide from real life. To roll around in mediocrity and feel good about it. And it's not! It's *not okay.*"

His words hit me in one big, physical push. Is he talking about his father here, or me? I didn't go away to school. All those Ivy League acceptance letters went unanswered—the money was too tight with my mounting medical bills, and when every attempt to eat and live a normal life was punished, I was too scared to leave my house, let alone go off to college. I took the easy route, because I *had to.* And even the easy route wasn't easy. Not for me. Yet here is Julian, staring me down like it's an affront to *him* that I haven't lived up to my potential. But what does he know about life? And why does he assume he's the one winning at it? He's mean and judgmental and approaches each day like it's already done him wrong and he'll make it pay. Ambition fueled by spite, where each goal surpassed isn't cause for celebration, but just another rung up the ladder. But where does that ladder lead, and why is he so desperate to get there?

A cold satisfaction ices over his eyes. "The fact *is*, Ms. Wyeth, it's still federally illegal, and legalizing it state by state is a shameless money grab that comes at the expense of people's well-being."

My lips part, and a small puff of air exits. So, this is what he thinks of me? That I'm an underachieving stoner who wants to shake people down and get them hooked on drugs?

Well, it's a good thing I know who I am.

This underachieving stoner wants to help people, and this is my chance to do it.

I smile ruefully. "Some of what you said is true, Dr. D'Angelo. Corporate cannabis, with their vertical monopoly capped by a big box store approach to operating dispensaries, shortchanges the people they serve in chase of the dollar. They slash prices to run small dispensaries out of business, then raise prices once they've killed the competition. Their cannabis is substandard and unvaried, they disregard its medicinal qualities, and they give nothing back to the towns and cities where they operate." I turn my smile back to the city council. "In other words, the antithesis of everything Stranger Drugs and I stand for. Voting to approve my license today will dissuade corporate weed-marts from popping up nearby, because Sparrow Nook deserves more than that." My gaze swivels back to Julian. "And no doctor, with his uninformed, prejudicial opinions, *who lives in Philadelphia*, can convince me otherwise."

Outrage spills from the chambers. Someone shouts, "Philadelphia?!"

Chester bangs his gavel with gusto. "Is it true that you reside in Philadelphia, Dr. D'Angelo?"

Smug satisfaction curves my mouth. The only thing that pisses off Sparrow Nook more than shore traffic is New Jerseyans who live in Philadelphia. Judging by Julian's panicked face, he's picked up on the major downshift in vibe. Before he can say anything, I lean forward.

"Worse. Dr. D'Angelo complains about New Jersey drivers now." I look at Julian and shake my head slowly. "As if he isn't just as bad as the rest of us."

The chambers immediately fill with booing.

"You're from Georgia!" Julian shouts. "You're not *one of us.*"

I step out from behind the podium and walk toward him. His eyes widen slightly, and I'm thrilled to see the rapid rise and fall of his chest beneath his perfect white coat.

I love scaring men.

"I live here because I love Sparrow Nook." I raise an eyebrow. "And you cannot say the same thing, Doctor." I turn my gaze out to the audience. "Sparrow Nook deserves compassionate care, free from judgment. We deserve respect and the autonomy to choose what's right for our bodies instead of ignorant, knee-jerk opinions that presume us too stupid to govern ourselves responsibly. More than anything, we deserve a good time!" I raise my fist in the air, and the audience rises to a standing ovation.

Ten minutes later, the final vote's entered into the record—3 yeas, 2 nays—and I burst into the happiest tears of my life.

JULIAN

The cheering chases me from the building. Or maybe it was Mom frowning at me, or seeing Nomi incandescently happy as Eve tackled her in a big, spinning hug, their limbs jumbled together in the kind of friendship I've never had.

And never wanted, frankly. Who enjoys being touched like that? That's how you get norovirus. Pink eye. Hit up for informal loans.

I click my key fob the second I'm outside, repeatedly unlocking it even though my car emits horn blips each time. I can't get out of here fast enough. I check my phone to distract my furious brain and nearly trip at an email from Dr. Riveras labeled: *Re: Update.*

Julian,

I received your request to immediately reinstate your position at Philly Gen: the answer is no. It has been three weeks. I don't care if you're unchallenged and bored and "wasting away in a sea of Type II Diabetes," and frankly, I don't understand what beer pong has to do with it. Your outrageous mistake could've cost the hospital its brand-new wing for autoimmune disease research and treatment. I implore you—take this probation seriously, learn your lesson, and after six months, we'll reconsider your employment at Philly Gen. More than anything, keep a low profile. I cannot overstate how important it is to keep your head down right now until the Corringtons forget you exist.

—Dr. Riveras

My eyes widen in horror. I never sent an email requesting reinstatement! I scroll down quickly, my stomach bottoming out when I see that actually I had, the message date-stamped the night of the Pot Luck after Nomi left me on the couch and before the drugs left my system. I don't remember writing a word of it.

I throw my head back and yell at the sky.

"Doctor." A man calls from behind me, his voice rough with a veneer of friendliness over top, like honey-coated gravel. "A quick word?"

"*What!*" I bellow.

The gravelly voice laughs, which catches me off guard. I glance over my shoulder. It's Mike Tonuto, one of the two reasonable voters against Nomi's weed hovel. "Sorry to bother you when you're *ah*, upset, but I wanted to discuss our mutual... *concerns* about that sweet girl's misguided venture."

I snort. Nomi, *sweet*? She was a besuited succubus with a PowerPoint in there. It was, admittedly, extremely hot.

"What is it?" I offer grudgingly.

"You brought up an excellent point that my fellow Council-friends failed to consider." Tonuto flashes that car dealer smile—genuine, sympathetic, deeply wise—as if he could fix all the world's problems with a gently used Dodge Charger. "Why would we allow a stoner hangout to open on Main Street, next to your family clinic, no less? The low-life clientele hanging around, the fumes—have you been to New York lately? It smells like weed and halal carts everywhere you go." Tonuto places a hand over his heart. "Are we really going to expose our sickly children to mind-altering substances like that?"

I point at him. "Exactly!"

"My Council-friends are taken by Ms. Wyeth's promises, but I feel that other minds—cooler, more rational, more *conservative* minds—would feel differently." Tonuto's chin dips. "Ones you could find, say, on the zoning commission."

The zoning commission... My eyebrows slowly lift.

"A well-pled zoning complaint can gum up the works for any new business." Tonuto shrugs casually, as though remarking on the weather. "Does a cannabis dispensary classify as general commercial use? Has anyone counted the feet between it and the local school, the arcade, the daycare? The zoning commission would appreciate hearing from you."

"Hey, Mike! Wait up!" We both glance over to see Wilson Phillips, which, come on, that name's *hilarious*, striding over.

"Ugh, constituents." Tonuto rolls his eyes playfully. "I better get out of here before I have to listen to literal cheese mongering. Consider what I said, Doctor. I'd support you every step of the way."

With that, Tonuto strides toward City Hall's side entrance at a clip, entering just before Wilson can grab him by the shoulder.

Nomi's words curdle in my gut, but all her *studies* do not change what happened to my family when my father threw away everything he had going for him—good looks, brains, and the kind of personality that drew everyone close. None of that mattered when all he cared about was staying home, smoking pot in our garage, and building models of our small town to rival that ghost's in *Beetlejuice*. His hobbies and drugs drained his meager disability checks. Rather than getting back out there and finding something that could support his family, he let Mom work twice as hard while he withered to nothing in a folding camp chair.

The same thing is happening to Nomi. So smart and wry, so funny. So capable. When she clinched our win at the state championship after delivering the most awe-inspiring smackdown I'd ever witnessed, my heart nearly burst. I felt every emotion seeing her behind that podium that night. Wonder, pride, jealousy, happiness, sadness, and this inescapable, profound *wanting* that ran so deeply through me, it hurt. When we won, I hugged her the way Eve did today, spinning her around, as happy as I've ever been.

But then, she kissed me. Right there, in front of the whole auditorium, and blew my world apart. My vision narrowed to Nomi, just Nomi, and the exceptional futures we'd have together. We spent one blissful month tangled in each other's arms. When she disappeared later without any explanation, then resurfaced at the end of our senior year paler and skinnier than before, smoking pot with that deranged Eve Ionides, it felt like Dad all over again. Choosing to wreck her brain and her life and all that we'd worked for, and for what? To get high? To leave me behind like I never mattered?

I slide into my car and blow out a long, tortured breath.

"Phone, call Dr. Sampson's cell number."

"Eric," I say when his voicemail picks up without bothering to say *hello* or who I am. "Can you get addicted to marijuana after eating one edible? Er, two edibles? Several edibles. Also, how do you file a zoning complaint?" I grimace as I turn the steering wheel, reversing out of the parking space. Before I end the voicemail, I tack on one last question that I'd been saving up. "And what is your opinion on *neti pots*?"

I end the call feeling...if not better, a little more focused. I have research to do, an unprincipled pothead to thwart, and also the feeling someone may be following me. My eyes dart to the rearview mirror, where a purple Kia Soul, the most unhinged of cars, follows close behind. I take a quick turn without using my blinker, the abject lawlessness of it nearly killing me, but the suspicion's confirmed when the Kia Soul hastily follows. From the front-mounted Grateful Dead vanity plate, a blank-eyed neon teddy bear head smiles at me through my rearview mirror. Dread prickles across the back of my neck.

Oh, no. I've angered the *stoners*.

"Phone!" I call out, more desperate. "Call Dr. Sampson's *home number*!"

CHAPTER TEN

NOMI

I'm not religious, but when I wake up the morning of move-in day, the spirit of, well, *something*, enters my body and levitates me out of bed. I throw off the covers, unceremoniously unseating Big Bird by accident, and leap to my feet, feeling true joy.

I rush up the stairs and bang on Eve's door before throwing it open. "It's move-in day, bitch!"

Eve's already up and baking in her kitchen, wearing a beautiful pale-green apron with *The food has weed in it* embroidered in cursive, a present from me for 4/20.

She grins and proffers a beautiful platter of freshly baked scones, muffins, and the infamous hemp protein bars. "Breakfast is the most important meal of the day!"

I hesitate in front of the platter. "I don't know... we have so much to do."

She *pshhaws* at me, then picks up a big, sumptuous blueberry muffin tinged the palest green and waves it in my face. "I used the high-energy Sativa blend—the one that made you clean the whole house two weeks ago and do your taxes. This is for our Wake and Bake menu."

I grab the muffin. The rich, buttery flake makes me groan out loud. "Eve. This is so fucking *good*. You're ridiculously talented."

"Funny." Eve smirks. "That's what Julian said to me at the party."

“Can we not sully this perfect morning with D’Asshole?”

“Fine.” Eve wraps up the platter to take with us. “But let the record show that my pot baking is *so* good, it turned Julian D’Angelo into a lovely person for one whole evening.”

“Truly witchcraft,” I mutter. Whenever I think about that night, a wave of angry, frustrated disappointment surges through me. Because Julian *was* lovely at our Pot Luck. Kind, open, earnest. Hilariously scared of raccoons. I was charmed against my better judgment. Seduced by the sheer physicality of him all grown up with too much horny pot in my system. I knew what kind of person Julian was, and I fell for it anyway. It hurt when he woke up the next day, horrified at what we’d done.

I didn’t ask you out, did I? The look of disgust on his face haunts me, and I cringe in mortification every time I remember how he accused me of drugging him so I could straddle him.

It shouldn’t have surprised me, then, when he got up in front of the whole town and said there was no excuse for my mediocrity to my face. That’s the Julian who hurt me all those years ago when I finally came back to high school, and that’s the one he *chooses* to be, every day. So what if there’s a lovely person trapped inside, accessible only by increased dopamine activation in his nucleus accumbens from the presence of cannabinoids? Who he chooses to be matters more.

And he chooses to *suck*.

“Come on.” Eve tugs my arm. “Let’s get to Stranger Drugs before the edibles hit.”

The morose mood Julian’s wasted potential put me in evaporates as soon as we park in front of *our building*.

“Our building!” Eve says, a perfect echo of my own thoughts. We smile up at the red brick façade. “Our *dispensary*!”

“We did it, Joe!” I hug her to my side, wishing I’d ordered a big ribbon and giant pair of scissors for the moment. Ooh, maybe for the grand opening! Where does one buy ceremonial scissors, anyways? In two thousand years, will some race of conquering aliens dig through the rubble of what was once Sparrow Nook and find my giant scissors? What will they think? How will they explain why most scissors fit our primitive human hands, but sometimes we made gigantic versions? I press my hand into my chest, empathy welling there for those little alien archaeologists. They'll be so *confused.*

Eve nudges me. "The muffin hit, didn't it."

My face breaks into a big, sunny grin. "Let's get cleaning, *bitch.*"

"You realize that all your motivational one-liners end with the word *bitch.* Not very progressive of you."

"Let's get progressive, *bi—*"

Eve drags me through the beautiful double doors as I cackle.

The morning disappears into a spirited haze of mopping, dusting, and after Graham arrives with his truck, unloading various furniture and supplies. While he's an absolute demon at trivia, Graham's also very strong, which is great since I've already tapped him to be our security guard and chief mover-of-heavy-things. The dispensary's main room needs almost nothing—the glass display cases intended for historical artifacts are perfect for displaying our cannabis selections. The booths, old soda fountain counter, and bar stools are all perfect for socializing and enjoying Eve's baking. We install an old commercial coffee maker Eve bought cheap off one of her Greek uncles and hang our thick, ceramic mugs with our dispensary's logo lovingly emblazoned in red along the copper wall hooks. While I don't drink coffee thanks to my angry colon, Eve convinced me coffee will go perfectly with her morning Wake and Bake line, so I gave in. As long as I don't have to learn that machine, I'm fine with it.

Graham helps me hoist the antique wooden desk I scored from an estate sale onto a hand truck for my office. *My office!* It's been like this all morning. Every time I touch something, the words *My ___!* fill my brain, making me smile in wonder. *My desk. My office. My bathroom. My giant pair of scissors*, I muse as I happily press *add to cart* during a break later that morning. When you've waited your whole life for something to be truly yours, the simple truth of it feels like a hug, whispering *you did it*, over and over.

My dispensary. My future. My life.

I've just finished installing a new desktop computer for my office when Eve's voice cuts through my concentration.

"Um, Nomi? Can you come out here?"

I break away from my new tech-baby and all the sweet, sweet spreadsheets I'm going to make and pad out to the front.

"*Oh.*" I startle back. There's an officer standing in front of the door, but I don't recognize the ruddy uniform or the patch on his chest pocket. Eve and Graham are standing motionless to the side of him, their eyes round, concerned, and aimed at me.

"Are you Nomi Wyeth?" he asks with the kind of pep that comes from loving your job.

"Yes?"

He hands over a manila envelope with my name and the dispensary's address on front. "The Sparrow Nook Zoning Commission has received a citizen complaint regarding your business's zoning eligibility. I'll be performing the investigation."

I stare at the envelope dumbly in my hands, then up at his face. The officer can't be older than forty, but it's difficult to tell since his face, hair, and facial hair are all the same, sandy color of old limestone. "You're a . . ." I squint at the embroidered patch on his shirt, "*zoning detective*?"

"That's right, Ms. Wyeth. May I ask you some questions?"

Behind him, Eve's waving her arms wildly, mouthing, "*Say no! You have rights!*" She watches a lot of *Law & Order*.

"No, I have rights," I repeat slowly. This appears to be the wrong thing to say, because the detective's jaw tightens.

"If you want to play it that way." A hostile sparkle gleams in his yellowish eyes. This man is jaundice personified.

"No, no, I mean—now's not a great time, is all." I make my tone as deferential as possible. "Can we make an appointment to talk over everything later this week?"

He sniffs, mollified. "I'd be happy to arrange a mutually convenient time with you, Ms. Wyeth." His eyes skim over me to the platter of Eve's baked goods with obvious interest. "In exchange for one of those scones." His pasty lips quiver into a smile as he reaches toward the platter. I jump in front of it.

"*No!* Those are—" I scramble for what to say as his eyes narrow at me once more.

"Filled with weed, sir," Eve blurts, rushing to pull the platter back and behind the counter. She smiles hastily. "Can't get intoxicated when you're pursuing uh, zoning justice."

The detective looks at us with shocked outrage, then pulls out a notepad from his belt. With giant, petty flourishes, he jots down what must be very thorough notes because this goes on for a while. We stand around in increasing discomfort until he finishes.

"I'll be back, and in the meantime, you're officially prohibited from conducting any marijuana business on this property." He takes one last look at the scones, scowls, then strides out the door.

As soon as he's gone, Graham and Eve descend on me like seagulls on pizza.

"A zoning complaint?" Eve plucks the envelope from my hands and dumps the contents on the counter. "What even is that?"

I hoist myself up on the stool next to Graham and groan. "Every part of town is zoned for a specific use. Commercial, residential, industrial, designations like that. If you try to operate a business in an area that's not zoned for that kind of business, you can get investigated, penalized, fined, even forced to move."

Graham frowns. "I don't understand. Who told on you?"

"All you need to know is *right here.*" Eve points at the signature at the bottom.

"*Julian?!*" Rage kindles inside of me, blazing to life. "That absolute dickhead!" I push off the counter and stomp toward the door.

"Where is he?!" I bellow two minutes later at the bored teenage boy manning Dr. Appa's reception desk. He takes in my crazed eyes, bandana askew, sweat-damp tank, and the fire of holy fury burning me alive. He's only slightly interested.

"You must be looking for Dr. D'Angelo," the bored teen says, not a question. How many furious people does this kid field each day because of Julian? With a sigh, he closes his graphic novel, its cover all in Japanese with badass girls in prim school uniforms throat-punching businessmen. God, when did the youth get so cool? I was reading the novelizations of my favorite CW shows at that age. Without missing a beat, the teen airdrops a note to my phone, which buzzes in my pocket. I glance in surprise between it and his bored face, then open it tentatively. You can't tell with these Gen Alpha teens.

"This is Julian's—address?" I stare at the kid. "You're giving angry people his home address?"

The teen nods, and a small, sly smile flickers on his face before the apathy wipes the slate clean again. "You asked where he is."

I make a mental note not to fuck with this kid. "Thank you... Khalil," I finish, finding his name tag. "I'm going to go yell at Julian now."

"Bet." Khalil reopens his novel.

I've been dismissed.

It takes all of five minutes to reach Julian's place, a sunny little beach cottage with no beach in sight. It's painted pale blue with cream-colored shutters, the sweet porch out front decorated in country chic. I close the door to my car, feeling the rage ebb and replaced by unease as I take in legit *flower boxes*, their greenery and lush summer blooms spilling out of them.

Maybe it's an Airbnb? A suspiciously well-kept rental?

I bang the heel of my fist against the door. He won't mistake *me* for a gentle, kind Jehovah's Witness or a well-meaning but deluded college student canvassing for the Green Party.

Nobody answers, but he's definitely home—his Volvo's parked in the driveway. I screech against the curved windowpane at the top of the door. "Answer the door, you asshole!"

I'm halfway through another set of pounding knocks when the door opens. Julian's black waves are sleep-mussed, and the shadow across his face foretells an aggressively masculine beard pattern with full-growth potential should he wait three days' max to shave. His eyes seem weirdly small, and then I realize they're barely open.

This asshole's been *sleeping*? His soft, gray T-shirt is too small to be decent. Thick straps of triceps peek from the sleeves, his muscular arms as curvaceous as a 1940s starlet, though one is still wrapped in a soft cast. And the sweatpants, *oh ho*, slung so low around his hips, I have to witness a solid inch of black waistband fitting snugly beneath?

Infuriating.

"Nomi?" the idiot mumbles. "Wha—"

I place a full palm against the flat of his sternum, enraged at the rise of chest muscles on either side, and drive him backward, inside, where I can yell at him properly. He may be sleep-dumb, but he has the good sense to look terrified as I slam the door behind me like a thunderclap.

I wave the manila envelope in the air hard enough to take down a hornet. "You filed a *zoning complaint*?!"

The evidence of his assholery works like a beacon, summoning the tiny, nefarious demon ruling Julian's brain to repossess its bumbling human host. I watch it bodily re-inhabit him, his spine straightening, shoulders rotating back, eyes cranked all the way open now. The fuzzy quality of sleep that made him so soft and dammit, *inviting*, has burned away. His armpits look like terrible cuddle zones now.

"I did, because it's valid, Nomi. You can't open your little weed bordello—"

"*Bordello?* Do you hear yourself, Julian?"

"—next door to a family medical practice! What message would it send our children?"

My eyes must bulge as wide as his does, because he hastily amends, "The children of Sparrow Nook, of course! Not *our* children, like ones we make together—"

My eyebrows stretch so high, it feels like facial Pilates.

"—but the proverbial, royal *Our*, as in—" His cheekbones have colored a bright red, and thanks to his skimpy ass T-shirt, I can see the blush travel down the planes of his neck and collarbone.

I shake my head in disbelief. "What, exactly, do you think goes on at a dispensary?"

"People making bad decisions about their health, money, and well-being." He folds his arms. "And maybe sex. In the back."

"What?!"

"I listen to rap, Nomi, I'm not naive!"

The single, wild laugh that escapes me quickly morphs into a groan because he *is* that naive. "Listen, zoning complaints take months to reconcile—you might not even be here by the time they set the hearing date!"

"So?"

"So, what is your end game here? Swoop into town to piss everyone off, burn everything I've worked for to the ground, ruin my life, and then leave again? You don't even live here!"

"I'm not ruining your life, Nomi. I'm saving you *and* Sparrow Nook from marijuana."

"Don't lie to yourself—you're not saving anyone!" I take a step forward, hating the vulnerable confession I'm about to share. "Listen, Julian. I need to open Stranger Drugs immediately, or else my savings will be wiped out by the time this zoning hearing resolves. Your scheme will make me go broke." I pin him with my gaze, imploring him to listen. "Do you understand?"

"See?" Julian huffs, completely unmoved by this declaration of my impending doom. "A terrible business idea."

Tears unexpectedly sting my eyes. I guess a small part of me thought hearing the very real consequences of his actions would have some effect on him, but the demon's at Julian's wheel right now, and it's happy to ram me over a cliff. "Why are you so desperate to turn me into the loser you're so sure I am? Is this about high school? Some pathetic need to get back at me for what—what happened?"

The stern, sneering set to his brow softens, his whole face falling, like it's me pushing *him* over the cliff right now. "No, I—that's not it at all! I—"

Just then, the front door swings open, making us both startle back. "Julie? Is my son that I am not talking to home?" Gisella calls as she tramps in, her arms full of stuffed grocery bags.

Julian lives with his mom? And she's mad at him??

Glee *floods* the caverns of my petty, petty heart.

"Nomi! Great to see you." Gisella shoves the bags at Julian, who stumbles back beneath the sudden weight of them, and then throws her arms open and wraps me in a big, lung-compressing hug. She holds me back to look at me. "You did great at the city council meeting, sweetie. How's your baby-maker—all healed up?"

And just like that, the glee is gone, replaced by absolute mortification. My eyes dart to Julian. "You told your mother about my—*area*?"

Julian looks like he's about to faint.

"No, of course not, your mother did," Gisella answers for him, frowning. She pauses, looking between the two of us like guilty children, before her eyes widen. "*Noooo*... it was *my* Julian that sewed up your vagina?" She caws out a laugh. "Oh, he must've *loved*—"

"*Mother!*" Julian finally splutters out, and one full bag slips out of his grip, sending clementines rolling across the floor.

"Clean those up," she orders him, then blinks at me. "Well? Did he do a good job at least?"

"Um," I whisper, unable to fully breathe. "Yes?"

"Ha!" Gisella sashays into the kitchen. "Now that's a ringing endorsement. As long as it still works, right, sweetie?"

I grab the wall for support, physical *and* emotional, while Julian gathers up clementines, cursing. He eyes the last one that's rolled in front of me. He plucks it cautiously, as though I might knee him in the face.

Fair.

He slowly rises all the way to standing, the bottom of his gray shirt now cradling twenty small fruits, revealing his vicious abs beneath. We stare at each other, both drowning in this abyss of mutual horror. "*I'm so sorry*," he mouths silently, eyes pleading, "*for my mother*."

But *not* for ruining my dreams? I laugh once, shaking my head, then take a menacing step forward. "Withdraw that zoning complaint, Julian. *Immediately*. Or you'll *really* be sorry."

With narrowed eyes, I slap the underside of his shirt basket, upending the clementines once more, and stomp out.

CHAPTER ELEVEN

JULIAN

It's an armpit of a day, ninety percent humidity and eighty-four degrees at seven in the god-forsaken morning. My left arm feels hot and gummy beneath the Velcro cast, but there's no rest for those with *pizza belly*.

It's been two weeks since the Pot Luck, but my body hangs on to cheese bloat like it's a piece of doorframe in icy Atlantic waters that was *definitely* not big enough for two, justice for Rose DeWitt Bukater. But maybe another long, sweaty run on the river trail will finally wring me out—my fifth one this week.

When I arrive, there's only one car in the parking lot. A *purple* car.

No. A purple Kia Soul.

My pulse quickens.

Whatever, lots of South Jerseyans drive unnecessarily flamboyant cars. If I were afraid of them all, I wouldn't be able to leave my house. Still, I take the path in the other direction. A minute later, a car door slams, and I whip around, but nothing. No movement in the lot. No one on the path. The cough-syrup car sits unchanged.

I swipe my slick forehead. I'm going crazy.

The fall of my footsteps resolves into a steady, comforting beat, and I slip in my headphones. I'm listening to a middling podcast because this guy I knew from med school named Todd who *sucked* is the guest, but on impulse, I switch the settings to allow background noise. There's nobody else on the path except for a runner far behind me. From the look of his tiny running briefs and racing tank, he's serious about his exercise, so he *can't* be a stoner. He won't bother me, but... still.

"A debilitating neurodegenerative disease is experiencing an uptick—what's been your clinical experience with Parkinson's disease in the emergency medicine setting, Dr. Todd?"

He goes by *Dr. Todd*? Insufferable.

"Well, Nancy, akinesia, or the sudden impairment of motor function, can become quite severe in Parkinson's disease patients."

No shit, *Dr. Todd.* I glance back. The runner's closing the distance, his ropy legs cycling toward me in a churning stride.

I pick up my pace.

"—in advanced stages of the disease, or with sudden disruptions of medication, concurrent infections, even a bad fall, a Parkinson's patient can enter a full akinetic crisis, which is life threatening and must be attended to immediately—"

Loose gravel crunches behind me, and I lurch around. It's the runner, so close now his mirrored sunglasses reflect my anxious face. His hair is buzzed bald, a Phillie Phanatic sweatband ringing his dome. He runs alongside me, his even strides effortlessly keeping pace with my panicked ones. I'm fumbling to turn off the podcast when additional footsteps crackle along my *other* side.

Except for the long, frizzy brown hair bouncing off his chest like unappetizing cotton candy, the man to my left is the other's perfect *twin.*

Same mirrored shades, same sweatband, same tiny racing briefs. It's like being escorted by a pair of Dickensian ghosts. Which one is my future? Which is my past? I run faster, but they easily match my pace. I slow down, and the same. The *fuck*?

The distinct, funky smell of men sweating out marijuana surrounds me like a cloud. My head flaps wildly between them.

These men are stoners. They sport an eerie, echoing smile.

"Look, I don't know what you want," I pant out, "but—*ahhh*!" My foot connects with stone, and I go *flying*, straight over the path's low, rocky border, down the short embankment below, and into a reedy patch of smelly, stagnant water. I come up gasping, spluttering dirty water out of my mouth. The creepy twins are in the distance now, their shoulders quaking in synchronized laughter.

I hobble to my car, sneakers farting in a wet, squelching harmony as I glance nervously over my shoulder. There's a message on my windshield, scrawled in sunscreen:

Withdraw the complaint.

Nomi sent *henchmen* after me?!

My windshield wipers smear the sunscreen into an impenetrable, mineral glaze, and I growl, grab my sweat towel, and start buffing the glass.

I'm still wet when I reach downtown, sloshing angrily toward Nomi's dispensary to confront her when my face stares back at me from a lamppost. On neon pink paper, there's a photocopied picture of me pretending to smoke a beer bottle, which must've been taken at Nomi's Pot Luck. In bold font, it states: HAVE YOU SEEN THIS CAT?

There are only three rip-off tabs at the bottom left, which feature my *actual* cell phone number.

As if on cue, my phone rings from an unknown number.

"Hello?" I answer in horror.

"*Yeah, I'm callin' about that free couch. Ever been urinated on?*"

I hang up on the unhinged laughter. I have twenty-seven missed calls, all from unknown numbers. I rip down the flyer, but on the next lamppost, there are *more.*

Me, lying in the bushes. FREE COUCH TO A GOOD HOME.

Me, staring dreamily at Nomi. LOSE WEIGHT AND FEEL GREAT WITH RX MAXUM PILLZ!

And in an incredibly low blow—me, passed out on Nomi's couch wearing her Kiss & Tale Bookshop T-shirt with my pizza belly on full display. LOOKING FOR BON JOVI TIX?

I race through downtown, desperately tearing down flyers while onlookers laugh behind their hands at the smelly, wet man from the pictures. If anyone from Philly Gen catches sight of these, I'll be fired for good. After I finish, I stand panting in front of Nomi's dispensary. On the door it states: "*Opening delayed due to Dr. Julian D'Angelo's unwarranted zoning complaint. For now, find the Stranger Drugs pop-up at the farm stand on HWY 5.*"

I shriek like a madman, then jump into my car and tear off for the dinky set of farm huts huddled at the edge of town. Fresh rhubarb, cartons of overflowing strawberries, and the reddest tomatoes I've ever seen spill forth from bins, baskets, and shelves, but it's the skunky smell of Nomi's goods that's drawn a line. She's set up in the second hut, a similar spread of edibles from the fundraiser arrayed on platters beneath glass cloches. I stomp up to the hut, but an old woman blocks me with her cane.

"Line starts back there, kid." She jerks her head to indicate the seven people behind her waiting. I have to *wait in line* to chew Nomi out? A small laugh bubbles up from behind the counter, but when I turn to glare at her, Nomi's smirking down at the stack of cash she's counting diligently in her hands.

"Fine," I bark out, then spin on my heels to the back of the line. Selling marijuana on the side of the road—how is this *possibly* legal? That sparks an idea, and I whip out my phone in glee and text the local police hotline.

"Illicit drug deals occurring at the HWY 5 fruit stand—come quick! Many criminals!!"

I'm about to close out the messages app when the family text chain blazes to life.

The D'Angelo Family Sex Gods

MOM

Julian, what have you done now? Your face is all over town!

JULIAN

If you see any of those flyers, please, tear them down!

MARCO

He filed a zoning complaint against Nomi's dispensary, that's what happened! People are upset.

VERONICA D'ANGELO-BORK

A zoning complaint?! What are you, Julian, a seventy-two-year-old republican with nothing better to do?

MOM

But you like her! You kissed! This is a hell of a way to treat a good woman!!

JULIAN

MOM. Can we not discuss this on the family text chain?

MOM

After your disappointing behavior at the Pot Luck, I'm not talking to you, remember?

How could I forget? Mom's version of the silent treatment is nonstop explanations for why she's giving me the silent treatment.

MARCO

Julian, you need to withdraw that complaint. You're embarrassing the entire family.

My head rears back. *Me?!* Embarrass *them?!*

JULIAN

I'm doing this FOR the family, for ALL of Sparrow Nook. If you saw HALF of what I've seen in the ER, you'd know how dangerous marijuana is!

AUNT EDNA

People insert foreign objects into butts sober, too.

JULIAN

?????!!!!

MOM

Oh, honey. ☹

ELLIO

You see what you're doing to your mother? Withdraw the complaint!

ALDO

This woman heard my last name at the bar last night, and then she wouldn't give me her number. Because of YOU, Julian!

JULIAN

You sure it's not because you were wearing last season's Armani Exchange jeans?

MARCO

HOOO

ELLIO

HOOOOO

AUNT EDNA

Now that was uncalled for.

UNCLE ROCCO

Can someone pick up a Stocks pound cake?

MARCO

Gotchu, Pop. JULIAN, WITHDRAW THE COMPLAINT!!!

Julian has left the chat.

I shove the phone into my back pocket, steaming. One person's in front of me, and he's taking forever. He asks about each item on the menu, what kind of cannabis was used, and what will work best for his anxiety.

"*Exercise,*" I say, interrupting Nomi's spiel. "*Exercise* will help your anxiety. Not drugs."

The man flinches as if I slapped him.

"Do not speak to my customers like that, or you will be asked to *leave.*" Nomi glares at me.

"*Me,* leave? You're the one operating an illegal drug trade on the side of Highway Five like it's the goddamn Silk Road!"

Nomi turns and offers the nervous man a soft smile. "Sorry about that. Where were we, Mr. Franklin?"

The man lowers his voice to a whisper, and the two continue to have the world's longest conversation. If Nomi's trying to bore me into leaving, she'll have to work harder than this, though. My morning was ruined in a modern-day reenactment of *The Shining*, I'm covered in an itchy layer of pond scum, and I just pulled a reed out of my ass crack.

I'm not going *anywhere.*

As the man's handing over the cash for his startlingly large haul of baked goods, a cop car comes to an epic, screeching halt in front of the hut, lights on, sirens hiccupping like, *wut wut!*

The nervous man shrieks, then hustles away.

"Don't worry, Mr. Franklin, it's completely legal!" Nomi calls after him.

I cross my arms, smug. We'll see about that.

The cop car opens, and Lil Dom swaggers out, hands already tucked into his belt. Oh Jesus, this guy? I haven't seen him since graduation, where he spent the whole after-party drinking Schlitz beer and retching in the bushes.

"Hey, you!" Nomi dons a big, flirtatious smile like a freaky Halloween mask and waves, coy as hell.

"Ms. Wyeth." Lil Dom smiles and tips his hat like he's the fucking sheriff, and now *I* want to retch in the bushes. "You're not causing any trouble out here, are you?"

"Oh, only the fun kind."

I groan, loud and disgusted.

"Officer, I'm the one who texted in the emergency," I step forward, inserting myself between this blatant display of hypermasculine posturing and Nomi's fawning *little ol' me?* bullshit. "She's selling drugs out here without a—without a permit!"

I don't *know* that she doesn't have a permit, but seriously, what kind of permit exists for selling weed on the side of the road?

"Oh, you mean this permit?" Nomi waves a copy of her new license to operate granted at the last city council meeting. "While I don't have permission to operate my dispensary in my building *yet*, I do have permission from Sparrow Nook to operate a dispensary within township lines. She holds out her hands, gesturing to her tiny hut. "Voila. Bake sale. What can be more wholesome and law abiding than that?"

Lil Dom makes a show of inspecting her license, then gazing up Nomi's tank top to her glossy lips and the swinging swish of her high ponytail. "Everything looks in order to me." His lips quirk into a suggestive smile beneath his *Top Gun* aviators. "Looks *fantastic*, in fact."

"Are you kidding me?! She's selling *weed* on the *side of the road*!"

Lil Dom ducks his chin and gives me a long, probing look over the rim of his sunglasses. He slowly straightens up to his full height, which is still a good five inches shorter than me, not that it's affecting his self-esteem at all, and saunters over. "Ms. Wyeth," he drawls, "is this guy bothering you?"

"Yes," Nomi nods emphatically. "*So* much. But I can take care of it, Officer."

"You sure?" Lil Dom cocks his head back, giving me a full view of his stubbled chin. "I can bring 'im in for you."

My eyes nearly bulge out of my skull. "On what grounds?!"

Just then, Lil Dom's radio buzzes from his car. He eyes it regretfully, sad he can't cop it up there and in my face simultaneously.

"Go, Dom. I've got it under control here." Nomi winks again. "Thanks for stopping by."

Lil Dom tips his hat to her once more, gives me a meaningful spit that lands by my foot, and disappears into his cruiser, cutting out as fast as he came in. *Wut wuuuuut*, his siren blips in parting.

"What an *incredible* douche." I fold my arms as he tears down the road. "You like that guy?" The thought sets the contents of my stomach to boil.

Nomi shrugs. "We made out a few times. Comes in handy."

I gawp at her. "You kissed him!" Then, because my brain can't stop screaming it, I blurt again, "You *kissed* him?!"

She smiles at me wickedly. "He's got a big—"

"*Ughhhh!*" I slam my hands over my ears, furious that I called the cops at all. Is this what passes for justice in this small shit-town?!

"—hat," she finishes, then bites her bottom lip, she's grinning so hard.

God, she loves torturing me.

She eyes my mucked-up clothes, brown socks, and green-tinged skin and snorts. "What happened to you, anyway?"

"You happened to me, Nomi Wyeth! *You!*" I grab my still-dripping T-shirt and wring it out in front of my body, sluicing off more of the disgusting water. I don't miss the way her eyes track across my abs, though, and it makes me draw my shirt up higher, just to prove my point. I don't know what point that *is*, exactly, but I'm gonna prove the *fuck* out of it. "You sent your hench-twins after me, and they threw me in the river!"

That's not exactly what happened, but it was clearly the intended outcome. So.

Nomi's eyes widen, as though she didn't plan the whole thing herself. "Ridge and Thorn threw you in the river?" She busts out an oversized laugh. "No, they did *not*."

"The monozygotic weirdos have hippie names? Ironic since they came upon me *with* violence."

"Their mom loves soap operas, and Ridge and Thorn would *never*."

"Sure, says the woman responsible!" I rake my hair out of my eyes and pull away gunk wrapped around my fingers. "*Ugh!* And the flyers? You're trying to ruin my life!"

"Wow. In case you forgot, my dispensary is under a zoning investigation, and I'm out here in a farm stand trying to make enough money to survive. Because *you're* trying to ruin *my* life."

"Just call off your hench-people, Wyeth!"

"Listen, Julian, you're clearly in over your head, so I'm going to let you in on a secret." Nomi leans over the counter toward me, the space between her delicate collarbones and her round, shapely breasts incredibly lick-able.

I cannot help but move closer, too, as though this secret she's about to share holds the meaning of life. Her skin looks so soft, and without my consent, my own body relives the feel of that soft skin pressed against my chest, the tight buds of her nipples bearing into me through two layers of clothing. Her voice drops to a low, husky whisper.

"I don't have to call off a thing because I didn't ask for any of this. These are *my* people. And *my people* hate *your guts*." Her whispered voice grates over each syllable, raising the hairs on my arms. "Withdraw. The. Complaint." She pauses to wrinkle her nose, then backs away. "And take a shower, my *God*, you smell like moldy bread."

CHAPTER TWELVE

NOMI

"Why can't I sell cannabis at the farm stand anymore?" I clutch the cell phone hard to my face, keeping my voice low since the zoning detective's back and currently poking around my inventory room. As if empty stash boxes and humidifier packs have anything to do with whether my dispensary qualifies as a "*pharmacy*," or an "*amoral weed bordello*," as Julian's complaint alleges.

"I'm sorry, Nomi," the city council clerk says through the receiver, sounding genuinely distressed. "A Council-friend saw you and asked whether it was legal, so I had to call the State Cannabis Regulatory Commission. They said you'd need a different license for that. She gave me a link to the paperwork; I can send it to you if you like."

Council-friend, my ass. This smacks of Julian's doing. "How fast is the approval turnaround, did she say?"

"Three months."

Fuck, I mouth silently at the wall.

I thank the clerk for the information and disconnect the call. Another three months of no income from cannabis, and we'll officially be destitute. The rent is too high to cover with no profits coming in, and judging by the detective's sour demeanor, I'm not acing this investigation, either. I rest my head on the counter, and I'm still lying here when Eve comes in twenty minutes later, high as a kite and carrying a box of hand-stamped shopping bags we spent all weekend making.

For *nothing*.

"Hmm," Eve says after I fill her in on the latest blow to our livelihood, then sits on a red vinyl stool at the counter. "We could set up an OnlyFans."

"Angle?" I ask, face still smushed against the glass.

"I could braid your hair while you pop bubble wrap." Eve revolves on her stool like Bella in that overly cinematic moment in *Twilight*. "Or you could show off your big flap. People like scars."

"*Eve.*"

"It'll be like Tiny Tim, but vulvas." Eve's eyes get big. "We could make it a little crutch and everything!"

"*Eve!* I'm not getting into flap content."

Eve frowns, which usually makes me laugh because it wrinkles her entire face like a bulldog. But even Eve's bulldog face does nothing for me now.

"We could sell coffee..." Eve begins. "For real."

"Our dream is to open an Amsterdam-style coffeehouse. Not an actual American one."

"How hard can it be? I've dated enough baristas. Some of it probably rubbed off on me." A wicked smile perks up Eve's mouth. "Other stuff did."

"Dammit, Eve! Now's *not* the time for double entendres!"

"Come on, just for a little while until we figure out what to do. I'll call Uncle Dimitri, see if he's got an espresso machine he can bring over." Eve begins idly scooping up her hair with a pair of bakery tongs and placing it over her shoulder. "Still think the crutch idea's gold, though."

I arch an eyebrow. Maybe *I* should get high, too.

The detective exits the inventory room, and we both sit up straighter. "My investigation inside the premises is complete." He's holding a long-poled object with a wheel at the bottom.

"What's that?" Eve asks, starry eyed. She loves toys.

"It's a measuring wheel," the detective says, pleased by her attention despite himself. "I'll use it to count the feet between this building and establishments that serve children." His eyes cut to mine. "Like family clinics. Afternoon, ladies."

My stomach cramps ominously as the door closes behind him.

"*Fuck.*" I press my forearm against my middle, hunching over, as another surge of pain grips my insides.

Eve's brow knits together. "Are you—"

"No!" I belt out, sliding from my chair behind the counter. "I'm not okay. Nothing's okay! Everything I have is riding on this dispensary, which that *detective's* about to ruin!"

"Then we'll appeal the decision and keep fighting."

"With what money, Eve?" Sweat collects under my hair, on my neck, in the curve of my lower back. I have to get out of here. "I'll be wiped out before we get a hearing date, and we'll lose everything. All our hard work. All my savings. It'll have been for nothing."

"Hey. You're not alone in this, Nomi. We're going to figure this out." Eve walks around the counter and wraps her arms around me, which my stomach can tolerate for about one second before I have to shake her off. Her face is hurt when I pull away, and another wave of pain crests inside me.

"I'm—sorry. I have to go." I push through the glass doors, praying I'll make it home in time, and knowing, no matter what Eve says, that I *am* alone.

JULIAN

Eight showers later, I *still* smell the scum of New Jersey's waterways. Somewhere on my body is a phantom patch of something mossy and unnatural, and it's driving me insane. Or maybe it's the memory of Nomi's threats sliding out of her lush mouth that's making me lose touch with reality.

She doesn't *own* this town.

I'm not in any *danger.*

I flick open my office blinds to glance out at the street. No Kia Souls in sight. That doesn't mean I'm not being watched, though. I haven't been physically harassed since the river park, but Nomi's lackeys are still messing with me. First, it was the flyers stapled around downtown, then the nonstop prank calls. Even the Ohs descended upon me one night at Mom's house in a cloud of competing cologne.

"Julie, seriously." Marco'd gripped me by the shoulders. "Withdraw the complaint."

"I'm a *medical professional.* Maybe that means nothing to you meatheads, but I took the Hippocratic oath and specifically swore to administer no poison when asked to do so, and guess what? Weed's *poison*!"

"That's a weird oath, man." Aldo frowned. "They really make doctors say that?"

"If weed is poison, why'd it make you such a decent guy that night? Huh?" Marco crossed his arms over his chest. "That was the first time you've been nice to us since we were kids, Julie."

"*What?*" I'd sputtered, feeling caught and entirely unprepared to handle their interrogation when I still smelled the river on me, still burned with anger at Lil Dom eyeing Nomi like she was a stuffed prize to win down the Shore. "That's not *true—*"

"It's true, bro," Ellio said. "You're a stone-cold dick when you're sober. Pretty decent when you're high, though."

"Yeah, pretty decent," Aldo agreed. "Everybody liked you stoned."

And the thing is, I'd thought the same thing. At the Pot Luck I felt... I don't know. Connected to everyone, somehow. My cousins. The townies who never left home, or who came back on purpose. Even the folks like me, who ended up back in Sparrow Nook through every fault of their own, but unlike me, were making the best of it. I felt included. Accepted. I made my cousins *laugh*, and for once, it wasn't at obnoxious Julie's expense.

Or . . . maybe it was. Maybe they only liked me when they *could* laugh at me, when I was stoned and pretending to smoke beer bottles and stuffing my face with pizza. Maybe they had to see me transformed into an idiot to forget how much they resented me the rest of the time. I learned early on in life that people don't like reminders of their own shortcomings. They transmute your success into their shame. They blame *you* for how *they* feel instead of facing the real source of their discomfort—their decisions not to try. Not to work hard. Not to grab hold of this one life we have and shake it for everything it's worth.

Well, that's not my fault. And I shouldn't have to debase myself so people like me.

I kicked my cousins out then, or tried to, at least. Mom busted in right as the door was swinging shut and dragged them all back inside for popsicles, and when they didn't want those, beers. Worse, Mom forced me to join them on the front porch while they visited. They hogged all the rocking chairs, laughing and chatting with Mom while I sat sullenly on the stoop holding a melting blue pop.

Humiliating.

I sink down in the office chair. I'm taking regular appointments today during the clinic's daytime hours. Dr. Srinivasan isn't convinced I'm "ready" for this type of patient interaction, but he needs coverage while he does errands, so here I am. I roll my eyes and bring up my next appointment's information. Does he think I can't handle annual exams and listening to people prattle on about symptoms that can be explained, nine times out of ten, by their sedentary, vice-filled lifestyles?

I take three long breaths. It's only mid-June. I have four and a half more months before I can prove to Dr. Riveras that I deserve to return to Philly Gen where I belong. To do that, I need Dr. Srinivasan's full support, which means playing nice and doing whatever the old country doctor requires.

I briefly review the next patient's records, a Mr. Franco Gutierrez. Sixty-two years old, with advanced Parkinson's Disease. Currently prescribed the standard course of treatment—levodopa to increase dopamine, as well as a dopamine agonist to prevent his brain from breaking it down too quickly. I squint at the last line in Dr. Srinivasan's notes: *Patient supplements with high CBD, low THC strains of cannabis to treat break-through tremors, as needed. Consult with Nomi Wyeth for cannabis treatment planning.*

My jaw drops. *Consult with Nomi Wyeth?* Getting the town giggly and stoned isn't bad enough, now she's "*treating*" people with serious neurological diseases? The buzzer on my desk sounds, followed by the dull, lifeless voice of our teen reception clerk. *Mr. Gutierrez is waiting in Room Four.*

I march toward the room. Who does she think she is, *Doctor Weed*?! I swing the door open without knocking, startling Mr. Gutierrez where he sits so badly he drops his cane and makes a small *oof!* sound.

"Good afternoon," I bark out. "I'm Dr. D'Angelo. You're Franco Gutierrez, correct?"

The old man nods, still grasping for his cane where it lies on the floor, his tremors evident with the difficulty he's having. With a short exhale, I lean over, grab the cane, and return it to him.

"Thank you," he says stiffly.

"You're here for a wellness visit today?" My words are short and clipped but professional, which is honestly impressive considering the amount of fury seething beneath my skin. I know she spouted off all those purported medical benefits at the city council meeting, but I didn't realize Nomi was actually dispensing *medical advice* along with all her dime bags and eight balls and bong hits. I cannot believe Dr. Srinivasan condones this.

"Yes, I see Dr. Appa for check-ins between my neurologist visits." Mr. Gutierrez tries to sit higher in his seat, but his left leg wriggles involuntarily beneath him, making him slide back down each time. The skin stretches tight over his knuckles as he grips the arms of his chair in a struggle.

"This movement," I indicate his wriggling leg, "this is dyskinesia from the levodopa usage?"

"That's right," Mr. Gutierrez grits out.

"How long have you been taking levodopa?"

"Eight years."

I nod tightly. Dyskinesia often develops after a few years of levodopa usage, but for it to be this pronounced is concerning. Parkinson's patients don't usually come into the ER for emergencies related to the actual disease—it's the secondary impacts that get them. Falls, primarily. Complications from pneumonia and asphyxiation when they can no longer swallow. I'm familiar with the disease, how you treat those secondary emergencies requires a basic understanding of the patient's underlying etiology, but I've never been involved in the treatment of the disease itself. It's an incredibly complex, debilitating condition, and *not* something you can solve by smoking a big, fat blunt.

Again, anger roils through me at Nomi's interference in this man's life. "How long have you been using marijuana, sir?"

"Excuse me?"

"Reefer. Ganja. Weed." I spin around on the stool to face him. "*Cannabis*," I say, making a face at Nomi's preferred term and its sanitized version of the truth.

Mr. Gutierrez leans back, both hands on his cane, and regards me coolly. "I don't like your tone, Doctor."

"Well, I cannot assess how your medications are functioning without understanding how your... marijuana habit may be impeding them," I manage through my flexed jaw.

His brows form a single dark thundercloud. "I don't have a *marijuana habit*. I use it when the dyskinesia gets so bad I cannot *walk*, or when my back clenches so tightly, my spine feels as though it will snap in half. It loosens and calms the misfiring muscles."

"And did you use marijuana before your Parkinson's developed?" I press, feeling my face pulse with heat. "Have you considered that it may be worsening your overall condition?"

"You know *nothing* about my condition. I will not sit here and listen to some hot shot doctor insinuating that I somehow brought this on myself!" Mr. Gutierrez huffs furiously as he struggles to his feet. "Nomi told me to reschedule this appointment until I could see Dr. Appa, but did I listen?" He shakes his head. "She was right about you."

"Oh yeah?" My head jerks up as Mr. Gutierrez shuffles out of the room, unable to keep my calm any longer. "And what did your drug dealer say about me?"

Mr. Gutierrez pauses in the doorframe, eyeing me with disgust.

"That you're the worst kind of doctor there is."

Surprisingly, the day devolved from there. The bad feelings brought on by Mr. Gutierrez's appointment stewed in a furious, rolling boil all afternoon that bubbled up every time one of Dr. Srinivasan's patients tried me. The number of people that (1) stormed out of the clinic today, (2) cried, and (3) placed very convincing hexes on me are *all* greater than zero. When I finally finish the last appointment, I exhale, feeling the fury leave my body, utterly spent. Four hours of appointments—that's all it took to bring me to my knees. I slump into the office and lay my head on the desk.

The door swings open, banging into the wall so hard I nearly fall out of the chair. Dr. Srinivasan looms in the doorframe, which is impressive considering he's only five foot six. Without a word, he stomps over to the IT'S BEEN ___ DAYS SINCE I'VE RECEIVED A COMPLAINT ABOUT JULIAN sign.

What's he going to write? He's never been able to change it from zero. But then he takes it off the wall and throws it down in a shocking display of emotion. For as long as I've known Dr. Srinivasan, he has been a bastion of calm professionalism, if a little snarky at times.

Not now.

His skin heats to a deep crimson as he struggles to form the words. "Julian," he finally utters, "you're fired. Get out."

My eyes bulge as I jump up from the chair. "Dr. Srinivasan, no! Please—I had a bad day, I'm sorry!"

"It's not working out. You haven't learned anything I've tried to teach you about treating patients with compassion, and after your behavior with Mr. Gutierrez today..." Dr. Srinivasan trails off, shaking his head. "Frankly, Julian, I'm disgusted. Embarrassed. And more than anything, disappointed. You have so much potential—you're bright and hardworking, with excellent training. But you're not cut out for this type of care. You'll have to finish your probation somewhere else."

Pressure builds up behind my eyes, stinging my sinuses. "Nowhere else will have me!"

"Well, now we know why, don't we?" Dr. Srinivasan frowns at the sign on the floor and leans over to pick it up. He grabs the cloth and wipes off the marker'ed message. "I'm sorry, Julian. Not to you, but to my patients, whom I've allowed you to hurt. I'm sorry to your mother, who is a deeply kind woman, and whom I wished to help with this favor. But I cannot give you access to my patients any longer."

"I'm a good doctor," I assert, louder than I mean to. "I save lives!"

"When you have your way, yes," Dr. Srinivasan agrees. "You thrive in emergencies with a top-down approach. You assess the damage. You make all the decisions. No one's in any state to argue with your judgment. But that's not how it works anywhere else, Julian. Here, you have to collaborate with your patients to find the solutions together. You have to put your ego aside and listen to someone else because your voice isn't the only one that matters. And that, I'm afraid, you're incapable of doing."

My stomach bottoms out. "I need this job, Dr. Srinivasan. If you fire me after six weeks, there's no way Philly Gen will take me back. My entire career's at stake. What can I do to change your mind?"

Dr. Srinivasan huffs humorlessly. "Become a different person?"

"Okay. I'll do it."

"Julian, be serious. There's no way to come back from how you acted today. How you've been acting this entire time."

"I'll apologize to Mr. Gutierrez, to anybody you want. I'll count to ten before I say anything. I'll—I'll go to therapy!"

"Will you study? Will you learn—"

I laugh, a burst of giddy relief at the tiny glimmer of hope. "—*yes!* I'll learn anything! I'll study so hard—"

"About cannabis, Julian? About its medical benefits? How it's used to treat different conditions, including Parkinson's?"

The words die on my lips. "I—but sir, it's—"

"See? You cannot do this job. You refuse to expand your narrow worldview, which is unacceptable."

I swallow, my heart thudding in my chest as I try, desperately, to sound reasonable. "But I believe cannabis use is unethical, sir."

"A significant portion of the medical community disagrees with you. Isn't it worth educating yourself before you take such a harsh, unyielding position on a complex subject?"

"I—I suppose so, but—"

Dr. Srinivasan strides over to the desk and reclaims the chair. "Though I absolutely shouldn't allow you to stay one more minute under my employ, I'm willing to *consider* it if you honor my conditions. All of them."

My face goes slack with relief. "I—thank you, sir! Anything!"

"First, you won't see any patients until you complete my conditions to my satisfaction."

"Okay."

"Second, I won't write you the recommendation letter you need at the end of this probation unless I see *real growth* in you as a doctor. I won't lie to protect your incompetence. Do you understand?"

Everything above my collar flushes with shame. "Of course, sir."

"Third, you will learn *everything* there is to know about both medicinal and recreational cannabis with an open mind."

The thought makes my stomach recoil. After watching Dad waste away in our garage, stoned until the very end, I already know what cannabis does to a person. A family. A future. Add that to what I've seen in the ER—car accidents from driving under the influence, psychotic episodes from overuse, and yes, lots of foreign objects in butts—and my mind's made up. But I also know this condition is non-negotiable. Dr. Srinivasan obviously believes in cannabis's value—he uses it himself. "I will read every medical study there is, sir."

"Not enough," Dr. Srinivasan counters. "You need to witness firsthand how cannabis helps people in their daily lives. I want you to shadow Nomi Wyeth and learn everything she's willing to teach you. She's an expert of great knowledge."

The hope blooming in my chest gets chopped down like a weed. "Uh, sir. That's impossible."

"Make it possible."

"You see, Nomi..." I pause, searching for the right words, but my brain supplies exactly none of them.

Is so pretty, it makes my chest hurt.

Kissed me and blew my world apart.

Makes me feel like I'm... I'm more and less, all at once.

"Hates you, I know," Dr. Srinivasan supplies succinctly, and I wince, my heart spiraling in my chest.

Yes. Those are the right words.

"She'll never let me shadow her, sir. Not after I filed that zoning complaint."

"Interesting predicament." Dr. Srinivasan's eyebrows rise as he dryly regards me. "What*ever* will you do."

CHAPTER THIRTEEN

NOMI

Uncle Dimitri stops by later in the week with either a homemade bomb or an espresso machine, hard to say. For all the shuddering, thunking, and weird gasping shrieks it makes, maybe it's both.

"Barely used, excellent condition, makes a beautiful cup of espresso." Eve's uncle slaps the machine as it spits out a tiny cup of dark, murky liquid. "Some sad Italian guy brought it in the pawn shop, got it for a song."

"Why does it matter if he was sad?" I frown at the belching machine.

"The sadder the person, the better the item they're pawning," Eve explains.

"Here, try it." Uncle Dimitri hands me a cup to taste.

I stare into it. "What *is* espresso?"

Uncle Dimitri's eyebrows bush together, like sentient shrubbery. "What's espresso?" He lifts his palms up to Eve. "What's *espresso*?!"

"Calm down, Nomi doesn't drink coffee. It uh, doesn't agree with her."

I give her a small smile, relieved that Eve and I are okay. I don't have many close friends, and the day I got sick this week is basically why. Not everyone can handle my sudden need to withdraw, or how, when I'm gripped in the kind of pain that makes you moan, I become someone different for a while. Someone they don't know and can't understand. Maybe even someone they don't like. But Eve gives me the grace to get through the pain however I need to, and I know she'll always be there, waiting for me on the other side.

"I better not." I push the tiny cup back.

"How are you gonna run a coffee shop if you don't know what it tastes like?" He huffs.

After two days of tinkering with espresso and brewing Costco brand ground coffee out of a substandard machine, the answer is *badly* and *to great critical condemnation.*

"Sorry!" I call out as the customer, a woman in her thirties pushing a double baby stroller *filled* with infants, chokes and splutters on her first sip of latte. She eyes the paper cup in her hand warily, grimaces, then glugs down another swallow before struggling out the door.

That's the first person I've seen go back for more. I must be getting better!

Stranger Drugs, now renamed Stranger Coffee thanks to Eve taping a piece of printer paper over our painted glass door, is in a great spot to serve coffee downtown. Literally five minutes after she taped up the sign, a big guy named Carl popped his head inside to ask if we were open. Like Carl, many city employees pass by on their way to work. Yesterday, the first day we claimed to sell coffee, we had a line for a solid two hours.

It was *horrible.* We only have the one coffeepot, and the little fucker takes ten minutes to brew a pot *every time.* I couldn't believe it! The espresso machine isn't much faster, though that's in large part due to user error. Uncle Dimitri must've shown me a dozen times how to brew the tiny cup of motor oil, but I still can't get it right. Half the time it doesn't work at all and spews out a thin, gruesome water flecked with black grounds. The other half of the time I have to use a spoon to dig it out. While I'm new to this world, I'm pretty sure espresso shouldn't have the consistency of facial scrub.

This morning's been much slower since the city employees that came in yesterday are now walking briskly past and avoiding my gaze. Only new, uninformed souls have come in today, like the woman saddled with babies. I check the receipts for the morning—a whopping eighteen dollars—and sigh before pulling out my laptop to work on the mobile dispensary license paperwork. What else can I do? Without the farm stand, we have nowhere to publicly sell our product and have resorted to quietly fulfilling orders via home visits for my longstanding customers. The irony isn't lost on me that I'm basically dealing drugs the old-school illegal way, but I'm sorry—I'm not going to let Mr. Gutierrez or Edna D'Angelo go without and suffer.

The door jingles as it opens, and the mail carrier enters carrying a package, which she leaves on the counter along with a thick stack of bills. "Here you go, sweetheart."

"Wait," I call out as she turns. "I didn't order anything."

"It's addressed to here." The carrier shrugs and continues out the door.

"Huh." I read the package's label and frown. It's addressed to here, alright, but the label states it's for JM Enterprises, LLC. Must be a mistake. I'm the first and only tenant since the deed passed from the original owners to the city council. I turn my attention to the envelopes, anxiety stitching like a needle through my heart, drawing it up, tight. After tallying what we owe and comparing it to the balance in my checking, savings, and emergency fund, the feeling only gets worse. Getting fired a month early and paying for expensive COBRA coverage while I wait for my marketplace health insurance to come through dealt a major blow to my cashflow timeline. If something doesn't change and fast, I'm not sure how we'll make it through August.

With no customers to wait on, I pull up an espresso machine tutorial online and watch for the fifth time, hoping for a miracle.

JULIAN

"It's coercion!" I spew into Eric's voicemail. "He's forcing me to drop the complaint! He knows if I'm dismissed from the clinic, Philly Gen will take it as proof that I haven't learned anything, and I'll lose everything—my entire career!"

I turn sharply into the Wawa parking lot. "Advise me, Eric, or I'm joining Doctors Without Borders and disappearing forever." I hang up with a percussive sigh, shut off my car, and review Mom's text again.

> Julian. I'm finally ready to discuss your disappointing behavior at Nomi's Pot Luck. Come to Aunt Edna's tonight with dinner for everyone, no excuses! You haven't seen her since you've been home, and she's VERY pissed about it! We want Wawa. Get my usual and loaded fries with extra ham chunks and a cheeseburger with barbecue sauce for Aunt Edna. Don't forget the ham chunks!!

Ugh. I'd intended to go for a rage run in the next town over, but Mom hasn't spoken to me directly in weeks, and living with a passive-aggressive South Jersey Italian woman who's mad at you is one of Dante's nine circles of hell.

I knead the stress knots in my forehead. The last thing I want is to spend the evening with Mom, a very pissed Aunt Edna, and her perpetually farting dog, BonBon Jovi, while they eat a metric ton of garbage.

But I don't get the things I want, do I?

Five minutes later, I'm punching in our hot food order one-handed on Wawa's touch screen. I have to laud Wawa's commitment to reducing human interaction, allowing me to order my family's trash food with as much dignity as possible.

When the ticket goes through, the Wawa worker, a thick, hairy thumb of a man, glances up from my order with narrowed eyes.

"You're Julian D'Angelo? That asshole who filed the zoning complaint?"

Shit.

I hold up a finger, briefly consider lying, but my name's clearly on my credit card. "Yes, but this entire food order is for my very sick Great Aunt Edna D'Angelo. *Please* don't corrupt her food because you love weed."

The Wawa man aggressively dishes out ham chunks onto Aunt Edna's fries, his eyes glued to me the whole time.

I squeeze my own shut. I was *supposed* to lie low. Keep my head down. Serve out my probation and learn some people skills. So why did I think the best way to do that was by starting a public showdown with Nomi over her dispensary?

Because you have ethics, my brain insists, then helpfully flashes through a slideshow of my most unethical hits—the semi-erection during Nomi's sutures, laughing aloud when that lifelong smoker asked why he'd developed a cough, the ill-fated night I called Lillian Corrington Van Dyke to her husband's bedside and put my career on a collision course with a brick wall.

Ethics . . . not the most compelling argument, no.

Because you care about Sparrow Nook's well-being!

Do I? I guess that's true, in the same way I wish for world peace, or for Costco to carry my preferred vegan protein shakes. Vaguely, and without a lot of effort.

Because you're hurt.

I immediately push that theory out of my head. So what if I hurt? I've *always* hurt, and it doesn't change a thing.

When I arrive at Aunt Edna's with her gas station cuisine, the first thing I hear is wild, witchy cackling and Billy Joel blaring over the stereo. "Mom? Aunt Edna?"

"Is that my son, ready to apologize?"

I trudge into the living room, and the sight takes me aback. The 1980s wood paneling is still here, along with the tan paisley velvet couch and coordinating orange armchairs, but a hospital bed's been shoved in the middle of the room. Aunt Edna's propped up to sitting, looking like the wrinkly, doll-sized version of herself. Her dyed brown hair has finally been allowed to fade to a soft yellow-white, and she looks, for the first time in my life, truly *old*.

Aunt Edna's always been a force of nature. Irish by heritage, she married into the D'Angelo clan in the 1970s and was louder and brasher than any of my Italian aunts by a long shot. They *loved* her, as did all of Sparrow Nook. She was involved in everything. Secretary of the PTO, president of the South Jersey Rotary Club, she even drove my Uncle Joseph, a Shriner, in one of those little cars in the parades. Every holiday was hosted here since her house was the biggest. The Ohs and I would be relegated to a wobbly card table in the corner, poking the bizarre casseroles Aunt Edna made while our girl cousins sat around a white, curly iron patio table set with fake roses and pink butt cushions.

More than anything, though, Aunt Edna's always been a stone-cold weirdo, and while she embarrassed the hell out of me growing up, I've always loved her, too. Grudgingly, yes, but she feels like home in a way no one else does. She's in her eighties now, and after a few rough years, she recently decided to forgo treatment for the leukemia storming her system. I can respect that decision, but I can't quite look it in the face, either. I know her end is near, but part of me has been desperate to preserve the monolith of *Aunt Edna* that's always been such a strong, supportive constant in my life. Seeing her so frail now punches me in the chest, just like I knew it would.

"Get in here, Julie!" Aunt Edna rasps out, then makes grabby hands at me. I walk over, doing my best not to broadcast my emotions, and lean in, closing my eyes for a peck on the cheek. So, when the Wawa bag is ripped from my hand instead, followed by the sound of Aunt Edna's satisfied grunts as she removes box after greasy box and places them on her TV tray, I'm surprised and slightly miffed.

"Oh, good—you remembered the blue cheese dressing. Can you heat it up?"

Hot blue cheese dressing? My mouth contorts into a grimace. "Abso*lutely* not!"

Aunt Edna cackles again. "Oh, my wittle Julie. Still such a fussbudget prissy pants."

She wipes at her tearing eyes, which are a startling bloodshot red.

"Jesus, Aunt Edna—what's wrong with your eyes?"

"I'm eighty-four years old. What's right with them?" She opens the box of loaded fries first, sniffs it appreciatively. "God, I love Wawa ham chunks." She picks one off the cheesy pile and throws it to BonBon Jovi, the ridiculous shih tzu fluff ball nestled between Aunt Edna's knees. "Best chunks in town."

The tiny, ninety-pound woman proceeds to destroy that box of fries. She eats with the gusto of a starved person, or a fourteen-year-old boy. My brow pinches as she makes actual carnivorous *noises*.

"What's going on here?" I whisper to Mom, who's smiling fondly as Aunt Edna tears into the cheeseburger with barbecue sauce next.

Even after three years in the ER, I have to look away.

"This is the first time she's had an appetite all week." Mom holds up a paper shopping bag stamped with STRANGER DRUGS. "Thanks to Nomi."

"Aunt Edna's *high*?!"

"If it's good enough for Martha Stewart, it's good enough for me," Aunt Edna says between gruesome bites. "Come sit with me, Julie. I'm gonna die soon, and you'll wish you had." She says this with zero fear or concern, like she's just remarked on the forecast or someone's unfortunate haircut. She slices an entire quarter off the burger and gives it to BonBon, who eats it one vicious gulp, then promptly farts.

"God bless you," Aunt Edna says.

Mom and I pull up chairs and TV trays to her bedside, close enough to hear each other, but far enough to avoid the barbecue splash zone. Though now *I* have no appetite, I pull out my garden salad with grilled chicken. It... looks normal? I check for pubic hair—judging by the Wawa man's knuckles, that man must shed like a dog—but find none. Tentatively, I arrange the napkin across my lap, then pour an exact measure of oil and vinegar across the greens.

Aunt Edna watches me, her face incredulous, as I sprinkle the tiniest amount of salt and black pepper last. "Oh, Julie. Your butthole must be so tight—"

"*Edna!*" Mom spews out, laughing. Laughing so hard, it's rather suspicious, now that I think about it. "Can we not discuss my judgmental son's butthole at dinnertime?"

My lips thin into a severe line. "Are you high, too, Mother?"

This makes them laugh even harder, but now my heart's hammering in my ears. I feel—*betrayed,* yes, *betrayed*—by Mom smoking pot. She lived in the same house I did, watching Dad waste away in the garage. Our power getting cut off in the winter when all our money went toward his weed and prescriptions until Mom called Aunt Edna or Uncle Rocco for help. How can she smoke it now, knowing what it did to Dad? What it did to *us*?

I exhale through my nose and cut my chicken into neat, even squares.

"Listen, Julie, I have wisdom to impart." Aunt Edna wipes her mouth daintily on one of Wawa's brown napkins. "Are you listening?"

"Is it about my butthole?" I arch an eyebrow.

Aunt Edna lifts her finger. "You must learn to loosen it."

Mom clutches her stomach and emits one long, high-pitched squeal.

"Okay, that's it." I throw my napkin down on my salad. It's probably covered in norovirus anyway. "I'm done."

"Your whole life, you're too uptight. Your entire existence is one long Kegel," Aunt Edna continues with no regard to how Mom is struggling to breathe. "One day, you're gonna be old, and you'll look back and ask yourself, why did I live my life with this tight butthole?" She presses her hand to her chest, looking philosophically into the distance. "Where did this tight butthole get me?"

"I don't have to take this." I shove the TV tray back into the little stand meant to hold it, surely the most unironically American piece of furniture that's ever existed, and brush nonexistent crumbs off my pants. "Thank you and goodnight."

"You sit that tight butthole down, young man!" Mom wheezes.

"Sit, sit, I'll be serious." Aunt Edna throws her hands in the air.

I groan. "No, you won't."

Aunt Edna eyes me sternly, and I sink into my seat.

"I know it's hard, but you need to hear this, Julie. So much of what upsets us exists only up here." She points a finger to her temple. "How much of what's bothering you is your own making? How much of it exists only in your head?"

"How do *you* know I'm upset?"

Aunt Edna tuts. "The whole town knows."

"Dr. Appa called me." Mom folds her arms. "Told me everything."

I frown. Since when do they talk on the phone? I lean my head into my hands. "Then you know these problems aren't just in my head. Dr. Srinivasan won't let me work unless I convince Nomi to teach me about cannabis. And if I don't—if I stand on my ethics or worse, beg Nomi for forgiveness and she laughs in my face—Dr. Appa will fire me, Philly Gen won't take me back, and everything I've worked for will be gone, just like that. All the prestige, awards, certifications, and research. The years I've spent sacrificing everything else to become the best won't mean a damn thing. All because of *weed*!"

I moan softly at the floor.

"Okay, here's what you do: go do a big workout, really get your muscles pumped, then shower but don't shave—leave some stubble. Show up to Nomi's dispensary wearing *extremely* short shorts, I'm talking Tom Selleck, I'm talking *Magnum, P.I.*, we're working for the female gaze here. If you don't have any, I still have some of your Uncle Joseph's nut-huggers in the back closet."

"No," I whisper futilely. "*No!*"

"Wear a button-down with the sleeves rolled up to your forearms, linen if possible. Bring flowers, good ones. Beg. Get on your knees if you have to—"

"Women *love* a good grovel." Mom takes a big swig of Arctic Splash. "And short shorts."

"Yes, we do," Aunt Edna nods. "Tell Nomi you're sorry for being such a know-it-all jerk—"

"*—hey—*" I look up, glaring.

"—and swallow that big ego of yours and actually learn about what you're trying to ruin for everybody." Aunt Edna wags a fry at me. "If I didn't take edibles, I'd have died years ago. Do you know what chemo does to your ability to eat?"

"Of course I do—"

"No," Aunt Edna interrupts. "You know about it in *theory*. If you really knew, if you really understood just how terrible it is when your own body's determined to starve you, you'd see cannabis for the miracle it is, for me especially." Aunt Edna blinks sleepily, then lies back in her bed, as if this lecture has cost her significant energy she's now used up. "Now come here and give us a kiss. I'm about to pass out."

I stand up, leaning over the tiny twig of a woman who's always loomed so large in my life, and kiss her soft, crinkled cheek. She lifts a hand to gently grasp my chin. "Remember, Julian. Very short shorts. Three inches or bust. In fact, they should look like they're about to bust."

"Yes, Aunt Edna," I mumble, though the thought of groveling for Nomi's forgiveness in slutty little shorts is unbearable. My jaw clenches with the same rush of frustration that's washed over me all day. I don't *want* to withdraw the complaint. I don't *want* to learn about marijuana. And I certainly, most ardently, do *not* want to apologize to Nomi Wyeth.

Aunt Edna pulls me by the collar until I lean over again, then whispers in my ear, "Remember, Julie. Loosen that butthole."

I'll do *no such thing.*

After Mom and I clean up, we return to Aunt Edna's light snoring, BonBon curled up against her side. Mom gestures for me to follow her to the screened-in porch. Ugh. The *talk.* She takes a seat on the swinging bench, and after a second, I sit beside her. The bench's chains creak lightly as we swing, loud in the quiet between us.

"We need to talk, Julie."

"You're high. It can wait until you're not." The words are clipped and hard, but she's not the only one who's angry here.

"Actually, it can't, because your stubborn, pigheaded behavior has landed you and other people I care about in real trouble. Dr. Appa has given you a very reasonable ultimatum that you have yet to agree to. What's going on in your head?"

I blink, turning to face her. "Dad's going on, Mom, *Dad.* Or did you forget about the stoner who lived in our garage?"

Mom lifts her chin. "I miss that stoner every single day. I loved him with my whole heart and part of me always will, and you better never, *ever* suggest otherwise again." Her voice is soft and hurt, but strong. Always so strong. She's always had to be.

"How could you do the same drugs he did, Mom?" My voice comes out strained.

Mom smiles sadly. "Oh, Julie. You're pinning the tail on the wrong donkey."

My brow creases. "What?"

"If your father only smoked pot, he'd still be here today. It was when he tried to get 'legit' by using prescription medication that everything went to hell. It was the oxycodone, Julian. The opioids. How do you not see that?"

"Of *course* I see that! But he'd been languishing in our garage for years at that point, Mom. He was constantly stoned. Marijuana came first."

"No," Mom says. "The *accident* came first. Then the wrenching pain. Everything after that was Anthony trying to stay in our lives the best way he knew how."

"Well, it wasn't good enough."

"It was for me."

"How can you say that?" I wipe my eyes with the back of my hand. "He was always out there working on that model, getting stoned, while you worked two jobs."

"Don't you know why? He was trying, desperately, to regain his motor skills so he could find a new job and take care of us again. Every house he painted, every little dog, every lamppost, he'd say, *I'm getting better, Gisella. Every day, I'm getting a little better.* And he'd go out there the next day and work twice as hard. You have a lot of his determination."

I blink, hard. *That* was why? My whole body shakes itself no, rejecting this statement and all it implies. "But he didn't get better," I insist. "He never made anything of himself again, and then he died and left us on our own."

"And he deserved our love anyway," Mom says. "He was there for us in the ways he knew how to be. You were so young, you may not remember, but he cooked every meal for us. After dinner, he'd sit with you at the table while you did your homework."

"He never helped."

Mom shrugs. "He didn't need to. But if you did need him, he was there for you, Julian."

"I didn't want to need him," I admit, remembering all those nights he sat beside me, asking me questions so I'd explain what I was learning to him. I thought he was quizzing me at the time, which triggered my competitive need to be right. But... maybe he was just making sure I didn't need him, after all. "I was so mad at him for—for not being more."

"He knew that, too. And he might not have been the dad you wanted, but you were the son of his dreams."

I sigh. "Because I was smart? Because I worked hard?"

"No," Mom says simply. "Because you existed."

The tears I don't want to cry are streaming down my face, and Mom clucks her tongue, bringing me in close for a hug.

"Julie. It's time to rewrite the story you tell yourself about your dad. Cannabis helps people. Nomi helps people. And your actions are hurting her and the people of this town." Mom runs her hand up and down my back, and it's simultaneously the most comforting and devastating thing I've ever felt. "I know you care about her, sweetie, and in your own way, you're trying to protect her. But it's time to listen to her for a change, and if you want to show you care, let *her* tell you how. You can't substitute your judgment for hers, and moreover, you don't deserve to. Do you understand that now?"

I suck in a deep, shaking breath, my chin still resting on my mother's shoulder. "I-I guess so."

"Good. Tomorrow morning, you'll go over to her dispensary and show off all this new emotional growth." Mom sits back and slaps my leg. "And your thighs. I'll find some of Uncle Joseph's nut-huggers."

Christ.

CHAPTER FOURTEEN

NOMI

There are many things I hate about running a coffee shop. First, my inability to make it. While I understand drip coffee now, the espresso torture device still eludes me. A very close second, though, is how *early* these coffee people demand to drink it. If I want to make any money, I have to be here at six in the godforsaken morning. It's brutal, unfair, and all Julian's fault.

When I pull into my parking spot this morning, there's already a person waiting outside the shop's door. It's not even that weird guy Carl, who always asks if we're open when we're not.

"Fucking *maniac.* Wouldn't *need* coffee if you slept to a goddamn reasonable hour!"

Which is, I'm learning, the reason I've never needed coffee—I've never *had* to wake up this early for work before.

Coincidentally, I've also learned I'm a huge bitch before eight a.m.

The keys are at the bottom of my bag because everything's difficult and life is terrible, so I'm too busy rooting around to give the maniac a second glance. To be honest, I don't want to see them. I just want to be asleep.

"Shop doesn't open for a half an hour, so back the *fu*—"

"You win, Wyeth."

My hand freezes in my bag, and I slowly lift my gaze to expensive canvas shoes, then fine ankles leading to shapely calves. Kneecaps, which are normal as far as kneecaps go, and then the thighs, grooved with muscle like walnuts. Then *more* thighs, and more, and *Jesus,* is the man Porky-Pigging it? Finally, my eyes hit fabric, then a full, physically present crotch. They flip upward in horror as recognition dawns.

"Julian?"

Julian thrusts a pot of sad, purple pansies at me, discounted to $4.99. "I know they're terrible, but it's all the twenty-four-hour Acme had. I'll get you better ones later."

"What's going on here? Why are your shorts so short?" I do *not* take the pansies.

"I couldn't sleep, and I've been waiting out here for you for over an hour, and Aunt Edna told me to—and *ugh,* just take the damn pansies!" Julian shakes them at me, frustration building in his face.

"No!" I finally grasp the keys, then shoulder past him to open the door.

"Please, wait, I'm sorry! I need to talk to you!"

"Well, I don't need to talk to you." I step inside quickly and shut the door, but he squeezes one of his obscenely toned thighs in to hold it open.

"Nomi, listen—I'm withdrawing the complaint!"

"You…are?" The fight goes out of my arms, and without the resistance, Julian's thigh cranks the door all the way open, and he stumbles inside.

"Yes! I've already completed the paperwork, it's here." His chin jerks toward his armpit, where a beige folder is tucked. "See for yourself."

I yank it out so fast, he hisses.

"Are you *trying* to give me a paper cut?"

Inside, a printed form creatively titled "Withdrawal of Zoning Complaint" is already filled out, Julian's signature slashed across the bottom.

"But why?" I'm still staring at the form, trying to understand how we got here, where I'm holding the solution to all my problems, and Julian's holding a pot of drooping pansies wearing a pair of retro polyester briefs. I glance up as he places the flowerpot down by the register. "You changed your mind?"

"Does it matter?" Julian plops down on a counter stool and runs his palms down his face. "I'll withdraw the complaint... on one condition."

My shoulders immediately tense. I should've known there'd be a catch. "*What.*"

"Can I have a cup of coffee first?"

"No."

"I'll buy it."

"It's not for sale."

"Of course it's for sale." His chin drops to the side, and he gives me an *oh, really* glare. "You sell coffee."

"Fine," I bark out, then slam a mug on the counter and pour him a day-old cup of coffee I should've cleaned out yesterday. Now I'm glad I didn't.

Julian looks down at the old, cold cup of coffee with sorrow.

"That'll be fifty dollars."

He flinches but pulls his wallet out and throws a fifty on the counter. "Can you heat it up at least?"

"Nope." I cross my arms. "And creamer's extra."

A stream of emotions pours over his features, but with great difficulty, he forces a smile and plucks a set of notecards from his pocket. He begins to read from the top. "Nomi, I—" His eyes snag on his loose cuff, and he pauses to roll both linen sleeves up to his elbows.

"Julian, what is this? I'm opening in twenty minutes. I have work to do."

"I'm groveling. Don't you want to hear me grovel?" His pale-blue eyes interrogate mine.

I blow out a long, tired breath. "Yes."

He clears his throat again. "Nomi, I first want to express how regretful I am for successfully thwarting your ill-advised and amoral business venture—"

"Good *God*."

"While plying a naive populace with intoxicating substances goes against my conscience, I concede that Sparrow Nook isn't where I live and thus, shouldn't be my sole concern when fighting on its behalf is directly impeding my own career."

"This isn't groveling, Julian."

He ignores me and flips to the next card, flexing his forearms unnecessarily, then checks my face to see if I've noticed.

"As you see in your—" Julian picks up the folder and thrusts it into my hands, "—hands, I'm prepared to withdraw my complaint in a show of good faith. Now it's *your* turn to show good faith by issuing a ceasefire to all your acquaintances, instructing them to immediately halt all planned attacks on my reputation, body, and otherwise, and then design a curriculum and shadowing schedule for me to learn everything about cannabis—"

He flips to the next card. "From you."

Julian taps the notecards on the counter, reapplies the rubber band, then tucks them neatly into his pocket.

"Wait, *what*?" I blink, trying to fuse together the last thirty seconds with reality. "Did you just ask me to do . . . what exactly?"

"Design a curriculum and shadowing schedule so I can learn everything about cannabis from you," he repeats, as if that explains anything.

"Why would I do that?"

"Because this is a deal. I'll withdraw the complaint in return for you teaching me about cannabis."

"Why do you suddenly want to learn about cannabis?"

Julian flexes his forearms again, then looks away. "Because . . . I want to."

I roll my eyes. "The truth, Julian."

His jaw clenches, and he exhales through his nose. "Because Dr. Srinivasan won't let me work again until I do, and if I don't complete my—*sabbatical* with his practice, Philly Gen won't . . . ah. They won't like it." His gaze darts back to mine. "Happy?"

"You must've really pissed off Dr. Appa." Understanding rolls through me, and my eyes widen. "You weren't mean to Mr. Gutierrez, were you?"

Julian says nothing, but shame colors his cheekbones.

"Let me get this straight. You do something spectacularly awful at Philly Gen, get slapped with some kind of conditional probation that requires you to work for Dr. Appa successfully for—what? Three months? Six?"

"Six," Julian says to the wall behind my head.

"But then you act like an ass all over town, and now Dr. Appa's given you his own conditional probation—where if you don't drop the complaint and learn about cannabis, from *me* apparently, he'll fire you, Philly Gen will never take you back, and your whole superiority complex will crumble to the ground." I fold my arms. "Do I have that right?"

Julian's bottom lip is dangerously pouty. For some reason, it makes me check the length of his shorts again.

Yep. Still short.

"At a rudimentary level, yes," he finally concedes.

"Then there's no deal to strike here." I huff. "You need me to rescue your entire career."

"*Fine.* I'm desperate, but you're desperate, too." His eyes flash, and he stands suddenly. "You're paying a lot of money to lease this space, and no matter how many rancid cups of coffee you sell, you're losing hundreds of dollars every day. Like it or not, Wyeth, you need me, too." He leans over the counter, meeting my gaze head on. "Now, you can teach me about marijuana, and I'll drop this complaint right now, or don't and we'll both go down in flames. What's it gonna be, Wyeth?"

His eyes are the color of pure, glacial ice, a blue so cold it burns everywhere it touches. *Goddammit.* Ever since Julian returned to Sparrow Nook, he's been like a rock in my shoe. Hobbling me, annoying me, hurting me, making it almost impossible for me to think of anything else. Every time I fish him out and fling him into the distance, he reappears a few days later, more annoying and intrusive than ever. And now, if I want to rescue my flailing dreams and avoid going broke for good, I have to work *with* him?

The last time we teamed up, we—

I suck in a deep breath. Whatever, we were seventeen, and Julian's so obnoxious now, there's no chance any of that would happen again. All I'd have to do is remind myself how much his bullshit opposition to my dispensary is costing me, and—*wait.*

An idea strikes. I lean over my counter, taking back control over my space and this deal.

"Pay me."

"What?" Julian looks momentarily baffled as I lift my chin.

"Pay me, for both the prep time and the shadowing. And you'll withdraw the complaint right now, while I watch. If you agree to these terms, we'll start immediately."

"How much?" Julian asks, his voice incredulous.

"Every month of rent I'm unable to sell weed during, *Julian.*" I cock my head to the side. "Or lest you forget, your entire career is riding on this."

His eyes widen all the way to the whites. Finally, he grits out, "Deal."

"Great. By the way, you work here for free now." I ball up a towel and throw it at his face. "You can start by making the coffee."

I saunter over to the door, flip the sign to Open, and smile for the first time in weeks.

CHAPTER FIFTEEN

JULIAN

After a week of early mornings at Nomi's "coffee shop" and evenings studying Nomi's assigned readings, quiz day arrives.

"Well?" She crosses her arms, which has the outrageous effect of hoisting her breasts even higher. Their rounded tops puff out of her black tank top ominously, like a blowfish about to strike. This helps quell the swirl of heat licking through my groin.

Theoretically.

"Did you do the reading?" She's looking at me as if I haven't, but I *have*. I read, I highlighted, I had an existential crisis about how I ended up back in Sparrow Nook apprenticed to a street pharmacist. Then, I read some more.

I clear my throat. "Yes."

"Everything?"

"Everything." And when I finished what Nomi hand-selected for me, I picked through the works cited, reading those articles, too. Let no one ever say I half-assed *my* homework. I've spent a small fortune on PubMed access this week, and I have the twitching eyelid to prove it.

Nomi's tawny brown eyes narrow, and she points to the counter where the quiz waits. "Then get started. You have fifteen minutes."

My mouth forms a hard line, and I snatch the pencil. The questions are straightforward but aren't playing around.

What functions does the endocannabinoid system regulate within the human body?

Explain the dopaminergic reaction of THC within the hypothalamus.

Cannabis with what ratio of THC to CBD is most effective for treating symptoms of Parkinson's disease? I feel a brief flush of shame as I slash out an answer to that one.

The timer buzzes, and I slam my pencil down on reflex. My cheeks heat as Nomi takes my paper. She may be wearing denim cut-offs and stacked black lace-up boots, but she is one hundred percent *teacher* right now, and it's doing things to me. She reads my responses through lowered lashes, absently pulling her bottom lip into her mouth. When she reaches the end, she sniffs, then tosses the paper in the trash.

"Well?" I know I aced it, but I want to hear her say it. I want my gold star, and I want *her* to give it to me.

Oh, God, I'm getting a boner.

She walks toward the door, her hips swaying in perfect rhythm back and forth, like a metronome ticking away the last of my sanity. "You passed," she calls over her shoulder. "Come on."

I grin, then bound after her.

After I squeeze into her car's tiny front seat and buckle in, Nomi puts on a pair of cat-eyed sunglasses and pulls out onto the road. I'm almost grateful for how bunched up my limbs are—being this uncomfortable is the only way I'll survive the way the shorts' frayed hem dances across her thighs, catching on the tiny blonde hairs there. The image of her legs spread open before me on the patient table flashes through my brain like a lightning strike, and I flinch, staring out the window instead.

"Where are we going?"

Nomi takes a deep breath. "You passed the quiz, so your shadowing can begin for my medicinal clients. I don't want to hear about how I'm not a doctor—"

"Point of fact: you're *not* a doctor."

"—how cannabis is a dangerous, unregulated drug—"

"Your own literature admits that THC and CBD levels can vary significantly within the same plant!"

"—or really, your voice at all." Nomi grips the steering wheel with both hands. "You're prohibited from speaking once we are inside with clients. Do you understand?"

"So I'm supposed to sit there while you engage in the unauthorized practice of medicine?"

"I'm not practicing medicine—I'm practicing listening, I'm practicing *helping*, I'm practicing compassionate care for people who are out of options." Nomi navigates into a parallel spot. "And you'll sit there as my shadow *silently*, or else the deal is off. Got it?"

"Fine." I fold my arms and sullenly look out the window, then do a double take at one of Sparrow Nook's biggest houses. "Your client lives *here*?"

"What's wrong, Julian?" Nomi grabs her bag from the backseat. "Doesn't gel with your *potheads are losers* narrative?"

I stare up at the beautiful, sea-blue Victorian mansion and the wide, grassy lawn flanking it on all sides. Nomi makes a curt zipper motion across her lips, then knocks on the front door.

"Nomi!" A woman with silvered black hair answers. She's in her fifties, fit and dressed sharply in cream-colored slacks and a silky tank. She glances at me. "This is the young doctor you're helping out?"

"Yes, this is Julian D'Angelo. Thank you so much for letting him sit in on our visit—he's here to listen and learn. Julian, this is Hillary Frankel, one of my favorite clients."

"Nice to meet you," I mumble.

"But you didn't mention how handsome he is, Nomi." Hillary winks. "Just how annoying."

A startled cough exits my throat as she leads us inside. Ms. Frankel settles onto a chartreuse velvet couch in the parlor. With her arms draped along the back and her long legs crossed at the knee, she explains she hasn't slept a full night without medical assistance since 2023.

"That's the year I started menopause. The doctor told me to exercise, that it'd wear me out. That's what doctors always say to women. In pain? Lose ten pounds! Have migraines? Go for a run! Can't sleep? Must not be moving enough. As if I haven't seen a personal trainer four days a week for the last twenty years." Ms. Frankel huffs. "It didn't matter—nothing could shut my brain off. It makes sense when you're the founder and CEO of a successful development company, but how can I lead my business effectively when I can't sleep? I was exhausted all the time. My doctor started prescribing pills, and while some would knock me out, I'd wake up groggy after these horrible, vivid nightmares. After I started sleepwalking and had to stop, my doctor just shrugged and referred me to someone else." Hillary shakes her head. "That doctor tried the same course of interventions and when those didn't work, he referred me to someone else, too. On and on. Everywhere, I heard the same thing—*everyone experiences insomnia from time to time. Everyone suffers from menopause.* Well, if everyone's suffering, why haven't we come up with a solution yet?"

"Menopause is a major cause of insomnia—more than half of women experience sleep disturbances that significantly decrease their quality of life." Nomi's eyes flash with righteous anger. "Loss of sleep is debilitating, and just because it's common doesn't mean it's something you have to live with."

I sit with that, turning their words and anger over in my head. The fact is, lack of exercise *is* a major problem for many Americans, but the idea that anyone would look at Hillary Frankel and think her problems could be solved with exercise is ridiculous. She looks like she could out-plank a piece of wood. It's a cop-out of a treatment recommendation, especially for a condition where the culprit is known. It's not lack of exercise—it's lack of *estrogen*, and no amount of push-ups and prescription sleep aids are going to change that. I feel annoyed on her behalf, and also, a little embarrassed of my profession.

"I'm not a candidate for hormone replacement therapy, so I tried every natural route next—melatonin, valerian root, ashwagandha, magnesium, warm baths—nothing worked. I felt like I was going insane." Hillary's eyes crinkle fondly at Nomi. "Until I found good old marijuana."

Nomi pulls her tablet out and taps the stylus against it in a rapid *rat-a-tat-tat*. "Last month, we tried the Frankenbush. How'd that work for you?"

"I liked it," Ms. Frankel says after a beat. "It certainly helped me sleep."

"But?" Nomi looks up. "Did you experience any unwanted side effects?"

"Unwanted? No, I wouldn't say that." She lets out a soft laugh, her fingers lightly touching her silky, straight hair as she pushes it over her shoulder. "Let's just say it had me looking for batteries and a juicy Beverly Jenkins novel."

My eyes widen. The *horny pot*.

Nomi snorts but makes a note in Ms. Frankel's treatment plan. "That's the linalool and limonene terpenes at play."

Linalool. Limonene. I commit the horny terpenes' names to memory. Just in case I'm quizzed later.

Nomi pauses, her stylus poised in front of her lips. "Would you like something with a similar ratio of THC to CBD but without the libido-boosting effects?"

"No, dear—I'd like more, to be honest. That's the kind of exercise I'd enjoy more of." Ms. Frankel winks at me again, and my entire neck flushes with heat. "Reminds me how good it is to feel things. There's more to life than working, you know."

Nomi procures a small, discreet jar of Frankenbush flower, the smokeable, dried buds of the cannabis plant I learn, and hands it to Ms. Frankel in exchange for an envelope presumably filled with payment. After Nomi promises to research other alternatives for Ms. Frankel, we head out, and it's official: I'm a drug dealer's accomplice. A legal drug dealer, dealing legal drugs, sort of legally, but still. A weird rush of taboo zings up my spine.

"Well, she liked you," Nomi says as we scrunch inside her car.

"I have no clue why. I barely said a thing."

"I'm guessing that's a big part of it, actually." Nomi smiles wryly beneath those cat-eye sunglasses as she navigates us downtown. "Let it be a lesson, Julian. When you keep your judgmental opinions to yourself, people respond positively to you."

"That's what being a doctor is, though. Observing a person's problems and telling them how to solve them. If their problems stem from their own behavior, I can't pretend otherwise." I fold my arms. "If they dislike me for it, so be it."

"Okay, but hear me out: What if being a doctor *doesn't* make you an all-knowing god?" Nomi's eyebrows rise over her sunglasses as she parks in front of Stranger Coffee. "What if being a doctor means standing *beside* someone in need instead of lording over them?"

I blink, reeling from the insinuation that *I* lord over *anyone*. That's not what I do.

Is it?

We head inside, Nomi flipping the sign to Open before throwing me my barista apron. "I've got some work to do in my office. Can you . . . do that thing you did yesterday?"

"Craft a signature coffee drink of the day and advertise it in neat script on the chalkboard sign outside?"

Nomi shoots a finger-gun. "That's it."

I straighten, tying the apron tight around my waist. Nomi's eyes track the movement before flicking up. "I suppose I could."

I only stayed up half the night coming up with iced coffee concoctions to last through the end of August. Now that I bought and installed the luxe commercial coffee brewing machine that can properly service the demand and arranged for high-quality beans from a local distributor, it's actually kind of *fun*, working here. I've always loved coffee—the smell, the taste, the electric way it lights up my brain. And after this week, I've realized I love making it, too. Word's gotten around that Nomi hired someone who knows what they're doing, and every day, the profits I bring her shop increase a little more.

"Good," she says coolly.

"Good," I mimic her tone, watching her disappear into the back with a misplaced pang of homesickness.

The following week, Nomi flips the sign to CLOSED for our second shadowing session. The midafternoon is a slow time for coffee drinkers, and thus, the perfect time to part me from my demanding customer base. "Ready to go?" she asks.

"Yep." I slide a tall, iced drink to Nomi and untie my apron.

"Oh." Nomi winces. "I don't drink coffee. Sorry."

"I know that. It's an iced chai latte with cardamom foam and ginger popping boba pearls."

"A *what*?"

I sigh. "It's delicious and tea based. Drink it."

She picks it up warily, sniffs. After a tentative taste through the big straw, her eyes go round. "Julian. This is—it's—"

"Amazing?" I smile, smug. "I know that, too."

"—art," she finally says after another long sip. "The boba pearls! They're so *fun*. Delicious." She sucks the drink down greedily all the way to her car, and I feel like a million dollars.

As she slurps the last of the tea, she asks, "Did you bring the apology letter?"

All the confidence the iced chai brought me quickly evaporates. "I—yes. Are we—am I—"

"Going to give it to Mr. Gutierrez today? Yes. Unfortunately, apologizing to Mr. Gutierrez requires you to speak, so I beg you—*please* don't mess this up. Dr. Appa won't care how much you learn about cannabis if you piss off Mr. G again. Got it?"

I nod, patting my shirt pocket and the terrifying shape of the folded letter within. Nomi read it for me, and it's taken four drafts to get an approved version. Even with her help, it still feels scary knowing that my future hinges in part on me successfully apologizing, something I'm not great at.

Nomi knocks first, then after a minute, slides a key into the lock of the small ranch home. "Knock, knock, we're here," she calls as we cross the threshold.

The hallway is flanked with metal handrails, several canes hanging from the end. The floors have been stripped to reveal a smooth, continuous base throughout the house. The rooms are painfully spare. Someone has thoughtfully taped cotton batting to the edges of the wooden dining table, the coffee table, and the corners of the kitchen bar. As we pass by, Nomi absently checks the tape, stopping to smooth the peeling edges flat.

Did *she* do this for him? The thought plucks at my heart.

"I'm sorry I couldn't answer the door today," Mr. Gutierrez calls from the living room where he sits twisted up on the couch. His left arm is pinned against his chest at an awkward angle, thumping there erratically, his right shoulder slumped downward. He's breathing shallowly and in clear pain.

"Mr. G, you should've called." Nomi rushes over. "How long has the dyskinesia been like this?"

"A few hours." He winces. "It's getting worse. I couldn't pack the vaporizer."

"I finally got the shipment of those sublingual CBD lozenges in—do you want to try one now?"

"Y-yes." Mr. Gutierrez's neck ticks to the right sharply. "Please."

Nomi carefully places a small, rectangular lozenge under Mr. Gutierrez's tongue. "These melt quickly, and the effects should hit quickly as well."

He groans as Nomi props up his straining neck with pillows for support, then releases a small, broken sigh. "Thank you, dear. That's better."

"We'll sit with you and monitor for impacts. In the meantime, Julian has something he'd like to say."

Nomi delivers a sharp elbow to my side, snapping me out of my silent observations of Mr. Gutierrez's state. Much of Nomi's required reading dealt with Parkinson's disease—not only how cannabis can help, but also the long-term impacts of levodopa, the standard course of treatment for it. I found the studies fascinating, grateful for the chance to slow down and dive deeply into a condition. Working in the ER, you become an expert in triage. Halting system collapse. Stabilizing the body's core functions, then moving the patient off your floor and into the specialized unit where their long-term well-being becomes someone else's job. There are countless ways to die, but those core functions that must be restored are all the same. It can be incredibly difficult to achieve when the damage is too great, but it's still the ABCs of life. Breathing. Pumping blood. Finding the energy to do it all over again. But just as there's more to language than ABCs, there's more to life than survival, and the part of me that compulsively craves harder and more challenging work was unexpectedly satisfied by learning about the complexities of Parkinson's disease.

I pull the letter from my pocket. "Mr. Gutierrez, I'm very sorry for how I behaved during your appointment. I treated you unkindly and worse, without the respect you deserve. I have much to learn about cannabis, and more importantly, how to treat people with compassion and a collaborative spirit." I inhale before reading the last line Nomi insisted on: "Also, I'm a huge asshole."

Mr. Gutierrez snorts, then straightens slowly from the pillow, his left arm unlocking from its pinned, cramped position against his chest.

At some point in the last few minutes, it stopped thumping against his chest. He sags backward against the couch, relief slackening his clenched jaw. "Thank you, Dr. D'Angelo." He reaches his right hand for the letter, which I pass to him, mouth slightly open at the fluid range of movement he's exhibiting. I check my watch, then look at Nomi.

"Four minutes since dosage administration, and the visible dyskinesia has almost entirely abated." I blink at her, then reach for the small bottle of lozenges to study them.

Her eyebrows raise in appreciation. "Well, the fast-acting claims appear legit. How are you feeling, Mr. G?"

"So much looser." He breathes deeply for the first time since we've been here. "And completely exhausted."

"After hours of dyskinesia that intense, I bet you are." Nomi briefly runs through a list of questions about Mr. Gutierrez's routines leading up to today, how often he'd consumed cannabis and in what method coupled with his current levodopa dosage and symptoms experienced. Each question is thoughtful, precise, with thorough follow-ups, and I marvel at the patience she has for his longer, more plodding answers. When she's finished, she asks him if there's anything else she can help him with, and unlike most people who ask that, you can tell Nomi means it.

"Yes, dear. There's a tub of birthday cake ice cream in the freezer. Could you get me a spoon, and—and some Doritos?"

Nomi's lips curve into a soft smile. "Does someone have the munchies?"

Mr. Gutierrez meets her smile with his own, sweet and silly and full of a personality I hadn't yet seen. It's lovely to witness, and I'm relieved knowing we're not leaving him here in cramped agony to fight against the slow, miserable progression of his disease untreated, unhappy, and unwell. The wildest part is, we've been here for thirty-seven minutes. It took only *thirty-seven minutes* to change his day from awful to bearable to maybe even good.

"Thank you, sweet Nomi. You, too, Doctor Asshole," he adds, chuckling as he yoinks the spoon and ice cream that I've retrieved for him from my hands.

I glance at Nomi, and she smiles, shrugging.

"Well, they're not *straight* CBD."

Another week passes at Stranger Coffee, making Nomi tea drinks, baiting her into delicious arguments, and going with her to appointments that rock my perception of medicinal cannabis. But today, for the first time, Nomi looks nervous.

"You know what? I'm having second thoughts. Stay in the car for this one."

"What?" I twist in my seat. "I've been on my best behavior!"

"I know," Nomi concedes, tapping her nails against the steering wheel, "but this is a very sensitive situation. I'm not sure you're ready for it."

"*Ready* for it? I piece people's bodies back together for a living." I point at the small house, only a few blocks away from the small house where *I* grew up. "There's nothing in there that's worse than what I've experienced at Philly Gen."

"It's . . . a child, Julian. He's twelve years old."

I blink at her slowly, an avalanche of disapproval within me cracking, ready to bury everything in its path. "What could *possibly* justify cannabis at that age?"

"He has a severe form of epilepsy—over fifty seizures a day unmedicated. His mother was desperate and dropped everything to move to New Jersey to gain access to medicinal cannabis for him. I've been working with them for a few months. It's very hard to witness, and if you can't refrain from judgment, you need to—"

The last bit of what she says is cut off as I launch out of the car.

"Julian! Wait!"

"It's one thing when it's an adult, Nomi, but a child with that serious a condition needs real medical treatment!"

"I completely agree!" Nomi catches up with me, grabs me by the arm, and pulls me back. "This child needs much, much more than I can give him. But *please* listen to what his mother has to say. They need our compassion and help. Not your outrage and not your judgment. Do you understand?"

I force myself to breathe deeply in, then out. I understand a grown woman's decision to get sleep however she can, and after seeing the damn-near miraculous effects on Mr. Gutierrez's dyskinesia, I can accept that some treatments are worth the unknown future impacts to make the present worth living. But there's no reason a child with severe epilepsy should be treated by a person without a medical degree, even one as knowledgeable, intelligent, and caring as Nomi.

"I'm not trying to be an asshole, I promise. I'm just really, really concerned."

"I am, too. The others, I wanted you to see because I wanted you to learn. For Charlie, though, I want your help. But you *must* remain calm."

"Okay." I blow out a breath. "I'll do my best."

She nods, and her fingers loosen around my arm. Part of me mourns the loss of the concrete, physical connection between us. Her hand holding me in place for once instead of pushing me away.

We walk up to the front door.

"Hello!" A small, harried woman answers after one knock. "Come in. I'm Deborah, Charlie's mom. You must be Dr. D'Angelo." She holds out her hand to shake, and I take it. Her eyes are exhausted but bright with hope, something I haven't seen since an early stint in the pediatric ER. It pinches my heart.

"Nice to meet you, Deborah."

She leads us to the living room where a skinny, long-limbed boy with a flop of brown, unruly hair sits playing video games. If Nomi hadn't told me, I wouldn't have known he suffers from epilepsy. He glances up with a big, goofy smile. "Nomi!"

"Hey, my man!" Nomi hands Deborah a package of glass vials filled with liquid. "Deb, please fill Dr. D'Angelo in while *I* beat Charlie at *Racing Raptors*."

"Aww, you wish!" Charlie says, then scoots over to make room for her.

I clear my throat, not realizing Nomi would be leaving me alone for this part. Her eyes find me, as if to say *I'm choosing to trust you*, and this feels like the *real* test.

Deborah and I sit at the scratched-up table. "So," I wrack my brain for the best way to start. *How long have you been dosing your child with marijuana?* is not it. Thinking back to our visit with Mr. Gutierrez, I remember how open Nomi was—how gentle. How did she begin that conversation?

I smile softly. "Tell me about Charlie."

Deborah, like most mothers I've met, lights up when she talks about her child. It's just the two of them, his father cutting out when Charlie started experiencing seizures as a baby.

"Some relationships can't pass the stress test," Deborah explains wistfully. "That was me and Charlie's dad. He still calls, sometimes."

I want to punch Charlie's dad. Hard.

She tells me about the long, difficult years in rural Kansas—trying to find care for Charlie, fighting for the state's insurance for children living in poverty, then fighting it to cover the neurology care Charlie needed. "When I finally found a neurologist that would accept our insurance, she was wonderful—fought so hard for us. Listened when others wouldn't, and stood by us as Charlie's seizures broke through each of the standard medications we tried." Deborah swallows. "It was her idea to try the Epidiolex, the purified prescription CBD oil for seizures? I didn't approve at first. Charlie's dad smoked pot and look how *he* turned out." Deborah releases a sad huff. "But the doctor told us how it was a godsend for her other patients with treatment-resistant epilepsy, and the seizures had gotten so bad, I was struggling to keep Charlie in school."

She glances over to where Nomi and Charlie sit, laughing as their characters ride the backs of raptors across a racetrack, dodging falling comets and meteorites. "He's really smart, my Charlie. Most children with epilepsy as severe as his have significant developmental delays, and while he has his difficulties, he thrives in school, when he can go. But his seizures were uncontrolled, and the school was scared. I was, too. Legally they had to take him, but how could I send him knowing he was suffering all day long? That's when I agreed to try the Epidiolex, and it was like night and day. Charlie's seizures became milder, then with regular dosing, stopped for days, weeks at a time. It was a miracle."

I blink. "Why'd you stop?"

"The free samples his neurologist gave us ran out, and Charlie's form of epilepsy is not an approved condition for Epidiolex—he'd need to be diagnosed with Dravet or Lennox-Gastaut syndromes to qualify. The state insurance refused to cover it, no matter how many appeals we filed, and I had to watch as Charlie's seizures came back and worsened. I couldn't afford to pay out of pocket, though I bankrupted myself trying."

Deborah looks at her hands, and the shame coloring her cheeks twists my stomach.

"That's when we moved to New Jersey and met Nomi, our angel. It's hard finding a CBD oil that works the way Charlie needs it to, and while nothing's as good as Epidiolex, Nomi's gotten us pretty damn close."

"That's amazing," I murmur, watching them laugh as Charlie beats Nomi, again. I turn my gaze back to Deborah, trying to keep my voice steady and devoid of judgment, mentally rehearsing before I let the words leave my mouth. "Have you found appropriate medical care for Charlie here? With his condition, a pediatric neurologist would be . . . a wonderful addition to his team."

Deborah smiles as though I didn't just utter the obvious. "We're on a waitlist for the only practice that accepts the state insurance for children in this area, though we'll still have the same issues with getting Epidiolex covered for Charlie. His condition simply isn't eligible for it, even though it's the only medication that works for his seizures. Our immediate problem is with his school, though."

"How so?"

"Legally, they're only allowed to give Charlie officially prescribed medications during the school day. Over-the-counter CBD oil doesn't count, and Charlie needs to take his second dose at lunch. Without it, his seizures become uncontrollable again. For a while, we got around it by me visiting him every day, but the school caught on." Deborah breathes deeply. "They love Charlie, but they have to follow the law."

"And a doctor can't legally prescribe medical marijuana..." My voice trails off as I fully understand Deborah's terrible predicament. "They can only recommend it unless they can meet the stringent special prescription requirements due to its federal designation."

"You see where we're at. We can't afford the legal medication that Charlie needs, and we're not allowed to take the medication we can at school. Charlie *needs* to be in school, Dr. D'Angelo. He gets depressed without it, so isolated at home with just his nervous wreck of a mother. But how can I let him go when his seizures are so dangerous?"

My mouth opens, but nothing comes out. This woman is in an impossible situation, hampered at every end by man-made barriers that hurt her son and his future. Deborah's eyes must register the utter loss I'm at, because the hope she had when I walked in has faded to a keen, piercing resignation.

Impulsively, I take her hands in mine. "Deborah, I don't have an answer for you yet, but I'm going to. I promise."

Deborah makes a small, choked sound that's part relieved laughter, part despair too set in to ever fully leave. "Thank you, Doctor," she whispers, then smiles.

Nomi looks up from her game, her eyes soft and grateful.

It's a somber parting for the adults, but Charlie seems invigorated by the ass-kicking he delivered to Nomi and her purple raptor. It's hard not to notice the difficulty he has walking us to the door, the way his thin legs struggle with an even gait. When he gives me a nod goodbye, the universally accepted *man's goodbye*, I smile and give it right back. I meant what I said—I'm going to help this family.

I just don't know how yet.

Nomi and I ride in silence back to the dispensary, but not because I have nothing to say. The truth is, I have *too* much I want to say, and none of it feels adequate enough to express how I feel. I want to tell Nomi how…how *impressed* I am with how she treats people. How much they trust her, like her, how much they appreciate what she does for their quality of life. I want to apologize. I want to take back all the digs I made about cannabis. More than anything, I wish I could take back how I accused her of manipulating people in need because nothing could be further from the truth. She truly cares about these people. These clients were once strangers, and now are so much more. How many patients have crossed my path with stories like Charlie's that I never cared enough to hear? How much suffering have I dismissed because it's common, or worse, *justifiable*, by blaming people's actions? I want to confess how guilty I feel for trying to stop Nomi's dispensary, for creating yet another obstacle to her clients' struggle to have better lives. I want to say all this, and more.

When we reach the dispensary, the sun's lazy rays paint Nomi's long, brown hair with strands of fire and bronze, the pale freckles that dot her cheekbones pronounced in the day's heat. Nomi's always been beautiful, but my chest could crack from seeing how beautiful she *really* is, just walking through this world, trying to help.

CHAPTER SIXTEEN

NOMI

My alarm starts bleeping at five thirty a.m., summoning an anguished cry from my sleepy soul. All night long, I dreamt of Julian. All my usual dreams, but now starring that absolute menace. The class I forgot I was taking until the day of the exam? Julian was the teacher. Wandering around a never-ending mall? Julian was at my side, sucking up an Icee that stained his lips a sweet, cherry red. Running from a faceless murderer? Julian hid me in his basement that had a cozy, roaring fire and wasn't a basement at all, but like, a very fancy ski cabin?

Why can't I stop thinking about him?

Julian's made incredible strides these last few weeks in understanding cannabis, but he still blames it for whatever happened to his father. And until recently, he was trying *enthusiastically* to ruin my dreams at great personal cost to me. More than that, he's annoying. He's obnoxiously competitive. And he looks amazing in short shorts!

I frown at the tangent, but the point stands. The man's got legs more mouthwatering than a Renaissance Faire.

Still. *Still.* Just because we have this crackling sexual energy between us doesn't mean we're compatible humans. He can't be a decent person for three weeks and erase all the bullshit he's put me through. But his passionate promise to Deborah yesterday sent me into an existential spiral so alarming, I ended up vaping Frankenbush so I could sleep.

It was a great plan, until the terpenes hit. Horny pot was the last thing I needed after Julian looked at me so reverently last night, like he didn't see all my wasted potential for once and instead saw *me*, who I am now, what I stand for now, and understood that I'm exactly where I'm meant to be.

I masturbated half the night.

I grab my phone to silence the buzzing alarm, but there's a text there, sent an hour ago.

JULIAN FUCKING D'ANGELO

This is Doctor Asshole. Stay in bed and get some extra sleep—I'll handle the morning rush. See you later.

I blink at the words. Am I still dreaming?

Nope, I'm awake and now suffering from an entirely inadvisable *swoon* that sweeps over me. My head sags against my pillow, and when I drift back to sleep, I dream of—who else?

Julian.

I roll into the dispensary at the lovely hour of ten a.m., just after the morning rush, but still during the steady thrum of business that Julian, with his delicious coffee drinks and fine fucking ass, has drummed up on his own.

"Welcome to Stranger Coffee," Julian announces without looking up. Eve is working alongside him, forking over pastries made with normal, undrugged butter for customers, while Graham sits at the counter. I take a moment to observe the unlikely trio before declaring myself.

"I'm not saying you're evil. But I *am* saying you're a complete prick." Eve's standing with her arms crossed, a look of grudging respect on her face. "It's almost pathological."

Julian huffs, then swings a white dish towel over his shoulder in this weirdly sexual way that, frankly, should be illegal.

Do *I* have a *Gilmore Girls* mean coffee-shop-man kink?

"Look, if you cut the line in my coffee shop, I'm going to make an example out of you." Julian shrugs. "Baby or no."

The possessive, bossy way he just said *my coffee shop* heats my neck with pleasure.

Oh, no. I *do.*

"Painful to watch, but necessary for her growth." Graham looks up, sees me watching from the doorway. "Oh, hey Nomi."

"Hey, bitch," Eve says. "Another package came in for JM Enterprises. I put it in your office."

Ugh. That's the third time this month!

Eve turns back to Julian. "But seriously, *can* you control yourself? You were really cool at the Pot Luck when you were stoned off your ass. Is that how you really are, and you just choose to hide it under this unhinged exterior? Or was it a neurological fluke?"

Julian absently dries a mug while he considers the question. "You know that phrase, *the cat's hackles raised*? I think my hackles are permanently raised. They are stuck in the raised position."

"They only go up," Graham adds, then lifts his finger. "But can they go *higher*?"

"Oh, definitely," Eve says. "I've seen it."

"Like when Carl came back in and asked for a refill on his latte," Graham muses. "The hackles definitely went higher."

Julian nods solemnly as I approach the counter, looking between my two best friends and then to Julian. "You know these two are *really* high right now."

Julian hangs the mug on its rack. "I had my suspicions."

"I think we should help him," Eve says to me. "We should teach Julian how to be nice."

"I am a lost cause, you mean, little lesbian."

"No, really. We can help you," Eve insists. "I'm great, Graham's a sweetheart, and Nomi's the nicest person there is."

Graham tilts his head to the side. "Weeeeelll—"

Eve slams her hand on the counter, now in full salesman mode. "What if I told you I had a *scientifically proven* method to make you a nicer person—would you do it?"

Julian frowns. "What kind of science?"

"*Science!*" Eve declares with jazz hands.

This, apparently, is enough.

Julian rubs his chin. "Today?"

"We could start this afternoon."

"Julian? Might I remind you—" I point at Eve, who's now drumming the counter in a frenetic reggae beat. "They are *very* high. Whatever she's thinking, I guarantee it's a bad decision."

"Gare-un-teeeeed," Graham says with a vaguely Cajun, almost certainly problematic accent. "What a weird word. Gare-un-teeeee. Garrrr-uhhh—"

"See?" I lift my palm like I'm serving up *pothead* on a very small platter.

Julian slaps his towel down. "Let's do it."

JULIAN

"You want me to wear a *shock collar*?" I run the hot-pink dog collar emblazoned in sparkly gems that spell out *REAL RUFF BITCH* through my fingers with mounting horror.

"Yes, you'll wear it around your wrist, like this." Eve points, and Graham fastens the collar on me. The metal shock box makes the whole thing resemble a very bulky, very gay smart watch. "We've designed a series of trying personal interactions for you, and one of us will zap you every time you're a dick."

"No!" Nomi laughs, her eyes wide. "Don't do this, Julian. This is batshit!"

"It doesn't hurt," Graham says mildly. "On the lower settings."

"Why do you have this?" I stare at it, my pink doom.

"My mom rescued a Chihuahua mutt that attacks everyone she sees," Graham explains. "Unless she's wearing the collar."

"See?" Eve exclaims. "Science!"

I swallow uncomfortably. *Why* did I agree to this? I made my peace with my unpalatable personality long ago. Didn't I?

Because you want your job back.

Because you want Dr. Srinivasan to sign off on your probation.

Because you want people to like you.

No.

Because you want Nomi *to like you.*

I look at her, trying to gauge her reaction to this ridiculous stunt. She's laughing—can't stop, actually. Her brown eyes curve into merry half-moons when she laughs, her freckled cheekbones lifted high and kissed by her dark, lower lashes. Her happiness eases something inside of me. There's this huge, fierce knot of anger and worry and irritation in my chest that pushes every other feeling out of me. But each peal of Nomi's laughter feels like fingers gently tugging at the knot until it loosens, giving me a relief I don't know how to give myself.

I take a deep breath and flip the collar's switch to *On*.

"So. What's first?"

"The art of casual conversation," Eve states. "We talk, you respond. The only rule is, don't be a dick."

"Got it."

Eve hands Nomi the remote to deliver the electronic stimulation to my wrist.

"No!" Nomi tries to give it back. "*I* don't want this!"

"Well, *I* can't be trusted," Eve says. "I've got a sensitive trigger finger when it comes to straight white men."

"So do I!" Nomi insists, still laughing, which should worry me, but honestly, I'm glad it's her. She's the one I want to impress.

I clear my throat roughly.

"Are you sure about this?" she asks me quietly, her lingering smile edged with concern.

If it keeps her happy and laughing, I'd do just about anything.

"Don't worry," I reassure her, my voice low and husky. "I'm a *real* ruff bitch."

Her cheeks flush, and she hurries to flip the sign to CLOSED for our regular afternoon break. The four of us gather into a booth, the air between us prickling with energy.

"So Julian," Eve begins, drumming against the table. "How 'bout that RFK, Jr.?"

"You wanna talk about *that* absolute orang—"

Zap!

"*AH!*" I jump half a foot in my seat, my collared wrist twitching wildly. "*Motherfucker!*"

"Sorry!" Nomi exclaims apologetically. "Maybe the setting's too high? I'll lower it!"

Graham leans over and examines the remote. "Huh. Princess Sugar takes level twenty like a champ. Lower it to fifteen, I guess."

"That still sounds very high," I grit out.

Graham ducks his chin at me. "It's out of a hundred, bro."

"I don't mind his whole crusade against food dyes, personally," Eve continues gamely. "His views on vaccines *are* a little overblown, though."

"A *little* overblown?" I manage out through measured breathing.

"You know, my mother never vaccinated me," Graham proffers, "and I didn't catch polio or whatever. Maybe," he wags his finger at me, "he's onto something."

I blink rapidly. "Are you fucking *serious* right n-*OW*!" I whimper, rubbing my wrist, but Nomi's laughing again, tears trailing down her cheeks.

"Julian, they're messing with you!" She wipes her tears, chest still shaking. "Can't you control yourself?"

"Not about vaccines, no," I reply glumly.

"Okay, that's fair," Eve says. "Started off too hot. Let's back it up a step. Julian, have you ever—"

Just then, the front door to the shop opens, and Carl sticks his head inside a full hour early. "You open?"

"Does the sign *say* open?" I spit out.

Zap!

The shriek bellows from my body. Carl jumps back.

"Um, it says closed?" Carl says tentatively, like this is the biggest mystery in the universe.

"Then it's CLOSED, CARL!"

Zap! Zap!

I flail behind the booth's table while Carl shuts the door quickly.

"Wow," Graham says. "This is worse than I thought."

"You're such a dick," Nomi says, though she's smiling at me fondly. She hates Carl, too.

Eve clears her throat. "As I was saying, have you ever noticed how women always have one big flap?"

Nomi's laughter dies, and she turns to glare at her. "*Eve!*"

I frown, confused but relieved I'm not battling an immediate spike of anger. "Uh, what?"

"The labia majora, scientifically speaking. One side's always bigger." Eve cocks her chin up and folds her arms. "Tell me I'm wrong."

I huff. "Well, they don't teach *that* at the Yale School of Medicine."

Zap!

I stare at Nomi, incredulous, but she just shrugs. "Condescending! Try again."

"Alright." I sit up straighter. "I think I'd *know* if women had—"

Zap!

Nomi raises her eyebrows. "You can do better."

I breathe in deeply, channeling patience. Jesus, my *teeth* feel weird. "In my experience, no, I have not noticed one big flap."

Nomi nods, satisfied.

"So you're saying you don't have a lot of experience, then." Eve smirks.

"I didn't say that!" I yell, eyes frantically meeting Nomi's just as she winces and presses the button.

Zap!

"I have some experience." I look anywhere but Nomi as I try to neutralize the words coming out of my mouth. "Though I do not date. Much."

"Really," Eve leans forward, intrigued, and to my surprise, so does Nomi. Her eyes flit to mine, curiosity blooming there.

"Nomi doesn't date much, either."

"*Jesus*, Eve!" Nomi shoves her shoulder.

"Well, there is Lil Dom," Graham says, meeting Eve's smirk with his own. "She taps that from time to time. And the old English teacher from Sparrow Nook High."

"Mr. Sanders?!" I breathe in, breathe out, breathe in, breathe out. I want to go rip the stupid elbow patches right off the *cool teacher's* arms that started teaching there straight out of college. But I breaaaaathe instead.

"How—*nice*," I finally growl with great effort. Nomi regards me suspiciously but ultimately does *not* zap me.

"Great job, Julian!" Eve slaps me on the shoulder. "This concludes the art of casual conversation. You showed real growth. Now. What's your cable provider?"

I frown, still sweating about Mr. Sanders. "Um. Comcast?"

"Perfect." She sets the timer on her phone. "You have twenty minutes to cancel your cable subscription. Go!"

"But…I don't want to cancel my subscription!" I look between Graham and Nomi pleadingly.

"Don't worry, they won't let you," Graham says. "That's the point."

"Step one." Eve sits back with her arms folded behind her head. "Find a working phone number and put it on speakerphone."

eight minutes and six failed phone numbers later

"No, I will *not* enter my account number again. I'd *like* to speak to a real human!"

Zap!

Suddenly, the hold music shifts to a real, human voice. *"Hello, this is Matilda. How can I help you today?"*

"Oh, thank God. I need to cancel my—"

"Before we begin, I need to verify your identity. Could you please provide your account number, your date of birth, and your last registered address?"

"I just entered *all* of that on the automated—*Ow!*" I breathe deeply and try again. "My account number is 459821JFP—"

"B as in Bubbles?"

"No, P as in, I don't know, Petunias."

"Okay, great. B as in Betunias."

I rear back in my seat. "Betunias is not a word!"

Zaaaaap!

"P, I said P, as in *please*," I whimper. "Please help."

Meanwhile, Nomi is losing it, she's laughing so hard. "Betunias," she whispers out, and Eve grabs her, laughing into her shoulder.

"I'm sorry, that information is incorrect."

"What?!"

Zap!

"I mean, let me give it to you again," I moan out, then provide the rest of the information, a broken man.

When the timer goes off, I hang up unceremoniously on Matilda, who I'm now fairly sure is an AI ghost in the machine. I did *not* manage to cancel my cable.

"That's okay," Eve says cheerfully. "These exercises are designed for frustration and failure."

"I think he did well, by and large," Graham says. Nomi chokes back a laugh.

"Is it over? I want it to be over." I collapse my forehead onto my arms.

"Too bad, because we have one challenge left," Eve says.

My head darts up. "What's the third challenge, Eve?"

"The one that matters most," she replies. "An appointment."

Surprise crumples my forehead. "For real?" I turn to Nomi. "Dr. Srinivasan's on board with this?"

"On board?" Nomi huffs. "He's holding the remote."

"Do you think I'm ready?" I thumb my chest. "Because *I* don't think I'm ready. We should cancel."

"Too late for that, I'm afraid." Nomi smiles apologetically. "But for what it's worth, I do think you're ready, Julian. You're a great doctor who just needed a new perspective. You have that now, even if you're still working on your temper."

We walk in just before the last appointment of the day, Nomi, Graham, and Eve trailing behind me, giving me last-minute instructions, helping me into my doctor's coat, and in Eve's case, waving the remote ominously in my face.

"I've set it extra high, Julian, because these are high stakes. You got me?"

I nod, and she thumps my chest, hard. "Don't fuck this up."

I sob nervously.

Nomi spins me around to face her, inspecting my hair, then straightening my collar. The feel of her light touch on my neck, nails scraping gently down the skin there, sends the biggest zap through me yet. I want to grasp her by the elbows and pull her to me, holding her close so I can bury my nose into her long, wavy hair. I spent the afternoon being mildly electrocuted by this woman, and it's the best day I've had in months. Years maybe. When was the last time anyone cared this much about me? Spent their time trying to help *me*?

"You'll do great," Nomi says softly, still holding lightly on to my lapels. "Just remember to take a deep breath before saying anything, and if it still feels hard, picture Deborah as your patient instead."

"Deborah," I say, still lost in my inconvenient yearning to touch Nomi. "Why?"

"Because everyone's a Deborah, in their own way. Everyone has a story. Everyone is struggling. We're all just trying to make it through our lives as best we can."

I frown, overwhelmed with the desire to stroke her hair. *Do you have a story, Nomi? Are you struggling?*

Dr. Srinivasan opens his office door and regards me coolly. "Julian."

"Dr. Srinivasan." I hold my hand out. "Thank you for the chance to come back today. I'm very sorry for how I've acted in the past, and I promise I'll do my best."

After a long beat, Dr. Srinivasan shakes my hand. "That's good to hear. Now, who has the remote?"

"Here you go, Doc." Eve drops it into his hand. "It's cranked extra high."

Dr. Srinivasan breaks into a diabolical grin.

"We'll be in the waiting room, rooting you on, buddy," Graham slaps me on the shoulder.

"I'm here for the screams, to be honest," Eve says.

Nomi smiles. "Remember. Deborah."

After a long, lingering look at her, I turn and follow Dr. Srinivasan into one of the most important appointments of my life. I'm *determined* to do this right. The door opens, and I suck in a breath.

Oh, *Jesus.*

"Carl!" I say, loud enough the poor man flinches on the examining table.

"The—the coffee man?" Carl gathers his paper nightgown close around him. "W-what are you doing here?"

"Bet you didn't know I was a doctor, too, eh?" I give him my winningest smile, tuck my sleeve over the pink shock collar, and open his records.

"Now, what's brought you in today?"

NOMI

The summer sun lingers late into the evening, as though it can't bear letting go of today, either. I haven't laughed like that in, *God.* Ages. Delivering tiny shocks to Julian was a surprisingly effective therapeutic device for us both. It taught him to think before he speaks, and it helped me forgive him, one zap at a time.

I didn't stay in the waiting room with Eve and Graham. I wanted to—I'm dying to know how Julian's appointment went—but the first warning bell of pain twisted through my abdomen, and I knew I needed to retreat.

It always starts with pain. Sometimes it's sharp and slicing, like I've swallowed a bunch of knives determined to make their way out. Other times it's a burning feeling tunneling through my insides, leaving me raw and tender. But whether it's cramps or spasms or the racking pain that bullies me to tears, it always ends the same way. The pain mounting until an urgency bottoms me out, sending me running for the bathroom, leaving me rocking and miserable and always, always alone.

I take a long pull from my vaporizer and exhale, watching the thin shimmer of air dissipate. I can't stop a Crohn's attack, not without medication that ruins me for the next week, but sometimes with the right cannabis, I can head it off for a while, pluck the sharpest teeth from its bite. This indica hybrid is good for blunting the pain and removing the lengthy, wretched prelude to the main event. It buys me time. It shortens the episode. It, unlike so many other medications I've tried, helps.

The dispensary's door to our brick patio whispers open. I turn on the old picnic table's top where I've perched to see Julian standing there in the mellow, melon light of the waning day.

"Can I join you?"

I release the lungful of cannabis vapor in surprise. "Oh, um. Sure." I turn back to hide my wince. I hate being around others when a Crohn's attack is brewing. People don't know how to coexist with another's suffering, and I hate seeing them try, and fail, to make me feel better. It underscores the hopelessness I already feel when I'm sick.

At least when I'm alone, I don't have to carry their discomfort, too.

I close my eyes, drawing in a deep breath of Blackberry Kush, before turning off the vape. The relaxing effects are immediate, and I sigh gratefully as the wringing, needling pain in my middle dampens. The metal picnic table reverberates slightly as Julian's weight settles next to me. When I open my eyes, his are trained on my face, his pupils flitting systematically across every inch of me, observing.

"You're not feeling well." He glances at the vape in my hand, then back to me, studying me still. "What's wrong?"

"I'm fine," I protest. "I'm just... anxious. Still haven't received the dismissal from the zoning commission."

He sighs. "I've called every day this week. I don't understand what the holdup is."

I nudge him with my shoulder. "Well, don't keep me in suspense. How did the appointment go?"

"Great, actually. Dr. Appa only zapped me once." A mischievous smile lifts the corners of his mouth. "It was worth it."

I laugh, and the sound seems to float on the air. "You called him Dr. Appa!"

Julian blinks. "Oh, God. I did, didn't I? How embarrassing."

"Don't be embarrassed. He can be your Doctor Daddy, too."

Julian groans, and the laughter comes easier to me now. The waves of pain sweeping through me earlier have crawled back out to sea, letting me enjoy this temporary low tide. I can afford to stay here a little while longer. I'll be gone before they come back, tucked safely out of sight at home.

"You really did do well today." I lean back onto the table, resting on my propped arms. The moon's already hanging above, patiently waiting its turn to light up the lavender sky.

Julian snorts. "Judging by the amount of times you zapped me, that's not true."

"It *is*, though." I turn to face him, and he leans on his arms, too, facing me back. "I know you believe you're prickly and defensive as a rule, but I think it's a learned response. A way you've chosen to be."

"Nomi," Julian exhales my name in a small laugh. "I don't choose to be this unlikable."

"No," I concede. "But you do choose to come out swinging. And I think, if you wanted to, you could learn to lower your fists."

The knowing smile on his face fades in degrees, replaced by contemplation. Julian is beautiful when he thinks. The way he turns over his thoughts methodically, doggedly, searching for what makes sense. In a world with so much apathy, Julian and his determination stand out like a pillar of stone in a sea of gently swaying grass. Something you can depend on, a place where you can rest, even if some of his edges are still sharp.

"And I did that today? Lowered my fists?" His body's angled toward mine, as if all of him is listening.

"Today was more about noticing when they're raised, I think."

Julian blinks, then shakes his head. "Are you always this philosophical when you smoke pot?"

"No. Sometimes I'm potato chips." I gesture to my body, now angled toward his, too. "Just entirely, potato chips."

A single laugh bounces out of him, and he leans all the way back, lying completely flat on the tabletop. I join him, relishing the feel of cool iron latticework on my warm back.

"I wish I could be more like you," he murmurs up to the night sky. "You're impossible not to like."

I huff, even as my cheeks burn with heat. "It seemed pretty possible when you first returned to Sparrow Nook."

Julian faces me again. "I've felt about a thousand different things for you over the years that I've known you. But I've always, always liked you."

I blink back at him, shocked, even as his words glimmer in my chest, the first stars of the night to shine.

"I've just gotta learn to stop throwing punches at the same time." He smiles, sad and wistful. "I'm so sorry, Nomi."

I swallow. "I—know you are, believe it or not."

A thrumming sound reverberates through the iron table, and Julian startles, then fumbles for his pocket. "Sorry—that might be Dr. Appa." He checks his phone, then sighs, resting it on his chest.

"Do you have to go in?"

"No, just Mom reminding me about a party this weekend. Marco's son is turning four." He removes his glasses and rubs his eyes with his palms. "There's nothing worse than a D'Angelo family birthday party."

"Oh, yeah? Bring me," I blurt on impulse. *Damn Kush!*

He stares at me without his glasses. His eyes are so blue, so unadulterated like this, it steals my breath.

"You want to come? *Why?*" He puts his glasses back on, and I can breathe again.

I shrug shakily. "Keep an eye on you so you don't make any kids cry. Birthday cake. Your hilarious Aunt Edna. Take your pick."

His mouth opens and closes, and I can tell he's choosing his next words carefully.

Progress. I smile.

"So, you're going to spend your Saturday afternoon at my nephew's birthday party, with me, after everything I've put you through? How can you be so nice to *me*?"

I sigh. "Because, Julian D'Angelo, I've always liked you, too."

CHAPTER SEVENTEEN

JULIAN

By the time Saturday arrives, I'm an anxious mess. Nomi's words have ricocheted around my brain nonstop for the last three days.

Because, Julian D'Angelo, I've always liked you, too.

It's terrifying knowing I have something to lose. If you remain at rock bottom with people, there's no way to disappoint them. But somehow, I've earned, or more likely been gifted, some of Nomi's regard, and it's mine now to destroy. It's enough to drive me insane.

"This is Dr. Sampson."

"Eric!" I bellow. "Quick, I need your advice. I'm going to my nephew's birthday party today, and I'm bringing Nomi. How do I *not* fuck this up?"

"Nomi? The special stoner from your past? That's great!"

"Yeah?" I ask breathlessly. "I feel like it's not great."

"Why?"

"Because I'm the worst possible version of myself around family?"

Eric whistles. "That's... Okay. That's saying something."

"*Help me*, Eric!"

"Alright, have you bought a present yet?"

I blink, then eye the unwrapped box in the back. "Yes. A farm puzzle."

"That's not gonna work."

"Why not? That's the one thing I've accomplished!"

"Because you're a doctor. They know you make bank. If you show up with a ten-dollar cow puzzle, you're gonna be the cheap uncle. Don't be the cheap uncle."

"Fuck, okay. What else?"

"Can Nomi bring you some weed?"

"E-*ric*," I groan.

"Okay, fine. Grab a beer as soon as you go in. You've got to alter this intense brain chemistry you've got going on."

"Beer, check. Anything else?"

"If provoked, don't say anything. Take a deep breath, deflect, pretend you didn't hear if you have to, but whatever you do, *do not engage* in family drama in front of a woman you like. That's major red-flag behavior."

I blow out a long breath. "That's gonna be hard."

"You can do it, Julian. And if you can't, hide in the bathroom until cake."

"This is why I call you, Eric. Your advice is incredibly practical."

"Yeah, yeah, I bet you say that to all the professionals whose boundaries you've crossed. Good luck, buddy."

With that, the call disconnects, and I'm on my own. I hammer out a quick text before I second-guess myself.

JULIAN

Hi Nomi. This is Julian D'Angelo.

NOMI

😃 Hello, Julian D'Angelo. How may I help you?

JULIAN

Can I pick you up an hour early?

NOMI

that's . . . now?

JULIAN

Yes.

NOMI

You're freaking out, aren't you.

JULIAN

Yes.

NOMI

♡ Sure. Come on over.

JULIAN

Great. I'm already here.

NOMI

lol, ok. Come on in.

I knock on her door, willing myself not to pace. As soon as it opens, I thrust the bouquet toward her, startling her back.

She blinks at the fulsome bunch of pale pink peonies, then reaches for them. "You're getting better at this."

"Do you like them?" I study her reaction. She leans reverently over the blooms, breathing them in.

"What do you think?" She gives me that half smile I associate with her teasing.

"I think so." I take a small step forward. "I hope so."

The half smile stretches into something genuine that temporarily interrupts the rhythm of my heart. "You've always been a quick study. Let me put these in water."

I follow her to the kitchen but pause before her bedroom's open door. I can't *believe* that, a month ago, Nomi had me pinned beneath her on that bed, and the next day I declared war on her.

I may have been top of my class at Yale, but I've always been a dumbass when it comes to Nomi Wyeth.

"Okay." Nomi joins me in the hallway. "What now?"

"How are you at buying presents?"

Nomi flutters her eyelashes. "Amazing."

Twenty minutes later, we're standing in the toy store's dangerous vehicle aisle.

"Gisella says Nico wants a scooter, though." Nomi rests her hand on the most tricked out scooter in the store. "Walk me through the problem again?"

"Do you know how many ER visits are children flung from '*recreational vehicles*'? I'm trying to give him a present, not a compound fracture."

"Getting hurt is a part of life—you can't protect a child by not allowing them to live. Besides, this scooter's super stable—it has three wheels! We're obviously buying him safety gear, too."

"Any closing arguments?" I fold my arms.

She places one hand on her hip. "You want to be the cool uncle, don't you?"

I buy the fucking scooter, as well as every protective pad, helmet, and shock absorber there is. If the kid manages to break a bone in all that, well, he had it coming. We cover everything in big red bows, and Nomi slaps on tags loudly proclaiming To Nico, From Uncle Julian on the sidewalk in front of Marco and Jessica's house.

"We've got to lock this honor in for you," she explains, then stretches to standing, pleased.

"Hmm. Something's missing." I take the Sharpie and add: & Nomi. We stare at our names together for a long second. Nomi clears her throat, then smiles.

"Come on." She gestures toward the backyard. "It's party-time, Uncle Julian."

I shudder involuntarily. "Don't *ever* call me that again."

She laughs as if we're not entering a minefield full of dangers. But walking in with Nomi feels like safe passage within an armored car. Everyone's so happy to see *her* they barely notice me, which is a bliss I didn't know existed. I grab two beers before anyone manages to insult me, and judging by my stack of presents, *Coolest Uncle* is in the bag.

"Edna!" Nomi leans over my great aunt's wheelchair to give her a long, sweet hug. "How are you feeling?"

"Absolutely terrible when I'm not stoned!" Aunt Edna laughs, though it sounds considerably weaker than the throaty, buoyant laugh I grew up hearing.

Nomi winks at her. "We can disappear behind the garage any second, just say the word."

"If my ornery nephew doesn't kiss me right now, I'll need my own blunt." Aunt Edna flaps her hand at me, and I lean over and brush my lips against her smooth cheek. She smells like blush and Elizabeth Taylor's White Diamonds. "Julie," she says as she draws me close. "How's that butthole, kid?"

A flare of irritation sweeps through me, but everything I've learned these last few weeks does, too, and before I snap, I take a deep breath in and remember: I don't always need to swing.

"It's . . . okay," I admit. "As far as buttholes go."

"*That's* what I like to hear! But where are your Uncle Joseph's nut-huggers? These aren't short enough. How will Nomi know what she's missing if you don't put 'em on display?"

"*You* told him to wear those short shorts?" Nomi intercedes, delighted. "When he apologized?"

God.

"Of course! Julie's smart, but not that smart." Aunt Edna winks. "And they worked, didn't they, honey?"

Nomi shrugs, smiling impishly. "A muscular thigh never hurt nothing."

"This one gets it. Julie, you should propose," Aunt Edna announces. "She's the one!"

I clap my hands together. "O-*kay*, Aunt Edna, can I get you anything? A filter, perhaps?"

"Such a tight butthole, this guy. You've gotta loosen him up, Nomi. Make him remember not to take life so seriously."

"I'm trying." This time, her smile's for me.

"I invited someone very special today for you. Jackie Lombardi." Aunt Edna waggles her eyebrows, as if we should know who that is.

"Holy shit, Jacqueline Lombardi?" Nomi's eyes go big, and Aunt Edna nods.

She really *does* get it.

"Who's that?" I look between the two women, fifty years apart but both just as shrewd.

"The zoning commissioner," Nomi says. "Where is she, Edna?"

"Over by the piñata. She loves violence." Aunt Edna thumbs over her shoulder. "Go and schmooze. Fix what you started, Julie, though I do wish you'd worn the short shorts." She shakes her head. "You'll learn one of these days."

Nomi and I sidle up to a middle-aged woman plucking at a bowl of watermelon while watching the frenetic piñata attack. Standing beside her is Wilson Phillips, that weird guy from the city council meetings that complains about Sammy's all the time.

"Ms. Lombardi!" Nomi holds out her hand. "I'm Nomi Wyeth, owner of the future Stranger Drugs dispensary downtown. I'm *so* glad to meet you." When Ms. Lombardi just looks at her, Nomi drops her arm, recovering quickly by gesturing to me at her side. "This is Dr. Julian D'Angelo."

Now *that* gets a reaction.

"So, you're the new Wilson." Ms. Lombardi's eyebrows rise as she looks at me, then Nomi, then zeroes in on how closely we're standing together.

I frown. What's that supposed to mean?

"He's not the new *Wilson*." Wilson's pitted cheeks pinken.

Lombardi rolls her eyes. "He filed the complaint, didn't he?"

I clear my throat. "Are you aware I've withdrawn it, though? Neither Ms. Wyeth nor I have received a notice of dismissal yet."

Lombardi's mouth quirks into a sour lemon of a fake smile. "Thank you, but I'd rather not discuss zoning business at social gatherings."

"Is this squirt bothering you, Jackie?" Uncle Gino walks up and delivers a thunderous clap on my back. *Fuck.* He's my dad's eldest brother and my number one family member to avoid. "Wouldn't be anything new—Julian's been bothering me for—how old are you again, squirt?"

"Gino!" Lombardi's eyes light up, and if she likes my uncle, that's a bad sign. "You ol' troublemaker."

"Sup, Gino!" Wilson goes in for a fist bump, but Gino ignores him.

Nomi's eyes dart to mine, and I smile tightly back. I will *not* engage with the worst dregs of my family in front of her or the zoning commissioner.

I turn back to Lombardi, smiling graciously. "My apologies. I'd love to get some time on your calendar next week if that works better. I'm anxious to get this matter settled." I straighten my shoulders, commanding my eyes to twinkle *just so*. I'm well aware of my eyes' effect on women, especially those who came of age during the Christopher Reeve era of *Superman*.

But Lombardi must be a Lex Luthor stan because she's having none of it.

"I'm sure you are." She pokes the watermelon around her Dixie paper bowl, pointedly side-eyeing Nomi's sundress.

"So, Julie's changed his mind about the weed shop, has he? I guess I can see why." Grinning, Gino leers at Nomi, and I sustain a brief, violent urge to grab the piñata stick and see what comes out of *him* after a few swings. He throws his arm around me, and I stiffen beneath the meaty weight of it, his peppery armpits enough to make me gag. "It's not surprising, seeing how Julie's old man loved reefer so much. Did your dad ever take you back in that garage and get you high, too?"

"My father wasn't like that. Now get your arm off me," I say to Gino coolly, even as my blood boils. Vinny, my lawyer cousin, comes over, as though sensing an assault action brewing.

"Pop, come on." Vinny prods his father with water. "You need to hydrate." But Gino *p'shaws* him away.

Nomi turns to Ms. Lombardi. "It was nice to meet you we hope to hear from y'all soon!" Then to me, softly, "Let's go."

"Aww, don't be like that, squirt!" Gino brings me in even closer. "You've always been such a little *bitch*." His breath reeks of alcohol and Marlboro Lights, and I just can't. I *can't*. I shove him off, and he loses balance, skidding backward on the lawn in his pale denim shorts.

Footsteps rush over. Marco yells, "Hey, is Gino okay?"

I can't say anything. I still smell Gino's sweat and hear his nasty, belittling words, and I just—

"I'm so sorry, Gino!" Nomi exclaims, clapping her hands over her cheeks. "I didn't mean to trip you! Here, let me help you up." She holds out a hand, smiling apologetically at my skeezy uncle, who looks confused as to how he ended up on the ground.

"It's these shoes; they always trip me in the grass." She hoists him back up.

"I—tripped?" Gino looks to his son for confirmation.

"Sure did, Pop," Vinny confirms, which... I did *not* see coming.

"He's alright, everybody!" Nomi pats him on the shoulder, and Gino decides to accept the truth as presented to him by the pretty young thing fussing over him. It must be easier than believing Julie, that *little bitch*, pushed him.

Nomi ushers me away quickly.

"Fuck, *fuck*! I'm sorry, Nomi." I cover my face with my hands. "God. Level 2000 red-flag deluxe."

"Come on, let's disappear for a while." She opens the door to Marco's garage then searches for the light switch.

"You probably think I have anger management problems." I run my palms down my face, hard. "I tried to stay calm, but then Gino said that about my dad, and I just—I'm sorry. And right in front of Lombardi, too."

"You don't have anger management problems. You have a *profoundly* shitty uncle. It's different."

After a second, the lights switch on, and she gasps.

"*Whoa*, look at this."

I open my eyes, and my heart momentarily stops. Nomi, eyes wide in wonder, stares at a massive model of Sparrow Nook, complete with the downtown, river park, even a backdrop of Philly's skyline in the distance.

I haven't seen it in twenty years.

I stagger back a step and slam into the door.

"Julian? What's wrong?"

"It's my...dad's." I feel lightheaded and unaccountably scared, as if my father's ghost appeared instead of the miniature town he poured all his energy into the last five years of his life. Maybe they're the same, in a way. "He built this. I didn't know Marco had it."

"Oh my God," Nomi murmurs, then leads me over to a camp chair. I shrink back from it, but it's not Dad's. I collapse into the seat, and Nomi sits beside me. "That's...wow. Really intense. Are you okay?"

After a second, I shake my head, dropping my eyes to the floor.

"Do you want to talk about it?"

Do I? I take several deep breaths, her question lingering in the air before I rise to my feet and feel for the switch hidden beneath the table. With an audible *click,* the town comes to life. The streetlamps light up, the storefronts blink on, and the traffic lights hanging over the intersections begin alternating between green, yellow, and red. "Dad always intended to add a motorized track for the cars." I drag my fingertips up Main Street. "But he hadn't figured out how to make the cars sync up with the traffic lights yet." I let out a small huff. "He would've, though. If he'd had more time."

"What happened?" Nomi asks softly beside me.

Whenever I've been asked about Dad before—by women from short-lived relationships, a few times out of professional interest by other ER doctors, once by Eric—I usually give the short answer: he was disabled and died when I was young. To Eric I gave the full story, though, and I've been glad many, many times that I did. Having someone I know and trust help me hold the truth, who sees me and understands me in my fuller context—it's why his advice is so good. Eric knows me. And as much as I hate the truth, I want Nomi to understand me, too. I want her to know, because I want her to know *me.*

"Dad was a mechanical engineer. Worked at the engine plant on all the assembly line machines. There was an accident one day, when I was pretty young. He got pulled halfway into a machine—it crushed his right arm and several of his vertebrae. If they hadn't pulled the emergency brake when they did, it would've—well. He'd have died on the spot. As it was, he was very badly injured. After several surgeries, he regained some function and mobility, but he couldn't work anymore. He had pretty severe PTSD around motorized machinery after the accident, and due to some poor decisions made during the initial surgery, he was in constant pain."

Nomi's brows draw together as she listens. The concern and empathy on her face is too much to bear, so instead I keep my eyes on the model and all the little details I used to resent so much.

"He went on disability, which was less than half of his old salary, and Mom had to work two jobs because of all the debt accruing from his care. I was only seven years old, and suddenly my dad, the funniest, most charismatic man you'd ever meet, barely left his bed, and my mom disappeared into work at the same time so we'd have enough to pay for Dad's treatments. When Mom *was* home, she was always tired, and I—I blamed Dad for it. I didn't understand why he couldn't get out of bed and take care of me. I didn't understand why Mom had to work twice as much."

"That must've been so hard on you. To be so young and lose that time with your parents."

I bite both lips in. "I had Aunt Edna. That's how we got so close, you know. During that first year after the accident, I practically lived at her house. She took care of the Ohs, too, and sometimes Vinny and Veronica."

Nomi huffs. "My god, what a brood."

"The first year was the hardest. Eventually, the surgeries stopped, and Dad could move around again. As part of his physical therapy, they encouraged him to do tasks that would improve his gross and fine-motor skills, and that's how this started." I gesture a hand at little Sparrow Nook. "You can tell which parts of town are the oldest because the painting is the sloppiest, and the buildings came from kits. Eventually, he built all the houses himself."

"It's amazing." Nomi runs her finger over the top of the STRANGE DRUGS Rx sign that hangs over the tiny sidewalk, facing the old Belly's Steaks shop across the street.

"It is. But God, I hated it growing up."

"Why?"

"It became all Dad cared about. He spent all day, every day, in our garage, working on this town instead of living in the real thing. He rarely left the house. If I wanted to see him, I had to go into the garage, and it always reeked of enamel paints and—and—"

"Weed," Nomi says, understanding. "He smoked to deal with his pain, right?"

"That's what Mom said when I asked why Dad was doing illegal drugs in our garage every day. But all I saw was a stoner sitting in a camp chair painting tiny things instead of being my dad. Instead of working, so Mom could be my mom."

"Oh, Julian." Nomi reaches out, and in Sparrow Nook's twinkling lights, touches my arm. "I'm sorry."

"It was hard, hearing people talk about my dad in the past tense before he was dead. Or worse, hearing people like Gino call him a worthless stoner. And it was even harder to believe Mom when she said it wasn't true, because it seemed true to me." I shake my head, hating this part most of all. "Then one day, he made this big announcement during dinner that he was giving up pot because his doctors had prescribed him this new miracle drug for pain relief, covered by insurance and everything. He was so proud, and Mom was so relieved." My breath twists in my throat. "The opioid crisis was just beginning, and Dad was one of the countless people trampled by it. On a bad pain night, he overdosed by accident and died in his sleep. I was twelve."

Nomi pulls me to her. Wraps her arms around my middle, rests her head against my chest. The weight of it there makes the first tear feel safe enough to run down my cheek. After a brief, terrified pause, I fold my arms around her woodenly, then melt into her, wishing that I could wear this hug like armor every day of my life. A new layer of skin that'd protect me from all the bullshit. If I had this, I could be nice, I think. I could finally lower my fists.

I wouldn't need them anymore.

"No wonder you hate pot," Nomi says into my chest.

"But I don't now. It took a long time to accept, but if Dad was just a stoner in our garage, this model would have motorized tracks."

Nomi's lips quirk at the corner as she regards me. "So. That's Dr. D'Angelo's origin story."

"You make me sound like a villain." My voice comes out husky and low, hands forming a warm knot at the base of her spine.

"Hey." Her mouth curves higher. "If the dastardly monocle fits."

I hold her to me, a little embarrassed by how much I don't want to let her go. "I was the son of a disabled, out-of-work, drug addict who eventually overdosed. After that, no one expected me to become anything, even my family. So, I had to become everything they never expected. The best."

"Did you, though?" Nomi asks softly. "Or did they love and accept you no matter what you did?" She reaches up and, tentatively, brushes a lock of hair from my forehead. "I think it's a good thing, to be loved without conditions or expectations. To be loved just because you're you, and you exist. That's enough."

My throat tightens painfully as I look down into Nomi's beautiful, open face.

Is it enough? Could *I* be enough, for her?

CHAPTER EIGHTEEN

NOMI

It's a busy day at Stranger Coffee, made busier now that Julian's working full time at the clinic again. He left a comprehensive regimen for when to brew coffee, mix syrups, and make various whimsical foams that Eve and I try to follow, but two stoners who get stressed out by crowds does not a Barista Julian make. His many admirers still come in, hope writ large upon their faces they might see the grumpy beaut with a heart of Arabica. Alas, they get us and our substandard coffee instead, their disappointment palpable.

The weird thing is, I miss him, too. Eve's not nearly as fun to bicker with, and I'd gotten used to his broad shoulders and busy hands behind my counter. Julian's beautiful in all his iterations—the surly doctor, the outraged citizen, even the mouthy debater—but Barista Julian is the most attractive one yet. He has this never-ending supply of soft, thin button-downs in dark plaids that he wears open-throated and rolled up to his elbows with well-worn jeans and leather boots. And the man was *made* to wear an apron—the rectangle of white cutting across his mid-section, the strings looped around his hips and tied tightly in the front—straight *porn*. But it's the joy, I think, that makes Barista Julian so appealing. He loves making coffee, and contented, passionate, *happy* Julian takes my breath away.

When the clock strikes two, I emerge from the bathroom changed, freshened up, and ready to go. "I'll be back soon."

Eve gives me a once-over from my clay-colored jumpsuit to my heeled clogs. "Why are you dressed so cute? Are you wearing *makeup*?"

"I'm not." I reapply my tinted lip balm, which is by definition *balm*.

She raises one eyebrow.

"I have my annual physical with Dr. Appa."

"Ah. You might see Julian, so you want to look hot."

"No, I don't!" I cringe. Is it that obvious? Will it be obvious to Julian? "I probably won't even see him."

"Just because I'm for ladies doesn't mean I don't understand the complicated games heterosexuals play. And honestly, everybody plays this game. Don't worry. You look smokin' hot."

"Yeah?"

"Yes. Your ass looks like an upside-down bubble heart in that jumpsuit."

I flush happily. Lesbians give the *best* compliments.

The second I enter the frosty air-conditioning of Dr. Appa's clinic, my nipples immediately *ping*.

Shit. Okay, yes, I admit I want to look hot, but I'm not trying to put Dr. Appa's eye out, either. I fold my arms over my chest and approach the desk. Khalil, the Gen Alpha receptionist, doesn't look up. "Nomi Wyeth?"

"Yes?" Why do today's teenagers always make me feel so uncertain? I clear my throat. "I mean, *yes*."

"Patient Room #2."

Of course it's that patient room. *Of course*.

I see myself down the hall and enter the empty room. I inspect it closely, but there's no sign of the horrors I endured in here. Not that I expected there to be physical evidence, but some events are so traumatic, surely they leave an indelible stain on the fabric of space-time or something.

The door opens after a perfunctory knock, and I spin on my clogs to see Julian frozen in the doorway.

"Nomi." His face blanks, a panicked, *play dead!* response, and he checks the file in his hand, then my face again. "Um, hi."

"Hi." I smile hastily. It's been a little weird since last weekend's birthday party, to be honest. Now that we don't work together and he's graduated the Nomi Wyeth School of Cannabis, we're out of rhythm, evicted from our old routine, and everything feels uncertain. "Where's Dr. Appa?"

His eyes drop to my lips, my collarbone, then the outrageous peaks of my nipples like an elevator stopping at every floor before shooting back to the top.

"He's running behind due to a walk-in and asked me to take his next appointment, which is . . . you." Julian frowns. "But I don't think it's a good idea, Nomi. Now that we're . . . um."

"Friends?" I offer.

"—yes, *friends*—I'm not sure it's ethical for me to treat you."

I shoulder my bag back on. "Totally understand. I'll wait for Dr. Appa."

"You'll need to reschedule then. He's leaving after he finishes with the walk-in patient."

I blink at him. "I can't reschedule. I have to have this physical today. If I don't, I won't get approved for my new marketplace healthcare insurance for another month."

What I *don't* add is that another month of outrageously expensive COBRA benefits will ruin me.

Julian's face is full of chagrin. "I'm sorry, Nomi. I don't know what to tell you."

"I really need this done today." I bite my lip in, feeling my cheeks burn. "I know it's a little weird, but could you please do it?"

His brow furrows together, his face tortured. He blows out a long breath. "Yes, okay. Hop up on the table."

I do as I'm told. He sits at the computer, but his eyes keep flicking to the table, the stirrups folded neatly at its sides, and me. It's obvious we're both remembering the last time we were in this room together.

Julian starts to bring up my records, when I suddenly realize the implication of that.

"No!"

He looks up at me, startled.

"Is there any way you can, you know." I gesture at his stethoscope. "Just do the basics?"

"You want me to . . . half-ass it?" His face is so pained at the thought, it makes me laugh aloud.

"Yes, please. All you have to do is check my blood pressure, listen to my chest, that sort of thing, then fill out this form. Okay?" I half smile, half wince. I know this is really pushing his boundaries.

After a long second, he says tightly, "Alright."

"Great!" I lie down on the table.

"You don't need to lie down yet."

"Okay!" I say too brightly as I sit back up, trying to muster a carefree attitude, but no dice, that was embarrassing.

Julian slips the blood pressure cuff around my upper arm, which is probably going to give me a bum reading since I'm so weirdly nervous right now. I exhale at the ceiling. His fingers are gentle as he releases the cuff, though, and when he dons his stethoscope, he warms the cold, round end in his palm before he presses it to my upper chest.

That was, admittedly, nice.

Julian clears his throat. "Breathe in for me? Good. Again." He moves the stethoscope around my chest, pressing softly, then firmly, listening intently with his eyes trained on the wall beside me as he instructs me when to breathe. The flat of his left hand is placed between my shoulder blades, steadying me, and the warmth of his palm sends goose bumps down my arms, hardening my nipples even more. When he moves the stethoscope to listen to my back, he carefully, almost reverently, gathers my long fall of hair and pushes it over my shoulder to expose the skin there. The warm bell of the stethoscope traveling down my ribs, coupled with the knowledge that his eyes are there, too, the stiff, white cuffs of his doctor's coat brushing against my skin...A hot, giddy flush floods my neck, cheeks, and forehead. Even my ears burn as his gloved fingers trail down the lymph nodes beneath my jawline.

"You can lie down now," he says gruffly, at complete odds with the soothing touch of his hands. A furious blush blooms across Julian's cheekbones as I swing my legs onto the exam table, his icy blue eyes finally meeting mine as I lean back on my elbows, then drop all the way down to my back. The déjà vu is *intense.* His eyes burn into me, and I can't blame the resulting ache between my legs on horny pot this time. His gaze fixes on my stomach as he begins to gently palpate the area. I'm so distracted by his touch, I flinch when he presses lightly into the lower right side of my belly, the source of all my pain.

"Did that hurt?" He frowns down at the area, then at me, watching closely.

"No," I lie. "I'm just...ticklish?"

"Hm," he says noncommittally the way doctors do when they don't believe you. I'm incredibly familiar.

"Are we done yet?" I ask, too chipper by half.

"Almost." He stands abruptly, removing his gloves, and opens the folder he'd plucked from outside the door.

"Don't look at that!" I reach for it, but he holds it away from me.

"Relax. These are just some notes Dr. Appa wanted me to mention with you," Julian reassures me, but I feel incredibly anxious all the same. There's no version of reality where Julian finds out I have Crohn's disease that doesn't end in me feeling vulnerable, ashamed, or embarrassed, and likely, all those emotions combined. I don't *want* Julian to look at me as a patient, as someone he needs to fix. I like the way he already looks at me so much.

He scans the notes. "Dr. Appa strongly encourages you to schedule the routine monitoring for your condition as you are long overdue. He says you know the risks of failing to do so."

My cheeks flare hot. My *condition*? Thanks a lot, Dr. Appa. He's talking about a screening colonoscopy, something I'm supposed to do every two years but haven't in over five. Colonoscopies mean GI specialists, and specialists all want the same thing—to prescribe me another biologic, even though I've had major allergic reactions to the two I've tried. I get that biologics have improved life with Crohn's for so many. They are a modern medical miracle that give most people back their lives. *Most.* But if they don't work for you, if you're one of the few they make sicker, the specialists don't know what to do. They just prescribe the newest biologic on the market, and the cycle repeats all over again.

Well, I'm done trying to dismantle my body's faulty immune system with medication only for it to roar back and try to destroy me harder than ever. I want to address the root causes of my disease, but every specialist I've ever seen is too busy to help me search for actual healing, to meet me and my body where we're at and help us improve from there. I get that there's no conclusive answer to what causes Crohn's, but there doesn't need to be one, either, to try and find what works best for *me*. If I have a colonoscopy, that's choosing to submit to the medical establishment that's alternately harmed me or ignored me, all while saddling my mother and me with intense medical debt. And if Dr. Appa can't understand that, Julian, who hails from the same prestigious hospital as so many of my former specialists, won't, either.

"Is that all?" I lift my chin.

"And he says to quit being so stubborn," Julian adds, a bit sheepishly. "Nomi, if you're overdue for a screening, I'm happy to help you set it up."

"No, thanks!" I thrust the insurance paperwork at Julian that I have to submit by five.

He pauses before taking it. "Fine. But I'm ordering bloodwork at the lab. You'll need to stop by the lab for the blood draw, and Dr. Appa will review the results with you when they come back."

"I don't need any bloodwork." I smile sweetly and shake the papers at him, pushing down the hurt and frustration rising inside. I don't know why I'm surprised. Of course, Julian would be like this. Not listening. Substituting his judgment for my own about *my body*.

"Ah, but you *do* need me to sign off that I gave you your annual physical, and bloodwork is part of that." He folds his arms.

I glare at him, long and hard, but he just gazes back placidly. He has the power right now and knows it.

"*Fine.*" I roll my eyes, and Julian takes the paperwork, signs, then hands it back. He eyes me thoughtfully.

"I'm only trying to help you, Nomi."

"Thanks, but I don't need your help." The words come out too sharp, too brittle, and Julian flinches like I hit him.

I exhale deeply, willing myself to calm down. Bloodwork isn't a big ask, and my knee-jerk anger isn't entirely fair right now.

"I'm—*sorry*, Julian. Medical stuff is sensitive for me, but I shouldn't have snapped at you—you're doing me a favor, and I really appreciate you helping me out." I swallow, dropping my gaze from his intense one to the safety of the floor. "It's good to see you. I've... missed you. At the coffee shop, I mean. It's not the same without you."

A strangled sound emerges from his throat, and I look up in time to see a *whoosh* of hunger emanate from him that I feel on my skin like a hot breeze. It's not the cold hardening my nipples anymore—it's the way Julian's consuming the sight of me, his professional façade flickering in and out as he fights it. The folder he's holding slips from his hands, spilling its contents across the floor. He swallows roughly.

"Can I take you out Friday night, Nomi? Please?"

JULIAN

She *doesn't date*? Nomi can stare up at me with those soft, brown eyes, her long, wavy hair sliding across her *rock-hard nipples*, and look at me with such open affection *and rock-hard nipples*, but she *won't date me*? I must've looked as crestfallen as I feel because she hastily added she'd be out of town, anyway, so it wouldn't work even if she *did* date, but then reiterated how very fervently *she does not.*

It's unbearable. I know she wants me, too. I feel it in every touch of her smooth fingertips on my hand, my arm, and that day in Marco's garage, my face. The rapid fluttering of her pulse beneath my hands, her breath trembling as my palm slid down her back, amplified through the earpieces of my stethoscope. The heat in her playful, bewitching smile.

But she won't date me?

"Dr. D'Angelo? Is now a bad time, or—" Dr. Riveras frowns from my laptop screen, her face one of several currently frowning at me. A veritable grid of disappointment.

Great. It's been two minutes, and I'm already bungling the three-month check-in with the probation committee. I exhale shortly. "My apologies. My last patient presented an intriguing set of—

Breasts? Say breasts.

Breasts.

Br—

"—symptoms. I'm a little preoccupied with them. The symptoms, that is. I'm all yours now, though." I summon my most reasonable smile and banish the image of Nomi's nipples from my mind.

Dr. Riveras assesses me. "Glad to hear you're finding the role engaging, Dr. D'Angelo."

"Very much so. In fact, while I regret the circumstances that led to my probation, I'm incredibly grateful for the opportunity to acquire new skills afforded by a primary care physician's role."

"Could you speak more to that?" Dr. Washington, a kindly older doctor from the infectious diseases unit, asks.

"Certainly." I adjust my frames. "I won't lie to you; I found the switch in tempo from the ER to a small-town clinic jarring at first. This role requires a level of patience I didn't have before, but I've made great strides. I've also appreciated learning more about the day-to-day management of serious diseases, like Parkinson's and type 2 diabetes, which will inform my treatment of patients with these conditions when they come in for emergencies. It's rounding out my perspective, sir."

Question by question, the committee's faces transition from frowning to grudging interest. I have Nomi to thank for that. There's been more than one dig at my expense on this call, but rather than rising to take the bait, as *well* as the hand dangling it, I've breathed through it. I half wonder whether they've been goading me on purpose, seeing if they could make me snap.

Pride swells in my chest. I'm not as easily manipulated as I used to be.

"This is very gratifying to hear, Dr. D'Angelo." Dr. Riveras opens a folder. "Dr. Srinivasan's preliminary reports on your progress have been interesting to read as well."

Oh, *no.*

"He says you've experienced particular growth in your understanding of medicinal cannabis through collaboration with a local dispensary. Is that right?"

I swallow, unsure where this is going. "Well, yes. I've read a lot of literature on the subject and even shadowed a medicinal cannabis counselor with some of her clients, who are also patients of my clinic."

"Very good," Dr. Washington says. "We're always glad when our doctors try to broaden their understanding of popular medical alternatives, but we do want to caution you, Julian. Don't take this too far."

"What do you mean, sir?"

"Do you want to return to Philly Gen after this probation is complete?"

"More than anything, sir." A hint of desperation seeps into my words. Dr. Washington clears his throat, but it's Dr. Riveras who answers.

"Then it's best not to associate with any dispensaries. The Corrington family is still quite furious with you, and they're very conservative on such topics. If they become aware of this association with cannabis, they'll use it to block your reinstatement."

Dr. Riveras taps the folder on her desk, then smiles briskly as if she didn't just deliver a dire proclamation. "Keep up the good work, Julian. You may not believe this, but we're rooting for you."

The organizer has ended the meeting.

Well, *fuck.*

My phone buzzes from my desk. I pick it up.

THAT MEAN, LITTLE LESBIAN

Julian. It's Eve.

JULIAN

Still looking into the purported "Big Flap." Please refrain from sending additional pictures to support your theory.

THAT MEAN, LITTLE LESBIAN

They were just Georgia O'Keeffe paintings.

JULIAN

They were screenshots of Google Image Results.

THAT MEAN, LITTLE LESBIAN

Okay. Inspiration FOR Georgia O'Keeffe paintings then. Listen, this isn't about vulvas.

JULIAN

I'm less interested now but go on.

THAT MEAN, LITTLE LESBIAN

We're going down the Shore this weekend. Wanna come?

My breath stutters in my chest. Is this Nomi's trip?

THAT MEAN, LITTLE LESBIAN

And yes, Nomi will be there.

JULIAN

ME? You're inviting ME?

JULIAN

Is this a joke? This is a VERY mean joke if so, you mean, little lesbian.

THAT MEAN, LITTLE LESBIAN

Not a joke.

JULIAN

I'm in.

THAT MEAN, LITTLE LESBIAN

Ok. Don't make me regret this, D'Asshole. I WILL be bringing the collar.

JULIAN

How…shocking.

THAT MEAN, LITTLE LESBIAN

JULIAN!!! 😠

CHAPTER NINETEEN

NOMI

It's eleven p.m. the night before our shore weekend, so you know what *that* means.

Absolutely nothing because I'm not *ever* bringing motorized blades around my labia *again*. I rummage through my drawers until I find the bikini with the boy shorts, the only bottoms that can contain my multitudes, and toss them on the bed. Somewhere within the covers, my phone buzzes. I pat around until I find it, then flop onto my back to read the text.

JULIAN

As your doctor

NOMI

Not my doctor

Julian is typing...

NOMI

Oh, God. I already see where this is going

Julian is typing…

NOMI

Don't do it!!!

JULIAN

On the night before a beach trip, I must caution you against any ill-advised attempts to visit "folds town" with an electric hair removal device.

NOMI

🙄 We swore never to speak of that night again.

JULIAN

We never swore to that. I would've NEVER sworn to that.

NOMI

It was an implied swear.

JULIAN

So . . . are you . . . going to? 👀

NOMI

Chill, I'm not going to slice open any labia and ruin another shore weekend.

JULIAN

Good, because I'm on call tonight, and I still need to pack. I simply don't have time for another trip to "folds town" in a professional capacity.

NOMI

Quit saying "folds town," or I'm rescinding your invitation.

Julian is typing...

NOMI

JULIAN, GODDAMMIT

JULIAN

Folds town. 😈

JULIAN

EVE INVITED ME, SO YOU CAN'T RESCIND SHIT, WYETH!!

NOMI

You are *so* annoying.

JULIAN

Can't wait for tomorrow.

NOMI

I roll over onto my stomach and smile into my pillow. Somehow, against every rational impulse in my body, I've caught feelings for Julian freaking D'Angelo.

NOMI

quick question

NOMI

if someone says they don't have time for another trip to "folds town" in a professional capacity, does that imply they DO have time to visit in their individual capacity? 👀

EVE

I cannot believe you're texting me about this. It's eleven thirty at night. I am BUSY. Making POT de crémes! YOU'RE WELCOME BTW!!!

NOMI

Wouldn't it be pots de créme?

GRAHAM

Nomi, as the resident male in this group chat, that's ABSOLUTELY what that means.

NOMI

I was afraid of that 😬

EVE

Do NOT encourage her, Grahamuel!

GRAHAM

why afraid? you liiiiiiike him!

NOMI

I do not!

GRAHAM

You want to pull on the doctor's little curls and watch them spring up.

EVE

This is literally the opposite of not encouraging her.

NOMI

...ok. I do want to do that. They're so cute!! But you both know I don't date.

EVE

...do we tho?

GRAHAM

do we, tho???

GRAHAM

jinx!

EVE

Seriously Nomes, what's holding you back from riding that annoying man's face and shutting him up for the greater good?

GRAHAM

Solid point. Nomi?

NOMI

Whatever Eve, don't act like you don't like Julian now, too.

EVE

The rich man pays our rent. We like the rich man.

NOMI

Hey, I earned that money by teaching him about cannabis.

EVE

notice how she's dodging our very valid question, Grahamuel?

GRAHAM

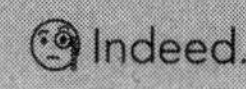

Indeed.

NOMI

I'm not dodging it, per se . . .

EVE

incredibly dodgy thing to say

NOMI

I just don't know how to answer.

EVE

Well, you might want to figure that out b/c I've got you and Julian sharing a room at the shore house. OK BYEEEEEEEEEEEEEEEEEEEEEEE

NOMI

WHAT?!?!?!

I blink down at my phone, heart racing.

SMS silence. Nobody is typing.

NOMI

YOU COME BACK TO THIS CHAT RIGHT NOW, EVE IONIDES, OR ELSE I'M COMING UP THERE!

Then, from above: "FUCKING GET OVER IT, NOMI! IT'S HAPPENING!" muffled through the floors.

I yell up at the ceiling. "*NO*, IT'S *NOT*!"

"YOU NEED TO GET LAID. WE'VE ALL DECIDED, IT'S FOR YOUR OWN FUCKING GOOD!"

An outraged huff exits my body. I march up the stairs and throw open her front door. "Who the hell is *we*?!"

Eve whirls around in her kitchen, apron on, whisk raised in self-defense. "The *royal we*, of course!"

I fold my arms. "Names. Now."

Eve points the whisk at me. "You want names? Fine. Your mom, Graham, me, the bartender at the Salty Taco—"

I blink at her. "You're discussing my sex life with strangers at the lesbian bar?!"

"Kaleigh is a close, personal friend!" Eve yells. "With sage and timely advice!"

A clot of pale green cream drips off the whisk and splats onto the vinyl floor. We both look at it, then back at each other. "*Eve*," I moan, then throw myself onto her couch. Big Bird promptly hops into my lap and begins batting at my chin, which I try to dodge. "You already invited him against my will. Don't do this to me."

Eve takes a deep breath, tosses the whisk into the bowl, then joins me on the couch. "First of all, it wasn't against your will. You were horrified for two seconds, then I saw the excitement form on your face in real time. You *like* him, Nomi. You never like anyone! Don't you think that means something?"

"No," I cross my arms, and Big Bird uses them like a ladder to get closer to my nose. "Not really."

Eve rolls her eyes. "You've always been able to say *no, thanks* to the guys that like you, but you can't with him, and that scares you."

"He annoys me!"

"He wakes you up, and that's a good thing, Nomi. Someone needs to." Eve exhales through her nose. "Listen, if you were happy living this acetic hot-nun lifestyle where you never date or have sex or even entertain romantic relationships, I would gladly leave you be. But you're not happy. I can't endorse your decisions that ultimately harm you, and that you're making out of fear."

My mouth opens, but surprise hinders my words. "I—*what?* I thought you were stoned! Where's this coming from?"

"I *am* stoned. You know that Sour Diesel sativa blend you got me for creativity? Pretty sure it's jacked up my IQ by thirty points. I solved the *New York Times* Crossword in like, three minutes today." Eve holds up one finger, runs to the kitchen, then returns with a spoon heaped with budder cream. "Here. Emotional support frosting."

I take a small lick and sigh miserably.

"I know you don't like to talk about your health problems, which means that, even as your best and hottest friend, I don't know exactly what you're facing. But I do know that life is easier when we let others love us. *All* of us, the good parts, and the bad. And there is so, so much good in you, Nomi. You deserve to love and be loved." Eve smiles kindly, which is altogether a very frightening look for her. "And when you don't make your own moves, that means *I* have to for the good of the order. Plus, Kayleigh's really invested in you two getting together, and it's giving me a reason to text her, so." Eve claps her hands. "Chop chop, as they say."

"I'm cutting you off from Sour Diesel." I take another big lick. "And Kayleigh."

"Ha! I'd like to see you try."

I exhale a long, deep breath. "Look, I hear what you're saying, and it all sounds really wise, but I'm not sitting here thinking stuff like, *boo hoo, I'm sick, I don't deserve to be loved*!" I shake my head, annoyed that that's how it looks to my own best friend. "And my feelings for Julian are... complicated."

"Complicated how?" Eve asks. "Tell me. Open up. Do you need more budder cream?"

I hand her the spoon, and she brings it back, refilled.

"I *do* like Julian a lot," I begin, taking another lick. "But he's... like a mosquito bite."

Eve arches an eyebrow. "If you thought that was a clear and complete thought, you're wrong."

"Ever since he moved back, he's been this—*itch*—constantly reminding me of his presence, driving me crazy, you know?"

Eve stares at me, disgusted. "Go... on?"

"And that night at the Pot Luck, I finally scratched it, and it felt so good, like *heaven* scratching that itch. But as soon as we stopped, the itch came back, worse than ever. I wanted to scratch him even *more*."

"This metaphor's really starting to bother me."

"That's what this whole working together, hanging out together, becoming friends thing has been like. This maddening itch I want to scratch so bad, but I know that if I do, it'll never be enough. He's leaving in three months, Eve. They'd be crazy not to reinstate him at Philly Gen, and then what will happen? I don't fit into his life there. He'll go back to working all the time, I'll never see him anymore, and I'll be left here with this horrible itch I can't scratch."

Eve sits there, face rumpled in comic displeasure.

"Well, you asked." I huff. "Why would I date someone when I know it's going to end? Why would I open myself up and get all vulnerable for three months, at best?"

"Because you just said kissing him felt like *heaven*." Eve blinks at me. "You're thinking about this all wrong. Scratch the itch, Nomi, be*cause* he's going to leave in three months! You don't have to open up about anything if you don't want to—just have fun!"

I frown, feeling slightly outmatched. Whatever's in this budder cream is *not* making me smarter. "I don't know..."

"Listen. Julian is the most intense person you've ever met. How do you think that translates in bed? Hmm?" Eve's eyebrows are raised halfway up her forehead. "Plus, he's already handled your vulva once without making you come—the man's indebted!"

"Okay, you've made your points, genius. I'll think about them. But in the meantime, can you please trust that if I want to hook up with Julian, I'll do it on my own terms? In a bedroom of *my* choosing? I don't need to be forced. And tell Kayleigh to get off my dick."

Eve sighs. "Fine. I'll shift things so we can room together, and Graham will stay with Julian. But if you change your mind, let's use a code word." Eve pauses. "Pumpkin."

I massage my temples. "Pumpkin it is."

Eve points at me. "And pumpkin goes both ways! If I need to claim the room, you have to respect my pumpkin."

"Okay. I'll respect your pumpkin." I stop in the doorway, then give her a small smile. "Thanks, Eve. For looking out for me and going way too far, as usual."

"Yeah, yeah, yeah." Eve waves a hand at me. "See you tomorrow."

JULIAN

Is there anything scarier than spending the weekend with new friends?

I honestly don't know; it's never happened to me before. This *being included* is a whole new world to me, and I'm oscillating between giddy joy and abject dread that I'm going to screw it all up.

I consult the to-do list on my notes app, even though every item's been checked off. My car has been washed and vacuumed, my bag packed with the least country-club-adjacent clothes I own, and three iced coffee drinks and one chai latte are sitting snug in their cupholders, sweating lightly in the August morning air. All I need now is to pick up my friends.

My friends.

I sweat all the way to Nomi's house, the pick-up point. I volunteered to drive because I'm never quite sure when Eve and Graham are sober, and if I had nothing to do for the hour drive to the shore, I would stare at Nomi the entire time. Also, if I didn't offer to drive, what if they went without me? They'd already be having so much fun by the time I got there, I'd be on the outside looking in all weekend, too far behind to catch up.

No, this way I can control the situation with the right coffee drinks, a comfortable luxury car, and the perfect playlist, with *me*, squarely included, from the outset. Things with Nomi are... I don't know. Approaching a precipice. And for better or worse, this weekend has started to feel like another test. If I fail, I'll be demoted back to the obnoxious doctor serving out his probation next door, and when they talk about me, it'll be reminiscing about that time they strapped a shock collar on me and tried to train me to be good. A failed experiment, a person they knew in the past tense.

But if I *succeed*, if I show them I can be fun and not a complete dickhead for a whole weekend, I...don't know. Maybe this could be my life? Having friends, going on trips, and...Nomi?

Nomi.

I've never wanted an A-plus more.

When I pull up to the curb, so excited it's bordering on panic, nobody's waiting outside as we'd discussed.

JULIAN

I'm here!

NOMI

Great! Come on in.

I frown briefly, glancing at the clock. It's exactly eight a.m., which we agreed was the best time to depart to beat the worst of the weekend traffic. I cut the engine. Maybe they're doing last-minute bathroom trips so we won't have to stop.

Respectable. Honorable. Lawful good.

I jog up to the door. "Hello?" I call, pushing it tentatively open.

Eve bustles past me wearing bikini bottoms, flip-flops, and a Bruce Springsteen muscle tank tied at her waist. In her arms are three stacked trays of plastic-wrapped desserts, which she thrusts at me.

"Finally!" She scurries off without further instruction.

Graham, who's shirtless, visibly confused, and wearing one sneaker, hobbles by. "Hey, man."

"This is a *wildly* irresponsible amount of dessert." I stare at the heavy trays. Where am I supposed to put these? My trunk is not temperature-controlled to safely contain cream-based desserts. I close my eyes, willing myself not to *be* myself about this. "Where's Nomi?"

"Here!" Nomi walks out of her bedroom, fully dressed in black denim cut-offs, sandals, and today, a Joan Baez T-shirt with its sleeves removed.

She looks *gorgeous.* Her brown hair hangs in loose, shower-damp waves down her back, her bangs long and parted to reveal her big, brown eyes and the cluster of freckles that dapple her nose and round, apple-pink cheeks. She has a duffel on one shoulder and her giant leather bag on the other, wearing a big, bright smile in between.

"Watch it!" Eve yells, and I snap back to attention as the trays list to the side. I correct just in time but not without pinching a finger in the process. I hiss out a curse as Eve glares at me.

"If you can't be trusted with desserts, you can't be trusted *at all.*" Eve hoists shorts up and over her hips, zipping them without breaking eye contact.

It's the most intimidating thing I've ever witnessed.

"Come on, Julian." Nomi scoots past me in the hallway. "We don't want to be late!"

I grunt, then follow her out to the car. It's a little easier to breathe outside, away from the chaos of Graham's bumbling efforts to pack and Eve's gremlin baker energy. It's also 8:14 a.m. I lower the trays into the trunk first, scooting them as close to the air-conditioned interior as I can. If people experience dairy spoliation–related diarrhea due to the proliferation of food-borne bacterial pathogens after eating these, well. I know how to write a prescription.

"I see the short shorts are back," Nomi says as I straighten to standing. The little smirk she's wearing brings down my blood pressure by a full ten points, more or less. Hard to say without the cuff.

I lean against the trunk, subtly flexing my forearms across my chest. "Well, someone once told me a muscular thigh, and I quote, 'never hurt nothing.' "

"Who said that?" Nomi pulls her sunglasses down and over her eyes, her crooked smile creating heat in my chest. "Sounds pretty smart."

My throat bobs involuntarily as I smile for the first time all morning. "Smartest person I've ever met."

Her own gaze lingers on my face, a pleased flush pinking her pretty cheeks, and I feel the heart-soaring joy that I might be able to pass this test after all.

"Quit standing there flirting and help Grahamuel find his shoe!" Eve bellows from the front door, then slams it shut again.

"Mornings stress her out," Nomi explains. "And sobriety."

By the time we find Graham's shoe (it was in the trash can), Eve smokes up, and Nomi turns off the lights and locks all the doors, it's after nine a.m., and my eye's begun to twitch.

"Ugh, what is this!" Eve complains as we enter a long line of backed-up cars for our first turn, all headed to the same place.

"Well, we were *supposed* to leave at eight," I say, unable to resist. "So, this is traffic."

"Sorry, DAD," Eve says belligerently from the backseat. Then, "*Ooh*, coffee! Thanks, Dad!" A beat later. "Is this supposed to be iced?"

"It was iced. An hour ago." I breathe deeply through my nose. "When we were supposed to leave."

"Oh, *honey*." Nomi looks at me over the rim of her sunglasses and places her hand lightly on my thigh. "Did you really think a car full of stoners would leave on time?" Her palm is warm and soft, and my muscle tics upward, jumping to meet it. She's so foxy right now, I'm regretting the length of my shorts. I don't *think* there could be a jailbreak incident? But I didn't try these on aroused, either.

"I—guess that was naive, wasn't it." I smile tightly. *Be cool, be cool, she's gorgeous and for some reason likes you, so for God's sake, BE COOL, JULIAN.* "But we're on the road now, and I love going—" I check the speedometer, "twenty-three miles per hour on highly congested highways."

"Good." Nomi withdraws her hand as she stretches back in her seat, content as a kitten in a patch of sunlight, and yawns. Meanwhile, my forgotten thigh enters a state of mourning. "Because this one-hour drive's gonna take two and a half hours now."

Even though the iced drinks have gone watery, and Graham seizes my phone because "*NPR podcasts are not a playlist,*" the morning skies are a seamless bolt of blue, and Nomi's sitting in my front seat, drumming her fingers happily to music I didn't know existed. The dual feeling of *euphoric!/terrified!* takes turns letting me float away then snatching me back down again, like a bored kid playing God with a balloon. I'm the balloon.

I almost lose it though when, twenty minutes before we arrive, Eve announces we have to stop at the Bruce Willis Service Area.

"You seriously can't hold it a little longer?" I plead with the backseat tyrant.

"Of *course* I can hold it, I have a bladder of vast and epic proportions! Rubbery, tough, discerning." She punches her fist into her palm with each emphatic word. "I've been training it since I was a kid."

"*What?*" My eyes widen in alarm.

"It's tradition, bro," Graham pipes up.

"A traditional pee," I say, fully scornful as I make eye contact with each of them in the rearview mirror. "*Twenty minutes* before we arrive."

"It's *Bruce Willis's* Service Area, man!" Eve points at the standard rest area. "What's *wrong* with you?"

"Are you even from New Jersey?" Graham tuts.

"Just pull over," Nomi says.

Groaning, I do. Eve launches out of the car first, then greets everyone she sees with a tip of her imaginary hat and "*Yippee-ki-yay, fellow truckers.*" Graham promptly holds up an imaginary mic to each of their faces and asks them what their favorite Bruce Willis movie is.

I blink slowly. "*This* is why we stopped?"

"Whichever movie gets the most votes is what we'll watch tonight," Nomi explains. "Tradition."

I cover my face with both hands.

"Hey. Breathe deep. You're going to be fine."

"I don't get it." I shake my head. "My whole life, people have complained that *I'm* obnoxious. But this—" I jab a finger at Eve and Graham's impromptu interview corner where a small crowd is engaging in friendly debate over the *Die Hard* franchise. "—is objectively the most obnoxious thing ever."

Nomi tilts her head. "Not objectively, no. It comes down to priorities."

"What do you mean?"

"Well, your priority is to get to where you're going as quickly and efficiently as possible."

"Exactly!"

Nomi shrugs. "Their priority is to have fun. Maybe your normal priorities are what's putting you at odds with this situation. Maybe if you consciously shift your priorities to align with ours, and you try prioritizing fun, too, it'll get your head in the right space."

I stare at her. How does Nomi do this? How does she know exactly how to help me understand? I've spent this whole drive fighting my own frustration and worse, feeling defective for feeling it. But she just transformed the cacophony of unnamable feelings inside my chest to an explanation as clear as a bell.

"What if I don't know how to prioritize fun?" I swallow, feeling oddly vulnerable admitting this, though it's pointless. Nomi already understands me better than almost anyone I've ever met. "Even though I want to?"

Nomi's smile is slow and sweet, like honey dripping from a spoon. "I'll show you how."

CHAPTER TWENTY

NOMI

There's something endearing about Julian really, earnestly trying to be cool. It's easy to forget how anxious he naturally is. His sharp jaw, piercing eyes, the strong, compelling architecture of his face—all of it suggests a confidence you'd presume is his birthright. How could anyone so attractive worry what the rest of us thinks?

But then this beautiful, successful man appears on your doorstep vibrating with nerves, armed with extravagant drinks he made to everyone's exact liking and a playlist curated to encourage conversation. At one point, I saw him scrolling through a lengthy to-do list on his phone, mouthing the word *check* over and over again.

And for what? Spending a weekend at the shore with a bunch of silly potheads? I hadn't meant to touch his thigh on the ride here, but he was so worked up, I longed to smother out all the little sparks of nerves burning him up. The way he stilled beneath the press of my palm, his tight muscles releasing—it was heady having that effect on him.

But Julian's always made me feel powerful.

After we exit for the Wildwoods and wend our way to Graham's family beach house, a 1950s cottage by way of a very enthusiastic 1993, Julian hoists Eve's heavy dessert trays through the sunny yellow door to the kitchen. Eve, Graham, and I trail him like puppies, lured by the siren song of Eve's baking.

"Finally! The moment we've all been waiting for." Eve scrambles to unwrap the first tray, revealing happy red ramekins filled with green custard clustered together like coral. She pats one with a spoon, then dips it in and brings a full bite to her mouth.

Julian watches this with fingers gripping the counter, until he bursts, slapping the spoon out of her hand before she can taste it. "Eve, no!"

"What the fuck?!" Eve gapes as he pushes between her and the counter full of dessert.

"Do you *know* the rate of bacterial proliferation in a milk-based product left at room temperature for two and a half hours?"

"Of course I don't know that!" Eve tries to move him aside, but Julian plants his feet. "Furthermore, I don't care! They weren't at room temperature!"

"Oh, *shit*," Graham whispers.

"You're right—they were in a hot trunk!" Julian darts side to side, effectively blocking Eve from her pots de créme.

My eyes widen. He doesn't know the danger he's in.

"STEP AWAY FROM THE DESSERTS, JULIAN!" Eve grabs a spatula from the drawer, wielding it like a weapon.

"E. coli! Listeria! Salmonella! Campylobacter!" Julian yells as he dodges Eve's wild swings. "You'll send everyone to the hospital if they eat it!"

"Okay, OKAY! Stop it, both of you!" I pluck the spatula from Eve's upraised hand before she has a chance to put permanent grill marks across Julian's pretty face, and Graham pulls Eve back.

I point the spatula at Eve. "We do *not* maim our guests, Eve."

She glares at me incredulously. "We do when they fuck with dessert!"

"And *you*." I spin on Julian, then break into a soft smile. "It's very sweet to risk your life protecting us from—"

"E. coli!" Julian begins again. "Listeria! Salmo—"

"Yes, we get it. But Julian, the desserts were frozen when Eve put them in your trunk." I glance at the contraband behind Julian. "They're not even fully thawed yet. They're fine."

"They were frozen?"

"Yes! I'm not an idiot." Eve shoulders out of Graham's grip. "Now, step aside, D'Asshole."

Tentatively, Julian does as he's told, and Eve gets a fresh spoon and bite, then holds it up to his lips. "Would *you* like to do the honors, Doctor?"

Julian's eyes flick nervously to mine.

"You don't need to have any cannabis this weekend if you don't want to, Julian. We'll have fun no matter what."

"Will it make me feel like it did at the Pot Luck?" He looks so tentative, so trusting right now. I really consider his question.

"Eve, you used your regular budder for these, right?"

Eve nods, her fury having disappeared into a strange, maternal encouragement as she holds the spoon near his mouth.

"Then yes, though it'll be a lot milder since you consumed so much that night."

Julian stands straighter, takes a deep breath, and after a long second, opens his mouth. Eve jams it in before he can change his mind. His jaw moves slowly, his eyes rolling back as he swallows.

"Oh my *God*," he says, grabbing the ramekin from Eve's hand and going carnal on the pot de créme. "This is amazing. Is that…pistachio? And black cherry?"

"Yes!" Eve claps her hands with delight. All has been forgiven in the face of Julian's unbridled French custard lust.

"You're really going to town on that." I frown slightly as Julian viciously scrapes the bottom of the ramekin with his spoon.

His eyes slide up to mine, and he winks. "It might help with shifting my priorities." He turns to Eve. "Thoughts on eating *two*?"

"That depends." Her lips press in a thoughtful line. "Do you enjoy mild hallucinations?"

"Ooh, I do!" Graham takes a second while the rest of us stop at one.

"Okay, enough screwing around. Time to suit up, Doctor!" Eve slaps Julian on the ass, rather hard judging by how high he jumps, then throws her arms in the air. "We're in Wildwood, baby!"

Wildwood, New Jersey—best boardwalk on the Jersey Shore, fight me. Two and a half glorious miles of fudge shops and crass T-shirt stands, broken up by three piers filled with water rides, coasters, and a massive Ferris wheel that lords over the beach, glowing rainbow all night. It smells perpetually of fresh French fries and salty ocean, and I love it. There's nothing more quintessentially *summer* to me than the cold sweet of Polish water ice on my tongue as I stroll down the boardwalk on a hot, humid night.

Our first stop is a pool party at one of the retro beach motels just off the boardwalk. The mid-century pop-art aesthetic is strong here, with smiling, bubbly-eyed cartoon heads emblazoned on its sign, along with stylized beach balls bouncing across its squat, cream-colored stucco. Julian takes everything in with parted lips, and when he strips off his shirt and throws it on a lounge chair, baring the trim stack of abs, broad chest, and the dips, lines, and mounds of shoulders trained to be strong, it's all I can do to keep my *own* mouth from hanging open. With all that Italian heritage, Julian's meant to be sun-bronzed and glowing, but his olive-toned skin is unnaturally pale from too many summers spent indoors serving those different priorities. He's about to jump in the pool when I call his name with zero chill.

"Yes?" His eyes are slightly alarmed. Mine probably are, too, as I limply hold up the long tube of sunscreen with an uneasy smile.

A minute later, he's sitting between my legs on the lounge chair, the long expanse of his back presented to me, waiting for my touch.

Oh, Jesus. What have I *done*?

"Thanks for reminding me," he offers casually, as though I'm not back here completely winded from the proximity of his ass. "Skin cancer is serious."

I squirt a line of cool sunscreen across his hot shoulders. He shivers, his back arching into my space, and a giddy, cloying kick of lust pulses low in my belly. I stare at the ludicrous stripe of cream. It's *obscene.*

"Yes, very serious." I repeat stupidly. My hands hover over his back. *Touch him*, I command myself. *You're making this weird!*

With a burst of resolve, I press both palms into the cream, then deliberately smear it across his skin. Fucking outrageous, the way it gathers in the dimples of muscle, how eagerly his skin sips in the moisture from my hands, leaving him coated in a dewy, coconut-scented glow.

"*So* serious," he murmurs. "That—skin. Cancer."

God help me, but I'm losing myself in this sunscreen's application. It feels so intimate, touching him like this. It makes the myth of *Julian*, this beautiful, difficult, admittedly brilliant man, more human and more vulnerable, seeing the freckles dotting his shoulders. A small scar on the back of one arm. When I push my thumbs experimentally into the tense ridge of muscles flanking his spine, a small, plaintive sound sighs out between his lips, and my thighs involuntarily clench. My fingertips trail down his sun-warmed skin, resting lightly against the waistband of his swim trunks. I want to dip my fingers within, continue this exploration with my palms flat against him, cupping his ass before grabbing his hips and grinding myself against him.

Eve's words *just have fun* echo in my brain. We don't have to date. We can have fun, right? Is it that easy?

He eyes me over his shoulder and swallows, throat bobbing, his eyes wonderfully electric. "Your turn."

I almost whimper. He stands quickly, then settles behind me on the long lip of the lounge chair. "Is this okay?" He murmurs into my ear, his chin's fresh stubble grazing my shoulder.

I vigorously bob my agreement. He sucks a sharp breath in, then the cool kiss of sunscreen licks down my hot back.

"*Pornographic*," he utters under his breath, then both of his hands land heavily, possessively there. My taut shoulders relax under his touch, and with the high THC, high CBD sativa blend singing through my system, my nerves buzz alive with every liquid pass of his hands over my body.

After what feels like a third comprehensive pass over my back, shoulders, and arms, he clears his throat roughly, sending warm breath prickling against my neck. "Um, is that enough?"

"Yes," I breathe, even though it's an outright lie because I want *more*. It's a steamy eighty-five degrees, but the tops of my breasts are covered in goose bumps from the nearness of his palms, my nipples so tight, they ache. His careful, life-saving hands feel like they could end mine with a simple slip of his finger beneath the warm cuff of spandex encircling my thigh, finding where I burn for him, dipping within, stroking me until I come nestled in the warm confines of his chest.

Jesus, this got out of control *fast*. We're barely five hours into this weekend, and I'm ready to scream *PUMPKIN!* and drag him by the hair back to the cottage. But haven't I been aching for him since he carried me to Patient Room #2 and stepped between my legs, cheeks blushing, and pressed the flat of his hand against me, *hard*? Haven't I wanted him even longer than that, when he drew me nervously into his arms in the back of the debate team van our senior year and pressed a dozen fervent kisses into my hair, my neck, my mouth? We were so young, but the chemistry of *us* reacted just as violently then as it does now. It may kill me to admit it, but I've always been drawn to this tense, difficult man who feels everything so furiously, even, and especially, his desire for me.

Before I can turn and straddle his lap with God and this motel pool's intoxicated revelers as our witness, I bolt upright, shuck off my sandals, and launch myself into the biting cold water. Julian splashes next to me an instant later, and our slick limbs slide against each other's as we tread in place. When I try and fail to unseat Graham from his unicorn float, Julian turns and offers his back to me.

"Here, ride me instead."

Eve crows, and I pelt her with a beach ball right in her face. From Julian's back, of course. I'm not passing up an opportunity to attach myself to him like a horny koala. This devolves into an all-out game of pool dodgeball, with everyone sloshing for cover and laughing wildly. Julian's cutthroat tendencies serve us well, but I'd be lying if I pretended to care more about destroying Eve and Graham than relishing every bounce, every slow grind and smooth slide of our pool-chilled bodies against each other.

When the Jell-O shots run out and the sun's sunk low in the horizon, the party breaks off into clumps, with us trailing behind Eve and Graham and their friends toward Surfside Pier. The pots de créme have hit in full glory, their effects buoyed further by the spiked water ice we drank, staining our lips and tongues a bright cherry red. The evening breeze ruffles the hem of my sundress, tickling the backs of my thighs, as we lose our friends to various rides and snack lines, and in Eve's case, the Whack-a-mole game.

"She'll be there until she earns enough tickets to buy whatever stuffed animal's the biggest."

Julian shakes his head in admiration. "Eve's my hero."

The pale-blue palette of his eyes reflects the reds, oranges, and golds of the pier's blinking lights, his black curls never wilder and more alive than in the ocean's humid, salty breeze. His face is open and relaxed and, best of all, *curious*, which I've come to realize is Julian's most natural, purest state of being.

"You've never been to Wildwood?" I nudge him slightly with my arm, bringing those kaleidoscope eyes down to mine, where I like them best.

"Nope. Mom's a Cape May type."

"*No!*" I press my hand against my chest. Don't get me wrong, Cape May is lovely and magical, but it's for grown-ups. It's candy-colored Victorian inns, interminable waits for brunch, and high-end beach boutiques. The magic of summer lives *here*, complete with booty shorts and questionable aquariums. It's rowdy and happy and cheap enough for folks to enjoy. Cape May doesn't even have a boardwalk.

I stop dead in my tracks. "So that means you've never ridden the Runaway Tram Car?"

Julian frowns. "What's that?" The real tram car, a yellow and blue institution, passes us then, car after car toting the drunk, elderly, young, and whiny up and down the boardwalk. "It doesn't seem like it's running away."

I blink at him, then yank him by the hand until we reach the best roller coaster on the Jersey Shore. "Prepare to be *amazed*."

"Oh, no. I don't do roller coasters. Ever."

"This one isn't scary—it's just fast and fun. Even little kids love it. You'll be fine!"

Julian's eyebrows raise in alarm. "I really have to do this?"

I stand on my tiptoes to whisper into his ear, "You do if you want to keep holding my hand."

We both look down at our joined hands, his so much bigger than my own, and he squeezes it tightly. With a deep breath in, he follows me through the turnstiles, never letting me go. When we're seated in the tiny blue car, and the lap bar descends over us, he checks my bar to make sure it's locked in position, then his, then mine, this his, then both at once. Laughing, I take his hand back firmly in mine.

With wide eyes, he clutches me tight, and then the train's off, chugging up the small hill before looping sideways into a quick downward rush, and Julian's *screaming*, louder than all the kids combined. But as the train lifts and falls, then dips sideways again, his screams transform into wild shrieks of laughter. I watch him, grinning, as he vocalizes more joy than I've ever heard him make, his eyes bright and glazed from the whip of the wind. Our train re-enters the station where we boarded, and he's grinning now, too.

"That was *amazing*, you were—*wha?!*" His words fall away as the train suddenly jolts forward again, beginning its second full lap of the track. "*Again?!*"

"It goes twice!"

I laugh into the sunset skies as my heart lifts and leaps, right along his.

CHAPTER TWENTY-ONE

NOMI

The sun never wants to let go of a Wildwood summer's day. The light lingers long after it's set, the skies flaring from pink to orange to an electric violet lit from within. When night finally does fall, the ink black wipes everything else away except streaks of neon and the glow of bulb-lit rides chirping for money. The ocean is only visible by the suggestion of one, the roar of waves you can't see until the moon finally rises, low and fat, wedging itself between dark water and darker air.

With sandals in one hand, and Julian's fingers knotted in the other, I pull him gently down the beach toward the cottage. We lost the others after the Runaway Tram Car, but then again, are you really lost when you're hoping not to be found? It's easier, being with Julian alone. While Eve and Graham like him, too, I feel their smug amusement at my growing feelings when we're all together. It's the most embarrassing of *I-told-you-so*'s. The one time your mother was right that the playground bully pulled your pigtails because he likes you. And a small part of me feels ashamed for forgiving him. Because I have—I've completely forgiven him. For the mean, judgmental things he's said, for the way he fought the dispensary without understanding a damn thing about it. For the way he kissed me like I was the most wondrous thing in the world, then declared war on everything I care about most the next day.

But all those things feel small compared to how I feel about Julian now. He didn't understand anything then, but I didn't understand him, either. Every glimpse I get of how his mind works, of how strongly he feels, I understand why he did what he did a little more. It's impossible to hate someone when you understand them.

I pause at the water's edge, letting foam bubble between my toes. Julian's face is turned to the sea. His strong features are softened by the dark, and he looks so pensive, it pulls at my heart.

"What's wrong?"

A full beat passes, filled with the gentle *shusssh* of the water, while he thinks.

"Your life is so full. It makes me realize I've been doing everything wrong."

"Hey." I pull him toward me, his hair lifting on the whimsies of the wind. "Your life is full, too."

He releases a low, pained huff. "Full of work, maybe. Full of expectations that I kill myself trying to exceed. Full of anger and bad feelings and—and loneliness." He swallows as his eyes meet mine. "But you're doing it right. You have friends and a calling you believe in. You have all this." His eyes sweep across the rebellious blare of Wildwood's lights behind us. "And I didn't even know it existed."

"Come on. You knew Wildwood existed." I smile, because it's easier than letting his words inside the small, lit room of my heart.

"I didn't know that Wildwood existed like *this*." Julian's thumb runs lightly over my wrist's pulse point. "And I don't think it ever would have for me, without you."

He lifts his other hand gently to my cheek, cupping it within his warm palm. "You make me realize how empty I was before I met you. And being with you, here, now, is the fullest I've ever felt."

This time, I have no choice. The door to my heart slams open, and his words flood in, filling me with an aching, bittersweet relief that's as difficult as it is beautiful, just like him.

Because I understand him.

Because I hurt the same way.

Maybe my life seems full to him, but that's only because he's come along and stepped neatly into the hollow space I've spent my adult life ignoring, filling it so completely, the edges brim with him.

Julian.

My face leans into his hand, my lips pressing softly into the cradle of his palm, kissing him there.

"Nomi," he murmurs, his pupils dilating until there's almost no blue left. Just pools of hungry, pensive dark. He brings his other hand up to cup my face, his thumbs tracing the curve of my cheekbones, before he tilts my face up to his. The soft velvet of his bottom lip slides across my own, and when our mouths open to each other, the muffled sound of want rising from his throat feels as much mine as his.

I sigh into him, and he breathes me in, like life.

The softness of our kiss contrasts with the fierce press of our bodies. He gathers me into him, folding his arms behind my back, pressing us so tightly together his heartbeat thrums against mine. The jut of my hips digs into his, my nipples studding, his cock pushing. Everything in me *clenches*. I rake my fingers into his curls, gasping as he tilts my head back and devours my neck, the wet steam of his mouth leaving trails of rippling sensation across my collarbone, down my chest, beneath the round, heavy curve of my breasts. I keen against this slick worship, my hips offering me up to him, again and again.

He groans, a quiet roar to match the ocean's, and falls to his knees before me. He pushes the skirt of my short sundress up to my waist, eyeing me hungrily, before lifting his reverent face to mine. "Can I—"

"You can do *whatever* you want." I dig my fingers into his hair, pulling his head back even further. "And you fucking better."

His fingers grip me by the hips, hard, then usher me forward to his waiting mouth. Warmth builds around my clit as he exhales harshly into the thin cotton underwear, followed by the hard press of his lips against me, his teeth biting fabric and dragging it aside.

I moan, weakness pooling in the backs of my knees.

The first slide of his tongue feels like every dirty thought I've ever had. Standing on this dark public beach, my skirt pinned against my stomach, Julian on his knees, his hot, wet mouth kissing, licking, sucking my clit, I feel unmoored.

"Your cunt is so pretty, Nomi," he murmurs into my crux, dragging his chin against me until I writhe against him. "And you taste—" he breaks off, groaning. "You taste like you're *mine*."

When every muscle in my core trembles, when I can barely stand, when I whimper and unabashedly grind myself against his chin, he whispers, "That's right, that's a good girl." His hands grip my ass, hard. "Come on my fucking face."

And I *do*, rocking into him, gripping him by his curly hair as every surge of pleasure entangles with the feeling of *him*, his mouth, his tongue. The gasp chokes out of me as the orgasm blows through every synapse. This time when the weakness hits, I melt into it, sinking to the ground. His hungry hands guide me down until I'm on my knees before him, and he rocks my hips into his, the column of his hard cock notching perfectly against me. Its presence sends another wave of aftershocks rioting through me. I lift my dazed face up to his, my hands still enmeshed in his hair, as he lowers me onto my back. The sand here is powder soft and still warm from the day's sun. It feels like a thousand pinpricks of pleasure against my skin as Julian settles his hips between my legs.

"You're so beautiful, Nomi, you feel so beautiful, so perfect." He slides one arm beneath my neck, so that I can rest there, while the other slides down the rumpled bodice of my sundress. He finds the vicious knot of one nipple through the fabric, pausing to rub circles around it, pinching it lightly between his fingers until I moan out his name.

"Was there ever anything so beautiful as my name on your lips?" His eyes are starrier than the night sky above us as he brings his forefinger to my mouth. He drags the pad of his finger against me, parting my lips, then diving in and kissing me as though jealous of his own hand. And I feel...

Precious. I feel right and good and perhaps just as obsessed with the man slowly grinding against me as he so clearly is with me.

"Julian." His name floats up and out of me, landing in his hair, the shell of his ear, as he tries to meld our bodies together by sheer willpower alone.

"What do you want, Nomi? I'll do anything."

I bring his ear to my mouth and give the lobe a long, slow suck, relishing the way his entire frame trembles in response. "Take me back."

He's on his feet in an instant, and then I'm up, too, gathered into his arms as he carries me princess-style, once again, through the sandy dunes up to the beach cottage.

The conditions are *infinitely* better this time.

The lights are off, the others still out. Julian lowers me to my feet in the dark backyard, beneath the outdoor shower.

There's something heady about Julian's attention. Intoxicating, even. It warms me up from the inside as it goes straight to my head. I don't feel quite like myself as I slip my sundress slowly off, and at the same time, I've never felt more quintessentially *me.* Julian's dark eyes watch it all, his lips parting on a small groan as I slide my saturated underwear off my body, leaving them in a pile by my feet. I step forward and unbutton his shirt, marveling at the feverish heat of his chest, the soft smattering of dark hair nestled there, until the shirt slides off his shoulders, falling to the wooden deck beneath us. His trunks are next, hampered only by the curve of his ass and the long jut of his thick, restless cock. I slide my hand in the front, grasping him in my fingers, and ease the shorts down over his hips unimpeded. His dick, already impossibly hard, swells further in my grip, and he exhales a small, helpless sound as I run my thumb over the head, sticky sweet with his own moisture.

I swallow tightly, taking in the sight of Julian D'Angelo, glorious and nude and thrumming with a hot, sexual energy that promises both the punishing intensity and unwavering commitment so uniquely his. I take it and commit it to memory. *He* is beautiful. *He* is perfect. And as I spin the shower's knobs to hot, stepping us both into its spray, and sink to my knees before him, *he* tastes like he's mine, too.

He allows me a long, slow suck before he digs one hand into my hair, gently tipping me back. He stares down at me in awe, in wonder, as the shower wicks my hair away from my face, my mouth filled with him. His fingers tighten in my hair. The sensation releases a flood of primal desire low in my belly, and I can feel myself drip with it, lightly down my inner thigh. He slowly withdraws from my mouth only to pump back in on an anguished groan.

"Oh, God, Nomi." A single bead of hot cum hits the roof of my mouth, and he withdraws again. "Your pretty mouth wrapped around my cock, *Jesus*. I don't deserve this. I don't." This time, I grip his ass and force him back in, my lips bearing down in a tight, demanding seal. When he throws his head back, holding on to me as if I'm the only thing keeping him upright, a long, satisfied *mmmm* escapes my throat, vibrating around him.

I *love* it.

It's been a long time since I've wanted to do anything sexual with a partner. I often feel completely divorced from my body. Not a part of it but held captive by it. My mind trapped inside its prison, forced to feel its pain and sickness and fear of *more* pain and sickness, leaving me so tired and beat down that I can't feel anything else.

But Julian is a feast. I want to taste every last bit of him, of what he can do to me, how he can make me feel. I want to gorge on this fantasy where girl fights boy, girl *defeats* boy, boy makes girl come into oblivion.

Julian bites his lower lip, his abdomen a tense stack of Jenga pieces about to topple. The pressure building in his thick cock stretches my lips wide.

"Nomi," he pants out, "can I please come?"

"In me," I say on a long lick, "on me," I drag his cock across my cheek, my lips, my chin, "wherever you want."

He grips me by the hair, harder, as his release builds, and the tight, prickling pleasure of it sends a shockwave down my spine. I work my own finger down, my clit a swollen heart beating furiously in the thick of me, and groan from the instant jolt of pleasure. The instant before he comes, he withdraws from my mouth, then presses the silky, burning brand of his cock against my lips, my chin, watching fascinated and helpless as he explodes hot and thick against my face, my neck, a knot sliding down and puddling in the hollow of my throat. A groan rips out of him as he shudders against me, his fingers gentling in my hair.

I'm working myself harder now, so close that when he slides his hand down my throat, smearing himself down my chest, over my breasts, rubbing his cum all over me, it's the last push I need. I come again, tumbling after him as I bury my face against his smooth, throbbing cock.

"I'm never going to be okay again," Julian whispers, cradling my face against him.

I laugh breathlessly between my own shivers. "Have I ruined you?"

"You laugh," Julian says, tipping my chin up as he sweeps a hand possessively across the breasts he just marked like a goddamn brute. "But my entire world just reoriented on its axis. All directions point to you now."

He helps me to my feet, then turns me gently around until I'm facing the wall, placing my hands on it, directly in the water's path. He begins washing my body, slowly running his hands over every part of me. Sand slides between my skin, the water, and him, the grit teasing every nerve ending. My clit aches painfully as his large hands glide over my body, soaping my breasts, my throat, the long line of my back. When his thumb gently trails down the cleft of my ass, dragging lightly over the rim where he starts to massage, I flinch and turn quickly beneath the spray to face him, pulling his hands to my front.

His face, transfixed in intense reverie, gazes down at me. "Did I do something wrong?"

"No, it's—I'm not into that." I smile hesitantly because I'm not sure what else to say. *After a lifetime of pain, my asshole and I are on bad terms. Do not give it a single ounce of affection.* I don't need to explain anything, though. Julian tucks this information away, like law etched in stone, leaving me certain that he won't try again without my enthusiastic initiation. I release a deep breath as Julian runs his hands over my body again, removing the last of the lather, then switches places with me under the shower head to cleanse the sand from his own body, too. I could watch him like this all night. Water streaming through his hair, over his body, down his long, thick cock, still partially engorged as though standing by, ready to go again. Julian is a work of art, as challenging and thought-provoking as the best art is. Even as the hot water goes, and he begins to hiss and shiver, making laughter build inside my chest, he is beautiful.

I could look at him forever.

JULIAN

After I wrap Nomi in a beach towel and lift her again, she throws her head back and laughs. "Are you going to carry me everywhere from now on?"

I scoop her tightly against my chest. "Maybe. Feels right." I shoulder open the door to her bedroom in the cottage.

She smiles at me, as sweet and salty as the caramel popcorn we shared earlier. Her long, brown hair is already setting into those mermaid waves, the makeup she wore licked away by the steady stream of water as she sucked every bit of tension out of my body. She is, by far, the most beautiful person that's ever lived, and I've pledged my eternal allegiance to her sweet, delicious cunt.

"I *can* walk, you know."

"Not for long." I grin wickedly as I throw her onto the bed, then jump on next, landing on all fours prowling over her. Her towel's fallen partially open, and I sit back on my knees, slowly pulling back its sides to reveal her pale, moonlit body, all creams and pinks, curves and dips, beneath me.

"Fuck," I breathe, the sight of her undoing me all over again. My hand's on my cock, already beginning to stroke.

She squirms, blushing, beneath my heavy gaze. "You're making me feel self-conscious."

"Good," I murmur, as I take each of her hands and hold them in mine on either side of her head, lowering myself between her legs. "You should be conscious of yourself, Nomi. You're beautiful, an absolute wonder. I'm going to study every inch of you, memorize every fact." I lick her from the base of her throat all the way to the hollow behind her ear. "What you like, what you love. How to make you scream my name." I grind my hips between hers, our bodies colliding in slick, teasing want. Her pussy is soaked for me. It'd be so easy to slide into her, feel her wrap around me as I fill her to the brim. We groan in tandem.

"Get the fucking condom, Julian," she pants out. And I'm on my feet, racing naked to my room without a single fuck if anyone sees me. Nomi could tell me to run a marathon right now, and I'd leave without my shoes on. Some core internal tension snapped when I came against the bell of her pretty throat. I feel loose, pliant, pliable, every doubt I've ever had erased by the certainty of *her*. As someone who's made success my guiding beacon because no other light's been bright enough to follow, it's like the long, cold night of searching for purpose has finally ended, and a new sun has risen. Everything is illuminated in her fresh, morning light.

I'd forgotten what it feels like to truly want something.

But I knew this feeling, long ago. When the pretty goth girl with the subtle accent strode into my debate team's practice, I knew this wanting then. Only I never let myself give in to it, not fully. Not until now. The relief of surrender is so palpable, so complete, I want to cry and laugh and bury my cock within her soft cunt again and again. I throw the door open to her room, my dick as big as it's ever been, condom box raised over my head in victory.

And she laughs, the sweetest, silky sound, and I feel my own grin rise to meet hers as I tear open a wrapper and roll the condom over the broad bolt of my cock. I approach the bed, encircling each of her ankles with my thumb and forefinger, gripping tight, then push until her legs open and her shining cunt is splayed wide. I look, long and slow, because this time, I'm allowed to. No doctor's coat. No whining fluorescent bulbs overhead. My dick throbs at the sight of her, so exposed, so wet, so *impatient* for me.

I climb onto the bed, one knee at a time, still holding tightly to her ankles. Nomi's as locked in as I am, her eyes like pools of honeyed lust as she stares at me, lips slightly parted, heart rate elevated and pulsing through her limbs. But still, I hold on to her tightly, like she might float away and leave me stranded on Earth, a perfect dream I'm not meant to hold in my hands.

"Julian," she warns, then whimpers. "I can't wait anymore."

"Just one more thing." I drop to my palms, deliver a long, languid lick up to her clit that makes her shiver and moan, then gently search her with my tongue until I find it. A slightly thicker stripe of skin, deep in the heart of *folds town.* I spread her apart to examine it.

"What are you doing?"

I grin up at her incredulous face. "Barely left a scar."

"Oh my *God.*" Nomi swats at my head.

"I'm *amazing.*" I whistle, eyeing my work. "First time stitching up labia, too."

"Julian!"

"And under great personal duress." I sit upright on my knees, grip her by the hips, then yank her flush against my hard cock. "Do you know how badly I wanted to do this to you? Pull you to the edge of the examining table and stick my dick in you?" I slide my cock up and down between the halves of her pussy, teasing us both. "I almost resigned from the medical profession over it."

She laughs breathily, her smile loose and lazy. "I wanted you, too." Her hands slide over mine where I squeeze each of her knees, tugging me toward her. "I thought I was going insane."

"You felt it, even then."

After a second, she nods, her eyes earnest and maybe, a little scared. I fall over her, cradling her shoulders in my arm, gathering her perfect body to mine. She works a hand between us, grips my hard cock. I moan into her hair, and she aims it lower, poising it just right. Together, we breathe, our chests expanding as if bracing for impact. The impact of what this means, maybe. Of how this is rewriting my DNA in real time. Of life before, now, and *after*, as we set this alchemical reaction in motion and see if it makes gold.

I push in, she clasps my face in her hands, staring into my eyes as she cries out in pleasure, and it is—it's *gold.*

A thousand glimmering shades of *gold.*

CHAPTER TWENTY-TWO

NOMI

The first thing I'm cognizant of is *happy*. The emotion stretches luxuriously within my body as I blink toward consciousness, without me fully understanding why or where it came from. The warm cocoon wrapped around me feels safe and complete, putting me at perfect temperature equilibrium in the cold air whirring from the window unit. I just had the best sleep of my life.

Perhaps wildest of all, I feel *hungry*. Not from weed and not the false hunger that sometimes precedes a Crohn's attack, either. Just pleasantly, normally, hungry. A body asking for what it needs. I let my eyes flutter shut and relish the feeling.

With chronic illness, you learn to notice and celebrate the brief interludes where nothing hurts and everything's working as it should. Then you systematically interrogate everything you did, looking for answers to finally escape the locked dungeon of your disease. But as my sleepy brain trawls over the food I ate yesterday, the strain I vaped, it doesn't add up. A greasy, decadent spread of boardwalk food doesn't make me feel like this.

The warm pressure at my hipbone materializes into a hand, flexing one finger at a time. The cool tip of a nose burrows into my hair, warm breath cascading across my neck, coalescing into a word as soft as my pillow.

"Nomi."

His hand skims down the slope of my stomach, pinkie brushing the edge of my dark, unshaved curls, lighting up my entire core with a giddy rush.

Julian.

That's what's different. I don't believe Julian and his magical cock fucked my disease away or anything, but maybe giving in to these feelings that have been building within me for months released a stress my sensitive body has struggled to handle. There's also fascinating evidence that orgasms activate your parasympathetic nervous system, inducing a state of calm at the biochemical level, which can in turn dampen the damaging impacts of increased cortisol so common in those who suffer from inflammatory bowel disease. Simply put, Julian didn't fuck me cured, but he *might* have fucked me chill.

Maybe he's my doctor, after all.

He draws me against him. I've never fit so perfectly anywhere in my life as I do in the crescent moon of his strong, sheltering body.

Spooning. I finally get it.

"Good morning." I turn so that my cheek brushes his lips. My hand caresses his stubbly jaw, and he kisses my palm, drawing a fingertip into his mouth and gently sucking. I exhale a soft rush of air as his hand travels lower, finding my split and stroking the quickly swelling bud there. I press greedily against his palm, delighted with how much of me can be covered by one of his long, graceful hands. He slides down until the heel of his palm presses against my clit, slipping his middle finger inside of me, then another, stretching me deliciously as he strokes into me. His thick erection nestles between the halves of my ass, waiting to explore me next as I tremble against him.

"*Nomi, Nomi, my Nomi*…" he whispers into my hair, then licks the back of one ear. His hips grind against me while he works me, easily, with his hand. "I was so afraid it was all a dream."

I come hard, sandwiched between the pressure of his hand and the wall of his groin. "Can I, baby? *Please?*" he asks into my ear, and I moan out a desperate *yes*. God, I love it when he begs. Before the shudders are done, he flips me onto my stomach, rolls on a condom, and enters me from behind. My muscles clench and release around the sudden presence of his cock, the orgasm renewed, heightened, amplified, his palm reaching around to press hard against my clit once again as I rock against him, around him, *with him*. He pushes deeper and deeper still, as if he'd lose himself in me if he could.

Up until now, we've both tried to be quiet, but when he comes, he releases a straight-up roar. We collapse against the mattress in a heap of limbs, then he rolls onto his back, and I curl into his arms, my cheek pressed against his chest.

"How am I supposed to live now?" He idly brushes my hair back from my face. "How am I supposed to get out of this bed and eat breakfast? Go to work next week? How am I supposed to do anything else, ever again?"

I laugh into the divot between his pecs, where the hair is softest, completely blissed out. I feel almost stoned from the rush of serotonin and dopamine flooding my body. "I don't know. How have you coped with this issue in the past?"

He tips my chin up. "What past? This has never happened to me."

I arch an eyebrow. "Julian D'Angelo, the most intense man alive, has never gotten this horny before?"

He frowns at me, his hair so adorably mussed and imperfect that it makes me want to hide every brush and comb in New Jersey. "I'm telling you that I have never, not once, looked at someone and felt like my entire life's finally begun."

My throat tightens, and I struggle to swallow as the pale-blue lakes of his eyes reflect my face back to me. "You can't say stuff like that after one night together, Julian. You'll scare the women away."

"Good. I don't want other women. I only want you."

"Fine. You'll scare *me* away."

"I don't believe that." His serious face transforms into a slow, knowing smile as he brushes his finger against my cheek. "You've seen all my scariest sides, Nomi, and you're still here with me now, looking at me like that. So, forgive me for telling you the truth, even when it's scary, even when it's too much. Besides, I think you like my too much."

"I do," I whisper, still strangely choked. In a world where so many are terrified of being cringe, of being seen and judged and found ridiculous, Julian's unabashed insistence on being himself might be my favorite thing about him. It's a form of bravery, I think. A confidence that transcends the small-minded fear of others' opinions. In *this* day and age? Where every text is carefully calculated to show just enough interest not to be embarrassing, to never fully put your feelings on display, always maintaining your ability to walk away and appear utterly unscathed, Julian's full-throttle devotion feels like a homecoming. A relief.

And also? Way, *way* too serious.

"We should talk."

"Alright. Let's talk." He regards me patiently, almost amused, as I clear my throat.

"As I have mentioned, I don't date." I watch him closely, but his expression doesn't change.

"Good. Me, either."

"Good?" I blink, wondering how I got off so easy here. "Okay, then. We're in agreement. We're *not* dating."

"Right," Julian agrees, pulling me fully atop him. "We're skipping dating and going straight to being together."

"*Julian!*" I laugh despite my intentions to be serious as he bites his bottom lip into his mouth and bucks me lower onto his lap, where his thick cock swells between my legs. "I thought we could, you know. Be casual. Have some—*fun*." My moan splits up the sentiment.

"What a pretty little liar you are, Wyeth," Julian pants out, smirking as his thumb finds my clit and bears down, hard. "You never thought that *I* could be *casual* about you. Admit it."

I whimper as I settle onto his cock, and his slack-jawed smile curls into that insolent grin, all the confession that he needs.

By the time we mosey into the kitchen, Eve is already up and baking. "Muffins," she announces grandly. "With honeyed peaches and oats."

"And weed?" I ask.

"Without, actually," Eve responds airily. "I figured the doctor might enjoy some sobriety this morning. But these are for the rest of us." She reveals a platter of pale-green blondie bars under aluminum foil and grins wickedly.

She delivers a muffin and banana to Julian, along with a mug of coffee and a little smile. "Thanks for taking care of my number one all night, Doc. Glad you're here."

Julian's expression goes impossibly touched at the gesture, his eyebrows folding into a single, perfect arch. "Thank you for inviting me. This has been the best weekend of my life."

Eve presses a hand quickly to her chest and sniffs, a frankly *wild* display of emotion for her toward a straight white man, then pushes his plate to him on the bar. "Go on, eat up. I even added some protein powder. You've got to keep your strength up the way you two are going." She winks, and Julian salutes, while I sigh and grab a blondie. I knew she wouldn't let us off the hook today, not after she came stumbling into our room at two a.m. while I was riding Julian like a seesaw, screaming "*Pumpkin!*" but unwilling to stop for even a minute. But if there's one thing I'm picking up from Julian, it's that feeling embarrassed is overrated.

I make my way to the couch, not quite bowlegged but pushing it, and grab my phone from where it's been charging overnight. I flip through all my usual notifications—texts from Mom, pictures sent from Graham and Eve as they terrorized a mini-golf course last night, then flip over to email. Most of it's trash, but one subject line makes my heart rate spike:

NOTICE OF ZONING HEARING

I toss down the uneaten blondie and click on the email, my eyes racing over the lines of text.

Ms. Wyeth:

You are hereby summoned to appear in front of the Sparrow Nook Zoning Commission on August 15th at 6 p.m. for the hearing referenced above. While the zoning commission received a request to withdraw the complaint initially filed against your dispensary by Dr. J. D'Angelo, the commission finds merit in the complaint as presented and as further supported by its independent investigation. Accordingly, the zoning commission has decided to hear the case, sua sponte. As per your rights under City Ordinance 25-23489(b), you may present your case for the legality of your proposed use, along with any supporting evidence you deem relevant.

Sincerely,
Ms. Jacqueline Lombardi,
Zoning Commissioner

My hand falls limp to my side.

"Nomi?" Julian calls from around a mouthful of muffin, already noticing the shift in my mood, already concerned. The Eye of Sauron in human form. "What's wrong?"

Eve's staring at me, too, and Graham, who's just emerged from his bedroom in yesterday's swimsuit, pauses groggily in the doorway. "What did I just walk into?"

"The zoning commission granted Julian's hearing request—"

"But I withdrew—" Julian cuts in, his eyes large and panicked.

"—sua sponte," I finish. "Whatever that means."

"Latin." Graham takes a bar seat and reaches for the largest blondie. "Means *of its own accord*. When a court takes an action unprompted by a party to the case."

"This isn't fair," Julian insists. "Lombardi *knows* I withdrew it!"

Something's not adding up. This letter, Lombardi's attitude at the party, the weird things she said... My spinning thoughts catch, and I look up. "She said you're the new Wilson Phillips."

Eve frowns, full bulldog. "Like the *band*?"

"No, that weird guy at the city council meetings. Lombardi said Julian's the new Wilson." It was so weird, it stuck in my memory like a bur. "Did he give you the idea to file it?"

"No." Julian scratches his head. "Tonuto did, actually."

"What?!"

"After the city council meeting, he found me in the parking lot, and he said..." Julian pauses, remembering. "That I'd find more conservative minds on the zoning commission and to file a complaint there."

"Do you feel like he put you up to it?" I ask.

Julian frowns harder. "Everything's a sale to that guy, so...yeah. Kind of."

"Huh." Graham finishes off his blondie. "Maybe Tonuto puts people up to doing what he can't as a sitting city council member."

"And maybe Wilson's Tonuto's usual patsy," Eve says.

Wilson *does* complain a lot. The man singlehandedly keeps Sparrow Nook's municipal government in perpetual investigative mode. I always wrote off his random attacks as a retirement boredom crisis, but what if he's actually a mouthpiece for Tonuto, saying all the things Tonuto can't?

"But why's Tonuto after my dispensary?"

"He must stand to benefit by keeping you out of business," Graham ponders. "Is he tight with Damon? Do you think Tonuto's bringing you down to protect XYB?"

I press my knuckles to my mouth. "Damon was at the city council meeting that day. Maybe?"

"We've got to go to the press with this!" Eve starts scrolling through her contacts list. "Does anyone know a press?"

"Pressss-sah," Graham hisses. "Pressssss-SUH?"

Well. The blondies have hit.

I glance at Julian, the only other straight-brained person in the room. He's as flummoxed as I am. How do I figure out what Tonuto's really up to? I could go to Min or Shar *if* I had a shred of evidence. But I don't.

All I have is a zoning hearing, two weeks to prepare for it, and an ill, clenching feeling in my gut that everything's about to go very, very wrong.

JULIAN

Dread grips my chest as Nomi crumples on the couch. I rush over and sit beside her, placing my arm around her back.

She lets me.

For now, a knowing voice whispers inside of me. *But you both know you've fucking ruined it.*

Is that all I'll get? One perfect night with Nomi before it all comes crashing down? While she slept so soundly, I barely slept at all, practically vibrating with the intensity of my happiness. I held her close to me, tucked her into the shell of my body, and nothing's ever felt so right.

I can't lose her.

"I promise you, I'm going to make this okay." My words are too loud, pitched to drown out the nasty certainty buzzing through me that I *can't* make this okay, and everyone knows it.

Nomi meets my eyes with a distant expression. She looks as convinced as I feel.

"I'll hire a lawyer—the best. We'll work night and day to put our case together. When's the hearing?"

"Two weeks." Nomi exhales shakily.

"Then we better get to work."

She nods, then turns to Eve. "Sorry to bail, but I'm not going to be any fun with this looming over me. I need to figure this out."

"Are you sure you're okay? Leaving with *this guy*?" Eve gestures at me with such comic disdain, I'd feel offended if she hadn't just made me breakfast.

Nomi's lips draw up into a sad smile. "Yeah. He's got to make this up to me, and besides, I love a good grovel."

A metric ton of pressure lifts from my chest. I sink to my knees in front of her, taking her hands in mine.

"Baby, I'm gonna grovel so hard."

"Ew, *gross*." Eve recoils, then points toward the door. "Get out of my beach house, the both of you."

"*My* beach house, you mean?" Graham reaches for another blondie, which, bold. "Oh, and can you make us some coffees before you go, man?"

After coffee chores are complete and Nomi hops in the shower, I grab my phone. "Going for a walk—I'll be back in twenty."

Graham's lying in the middle of the floor while Eve finds *Live Free or Die Hard*, the controversial winner of the Bruce Willis Service Area poll. Neither pays me any attention.

The second my flip-flops hit concrete, I pull up my messages. I consider calling Eric, but he can't help me with this. I need a special bench of expertise, and a deep one. The fact is, the D'Angelos know everyone, and chances are high that my family's got a connection we can take advantage of.

I blow out a breath, rejoin the family chat I keep deleting, and draft a multiparagraph explanation of the entire situation, complete with how important Nomi is to me, how badly I've screwed up, and how desperate I am for this hearing to resolve in our favor. I also throw in a sincere apology for not texting more, just to sweeten the pot. It takes mere seconds before the first text rolls in.

The D'Angelo Family Sex Gods

AUNT EDNA

New phone, who dis

MARCO

HEYOOOOOOOOO

ALDO

Bro, congrats about Nomi! Also, Aunt Edna just OWNED YOU, SON!

MOM

I have a son?

MOM

A son who knows how to text?

JULIAN

I knew this was a mistake. If you're not willing to help me, just say so.

AUNT EDNA

🤣🤣🤣 of course we're going to help you! What did I tell you about that butthole 😠

MARCO

👀 What DID Aunt Eddie tell you about your butthole???

ELLIO

This sounds concerning.

ALDO

My interest is peeked. Peaked?

MARCO

Piqued.

ALDO

Thanks, bro.

ALDO

Your butthole has piqued my interest.

VERONICA D'ANGELO-BORK

OMG, does Nomi know there's something wrong with your butthole?

JULIAN

There's nothing wrong with my butthole!!

AUNT EDNA

Acceptance is the first step to unclenching.

VINNY D'ANGELO, ESQUIRE

if you clowns are done talking about his butthole, can we get down to business?

JULIAN

VINNY D'ANGELO, ESQUIRE

Let's meet today to discuss. Who can host?

AUNT EDNA

Let's meet here. I'll lie in my hospital bed and help you scheme.

MOM

Let's make it a cookout! I'll send a spreadsheet out for dish sign-ups.

MARCO

Say... 3 p.m.?

ALDO

Party O'Clock!

ELLIO

I'll bring the ping-pong balls.

JULIAN

...really?

I swallow, weirdly touched by the messages streaming across my screen. It's a mix of arguing over who makes the best potato salad and who knows who on the zoning commission, and in Vinny's case, a piercing interrogation over the original complaint's contents, whether Nomi has been contacted by any zoning investigators, and if so, who. I didn't realize he had so much experience in front of the zoning commission, but apparently him and Veronica often team up to get the zoning outcomes their clients need, a tit-for-tat, keep-it-in-the-family situation between a real estate agent and the lawyer that helps her get her way. I hadn't known, but why would I? When have I *ever* deigned to talk to Vinny? I always avoided him because he's Gino's son, but Vinny saw what went down at the party, and he didn't call me out. There's clearly more to Vinny than I thought.

To *all* my family, really.

The fact that everyone's pulling together for me and Nomi, thinking hard about how to get us out of this trouble, means more than I can say.

Maybe Nomi's right, and I haven't given them the chance to love me the ways they know how. But I feel it right now.

I *feel it.*

CHAPTER TWENTY-THREE

NOMI

I wish I had a nice, normal self-destructive habit. Drunk-texting exes, like Graham. Falling in love with bartenders, like Eve. Spending two hundred bucks at the Container Store on organizational systems I never implement, like Mom. But no, in this regard, I am a classic overachiever. Whenever life is going great, I get sick. When life is going badly, I get even sicker.

I haven't been able to eat for three days.

Every time I do, the cramping begins. Painful, gripping cramps that feel like burning ropes wrapped around my insides, searing into me. I spend half my days in the bathroom, begging for the attack to begin so the painful cramps will finally stop. But that's another way Crohn's screws with you. When there's no bathroom, or you're stuck in traffic, or your plane's beginning the ascent and it's *federally illegal* to get up, that's when the urgency hits. But when you're home, safe and alone? The cramps persist for hours. The kind of pain you can't watch TV through, or play on your phone, or do anything other than rock back and forth and beg for it to stop.

But tonight, I'm *not* home, safe and alone. I'm at my dispensary-that-can't-dispense, in a booth with Julian, Veronica, and Vinny, discussing our case for the fourth night this week, which means I'm on borrowed time. The only way I've been able to hang as long as I have is by starving myself and taking frequent hits off my heaviest CBD strain. It's very low on THC, and my mind's still clear, but I *feel* Julian's eyes every time I press the vape to my lips.

I take a small sip of my protein shake, the only thing sustaining me this week, and nod at whatever Veronica's saying. She's listing other boundary-pushing businesses that have been granted approval, outlining how they're similar to Stranger Drugs so we should be approved, too. Vinny's taking notes, making thoughtful arguments, and Julian's sitting there, half in awe of his cousins' fast-paced back-and-forth strategizing, half with a worried eye on me.

After Edna's impromptu Save Stranger Drugs cookout last weekend, it's been a D'Angelo full-court press ever since. While Vinny and Veronica are heading the legal front, Edna is overseeing the family's social-political machinations, all from her bedside. It was truly something to behold, how this tiny, sick woman lit up with a problem to solve and a mission to execute, surrounded by her loving family. I felt guilty seeing Edna muster so much effort when my own motivation feels like air leaking from a punctured tire. But that's always what happens when I have a bad flare-up—my will gets drained away as weight peels off, and my disease starves me into depressed, resentful submission.

"I'll draft up the business comparators section of the brief, you take the introduction, legal standards, and persuasive case law supporting the commercial zoning designation." Veronica pins Vinny with her gaze, but he just gives her a thumbs-up as he jots more notes. He glances up at me, a thick, shiny lock escaping his slicked-back hair. "How're the community testimonials going? D'you have your volunteers lined up?"

I shift in my seat, sitting straighter. "Yep. I've got three clients to speak on our behalf, and written letters of support from five others."

Vinny frowns. “We need more, a blitz. We need the Commission to realize that everyone they’ve ever admired and respected will go *apeshit* if they don’t have access to your dispensary.”

My belly instantly clenches, but Julian covers my hand with his. “We’re on it.” He looks at me, a half-smile exposing one slutty dimple. “If we can get half the people that terrorized me on your behalf to help, that’ll be plenty.”

God, he’s hot. But the cramp seizing me digs in, and sweat dots my forehead. I slip my hand out from underneath his and try to smile back. “I’ll—send another text out.”

He frowns a little as I make more distance between us, but I hate being touched when I’m sick.

“What about the Tonuto sabotage angle?” I ask.

Veronica’s lacquered lips form a straight line. “Tonuto’s the city council representative for the Commission and attends every meeting. We can’t afford to bring it up unless we have hardcore evidence against him.”

“I don’t know if it’s worth it.” Vinny grimaces. “We’ll be making an enemy for life, Veronica.”

“Everybody knows Tonuto’s up to shit.” Veronica takes a long pull from her seltzer. “We just have to catch him at it. Has anyone talked to his guy Wilson?”

Vinny rolls his eyes. “Wilson’s never gonna spill against Tonuto while he’s on the payroll.”

“What about Sammy DiFiore?” Everyone stops to look at me.

“From Sammy’s Steaks?” Vinny frowns. “Why him?”

“He seems to be Wilson’s number one punching bag.” I shrug. “Maybe he’s got Tonuto theories.”

“Can’t hurt,” Veronica says. “Nomi, you talk to Sammy. I’ll try shaking something out of Wilson.”

After Vinny and Veronica head out, Julian hangs around while I lock up.

"Alright, then. Good night." My voice chirps with a false brightness, and I start walking down the sidewalk.

"Nomi, wait." Julian places a too-warm hand on my shoulder. The feeling makes me cringe in the already muggy air. "Can I drive you home?"

I shrug off his hand. "No, that's okay. I want to walk."

"You've been vaping a lot tonight. Are you—"

"I'm not stoned, and even if I was, I'd be fine to walk home." My smile turns tight.

Julian frowns. "I know—I saw you pack the vape with the high CBD, low THC strain that you got for Ms. Peters's fibromyalgia. I was going to ask whether you're feeling alright." His eyes study my face, my sweat-damp hair, the dark circles beneath my eyes. "Are you okay?"

I soften beneath his caring, concerned eyes. I didn't realize he'd recognize what I was using. But of course Julian would. He's one of the most observant people I've ever known. The fact that he was watching me, not out of judgment like I'd feared but out of knowing concern, reminds me how much he's grown.

"Is it anxiety?" He offers his hand, and this I can take. I slide my palm against his, letting him clasp his strong fingers around mine. "About the hearing?"

I exhale deeply, grateful for the excuse that's as true even as it's not. "Yeah, it's just—really stressing me out."

"Let me take you home. Let me help."

"You're already helping so much." Even though Julian's full time at the clinic, he spends every non-working hour deep in case preparation beside me. He's been relentless, even when I've been too sick to work and forced to scrounge up excuses covering my absence, he keeps on anyway, carrying the work forward on my behalf.

"Nomi," he says my name so softly. "Please?"

Ugh, I'm a slut for his begging. I can't keep avoiding alone time with him forever, and more than that, I don't want to. This last week, I've missed Julian. It feels crazy since I see him almost every day at our working sessions, but every night, I've pushed him away, keeping my distance, trying to give my body the privacy it needs to be sick.

But a ride home can't hurt, can it?

I breathe out. "Okay."

The short, air-conditioned drive to my house is admittedly much more pleasant than the longer humid walk would've been. When he arrives, he runs his fingers along the steering wheel then smiles at me sweetly. "Can I come inside?"

"Julian, I—" I begin, feeling guilty and torn and so tired of my body making choices I hate for me.

"It's okay. I understand why you don't want me to."

My eyes widen.

"I've done nothing but make your life complicated since I've returned, and while I'm trying to undo all the damage I've caused, I haven't fixed any of it yet. I don't deserve to be with you when I've done so much wrong, but I swear to you, I'm going to make it right. I don't want you to pretend you're not angry with me when you have every right to be. I just—miss you, and I want to be with you a little longer, if that's okay." He leans his head against the headrest, still facing me. "I'll be quiet. I'll do your dishes, or laundry, or whatever you need. Just—please. Don't make me leave. Not yet."

My heart squeezes at the little boy staring at me through this man's eyes, still convinced he doesn't deserve love until he earns it. I hate that this hearing has become another external contest he believes he must win to be worthy of acceptance. But I'm not willing to tell him the real reason I've been hiding from him, either. This—whatever it is between us—just began, and I'm not confident it could survive the truth of my disease. I've only just gotten Julian to accept the value cannabis has for other people's health. How will he look at me when he learns *I* need it to cope, too? Like I'm something broken that needs to be fixed? That I'm his patient to be treated instead of a woman who wants his touch? How could a doctor who wholeheartedly believes in Western medicine understand why I've spent the last five years running from it? Would he really be able to hear how it's failed me, over and over again?

Would he believe me?

Because I don't think I could handle it if he didn't.

The cramps seize my middle, and my eyes sting with tears. I have to go, *now*. "I'm sorry, Julian. I—can't. Not tonight."

His face crumples in disappointment as I bound out of the car and race to my front door, barely making it inside in time.

CHAPTER TWENTY-FOUR

JULIAN

By the time my last appointment of the day rolls around, I'm tired, and in the good way. At first, I resented all these small-issue appointments. Physicals, sore throats, checkups—they felt like a huge waste of my time and knowledge. But that was when I was looking at them as one-offs, thirty minutes with a person I'd never see again. That's how it is in a big-city ER. Most patients are not repeat visitors, and while before, thirty minutes with me might mean saving someone's life, thirty minutes here meant me getting increasingly frustrated as I try to give a highly mobile, highly *vocal* three-year-old her vaccinations.

But now, I see this position clearly. These people with their broken fingers and flu swabs aren't one-offs—they're long-term subjects with case histories full of questions. By the third visit with Mrs. Binardo for a recurrent UTI, we finally figured out she was suffering from kidney stones that were caused by insufficiently treated diabetes, trapping her in a vicious cycle of UTIs. When a young couple brought in their colicky six-month-old in the middle of the night for a horrifying bloody diaper, I didn't stop researching until we worked out the culprit—cow's milk protein intolerance passing through the mother's breastmilk. And when Charlie received the first bottle of his Epidiolex prescription CBD oil through the special savings program I got him into, complete with a legal prescription he can take to school?

I felt like I won the Nobel Prize.

So, this morning when I saw Mr. Gutierrez booked the last appointment with *me* today, pride at how far I've come as a doctor surged through me. I'm grateful Mr. Gutierrez trusts me with his care, and moreover, I'm excited to be his doctor. Ever since Nomi assigned all that reading on Parkinson's disease, I've continued to seek out more information about the condition. I've always enjoyed the study of medicine, but having a real person looking to me to help them navigate their tricky disease adds so much urgency and meaning to the endeavor.

I want to help, and I feel good knowing I can.

When Mr. Gutierrez arrives for his appointment, I knock briskly on the exam room's door, then step inside.

"Mr. Gutierrez, good to see you," I say, finding I truly mean it. I hold out my hand.

He looks at it, then his own where it's pinned tense at his side, his teeth gritted. He exhales in a burst of frustration. "I'm sorry, Dr. D'Angelo. I'm having a bad movement day."

My face softens as I take in the rigid lock of his shoulder, the contorted posture of his spine, and his shallow, rapid breathing. "When did the inability to move start?"

Mr. Gutierrez closes his eyes briefly. His brow is beaded with sweat, despite the icy air-conditioning of the clinic. "Three days ago, maybe?"

"Any other change in symptoms?" I'm already drawing up his chart in the system, scanning the vital signs taken today and comparing them against the last visit. Both heart rate and blood pressure significantly elevated. A loss of five pounds. A *fever.*

"I've had a bad stomach virus this week. It's mostly passed."

I bite my lower lip in. A virus could explain the change in vital signs, but Mr. Gutierrez suffers primarily from dyskinesia—erratic and involuntary movement. This akinesia, or inability to move, is new. "Any change in medications or strains?"

Mr. Gutierrez tries to shake his head, then curses. "Just over-the-counter medication for my stomach."

I take the names and his guessed dosages, then run a search in the medical database for drug interactions, but nothing. On a hunch, I fill a small paper cup with water and hand it to Mr. Gutierrez's left hand, which is still able to move, albeit roughly and with effort.

"Please, drink this." I watch closely as he brings the cup to his mouth, then struggles to swallow the sip of water, choking and spluttering. I stand up immediately, taking the water and patting his back until the coughing subsides.

Difficulty swallowing.

"Mr. Gutierrez, I believe you're at the beginning of an akinetic crisis, likely brought on by failure to absorb your levodopa due to the ongoing diarrhea you're experiencing. You need to go to the hospital right now."

"The *hospital*?" Mr. Gutierrez cries. "Which hospital?"

"Your neurology team is out of Philly Gen, right?"

"Yes, but how am I supposed to get to Philadelphia?" Mr. Gutierrez tries to shake his head again and groans in frustration. "I had to call a car to get here!"

I buzz Khalil at the front desk for a wheelchair, then help him up to standing when it arrives.

"I'm taking you." I wheel him in a quick jog toward the door. "I'm your doctor, after all."

I send Nomi a flurry of texts since she's Mr. Gutierrez's emergency contact, but I can't wait for a response before getting him to the hospital. I just hope she reads them. I've been trying to give her the space she needs, but every day she's felt more distant. I keep telling myself that once we win the hearing, we'll pick up where we left off, but *can* we? Or is she making Wildwood a casual, one-off thing, after all? The thought feels like a screwdriver grinding into my sternum, taking me apart.

The drive to Philly Gen passes in a blur of brake lights, toll plazas, and insane New Jersey drivers, seriously, what is *wrong* with my people? As we cross the Ben Franklin bridge into Philadelphia, a sea of high-rises greets us. Crossing this bridge used to feel like an escape hatch out of being a D'Angelo and the baggage that name holds in Sparrow Nook, the city's skyline filling me with visceral relief.

But now, it's just a skyline. A perspective that no longer fits. And as I glance at Mr. Gutierrez's rigid body laid out in the front seat of my car, it's a means to getting my patient the help he needs, urgently.

We roll up to the hospital's valet, and I leap from the car, calling for a wheelchair as I throw my keys to the attendant. I push Mr. Gutierrez through the patient entrance to the ER. It's chilling, being on this side of the equation.

I charge through the reception area, ready to use him like a wheel-bound battering ram to get to the back.

"Excuse me, sir? *SIR.*" The reception desk attendant stands and yells through the hole in the glass safety partition.

Shit. Cynthia. ER physicians have a somewhat fraught relationship with administrative staff, and for good reason. They think we're dramatic entitled shitheads, and... well. We are.

Mr. Gutierrez whimpers as I abruptly freeze, then wheel him toward the desk. I take a deep breath as I approach, my left wrist tingling ominously like a dickhead portent.

Lower your fists, Julian, Nomi's voice reminds me, the proverbial angel sitting on my shoulder. *You don't need to come out swinging.*

"Dr. D'Angelo?" Cynthia's stern voice turns baffled as I smile through the window. "What're *you* doing here?"

"Hey, Cynthia." I smile at the second attendant, too. "Hey, Dashonda. Listen, I need your help getting this patient admitted to the Neuro ICU immediately, skipping straight past the ER wait. What can you do for us?"

"Why are you wheeling random old people up to my desk, asking for things you know I can't do?" Cynthia folds her arms. "We have a protocol, Dr. D'Angelo."

I breathe deeply. "I wouldn't ask you to break protocol unless I was certain that's what this patient needs. And he needs help right now, Cynthia. He cannot afford to wait."

Cynthia eyes me doubtfully.

"I'll take whatever heat comes for breaking protocol, I swear. And don't tell me you can't get around the rules. You know this place inside and out."

It's true, I'm not saying this to suck up to her. Cynthia's been here for twenty years and runs this whole floor.

Her eyebrows lift. "Something's happened to you." She gestures at the entirety of me with one finger. "This is weird."

"Please, Cynthia? I won't ask for anything else, ever again. And—and I'll make you a coffee and bring it to you after I get him settled." I clasp my hands together. "Heavy cream, light on the sugar, right? You want one, too, Dashonda?"

Dashonda looks alarmed. "Um, yes?"

Cynthia presses her eyes closed and sighs. "Fine, but if Dr. Riveras comes at me for this, I'm sending her your way."

"Thank you, Cynthia!" I call out over my shoulder as she presses the button, and the doors to the back open.

"And no Splenda!" Cynthia yells after me. "Cane sugar, you hear me?"

After I get Mr. Gutierrez buzzed into the Neuro ICU and snatch my favorite neurologist for him, I head to the breakroom to fulfill my coffee promises. I brew a fresh pot, get them fixed up just right, and am about to head back to the reception area when a throat clears behind me.

"Dr. D'Angelo. What the *hell* are you doing here?"

I wince, then spin slowly, holding the coffees. "Dr. Riveras . . . great to see you."

Her eyebrow's arched as she blocks the way out.

I sigh. "Listen, I'll explain, but can you walk with me while I do? I need to deliver these before they get cold." Dr. Riveras's frown deepens, but hot coffee is sacred at Philly Gen, so grudgingly, she follows me to reception while I tell her everything: Mr. Gutierrez's ongoing issues, the akinesia, my suspicions for diagnosis, and because Cynthia's already giving big narc energy as we approach, how I convinced the staff into letting me bypass the ER straight for the Neuro ICU.

Dr. Riveras grunts as I pass Cynthia's and Dashonda's coffees over the partition. "This is all very . . ."

I brace myself for the worst. *Out of line. Irresponsible. Entitled.*

". . . weird."

"Right?" Dashonda takes a big sip of her coffee and *mmms* to herself.

Dr. Riveras folds her arms. "It's frankly bewildering to see you taking your primary care position so seriously, Julian. I must admit, I didn't expect you to rise to the occasion."

"I didn't, either," I reply honestly. "But you were right, about everything. It's taught me how to listen, get my head out of my own condescending ass, and improve my nonexistent people skills," I say, repeating everything she said in that first fraught meeting when she decided to have mercy and not fire me on the spot. "It's been very good for me, Dr. Riveras. I owe you so much. Thank you."

Dr. Riveras's bottom lip drops open as I head back to the Neuro ICU.

"I've got to run now," I call over my shoulder. "I want to catch up with Dr. Adebayo about her recommendations for my patient's treatment. See you around, Dr. Riveras!"

I check my phone. Nomi's texted back, and my heart flutters in happiness at the three little words: *On my way!*

NOMI

The door chimes as I enter Sammy's Steaks, the crackling beef inducing instant meat lust. I've barely eaten all week. While a steak would destroy me right now, it smells like a great way to go.

"Ms. Wyeth," Sammy says from behind the cash register, pronouncing my last name as if there's no *h* sound, but with such propriety it makes me straighten my back. "Right this way."

I follow Sammy into a back office that smells like freshly baked bread. I breathe deeply and settle into the chair opposite his desk, which is inexplicably covered in a pretzel party platter, one of my only safe foods during a flare. The soft, unoffensive carbs and the little chunks of salt just go down easy.

"Care for a pretzel?" His hands hover over the plastic tray top.

"Abso*lutely*."

Pleased, he removes the lid, and I help myself. This is already the best interview I've ever conducted.

Sammy sits back, his hands folding across his stomach. "How can I help you?"

"Long story short, I suspect Mike Tonuto's out to get me, and I think you know what that's like." I watch him closely for a reaction, but there's no need because there's nothing subtle about Sammy DiFiore. He belts out a laugh.

"What's my brother done now?"

I blink. "Your *brother*?"

"*Half* brother, he'd want me to say. *Half*." Sammy's good-natured smile turns pained. "We're not close."

"Do you believe he's behind all the attention your business gets from the city council?" I take a big bite of pretzel and pull up my notes. Audits, inspections, health code complaints, Wilson even tried getting the building designated as a historical landmark so Sammy couldn't add a back patio. It was built in 1974! They've really put Sammy through the wringer.

"Oh, a hundred percent. Mikey thinks he runs this town, and he uses that sycophant Wilson to do his bidding." Sammy huffs. "Why, what'd you do to piss him off?"

"I don't know. I was hoping you could help me figure that out."

"I do have a theory." Sammy squints at me. "You're trying to open the dispensary across the street, right?"

I nod as I swallow the last bite of pretzel, then reach for another.

"Well, I guarantee you that whatever he's doing to you, it's probably intended to hurt me."

"But how?"

"Like you said—your dispensary will drive up people's appetites in the area and bring hungry clientele to the downtown restaurant district." Sammy tosses his hands. "Who's across the street? Who owns a restaurant? Me. Mikey's public enemy number one."

"Do you mind telling me what happened between you two?" I wince. "I'm not trying to pry, but I've got a hearing in two days in front of the zoning commission, and if I don't find a way to win it, I'm going to lose everything."

"No, I don't mind. It stopped hurting a long time ago." Sammy shakes his head. "Our mother, Belinda, married Mikey's dad first, Stan Tonuto. Stan was in the car business, and Mom always wanted to start her own steak shop. By the time she opened, she was six months' pregnant with Mikey."

"Belly's Steaks," I murmur, remembering the shop across from Strange Drugs in the model of Sparrow Nook.

"Aw, you know of it?" Sammy smiles, his eyes twinkling. "It was a great shop. Mom really knew how to make a steak. Well, Stan passed when Mikey was two or three, and Mom remarried *my* dad a few years after that, Buddy DiFiore. I came along shortly thereafter, and then Mikey had a new stepdad *and* a new little brother, and that didn't sit well with him. Mikey's never liked to share. Dad adopted him, and we grew up as brothers, only five years apart, but you'd have thought Mikey was my second dad, the way he bossed me around. We spent all our time in the shop, and when we were tall enough not to get a face full of grease burns, we started working here, too. Mikey worked the grill while I was on the line, but he constantly ragged me, even then." Sammy's face twists into a sad smile. "Poor Mom was next to go—had a heart attack right at the counter. She left Belly's Steaks to us in equal shares, which pissed off Mikey. He felt like he should be sole owner on account of him being oldest. We co-managed the shop for a while, but the quality really suffered. One day, your steaks would be finely chopped, another day, they'd be minced. Some days Cooper sharp, others provolone. Always Sarcone's rolls, thank God, but that's the only thing we agreed on. Until everything blew up for good."

"What happened?" I lean forward in my seat.

"Cheez Whiz happened, that's what. It was all the rage, and I wanted to offer it, too. But Mikey didn't want to change anything from how Mom ran the shop, and every time someone tried to order their steak wiz wit, Mikey'd shit a brick. When he found out I'd been offering it under a secret code word when he wasn't there, we had a huge falling out. Mikey demanded I buy him out, so I did, and he used the money to start his own car dealership, just like his 'real dad.' All's well that ends well, right?" Sammy shakes a pretzel at me. "*Wrong!* According to Mikey, I started making too many changes. First the Cheez Whiz, then offering seating, but once I renamed the shop to Sammy's Steaks, he's been out to get me ever since."

"Geez." I sit back. "Do you have any proof?"

"I consulted with a lawyer, but she said all I had was circumstantial evidence, which wouldn't be enough." Sammy sighs. "I keep hoping he'll get tired of ragging me so hard, but it's been fifty years of his bullying, and everybody just looks the other way. The city council doesn't care, I'll tell you that much. They're afraid of Mikey, too."

I blink. "But how do we catch him?"

"I wish I knew." Sammy munches on his pretzel stick thoughtfully. "The weird thing is Mikey's always had his eye on your building. Thought for sure he'd try to lease it himself so he could spite me from across the street. I was shocked when you got it instead."

"Really?" I frown, thinking back to all the strings Veronica pulled to get me the first showing. Did we lease the building out from under Tonuto somehow? "How could a city council member lease a building owned by the city, though?"

"Wilson, probably. That man lives with Mikey's hand up his puppet ass."

My phone buzzes in my pocket twice in short succession, and I pull it out. "Sorry, I need to make sure this isn't important."

JULIAN

Since you are Mr. G's listed emergency contact, I'm letting you know that Mr. G is suffering from an akinetic crisis, which is potentially life-threatening. I'm driving him to Philly Gen right now.

JULIAN

Could you go to his house and grab all his medications and whatever strains he's been using, along with a change of clothes and anything else he might want?

I blink at my phone, dread erupting in my chest.

NOMI

On my way!!

After a hasty goodbye to Sammy, I race over to Mr. Gutierrez's house. The kitchen's a mess, clothes strewn around, the TV still on. But today's appointment was not an emergency one—it was a standard checkup. My heart aches as I right the place as fast as I can while packing up what Mr. Gutierrez needs. How long has he been living like this? Unable to care for himself and suffering?

I reach Philly Gen in a fugue state of worry, texting Julian as I approach the reception desk.

"Hi, I'm here for Mr. Gutierrez—Julian, I mean, um, Dr. D'Angelo brought him in about an hour ago for a suspected akinetic crisis?"

The stern attendant looks at me through the glass, one eyebrow raised. "*Julian*, eh?" She elbows the other attendant. "This one knows *Julian*."

"Oh, are you responsible then?" The second attendant smirks.

"Responsible? Oh, yes—kind of? I'm Mr. Gutierrez's emergency contact."

"No, for *Julian*."

"What?" I blink down at them. "I don't—"

"He smiled at me." The second attendant presses her hands flat against her desk. "Then he brought me coffee!"

"Me, too," the first attendant adds. "It's not even a full moon!"

I exhale a helpless, confused sound, struggling to process their gentle conversation as the bright fluorescent lights whine overhead, the smell of hospital antiseptic stinging my nose. Philly Gen is a beautiful, well-funded hospital, but you can't decorate the terror out of an ER waiting area. Memories of the last time I was here sweep over me like a flash flood. I was struggling to breathe and kept blacking out, the spontaneous allergic reaction to the newest biologic hitting me harder than ever before. My body felt tight and hot, claustrophobic, and my consciousness kept backing out of it, like it wanted to escape for good.

"Nomi." The swing-doors open in perfect tandem, revealing Julian, broad shoulders stretching out the width of his doctor's coat, glasses flashing, curly hair perfectly disheveled. He could be the top-billed star in any medical drama, Dr. McFuckMe.

He takes me into his arms and holds me to him, large hand spanning the back of my head so gently, serotonin floods my system. "I'm so glad you're here."

"Oh, she's responsible, alright," the second attendant says under her breath. "God bless."

I peer up into his eyes, incredibly grateful to see their placid blue right now. "How's Mr. Gutierrez?"

"He's in stable but rocky condition. Come on, I'll take you to him." Julian takes the duffel I've packed for Mr. Gutierrez and my bag, slings them over his shoulder, and leads me by the hand through the doors. The calming neutrals transition to pure white, the light symphonic music replaced by beeping machines and intercom announcements, secured doors and keypad locks.

This is the true face of the hospital, and it fills me with dread.

I swallow. "So, what's an akinetic crisis?"

"I didn't know, either, until I started reading more on the disease. Essentially, akinesia is the absence of movement, and it's often a sign of dopaminergic withdrawal. Sometimes an akinetic crisis is triggered by medication resistance, but luckily in Mr. Gutierrez's case, it was a GI infection that caused it."

"How's that lucky?"

"Because we can treat the bacterial infection he has with antibiotics, which in turn will help his body accept his medications again. Medication resistance is much harder to remedy. Diarrhea leads to poor medication absorption, so when he told me he'd been suffering from a stomach virus all week, I suspected that might've triggered the crisis." He leads me down a hall lined with patient rooms and busy, serious-faced nurses. "Without his medication, his body began the process of shutting down. The risk of choking is very high, and eventually, the akinetic immobility would've affected his ability to breathe."

I press a hand to my mouth. "Oh my God."

Julian stops outside of a patient room, the name on the door identifying *Franco Gutierrez* inside. He runs both hands down my arms. "He's going to be okay because we caught it in time, though he may be here for the next few days recovering. He'll be really glad to see you, Nomi."

Julian knocks lightly on the door, then sticks his head in. "Mr. Gutierrez? Quit napping—someone wants to see you."

"Julian! Don't wake him *up*!"

He turns to me, grinning. "Just kidding, he's awake. Go on in. I'm going to chat with his doctor."

I enter the small room. Mr. Gutierrez is hooked up to an army of machines, his burnished skin sallow against the hospital gown he's wearing. Beneath the cannula fitted to his nose, he still manages to smile. "My friend. Thank you for coming."

"Always, Mr. G." I rush to his side and take his hands. "Though you should've called me sooner. Your house—" I pause, not wanting to criticize, but not knowing how to put it, either.

"Looks like it belongs to a madman, I know." Mr. Gutierrez grimaces. "I'm sorry you had to see that. I get so . . . I don't know. Proud isn't the right word." He thinks for a moment. "Angry, maybe. Resentful. I hate needing so much help. I get so angry at my body for standing in the way of my life."

My eyebrows soften, and I squeeze his hands, careful not to upset the IV taped there. "I understand."

Mr. Gutierrez smiles sadly. “I know you do. You’ve been sick lately, too. Yes?”

I blow out a long breath, then nod. When Mr. Gutierrez was a new client, he struggled to trust that cannabis could offer relief until I shared my story with him. It’s easier talking about my health with someone who faces their own body’s betrayal every day. “How can you tell?”

“You’ve lost weight, and your eyes look sad.”

“I *am* sad.”

Mr. Gutierrez swallows. “I am, too.”

We sit there, witnessing each other’s feelings of helplessness, and saying nothing. Because sometimes, witnessing without platitudes is what you need most. I get why the people who love me want to solve my chronic illness; I wish wanting to solve it was all it took. But part of coming to terms with it is accepting that sometimes, you’re not okay, and it may be a long time before that changes. It looks like you’ve lost hope, which makes others feel so uncomfortable. But when hope’s based on denial, that hope can haunt you, sour your days, push you toward a never-ending hunt for the cure so you can finally go back to normal. That kind of hope prevents acceptance, which has been far more healing for me than hoping to exhaustion ever was.

“Does Julian know?”

I shake my head.

“Nomi,” he says simply.

“He won’t understand.” My eyes find Julian outside the glass window, where he stands, chin in hand, listening thoughtfully to the on-call neurologist. “He’ll panic. He’ll make me into his patient and try to fix me.”

“People never grow if we don’t challenge them to try.”

“But what if he doesn’t respect the choices I’ve made?”

“What if he does? He’s come a long way, Nomi.”

"I want to be Nomi, *just* Nomi, with him. Not Nomi who can't eat. Or Nomi crying in the bathroom. Or Nomi who shits fire."

Mr. Gutierrez smiles. "But all of those Nomis deserve to be loved. Even Nomi who shits fire."

"No, she *doesn't*." I drop his hands suddenly, standing up. His brows draw together, and I sigh. "I'm sorry. This hospital is getting to me. I've... had a hard time here before."

"I understand, dear," Mr. Gutierrez says, though his voice is pained. I hate that I did that, but I hate being here even more. Part of me is terrified that I belong here, too. Not as the doctor I once wanted to be, or a visiting friend, but as a patient. A sick person who's getting sicker. If not now, soon. Someday. When I can no longer pretend I have my health under control, which feels imminent since I've barely eaten for weeks now. And when that happens, when I finally break down and submit to the testing and specialists, what then? What will they find?

I'm not ready for my name to be on the door.

I glance back, but Julian's no longer in view. "I'm going to see what the neurologist had to say. Be right back."

With effort, Mr. G gives me a thumbs-up. I find Julian at the end of the hall, chatting with a short woman in a doctor's coat talking with big, exaggerated gestures, who claps him on the back, then leaves.

"Who was that?"

"Dr. Riveras, the hospital director."

My eyebrows rise. "The one who put you on probation?"

"The very same."

"She doesn't seem like she hates you at all."

"Right?" Julian shakes his head in wonder. "It's not even a full moon."

I struggle to smile.

"Listen, visiting hours are over. We should say goodbye for the night."

We start to go back in, but a quick glance through the window shows Mr. G out cold, snoring. I pause there, my hand on the glass, watching. He looks so frail in that bed, surrounded by machines.

"He's going to be okay, Nomi. They're taking great care of him, I promise." Julian takes my hand, running his thumb over my knuckles. "I'd like to take care of *you* tonight, if you're up for it." He smiles tentatively. "Take you back to my place, grab some dinner, maybe? You could stay the night since it's already so late."

"Oh, I ate before I came." The lie comes easily, though all I've had is a handful of chubby pretzel sticks. But I'm feeling okay, for now, the carbs having done me some good. And despite the strange brand of melancholy being in Julian's world provokes, I want to see more. I'm not ready to leave it quite yet, or him.

I've *missed* him.

"But I'd love to see your place. For a bit."

"Yeah?" His face lights up, and he squeezes my hand.

"Yeah."

The smile he gives me stays put as we head out, leaving a trail of surprised doctors, nurses, and staff in his wake. It's weird, seeing him in this environment that knows him so well. Or the old Julian, anyway. It slips onto him like a well-tailored blazer, dressing up the man I know in a professional persona I don't. He's more important here, grudgingly respected even if openly disliked, like a crown of prestige appeared on his head the second he walked in. Even in his disgrace, he's more important here than I've ever been anywhere.

We walk in the bronze glow of Rittenhouse Square's quaint streetlamps, down the park's main path to his building. His condo has more square feet than mine and Eve's apartments put together. From the outside, the building's architecture is vaguely European, with balconettes and intricate scrollwork flanking the large windows, but inside, it's all sleek and modern lofts. Exposed brick and matte-black framing the glass. Julian's bed is a massive feather-duvet affair in soft neutral tones that lies across from a wall of windows.

He sees me looking and steps behind me, gathering me into his arms. "It's beautiful in winter, when they light up the square. They hang these colored balls of light from the trees, and it paints my entire studio in rainbow." He kisses the top of my head. "It's probably the only thing I like about this place."

"What?" I turn in his arms. "It's beautiful here."

"No. It's empty here. But it's beautiful now, with you in it."

My hands drape across his neck, finding the warm stripe of skin between his button-down and slightly over-grown curls. How I've missed touching him this week, being touched *by* him. He looks as relieved as I feel to be standing here, in his arms. He holds me closer.

"Thank you." The softness in my voice reflects the softness in his gaze.

"For what?"

"For listening. For getting Mr. Gutierrez the help he needs. For saving the day." I smile ruefully as his fingers tighten against my hips.

"Thank you for showing me how." He runs his hand down my cheek, my eyes fluttering closed as the feel of his skin against mine alights across my body. "I know you've needed space, what with the hearing and everything going on, and I've tried to give it to you, even though it's been killing me not to hold you like this, but... can I kiss you now, Nomi?"

"Yes." Before the word fully sighs out, his lips press against my temple, trailing down my cheek, the tender line of my jaw.

"Oh, thank *God*," he murmurs into my skin. With one hand enmeshed in my hair and the other gripped around my hip, he lavishes my neck with the gentle, sultry slide of his mouth.

"Is this what you want?" I manage, more to the ceiling than to him. "Philly Gen? This loft? This life?" *This life that I don't fit into.*

"I always thought so," he says after a long pause, then places a kiss gently on my forehead. "I don't know anymore."

"What do you mean?" I search his face.

"I want *you*, Nomi." He searches mine right back, his eyes the cold, wintry blue of a deceptively hot flame. "Everything about you. All of you. I want your smiles and your sighs and your arguments. I want your body lying beneath mine, across my lap, in my arms, holding me down, hugging me from behind. I want to be inside of you as much as you're already inside of me." His hand caresses my jaw softly, then holds it firm. "I want your first words in the morning and your last look of the evening. I want my name on your lips, and yours in my mouth. I want *you*, Nomi. So much," he whispers as he stares into my eyes. "It doesn't leave room for anything else."

A small, soft breath trembles out of me, and he lifts me, cradling me easily to his chest, and walks me to his bed.

CHAPTER TWENTY-FIVE

JULIAN

The morning sunlight illuminates all the reds and golds hidden within Nomi's dark, shiny hair on my pillow. I feel like an explorer must, discovering new land, as I twirl a long, shimmering strand around my finger.

I would like to explore her further.

Nomi stretches her arms over her head sleepily, which pulls up the T-shirt she borrowed, revealing her pale thighs. I am butter melting against a hot potato. I groan as my body absorbs the way the curved mound of her pussy peeks beneath my shirt and tucks this information straight into my hardening dick.

She opens one eye, sees me staring, and laughs.

"What," I purr as I pull her by her exposed hip toward me.

"You look like the horniest man alive."

"I *am* the horniest man alive." I roll onto my back, bringing her on top of me, her legs parting around my thick, swelling cock. She *mmms* softly as I run my hands up her thighs, under her shirt, trailing along her ribs, pausing there. They seem more pronounced than a few weeks ago. I frown, start to say something, but Nomi brings my hands to her breasts, and *what was I going to say?*

My thumbs find her tight, excited nipples, and drag roughly down until the buds spring up, free. "God, you're perfect."

Nomi flinches, and I freeze, hands still cupping the heft of her small, perfect breasts. “Are you alright?”

“I’m fine.” Her soft laugh feels like butterflies beneath my hands, and my racing pulse slows even as her smile fades. “It’s just—I’m not perfect, Julian. Not by a long shot.” Her face is uncharacteristically pensive as she sweeps off the T-shirt and tosses it on the floor.

“Ah, but your evidence supports the opposite conclusion, Wyeth.” Jealousy floods my bloodstream at how the morning licks her body with light everywhere my mouth wants to be. My fingers wrap around her hips and guide her gently forward so I can have her for breakfast. “Allow me to *rebut*.”

After a morning spent testing my expensive mattress’s non-bounce claims, we stop by Philly Gen to check on Mr. Gutierrez. One night with antibiotics and IV administration of his regular medications, and he’s much improved. He’ll need to be in the hospital for the next few days until the choking risks have passed, but the difference in his rigidity is already stark compared to last night. Though it physically pains me, I have to say goodbye to Nomi in the parking deck afterward. She needs to drive her car back and visit some clients today, and I’m scheduled for the afternoon shift at the clinic.

“See you tonight?” I murmur into her hair, kissing the soft lobe of her ear while giving zero fucks that various hospital staff see me doing so.

“Six p.m.,” Nomi agrees, then sighs into my arms. “Our last planning meeting before the hearing.”

“It’s going to go great,” I assure her. “Vinny and Veronica know what they’re doing.”

Nomi’s mouth twists. “I wish we could prove that Tonuto’s vendetta against Sammy is at play here.”

“Me, too. But we don’t need it to win tomorrow. We can prove the dispensary is a valid use within the Main Street business zone.”

Her brown eyes, like amber pots of dark, meadow honey, lock on to mine. "I hope you're right." She leans her chin up, meeting my mouth in a kiss so soft and sweet, it almost breaks my heart. I would go to war for this woman. Fight the whole town, all of New Jersey, if it meant I could give Nomi what she wants.

The hours at the clinic pass in a pleasant, steady thrum of appointments. At the end of the day, I'm responding to messages in our patient portal when an urgent test results notification pops up. I click on it immediately, my pulse picking up as the number of abnormal values screams down the PDF. Both the C-reactive protein and ESR levels are way too high, indicating significant inflammation, and the patient's potassium and B-12 levels are very low. I frown at the results, considering the implications. Malabsorption of nutrients most often indicates gastrointestinal conditions, though it could be other serious concerns, too, like liver disease, even cystic fibrosis. My eyes flit to the top of the report, and my stomach turns to ice.

Patient: Nomi Wyeth.

Nomi's sick, *actually* sick. Oh, *fuck*, is that why she's been losing weight? My mind vomits up every bit of information I've ever inadvertently learned about Nomi's health—she has a "condition," she's badly overdue for some kind of screening. During her physical when I touched her abdomen, she winced in pain and oh! That day early in the summer when I tried to apologize to her, I briefly glimpsed that MRI report diagnosing her with a *moderate stool burden*. You don't forget those words written back-to-back about the woman of your dreams. I quickly search that phrase on the internet, but it can be indicative of many things, mostly GI-related.

My finger itches over the button for her patient records, and a wave of sick dread crashes through me.

I can't look. I *promised* I wouldn't look. But she's sick, and she isn't doing anything about it. My chest has become a tight metal locker that my heart is now slamming up against, over and over. I close my eyes, try to breathe. *There is no emergency, everyone you love is okay. There is no emergency, everyone you love is okay.* But I don't—I *can't* believe it this time.

A voice clears behind me, and I swirl around in my chair, irrationally terrified it's Nomi. My excuse is already in my mouth, *I didn't mean to look!* But it's Dr. Srinivasan standing there, his brown eyes kind. "Julian. How are you today?"

"Oh, pretty good, Dr. Appa," I wheeze out, hand pressed hard to my sternum. "You?"

His face lights up into a smile. "You called me Dr. Appa!"

I blink rapidly. "It's ah...growing on me."

"Do you have a moment, Julian? I have something I want to discuss with you."

"Sure." I quickly minimize Nomi's lab report and turn back to face him fully. I exhale a deep breath, trying to bring my careening anxiety back to the present moment. "More complaints?"

Dr. Appa laughs. "You know, I haven't received a legitimate complaint about you in ages."

"What were the illegitimate ones?"

Dr. Appa waves his hand dismissively as he takes the patient chair by the door. "Oh, Ms. Beckler thinks you should wear tighter pants."

My eyes widen in horror. Ms. Beckler's *ninety-two.*

"I was very impressed with how you handled Mr. Gutierrez's emergency, Julian." Dr. Appa looks at me sidelong. "Many doctors would've increased his medications without pausing to consider why the current dosage was no longer effective. A delay in treating that underlying bacterial infection could've cost Mr. Gutierrez critical mobility for years to come, or even his life. But you listened. You observed. And you'd already done enough research into your patient's condition to know what to look for. Because of that, you got him the help he needed and likely saved his life."

"Oh." I run my hand through my hair, surprised. "Well, I'm an ER doctor. It's all part of it, I guess."

Dr. Appa tilts his head. "But that's just it—it's not. What you did for Mr. Gutierrez was pure family medicine and really, beyond. Because of your ongoing relationship with Mr. Gutierrez, you were able to draw observations that eliminated many of the likely culprits and instead zeroed in on a rare, high-stakes complication of his disease. That's what makes a general practitioner truly excellent—the willingness to know their patients. To stay curious and informed about their conditions. To refuse to settle when the easiest explanations don't add up. You showed true partnership with Mr. Gutierrez that day, which is what being someone's primary care physician is all about. I'm impressed with you and how much you've grown these last few months, and I'm very grateful."

My chest aches with sudden emotion, my throat tightening. "Thank you, sir."

"When Gisella asked if I'd take you on for your probation, I didn't want to say yes. But she's your biggest advocate, and I respect her judgment wholeheartedly. And Gisella was right, as usual! Now, three months later, I'm retiring and would like to give you my practice." Dr. Appa chuckles to himself. "Funny how life works."

I choke on my own spit. "*What?*"

"I'm retiring at the end of December, and I'd like you to take over my practice. Oh, don't look so shocked! I'm sixty-eight years old. I've wanted to retire for ages, but I couldn't do it without knowing my patients would be well cared for. And I believe you're exactly the doctor to do it, Julian."

"Me?" My breath is coming out in short little spurts. "Your practice?"

"Yes," Dr. Appa says gamely. "On both accounts."

Staying in Sparrow Nook, long term? The idea feels like pans clanging together in my brain. I was supposed to rise up through the ranks at Philly Gen, eventually replacing Dr. Riveras one day, or perhaps moving to an even bigger city to work at an even bigger research hospital. I'm not a primary care physician—I'm an ER doctor, and a damn good one. Despite all the stress and pressure inherent in working at Philly Gen, those halls still feel like home, offering me a life that still makes sense. After seeing Dr. Riveras this week, I'm almost certain they'll take me back.

Could I really give up everything I've worked for to take this massive professional detour, landing me back where I never wanted to return? It doesn't make sense, but I *have* enjoyed these last few months in Sparrow Nook. Making friends, building relationships with patients like Mr. Gutierrez, spending time with Mom and Aunt Edna and the rest of the crazy D'Angelos.

And *Nomi*. My chest floods with giddy longing.

Would she want me to stay? Or is part of my appeal that I'm only temporary? That at the end of these six months, I'll be headed back to Philadelphia, with a river, toll bridge, and state lines between us? Would I still be as attractive with my salary cut in half and a small cottage instead of a big studio in Rittenhouse Square? More importantly, would I be the *best* for her—the best partner, the best husband, and maybe one day, the best father to our children—if all I am is a small, family doctor?

Is that version of me enough?

Our time together feels so natural and right, almost preordained, and I'm convinced she feels it, too. But if she does, why hasn't she confided in me about her illness yet? Doesn't she trust me? Doesn't she realize I'd do anything to help her?

I press a hand against my thumping chest, feeling terrified and overstimulated and absolutely *dying* to talk to Nomi about it. But with the zoning hearing tomorrow, is now really the time? "This . . . is a lot to process."

"It is," he agrees. "You'll have to decide what your priorities are. Do you want to return to your old life at Philly Gen and all the prestige it offers? I will be happy to write you a glowing recommendation letter if that's what you choose. But if you find that choosing long-term partnerships with your patients instead of brief, life-saving interludes fulfills you professionally, and that partnerships with *other* people here fulfill you emotionally," Dr. Appa says, his eyes glinting with mischief, "perhaps you'll consider making my practice your own." He raises both hands, palms facing me. "No rush. Take your time. Talk to Nomi. And more than anything, listen to your heart, Julian. I'm not sure you ever have."

With that, Dr. Appa stands and leaves me to spin out wildly into space.

NOMI

"Vibe is very important, Nomi." Veronica stands in front of my closet while I sit mutely to the side. The hearing is in two hours, and I feel terrible. This is what I get for attempting soup today. Just a bone broth with simple noodles and low sodium, and yet my body is reacting as though I decided to suck down hot lava. How can so little food cause so much pain?

"You can't roll into the hearing with your hot 1970s aesthetic. These people are conservative. We have to be strategic." She *click-clacks* in shiny black Jimmy Choo heels over to the garment bag she brought. The first option is a pale-yellow sundress with an empire waistline and big homesteader energy. She holds it up, then glances at me.

"How is that one strategic?" I hunch over, cradling my stomach. "I'd look like a toxic purity culture maiden who doesn't vote because an influencer claims it interferes with ovulation."

"Exactly. Conservatives love innocent maidens. But we could go for a different spin." She holds up a pristine Lacoste tennis dress as white as Veronica's bleached teeth. "Country club drug user. A classic."

"Pass. Nobody's gonna buy that I sport."

"Fine. That leaves only one option." She throws a wad of flouncy, colorful polyester at me, then a pair of pale-pink skinny-legged dress pants. I hold up what appears to be a giant ruffle masquerading as a top.

"Jersey girl?"

"Specifically, *Sunday-night family dinner at Mom-Mom's* Jersey girl. Now get changed. I've got to do your eyebrows."

When we arrive fully dressed and contoured with cheekbones we were not born with, Vinny's standing out front of City Hall, wearing a black leather blazer, black shirt, and black tie while Julian paces back and forth. I get the feeling Vinny dressed him, too, or maybe Marco. He's wearing high-waisted black pleated pants and a thin leather belt, a slim-cut dark purple button down with a synthetic sheen, and somebody's gelled his curls.

Excessively.

"You picked Jersey boy, too, huh?" I wobble over to him on the pale-pink patent leather heels Veronica capped my feet in, and he grabs my elbow before I teeter over.

"Specifically, *First Date at a Four-Star Italian Restaurant* Jersey boy," Vinny says for him, eyeing me over. He turns to Veronica. "Nice work. She looks like your mother."

"Upsetting," Julian leans over and whispers into my ear. "But still hot."

I manage a weak smile. "You, too."

His eyes rove over me. I'm as bronzed as the Liberty Bell, but he still sees through it. "Are you feeling okay?"

"Just anxious." I squeeze his arm and try to ignore the peals of thunder rumbling through my belly as we make our way inside.

"This meeting shall come to order." Chief Commissioner Jackie Lombardi claps the gavel down with zero flair. As she leads the introductory hearing procedures, my face heats beneath the uncomfortable mask of foundation, back prickling with sweat against the semi-sheer polyester shirt.

I pat my pocket for the over-the-counter antidiarrheal medication, a.k.a. Satan's Bargain in a foil blister pack. These ruin me. They stop the attack if I take enough of them, but that's the problem—they stop *everything.* I won't be able to go for a week after taking them, despite the eventual return of the cramps that just crash ineffectually against my shore, the metaphorical tide never coming in. Pressure builds until the medicine wears off, and the attack picks up right where it left off, even worse than before.

I've already taken two today, and I hope that'll be enough. Thanks to Vinny and Veronica, I don't have much to do. I'll be called as a witness, Vinny will lead me through a series of planned questions, and then I sit here at the defense counsel's table and look New Jersey wholesome. Easy. I can do this.

I glance at the half-full chamber behind us, smiling when I see our witnesses sitting in order of their appearance in the front row: Hillary Frankel, Deborah, and even Mr. Gutierrez, sitting in his wheelchair at the end. He gives me an encouraging little wave. I tried to convince him to stay home and rest since he was released just this morning, but Mr. G is as stubborn as I am.

My eyes pore over the chamber, feeling buoyed by every familiar, loving face that I know, until they hit Mike Tonuto like a car lurching over an unexpected speed bump. He's busy glad-handing the room, walking right up to the Commission and moving down the line.

"Look who's here." I nudge Julian, sitting to my left.

Julian's eyes narrow. "He's going down."

"Ladies and gentlemen of the esteemed Sparrow Nook Zoning Commission," Vinny begins in full strut across the floor, his prominent Jersey accent hammed up to pure Joe Pesci. The word *esteemed* sounded more like *esteemt,* and *board* with two syllables *bohr* and *ahd.* "I am here tonight to make your lives easier. And isn't that what we all want?" Vinny stops and winks at the stenographer.

A spasm racks my body, making me sweat and shiver in tandem.

"You see, my client Nomi Wyeth is in full compliance with Sparrow Nook's zoning ordinance already, as is, case closed. She doesn't require a zoning exception because she isn't changing the building's historical use." *Use* sounds like *yoose*. "My client's dispensary, which would bring a new and significant source of tax revenue for Sparrow Nook, is in all practical aspects of the word, a *pharmacy*. A literal *drugstore*." Vinny spins on his stacked shoes' heels. "To speak on the intricacies of Sparrow Nook's zoning ordinances, I'm calling Veronica D'Angelo-Bork as my expert witness."

Veronica *click-clacks* to the stand, giving major Marisa Tomei energy, and I have to give it to them both—the zoning commission sits enraptured. "Ms. D'Angelo-Bork, you are a real estate agent by trade, is that correct?"

"Yes, ten years and counting."

"And in your professional opinion, Ms. D'Angelo-Bork, does Ms. Wyeth *require* a zoning exception for her intended use of the historic Strange Drugs Pharmacy building?"

"No, she does not." Veronica points a sharp nail to the sky. "First, pharmacies sell drugs, and so do dispensaries. Second, the Main Street business zone expressly prioritizes the respectful use of historic buildings in line with their fundamental historic character."

"And Ms. Wyeth would respectfully sell the drugs?"

"Very respectfully," Veronica says. "It's a very classy venture. I do *not* associate with unclassy ventures," she says reproachfully at the zoning commission, as if they might argue back. "Third, Ms. Wyeth's dispensary fits perfectly in the zoning plan. Not only does it comply with all physical requirements, it's also quaint, historic, and it adds to the town's tourist appeal. It will do good business and drive up revenues for surrounding businesses as well."

"How, exactly, will a cannabis dispensary help local businesses?" Vinny pontificates dramatically.

Veronica leans over her mic. "I've heard that people who partake get the munchies. Sammy's Steaks, Fredo's Italian Ice, the new ice cream parlor on the corner can all expect to do excellent business thanks to Ms. Wyeth's dispensary."

Across the room, Tonuto's jaw tightens. Now that I know his backstory with Sammy, it's clear how much he wants him to fail. How does nobody else see it?

Vinny spins through our carefully curated roster of client witnesses. Julian wasn't wrong—once we put out the bat signal, both recreational and medicinal clients of mine signed up in earnest to share their stories of how, over the years, I've made their lives easier, better, fuller.

Happier.

Hearing client after client gush about me and all I've done for them should touch me inside. I should be crying tears of joy, of validation, hearing and seeing that a life lived outside the rat race can still have meaning.

But it doesn't. And I can't. I can't feel *anything* but the pain cresting inside of me. It feels like I've been divided into two people. The external Nomi, who's smiling placidly, nodding at all the right moments, the good girl who helps people however she can. And then there's Nomi on the inside, a bag of suffering squeezed into too-tight pants she can't escape. Forcibly gagged so that nobody discovers she's trying not to explode, right here, in agony. I can't hear the compliments over the sound of my own pain. The friendly voices can't reach me where I sit huddled, terrified I'm going to be sick in front of all these people, terrified I'm going to ruin my dreams, and so incredibly *furious* that my body works against me every chance it gets. My fingernails are embedded in the soft underside of my forearm, the sharp welts an underwhelming counter to the awful blunt-force pressure gripping my insides. But it's all I have grounding me in this moment.

That, and my mounting anger. I know it's not helpful, and I know it's whiny, and I know, *I know*, *I KNOW* that other people suffer. That they have their own agonies, their own woes, and that my pain does *not* make me special. I know all of this, but I'm still so angry this is happening to me. That this *always* happens to me. I try to live, and my body knocks me down and says, *Stay down. You think you can do this? You really think you can do anything? Stay. DOWN.*

And if I don't? If I try to start my own business, or God forbid, date a person?

I pay. I suffer. I hurt, so much.

And the extra slap in the face is that, on the inside, you feel like you're dying. But on the outside, you're just a person about to shit their pants. You're the woman trying to cry silently in a public stall, hoping the line of impatient women waiting to pee can't see you rocking back and forth through the cracks in the door. You're the friend who's left the group dinner to go to the bathroom five too many times to be normal. You're the date who ends the night sweating and clutching her stomach and apologizing for needing to go home, *right then*. You're suffering in a way society finds embarrassing. In ways you're not supposed to talk about. When someone asks how you are, they don't want to hear that you're internally bleeding again, that you can't eat, that you're afraid to.

They don't want to know.

Julian places his hand lightly on mine under the table. The warmth of his palm sends a shockwave of revulsion through my body, raising the hairs on my neck and kickstarting another set of spasms. I cringe away from him. Hurt blooms in his eyes, and I avert mine quickly.

"Sorry," I whisper, "you scared me."

"Are you sure you're okay?" he whispers back. "You look…like you're not."

Well, that was diplomatic.

"I now call Dr. Julian D'Angelo to the stand," Vinny announces.

I can feel Julian looking at the side of my face, waiting for me to assure him that I'm fine, just nervous. But I'm *not* fine, and I'm barely holding on to this external lie that I am. "Go," I urge. "Just . . . go."

Reluctantly, Julian stands, a slightly darker purple down his back where he's sweating through his clothes. Poor Julian. I know that, in some ways, he's even more terrified of this going badly than I am. My stomach lurches, and desperate, I do the unthinkable: I reach for the pill in my pocket. One more goes quickly in and down.

God, I'm doomed.

"Dr. D'Angelo, you filed the initial complaint against Ms. Wyeth's dispensary, correct?"

Julian clears his throat directly into the mic. The Commission flinches backward at the feedback filling the speakers. "I did."

"But you later withdrew your complaint. Why is that?"

"Because I realized that I'd been very stupid about cannabis and all the good it can do." His big eyes look so soft without the structure of his glasses hemming them in. Tender. Or maybe, that's just how he's looking at me. "You see, I thought that because I was top of my class at Yale and received the prestigious Corrington fellowship at Philadelphia General Hospital, that that meant I knew everything about what it really takes to help people. But it took me coming to Sparrow Nook to understand the kind of compassion, patience, and personal investment patients need their doctors to have, and I learned all of that from watching Nomi Wyeth work with her medicinal clients. She is, without a doubt, a force of real good for the people in her life. She will do so much good for this town, if you let her."

One commissioner audibly sighs at these words, pressing her hand against her heart. Jackie, on the other hand, rolls her eyes.

"Thank you, Dr. D'Angelo, that is all." Vinny turns and is about to call up his next witness, *me*, when a voice calls from the back.

"Chief Commissioner, if I may question the witness?"

Mike fucking Tonuto saunters up to the front. Except for a dark red flush on his rounded cheeks, he looks perfectly at ease as he clasps his hands behind his back, approaching Julian.

"You *may*, Council-friend Tonuto," Jackie Lombardi announces with bloodthirsty interest.

"Objection!" Vinny cries out. "As a city council member, Mr. Tonuto is an interested party to the outcome of this hearing. It's inappropriate for him to intervene."

"Vinny D'Angelo." Mike Tonuto puts his hands on his hips. "I ask you, is it a crime to love my town?"

"No, but—" Vinny begins, but is quickly cut off by Mike's loud, theatrical laughter.

"Okay, then! Sit down and give someone else a turn to talk." Mike's eyes glint with meanness, even as his smile is cranked up to eleven.

Jackie bangs the gavel. "Objection overruled. Proceed, Council-friend."

"Dr. D'Angelo," he begins. "Is it true that you and Nomi Wyeth are now in a relationship?"

Julian blinks, visibly taken aback. "Um, yes, but I made the decision to withdraw well before that—"

"A *sexual* relationship?"

"Objection!" Vinny stands and shouts. "The nature of Dr. D'Angelo's relationship with my client is entirely irrelevant to the legal matter at hand, which is whether Ms. Wyeth's dispensary constitutes a pharmacy for all intents and purposes under the ordinance."

Jackie sighs, fully put out. "Mr. D'Angelo. Whether your witness's testimony is credible is of utmost importance to this matter. However, I'll sustain this objection. Council-friend Tonuto, please continue with a different line of questioning."

The objection doesn't matter, though, because the revelation causes shockwaves through the Commission's expressions. Looking from Julian, to me, to my painted-on eyebrows and Kardashian cheekbones, back to Julian, wariness radiates across their faces.

"I apologize for the indelicate nature of my questions." Tonuto salutes the Commission. "I have no further questions for this witness."

Vinny, obviously ruffled, stumbles through calling me to the stand. It's been a while since I stood up, and I wobble on the sharp points of my heels, feeling lightheaded and underfed. Vinny offers me an arm, and I take it.

"Ms. Wyeth, is it true that you majored in chemistry in college and went to pharmacy school after graduation?" Vinny runs both his hands through the stiff hair at his temples, grimacing at the resistance there.

I frown a little. This wasn't one of the planned questions we rehearsed. "Yes, but—"

"And is it true that you use your pharmaceutical knowledge to assist your clients in selecting the drugs that would best suit their conditions and needs?"

My heartbeat picks up even faster. "Well, yes, but—"

"Is it *also* true that you always wanted to be a pharmacist when you grew up, and now you basically get to be?"

I glare at Vinny, then Veronica. None of this is planned. "Well, I wanted to be a doctor, but—"

"Even better!" Vinny cries, clapping his hands. "There you have it, members of the zoning commission. Ms. Wyeth comes to the dispensary business by way of a true foundational interest in medicine that she nurtured through extensive formal education, ergo, this will be a pharmacy the way Ms. Wyeth plans on running it, basically a CVS!"

"Now that's not *entirely* accurate." I lean over to speak more fully into the mic, my entire body clenched like a fist. I try to laugh a little to diffuse the tension caused by openly contradicting my own legal counsel, but it falls flat. "Stranger Drugs will be like a pharmacy in the most classic sense of the word. A place where people can buy products that suit their medical or recreational needs after consulting with a trained, knowledgeable sales associate, but also a place where the community can gather and enjoy a soda, or a brownie, or even burn some cannabis flower on our back smoking patio. It's more than a CVS could ever be, but it's exactly the kind of classic pharmacy that our town's beloved Strange Drugs was for Sparrow Nook. Just with fewer poodle skirts in our booths."

I smile nervously, but the zoning commission won't even look at me. I glance at Veronica, terrified, and she subtly points up at her right eyebrow, eyes wide.

Oh, fuck. There's something wrong with my eyebrow? I *have* been sweating like crazy, and *oh, God*, I did briefly put my head in my hands, too. I flip my hair in front of my shoulder, hoping it will hang in front of the offending brow, only to see Veronica gesturing at her left eyebrow, too.

Internally, I whimper. The god-forsaken Imodium hasn't kicked in yet, and swells of cramping pain wash over me, bearing down on me like a tide crashing to shore.

"Thank you, Ms. Wyeth," Vinny says glumly to the floor. "No further questions."

"My turn, then." Tonuto smiles patiently as he's back on his feet, the only one in these chambers willing to look at me. It's a smug, pleased expression, which is how I know my makeup must be truly fucked.

"Ms. Wyeth, did you graduate pharmacy school?"

I sniff. I *knew* this is where it would go if my brief stint in grad school came up. "No."

"Did you finish your *first* year in pharmacy school?" Mike's eyebrows are high as he exchanges looks with each of the zoning commissioners in turn.

"No."

"Your first semester?"

"No."

"Why is that, Ms. Wyeth? Too hard for you?"

I was sick, you fuck! I was hospitalized for a systemic allergic reaction to the medication I was on! I nearly died!

"I... I guess you could say that." I look at my hands, trembling on my lap.

"So, you're not a pharmacist?"

"No."

"Will Stranger Drugs be licensed by the New Jersey Board of Pharmacy?"

"No."

"Hm," Mike says simply. "Are you on drugs right now, Ms. Wyeth?"

"Objection!" Vinny yells, suddenly coming back to life.

Mike raises both hands. "No judgment, sweetheart, but I saw you pop a pill twenty minutes ago, and you don't look uh... very put together?"

My mouth drops open. "That's over-the-counter medication! I'm—I'm *not* feeling well, it's true. I'm very nervous."

The Commission stares at me with shocked disapproval.

"Are you on marijuana right now, Ms. Wyeth?"

"No!" I yell, just as Vinny bellows, "Objection! You gotta be kidding me!"

My eyes well with tears as the audience murmurs in a collective strain of anxiety.

"Listen!" I spin to face the Commissioners. "Mike Tonuto is only trying to get me shut down so that it'll hurt his brother, Sammy DiFiore. He doesn't *want* my dispensary to drive up business for him. And he put Julian up to filing the zoning complaint against me in the first place!"

Tonuto cranks out a laugh and shakes his head. "Commissioners, I recuse myself from every issue involving my half brother, Sammy DiFiore, and I wish him all the best. Frankly, the connection Ms. Wyeth is positing here is so tenuous, it makes me question her... *mindset.*" He arches an eyebrow meaningfully, then stops in front of the witness stand where I sit. He smacks it with the flat of his heavy palm, his pinky ring *clink*'ing against the wood. "Ladies and gentlemen, I ask you, is *this* the face that Sparrow Nook wants to display to guests on our beloved Main Street? Because let's face it, Stranger Drugs is no pharmacy. This is one woman's exploitation of our sick and elderly via the legalized use of mind-altering drugs. I don't know about you, but I don't want stoners like her on *my* Main Street." He gestures at me with a pitying scorn. "Thank you."

The room erupts. Julian, on his feet, pointing and yelling. Mr. Gutierrez cursing. Eve tries to rush Tonuto in something like a tackle, Graham holding her back. All my friends and family and clients coming to my aid, as if there's anything left of me to save.

I slip off the stand and run to the bathroom before anyone can stop me.

The Commission's decision is announced twenty minutes later, I learn via text.

Approval *denied.*

CHAPTER TWENTY-SIX

JULIAN

"Nomi?" I knock on the restroom door. "Can I come in?"

"*No!*" Nomi's voice is thick and muddy from tears. "I'm fine! I just want to be alone."

Down the hall by the exit, the security guard eyes me warily. City Hall rapidly emptied after the zoning commission announced its decision, and it's late. "We have to go," I say gently. "The guards are waiting for us to leave so they can lock up and go home."

The soft sound of her sobbing creeps around the door's edges, melting my insides like acid. I burn with the shame of it all, knowing *I* started this, *I'm* the reason she's in there crying, and it's *my fault* that her dreams are falling apart. I never understood why she dropped out of school our senior year and abandoned her ambitious plans for the future. I still don't, to be honest. But I do understand she replaced all that with this different dream of helping people, of having fun, of living a slower, quieter life, and I've ruined it.

"I can't leave yet. You go."

"I'm not leaving you, Nomi." I knock on the door again, even though the rough texture hurts my knuckles. Maybe because it does.

"You don't get it. I *want you to leave*," Nomi says, her voice suddenly iron.

It knocks the air out of me. I stumble back, understanding now.

She won't leave until I do, because…

She doesn't want to see me.

I swallow, the knot in my throat horrible and sharp.

"I—okay. I'll go. I'll tell the guards you'll be right out." I slide my palm down the door one last time. "I'm so sorry, Nomi."

I walk away, dread weighing down each footfall as I enter the August night. When I get inside my car, I rest my forehead against the steering wheel, more defeated than I can ever remember. How will Nomi forgive me? I've failed.

When morning comes, I let it pass me by. I don't get up to run, or make coffee, or shower. I lie in my bed, the weight of my fuck-ups pressing the air out of my chest. When my phone buzzes on the nightstand, I lunge for it, but it's not Nomi answering the many texts I sent her last night, asking if she was okay, if she made it home, if we could talk.

MOM

Aunt Edna passed in her sleep last night, honey.

I stare at the words, willing them to reorganize, to mean literally anything else. It feels like a punch, delivered to my throat. My eyes burn, and I squeeze them tightly closed against today. Against these feelings drowning me, making it hard to breathe.

JULIAN

Oh, Mom. I'm so sorry. Are you okay?

MOM

Hospice came and handled everything. I'm okay. Just terribly, terribly sad.

JULIAN

I'll be right there.

The loss feels like regret. Sad and heavy, a circular train of thoughts and feelings looping through me ad nauseam. Regret that Aunt Edna is gone. Regret that the world lost such a person. Regret that death comes for everyone. Regret that I can't stop it. Regret that having someone wonderful means that, one day, we don't get to have them anymore.

Even though Edna knew the end was coming and had prepared accordingly, the days that follow are full of helping Mom execute her plans. In lieu of a homily, Edna wanted us to share her favorite stories—the time she punched my Uncle Joseph in high school, when she met Neil Diamond backstage on her fiftieth birthday, when Krimpet, her beloved poodle mutt, caught an actual rabbit during the family Easter egg hunt and traumatized all the children. During the after-party, we are to project a never-ending slideshow of all her favorite pictures separated by themes of her choosing, the most disturbing of which is *Edna, the Sexy Years*. It's so, so her, it feels like a last gift, a last joke. I half expect there to be an item on her close-out list for me to loosen my butthole.

Nomi texts when she hears, telling me how sorry she is, asking if there's anything she can do. She says nothing about how I've ruined her life, or how she never wants to see me again. She's probably waiting until I've had time to grieve before ending things officially.

When the service begins, I scan the room for her, feeling guilty for caring so much about the state of us on *Edna's Big Day*, which is what Edna wanted printed on the programs. But seeking her is a compulsion; every time I think her name, my eyes reflexively scan the room for her. I haven't stopped looking since I got here, and when I do find her, it feels like coming home.

Then remembering I've been evicted.

After the service, Nomi slips out of the church, and I all but tackle grieving family to get to her before she disappears.

"Nomi, wait!"

She turns, her face guilty and regretful, and it hurts almost as much as the rest of it. Knowing that she feels bad for not wanting to be with me anymore. Even though I deserve her anger, deserve this break-up, deserve her never talking to me again—she still feels bad. I can't seem to stop hurting her, can I?

"Julian, I'm so sorry about Edna. You know how much I loved her." Her big, brown eyes are rimmed with red, and her face looks thinner, sharper than usual.

"She loved you, too." How many times did Aunt Edna tell me Nomi was the one and not to fuck it up, and then I did just that? "Are you coming to Edna's Big Party?"

"I wish I could, but—I can't."

My voice momentarily fails me, so I just nod, eyes welling as she turns and walks away.

"Nomi, please don't go yet," I say to her back, running to catch up. "I know I fucked everything up, but I want to fix things between us." She looks so small and forlorn before me, so badly in need of someone to care for her the way she cares for everyone else. I bite my lips in, then blurt, "Come to Philly with me."

"What?" She blinks.

"Move in with me, and I'll handle everything. We'll get you out of the building lease, and you won't have to pay rent or any bills while you get your life back on track. We can make new dreams together, Nomi, just like we did in high school." I grasp both of her small, cool hands in mine. "You could even go back to pharmacy school if you wanted—I'd support you through everything."

"Pharmacy school?" Color rises high on her cheekbones, her eyes clouding with suspicion. "What are you talking about?"

"You have options, Nomi. The dispensary didn't work out, but there are so many other things you can do with your life. You're brilliant and capable and ambitious." My voice is pleading, begging for her to understand just how much I want to be there for her. "Let me help you figure out what's next.

A long second passes, the church lawn emptying around us as guests head to the reception in Aunt Edna's honor.

"You don't want to help me—you want to *fix me*." She pulls her hands from mine. "You want to turn me into some respectable version of myself you can bring to donor dinners for Philly Gen, someone worthy enough to be on your arm, who'll fit perfectly into your life in Philadelphia."

"No! I don't want that! It's just—*Jesus*, would it be so bad if you took a beat and explored another path?" I run my hands through hair, frustrated. "Or does it have to be weed?"

Nomi huffs out a small, angry laugh. "You know, I thought you finally saw me for who I am. But after all this time, you still like *her* best, don't you? Nomi the valedictorian, the one who was Ivy-league-bound with a bright future. You wish I was her." Nomi blinks, her eyes filling with tears. "But that Nomi doesn't exist anymore, and that's how I like it! I don't want my worth to hinge on how prestigious my job is. I want to be loved as I am, because I exist, because I have inherent value as a human being! Not because I went to *fucking Yale*!"

"That's not what I'm saying at all!" I splutter. "I just don't want to watch you self-destruct and waste away in Sparrow Nook when there's so much else you can be doing with your life!"

Nomi's eyes widen, and she takes a step back. "You think I'm like your dad, don't you? Wasting my life here, smoking weed all day in my proverbial garage? Well, you don't need to rescue me, Julian. I'm doing fine on my own!"

"Oh, sure, you're doing so great, refusing to even consider another future for yourself while ignoring your own health!" I'm yelling now, my frustration tipping over into real anger.

Her mouth parts, forming a shocked *O*. "What are you talking about?"

With great effort, I force myself to breathe. "I saw your bloodwork, Nomi."

"You looked at my medical records?" The hurt on her face is quickly swallowed by rage. "After I expressly told you not to, you—you didn't listen?"

"I didn't look on purpose! Because I ordered the bloodwork, it came to me first. The lab flagged it urgent because of the findings, and I reviewed it before I realized who it was for." I swallow back the anxiety clenching my throat. "I didn't look at anything else, Nomi, I promise, so I still don't know what you're facing. Just please, let me help you. You're *sick*." My voice cracks on the last word. "Your inflammatory markers are very high, and several values are significantly abnormal—"

Nomi's eyes squeeze shut. "I can't believe you didn't listen to me."

"Well, I can't believe *you*, Nomi!" I bite my lips in, a barely contained hurricane of feeling thrashing inside of me. "Were you ever going to tell me?"

A dent forms between her brows. "We've only been seeing each other for a month—"

"We've known each other for *years*. I knew something was wrong—I've asked you over and over again if you're okay, but you lied to me! How bad is it, Nomi? You've been losing weight, barely eating, and you were obviously in pain at the zoning hearing. Does Dr. Appa know how bad it's gotten? Does anybody?"

"Stop! Just *stop*!" Nomi's hands shake in front of her face as if she can brush this entire conversation away. "This is why I didn't want to tell you! You're not my doctor, Julian. My health is not your concern!"

"You were never going to tell me." I blink at her, reading the panic on her face, feeling it sink like a heavy stone to the depths of my stomach.

"I'm in *love* with you, and this whole time, you've just been waiting for me to leave."

"You can't be in love with me, Julian!" Nomi rears back. "That's ridiculous!"

"Well, guess what? I am!" I throw my hands in the air. "I'm fucking ridiculous, okay? I'm intense and obnoxious, and I'm fucking ridiculously, intensely, *obnoxiously* in love with you, so get over it!"

"Jesus, Julian, it hasn't even been a whole month!"

I swallow the knot in my throat, but it keeps bobbing back up. "I've known since senior year."

"Oh, come on, that's not true," Nomi says, her voice scoffing and tinged with tears.

"Just because you look at me and see some pathetic try-hard you mess around with every fifteen years until you feel like disappearing on me doesn't mean I don't love you, Nomi."

I run my hand through my hair a final time, not caring that my neatly arranged curls are sloppy and wild now, or that my shoes are dusty from pacing across this dead lawn.

"It just means I'm a loser you don't love back."

JULIAN

There's weed at Edna's Big Party, and it has my name on it. Aunt Edna left me her stash box with a note that says: *For Julian and his* followed by a picture of a star. Not a five-pointed classic, but the easy kind that's just intersecting lines. I stare at it for too long, dead-eyed and stuporous, until Mom looks over my shoulder. "That's supposed to be your butthole, sweetie."

"Oh." Aunt Edna got one last crack at me, after all. I poke through the box's many compartments, inspecting all the jars and tinctures labeled in Nomi's tiny, precise handwriting because it's easier than talking to family right now. One tray holds ten perfectly rolled joints, its label reading: Party Time! I run my finger over them and sigh miserably.

Mom nudges me with her shoulder. "Want to get high with your ma?"

I close my red, swollen eyes, face crumpling inward from zero provocation.

"Oh, Julie. Let's go." Mom gently tugs me upward until I stand, head stooped to hide the tears streaming down my face. She leads me onto Aunt Edna's back porch and the bench swing. "What's wrong?"

"*Everything.* Everything is wrong."

She smiles, then produces one of Edna's joints, lights it, and inhales from it gracefully. "My God, you sound like Grandpa Fabrizio. So dramatic. Please elaborate." She passes me the joint, and after staring at it for a long second, I accept it.

"I told Nomi I'm in love with her." I take a deep drag off the joint and spend the next two minutes coughing.

Mom pats my back. "Oh, Julie! I'm so happy for you."

"Don't be. She didn't say it back, and we had a huge fight."

"Well, it's only been what . . . a month? Two?" Mom chuckles, takes another big hit. "You D'Angelo men—you're so passionate. When you love, you love with your whole being. That's a lot for a woman. Give her time, Nomi's a smart girl. She'll see what an amazing partner you'll be." Mom passes back the joint. "That's how it went between me and your dad, anyway." She snorts. "He told me he loved me on the second date."

After a second, I lean my head on Mom's shoulder. "Nomi's very sick. I'm worried."

"She finally told you? That's a good sign. She doesn't tell almost anyone."

"No," I admit. "I saw her bloodwork and confronted her about it."

"Oh, Julie." Mom shakes her head and relights the joint. "That was stupid."

I glance up. "Well, how did you know?"

"Her mother and I talk. It's hard raising stubborn geniuses who love to argue. We commiserate."

"But why wouldn't Nomi tell me, Mom? I've tried so hard to become someone she can trust—"

"By looking at her medical records?" Mom arches an eyebrow at me.

"It was an accident!"

"She probably didn't tell you for the same reason your dad preferred to stay home. It's hard carrying that kind of pain around, for both the person who's in pain, and the people who witness it. It naturally isolates you. Makes you feel like a burden to those who love you." Mom sighs. "Nomi's barely dated anyone, you know."

"You mean lately?"

"I mean *ever*. Her mom worries about how lonely she is, but Nomi's always been too scared to put herself out there. Until *you*." Mom eyes me meaningfully. "Cut her some slack. Trusting someone with her illness is new to her, and a very big deal."

"I acted like a complete asshole about it." I run my palms down my face.

"Another trait you get from your father." Mom smiles. "Listen, all you can do is own up to how you acted, apologize, and learn what being there for Nomi looks like. You don't get to be the boss of her body or her health. Loving someone doesn't work that way. Hell, being someone's *doctor* doesn't work that way. You can't make her get better. But you can learn how to make her feel less alone and how to be there for her as a partner." Mom leans back on the swing. "If you do all that in a pair of short shorts, you'll be set, honey."

"Mom."

"That's why God gave the D'Angelo men great thighs. It's how you get by for having such impetuous personalities and tight little buttholes to match. Aunt Edna left you Uncle Joseph's entire summer wardrobe, by the way."

I huff out a bittersweet laugh, feeling lighter and yet, sadder, than I have all day. I run a hand down the smooth wood of the stash box. "God, I'm going to miss her."

"Me, too, sweetie."

Just then, a small ball of floof hops up onto my lap, two little brown eyes gazing up at me through shaggy bangs. I flinch at first, then tentatively hug BonBon Jovi into my arms. "Hey, little guy." I kiss the top of his head.

Mom smiles. "She left you BonBon, too."

I blink. "Are you serious?"

"She said caring for a puppy would help your butthole. I've already packed up BonBon's things so we can take him home later." Mom smacks my leg and stands. "I'm going to find Vijay. You think about what I said, honey."

"Vijay?" I arch an eyebrow, accepting BonBon's furtive facial licking because he, too, is in grief, and I suddenly love him with my whole heart. "Since when did Dr. Appa become *Vijay*?"

"Since we made out six months ago and started going steady."

"What?!"

"Julian!" Marco, Aldo, and Ellio burst onto the porch in quick succession, then promptly start coughing and waving their hands in front of their faces. "Damn, is there a fire back here?"

"Here, you can have the rest." Mom offers the joint to Ellio. "We were honoring Aunt Edna."

"You're—" I stare at Mom. "With Doctor... *him*?!"

She blows me a kiss, then disappears inside.

"Julian—*hey*." Marco snaps his fingers in front of my face. "You've got to focus. This is big. Tell him, Aldo."

"Tell me what?" I blink, my eyes feeling fully chapped by the weed.

"Last night, I was cleaning up the chambers late, and I overheard Mike Tonuto on the phone as he was leaving his office. I could've sworn he said the word *dispensary*." Aldo lifts his brows.

I snap up straight, which is impressive since I feel like a giant noodle. "Yeah?"

"I snuck up behind him so I could listen." He taps his ear. Aldo doesn't usually tell the stories in this trio of brothers, and you can tell he's enjoying it. "And you won't *believe* what I heard."

I lean over so far, the porch swing nearly deposits me and BonBon on the ground. "What, man?"

"He was talking shit on Nomi!" Ellio bursts out in a bell of smoke. "Said it was '*only a matter of time before the little lady folds and gives up the lease!*' "

Aldo narrows his eyes at Ellio. "Way to steal my thunder, bro."

"Huh." So Tonuto *is* targeting Nomi specifically. Does he want her lease for himself? How could a sitting council member rent a building owned by the city council?

"Can you guys stay on him? Keep an eye out for anything that might suggest Tonuto's benefitting personally from thwarting Nomi's dispensary?"

The Ohs nod, and I stumble up to standing, my head feeling light and airy even as the thick, molten sadness of losing Aunt Edna and my big fight with Nomi weigh the rest of me down.

"Bro, I almost forgot." Marco claps me on the back. "There's a guy out there asking for you."

I make my way back inside to Aunt Edna's living room, where a man with short, neatly combed hair stands, arms crossed, watching Edna's slideshow.

"*Eric?*" I press my hand to my chest. BonBon licks that, too.

He turns around, his eyes crinkled at the corners. "Julian. Hey, buddy."

"What are you doing here?" I stand rooted on the spot.

"Other than developing a crush on your late Aunt Edna?" He gestures at the slideshow, squarely in the middle of The Sexy Years. "I thought you could use some support today. Was I *wro—*"

Before he can get the last word out, I've wrapped him in a three-way bone-crushing hug. "Thank you for coming, I—" My voice comes out strained and raw. I might be getting tears on his suit coat, but I just squeeze him tighter. "I can't tell you how much this means to me, sir."

Eric sniffs pointedly from within my boa constrictor embrace. "Dr. D'Angelo. Are you *stoned*?"

"Very much so, sir." I release Eric, who's now grinning.

"I'm proud of you, Julian. Who's this little fella?"

"BonBon Jovi." A beam of pure love shoots straight out of my chest. "My son."

"Well, congratulations to the new father."

The party's winding down, with only a few clumps of family having beers and sharing Edna stories. "Are you and BonBon hungry?" Eric asks, squinting an eye at me. "It's been a while since I partook, but I recall munchies being egregious."

I shake my head in awe. "You are, simply, always on point."

"Let's go. I spotted a diner up the road on the way here. Pancakes on me."

Ten minutes later, the three of us are seated in a comfortable booth at The Silver Dollar, an old mom-and-pop diner I used to go to with Aunt Edna every Saturday growing up. Eric couldn't have known that, but it feels special, all the same. I get teary-eyed just looking at the giant accordion menu.

When the server reaches our table, Eric says, "Bacon for the dog, and pancakes for us. Blueberry for me, peanut butter for him. Extra whipped cream."

"How much extra?" the server asks.

"Does it come in a bottle? Bring the bottle."

The server salutes, and Eric turns back to me. "Okay, Julian, let me have it."

I lay it all out. The whole saga. Aunt Edna's passing, the fight with Nomi, her mystery illness, the feeling that Tonuto's out to get her, my promising conversation with Dr. Riveras, immediately followed by Dr. Appa's mind-exploding offer.

"AND I just found he's *dating my mom*?!" I grab the can of Reddi-wip one-handed and spray it directly into my upturned mouth, which turns out, is pretty dangerous when you're trying not to hyperventilate.

"Okay, don't aspirate on that." Eric pries the can of whipped cream out of my hand. "No wonder you're stressed out and smoking joints at funerals. This is a lot."

I don't know if it's getting it all out or just hearing wise, sage Eric, agree that what I'm going through is too much, but after a few minutes, I'm able to breathe again. This time, the emotional support whipped cream slides down my throat the way it's supposed to.

"What should I do, Eric?" I feed BonBon the last of his bacon. He farts. "Bless you," I whisper.

Eric smirks. "Well, you're already nailing step one."

"Which is?"

"Feeling your feelings. The only way out is through, my friend, and you're doing a great job feeling your grief."

I huff. "The one thing I wish I sucked at."

"Well, usually you do," Eric muses. "You've been letting your brain drive your whole life, from what I can tell. All strategy, no heart. Maybe letting your feelings take control for once would help."

"My feelings want me to cry and eat canned whipped cream and adopt gassy dogs. Not the smartest."

"Feelings don't have to be true, or right, or smart. They just have to be felt."

"I don't have time to sit around and mope, Eric. I need to figure out what the fuck I'm doing so I can keep my life from imploding." I fork a giant bite of pancake into my mouth, just to feel productive.

"Okay," Eric says. "Let's do a thought experiment. Imagine it's next summer, and you're happy. Form a picture in your mind. Where are you?"

"With Nomi," I answer immediately.

"In Sparrow Nook?" Eric cuts a bite. "Philadelphia?"

"Surfside Pier," I murmur, the glimmer of neon lights painting the scene in my mind. "In Wildwood."

"Okay, it's Saturday night, and you're at Surfside Pier with Nomi. You're holding hands, licking each other's ice cream cones, I don't know. Something romantic. Then you remember that Monday, you're scheduled for a shift at Dr. Srinivasan's clinic. How does that feel in your body?"

"What do you mean?"

"How do you feel thinking that your Wildwood trip ends with you reporting back to the clinic. Don't reach for thoughts. Reach for the feelings."

I try, but there are no feelings, really. Just the happiness at spending the weekend with Nomi. "I don't think this is working."

"Why?"

"I feel nothing. Or calm, maybe? It's just... a statement you said."

"Let's back up. It's Saturday night in Wildwood, but this time, you remember you're working a shift at Philly Gen."

I wince.

Eric leans over with interest. "How do you feel in your body now?"

It doesn't take long to find the ball of dread bobbing up and down in my middle. "Anxious."

Eric leans back, gesturing with his fork and knife like *bon appétit*.

I scoff. "Just because I feel anxious about Philly Gen doesn't mean I shouldn't work there. Sometimes life is hard, and we live it anyway. We make the hard decisions because they make us stronger, better—"

"Happier?" Eric asks, one eyebrow raised.

I fork another piece of pancake into my mouth instead of answering.

"See, this is what I mean. When your brain is in charge, you ignore your body's feelings. But what happens when someone lives their whole life pushing through anxiety and stress because they think it will make them a better person? Do they ever get to stop and choose what makes them feel happy instead?"

"I don't know. Maybe?"

Eric shakes his head, then cuts into another pancake. A particularly fat blueberry bursts under the pressure of his knife, which, relatable. "In a world full of leisurewear, you choose the hair shirt every time, Julian, because somewhere along the way, you became convinced *you* don't get to relax. *You* don't get to be comfortable. *You* don't get to be happy. Not unless you earn it."

"Exactly. I'll do all of that when I earn it, and I haven't yet."

"But when will that be? What will it take? It wasn't when you graduated college summa cum laude or aced medical school. It wasn't landing that fellowship at Philly Gen, either. I'd venture to say that, for as long as I've known you, I've never seen you truly happy. Just varying stages of stressed the hell out and miserable." Eric pauses to chew. "What if you're not a grouchy asshole at all? What if you've just been in a very bad mood your whole life because you keep making bad choices?"

"*Bad choices?!*" I clutch BonBon in outrage. "I'm incredibly successful—I could hardly *be* more successful!" Frowning, I add, "Except for the last four months."

"So, is it enough?" Eric asks mildly. "Can you let yourself be happy now?"

I gape at him. Eric tilts his head to the side.

"It doesn't matter what I want." My head droops. "I've ruined Nomi's chance at opening her dispensary, and now she'll never forgive me."

"Has she said that?"

"No," I bite out, sounding surlier than I mean to. "But then I went and freaked out about her hiding her illness, and now she wants space. How am I supposed to win her back when she doesn't want to see me?"

"There's no *winning* someone, that's your toxic achiever speaking. Ask yourself why Nomi might not want to share something major with you specifically and see if that gives you insight. And honestly, Julian, this is the perfect time to be your most obnoxiously tenacious self and show her you'll be there for her, no matter what she's going through. Give her reason to trust you, and she will. What are you doing?"

I look up from my napkin. "Taking notes. How else am I supposed to remember all this?"

Eric smiles. "A star student, to the end."

"But what about Tonuto?" I use the pen to scratch BonBon's chin. "How do I prove he's up to something?"

"I don't know but sounds like you've got the D'Angelos on the case, and if they're as tenacious as you are, they'll help you figure it out."

"They're nothing like me," I say on reflex, but that's not true, is it? Marco's just as driven about owning his own small business as I've been pursuing medicine. Veronica's as cutthroat a real estate agent as I was a medical school student. Vinny, Aldo, Ellio, even Aunt Patty in the Acme checkout line—they're all as dedicated to doing what they love as I've been to the things I don't. So, who has really been more successful?

And can I *finally* stop pretending that it's me?

With the pancakes eaten and the bill paid, Eric extends a hand to me, then pulls me and BonBon in for a tight, bracing hug. "You're doing great, kid."

"You're ten years older than me. At *most*." But Eric doesn't hear me because the hug's somehow morphed into a headlock, and he's too busy giving me a vigorous noogie to listen to anything I say. "E-*ric*!"

"Ahh..." He finally releases me with a satisfied grin. "I've wanted to do that for *so* long."

"That was completely unprofessional." I fumble to straighten my glasses. "And inappropriate!"

"What can I say?" Eric grins. "You make it look fun."

CHAPTER TWENTY-SEVEN

NOMI

There are two main states in Crohn's disease—being sick or *fear* of being sick—and they're both disruptive to living my life. But it's the rare third state that devastates me most. When I go long enough without a flare that I start to wonder if I'm cured. *Maybe that expensive probiotic actually worked. Maybe I grew out of it. Maybe I never had Crohn's at all.*

But then some mysterious internal switch is flipped, and I realize I've been standing on a trapdoor the whole time. The floor opens beneath me, and I fall back into my illness, spending the next day, week, month in pain, wondering if I'll ever crawl out again. Crohn's is a trickster, a disruptor, a reverse *deus ex machina* where suddenly, out of nowhere, your plans blow up for no reason at all. It turns my body against me. It whispers *why bother* as it forces me to bow out of the life I've tried to build.

And I'm so fucking tired of it.

I roll onto my side, tears trickling over my nose, wetting my hair and pillow. I hate how I left things with Julian yesterday. But how can I make him understand that I can't be there for him when I can't even be here for myself? That loving me means empty seats beside him at family gatherings and plans canceled last minute. Lost deposits, late arrivals, and trips never taken. It means pain and a level of helplessness to stop it I'm not sure he can handle. He deserves someone who fits neatly into his high-achieving world, with as much ambition as he has. Not a sick, sad stoner puffing away at her vape in the bathroom stall, broken and unfixable. As angry as his words made me yesterday, I don't blame him for preferring the Nomi who still believed she could have whatever she wanted. I don't miss her priorities, but do I miss her optimism.

I'll get through this flare, and then I'll explain everything to him. Let him down as easily as I can. *My body feels like it doesn't belong to me,* I imagine saying to his disappointed face. *And I didn't tell you because I don't want it to be true.* Until then I'll hide out here, confined to my green, velvet bedroom like a consumptive Victorian invalid with the shits.

The distinctive *whir* of an expensive vehicle stops outside. I squint through the narrow sliver of window and see Julian's Volvo parked out front.

My eyes widen as he shoulders several bags up to my door and knocks, guts clenching on cue, a warning not to engage. *You belong to pain right now.*

"Nomi?" He knocks again. "Can we talk?"

Fuck! I stagger to my feet, feeling a rush of lightheadedness. I haven't eaten today and couldn't manage much yesterday, either. Still wearing the funeral makeup, too, though it's smeared from tears and sleep. I'm a mess, but I guess he already knows that. I reach the front door as he knocks again.

"Julian, it's not a good time."

"Just hear me out," he pleads. "You don't even need to open the door."

This isn't how I want to have this conversation. I close my eyes, exhaling to the ceiling, and let my body slump against the wall. "Okay."

"I don't expect you to forgive me, but I need you to know I'm so incredibly sorry. You don't need to go to Yale or pharmacy school or do anything, to earn my love or respect because you already have both, just for existing, just for being you. I'm a better doctor and a better person because of you, and if I'm able to rescue my career from the ledge I pushed it to, that's because of you, too."

There's a soft sound on the other side of the door, like a palm pressed flat against wood. I place my hand against it, an ache growing in my throat.

"It can be so humbling, to be understood by someone else. And terrifying, to see yourself through their eyes. But when you look at me, I think that maybe, for the first time in my life, I could learn to love myself. You teach me more about who I am and who I want to be every day. And now that I've experienced what it's like to be known by you, seen by you, *touched* by you, I can't go back to my life before, Nomi. It doesn't fit me anymore."

His ardent words travel through the wood, around the door, through the cracks, and find me. *Reach* me. Pulse through my veins like blood.

"You are the smartest, funniest, most incomprehensibly beautiful woman I've ever known. You mean everything to me. I haven't earned your trust yet, but I want to, Nomi. If you let me try, I'll start right now."

"Julian." I rest my forehead against the door, wishing it was him. His chest. "It's not just trust. I didn't want to tell you about my illness because every time I tell someone, it becomes part of my identity to them. And I don't want this to be my identity. I don't want it to be true. And more than anything, I don't want to be your patient, Julian, but I'm scared you'll make me into one."

"I understand, and I promise you that's not why I'm here."

I unlock the door and slowly open it a few inches. "Why *are* you here, then?"

"To be here for you. To love you." Julian's eyebrows knit together. "And install a bidet."

A surprised sound huffs out of me. "*What?*"

"Can I come in?" Julian lifts the bags. "I've brought provisions."

"I don't know..." My voice comes out small. "I'm very sick, Julian."

His soft, gentle smile wraps around my heart. "That doesn't mean you have to be alone."

Despite the fear and shame telling me to withdraw, to retreat, to hide this embarrassing version of myself and deny it any exposure to air, I want to believe him. I want to be with him.

And dammit, I've *always* wanted a bidet.

I let him in.

He bustles to the kitchen, where he begins systematically emptying his bags and arranging the items on my table. Wawa chicken noodle soup and soft pretzels, a heating pad, electrolyte packets, bananas, more of the protein shakes I like, and no less than three types of toilet paper.

"I got you a range from no-nonsense to super soft. I didn't know what you preferred." He pulls out the fancy bidet next, then jogs to the car and returns with two sleek oscillating fans with remotes.

"What *is* all this, Julian?"

"I joined the sub-reddit for IBD and read up on people's must-haves for bad flares." He winces as my face falls. "The inflammation, your weight loss, the pain in your lower belly... it's IBD, right?"

"You cracked the case. I have Crohn's." I smile ruefully, staring at the fans instead of him, feeling the truth in the words he said outside. It is humbling, to be seen and understood and then, loved anyway. "Why fans?"

"Many people experience hot flashes during bad flares, especially during cramping, so I bought a fan for your bathroom and one for wherever else you'd like it. Maybe by your couch?" He waits for me to answer, and finally I nod, my brain processing all this on a three-second delay. Then he's off, setting up the fans as directed.

"How are you feeling right now?" He expertly fits the bidet onto the water line next. "Hungry? Crampy? Fatigued?"

"Bewildered, mostly." I wrap my arms around myself in the doorway, watching him tighten everything with a wrench, my heart included. The sight of tall, handsome Julian, sleeves rolled up and working on my *toilet* of all things, is so unexpectedly domestic, it's like a vision of some happy future I can't have.

But... says who? Me? Or Crohn's?

"How did you know to do all this? To be here for me in this way?"

"You once said that creature comforts are how you get by. I understand that more now." Julian stops and pushes his glasses adorably up his nose. "I also know what it's like when someone lives with chronic pain, and thanks to my mom, I know how to love them through it."

My throat tightens painfully. "Your dad."

Julian gives me a small, sad half-smile as he stands, then washes his hands. "When he'd experience a bad pain flare, he'd isolate himself, usually out in our garage or in my parents' bedroom. I didn't understand back then. I thought he didn't want to see me, or didn't want to work, or some other horseshit reason that made his pain seem like a personal failing, instead of what it really was—this relentless struggle he fought every day, on his own, to try and remain a part of our lives. Mom understood that, and though she couldn't take his pain away, she did whatever she could to make him feel less alone in it."

Julian approaches me, his hands cupping my face as he peers down into my eyes. His thumbs brush away the tears collecting on the tops of my cheekbones so gently that more fall.

"You're going through the same thing, aren't you? Feeling alone in your pain? Separating yourself from everyone else to spare them the burden of your illness?"

I can't say anything, the words resolving into a single, choked sob. So, I nod. I nod, and Julian's arms wrap around me, holding me to him.

"Spare me from nothing, Nomi. Every part of you deserves to be loved, and I want it all. When I imagine the best, happiest version of my own future, all I see is you."

"I'm sorry I didn't tell you," I whisper into his shoulder. "I wish I'd been brave enough."

"Tell me now." He tucks a lock of hair behind my ear. "Tell me everything."

And so, I do. First at my table, then later, curled on my couch when the cramping hurts too much to sit. I tell him when the symptoms began, how hard high school in Georgia was, how I'd started to improve in Sparrow Nook but took a sharp turn during the most competitive stretch of our debate team season. I told him about going on Hospital-Homebound, and weird Ms. Middlecooks who'd come over with my assignments and proctor tests. I told him how much I missed him, how I wished I could tell him why I'd disappeared.

"It's very hard to admit you have a shitting disease to the boy you like."

"The *very hot guy*, you mean," Julian corrects.

"The extremely intense, underweight, big mouth teenager that I, for some reason, desperately wanted to make out with."

"I'll allow it." Julian folds his arms. "And then, when you came back, and I saw you smoking pot with Eve. All those things I said..." He swallows, the sound rough in his throat. "I'm so sorry. It wasn't really about you."

"I know that now," I reply softly.

"You *may* not have noticed this, but historically I've had some major emotional hang-ups with cannabis."

"Oh, really?" I smile, then wince as a spasm hits my lower belly. It's an empty threat, being that I've eaten nothing to fuel a true attack, but it doesn't stop the pain from radiating through me periodically. Julian's big, blue eyes see it, see *me*, but I don't see pity in him, or disgust, or dismay, or any of the reactions I've always hated so much. I see acknowledgment and understanding. I see love.

This intense, gorgeous, brilliant man *loves* me, all of me. And though I'm not ready to say it, I think I love him, too.

I tell him about going to the Rutgers regional campus instead of Yale and the rough college years when I was so sick and starting biologics therapy. The allergic reactions, the doctors who refused to try anything else. Julian bites his bottom lip in, clearly angry on my behalf, but also, chastised somehow, as though he's partly taking responsibility for his profession. I tell him how cannabis pulled me out of the worst of my illness, but how difficult it was to find the kinds I needed for Crohn's prior to legalization, and then, what a miracle getting my first medical card was and how I knew that's what I wanted to do. I'd quit pharmacy school because of an epic stress-induced flare and the worst allergic reaction to a biologic yet landed me in Philly Gen. I was back home, not knowing how I was supposed to pick up the pieces of my life or what my disease would allow me to do. But if I could help other people find relief through cannabis, the way I had, that was a calling I could answer.

I tell him about the years that followed, working for Damon, the ebb and flow of my disease. The disappointments I experienced with the medical industry, one doctor after another, until finally, I gave up seeing doctors and specialists altogether.

"Except for Dr. Appa," I amend. "He's always been good to me."

Julian's brows pinch together, though he doesn't say anything.

"What are you thinking? You want to say something."

"Nomi, I want to respect the boundaries you set around your illness and how we talk about it. But it may be hard for me to know where those boundaries are intuitively. If I ask or say things that go too far, especially in the beginning, will you give me some, I don't know. Amnesty? Without getting too angry right away? I'm really trying, and I want to do this right."

I run my hand down his arm, squeezing lightly, appreciating him so much in this moment it hurts. "Okay. That sounds fair. What do you want to say?"

Julian takes a deep breath in. "If you haven't seen a specialist in—"

"Five years," I fill in.

His eyebrows lift. "That means you haven't had a colonoscopy to monitor your disease progression recently. Is that right?"

I swallow. "That's right."

Julian bites both lips in. "I understand how frustrated you are with the medical industry, but you've been very sick, and your normal interventions haven't been helping lately. Maybe it's time you had some testing done to see what's going on in here." Julian places his hand directly over where it hurts the most, and the touch feels so comforting, a tear rolls down my cheek. "I'm suggesting this not as your doctor, Nomi, but if you'll have me, as your partner."

He watches me closely. "Was . . . that okay for me to say?"

I breathe deeply in, eyes closing on reflex. This is part of why I don't talk about my disease, too. I don't like hearing what I don't want to do. I don't like facing what I've been running from. And I don't like feeling accountable for ignoring my own needs to someone who cares about me.

But maybe this boundary isn't fair to ask the people in my life to respect. If I'm sick and getting sicker, is it right to pretend I'm not and then get angry when someone refuses to buy my heavily edited version of reality? Or is that just me choosing to be alone with my fear, *again*, instead of together with someone who loves me, where I have to be brave and vulnerable and honest?

Defiance surges through me, because I don't *want* to be alone anymore. Not when Julian's here beside me, the jagged, difficult angles of who he is fitting so neatly against my own. And if that means hearing the uncomfortable truth, if that means I have to be fucking brave and bravely allow some doctor to plumb my ass looking for answers, so be it.

"Yeah. It was." My mouth quirks in a half-smile. "The bidet doesn't hurt, either."

Julian's brows lift earnestly as he pulls me into his arms. "It'll change your *life*."

He holds me, the new fan keeping me cool in his embrace, and I sigh against his chest. "Now you know all my secrets."

"I do? There isn't anything else about, say, Lil Dom?"

I snort. "Nothing you can handle."

Julian groans, and I use the opportunity to nuzzle in closer. "Now you have to tell me your secrets, too."

"Anything." Julian's lips brush against my forehead.

"What happened at Philly Gen?"

He freezes in my arms. "I signed an NDA!"

I look at him sternly. "Spill it, Julian."

He sighs heavily, his head leaning back against the couch as he regards me. "I'm physically and emotionally unable to deny you anything."

I smile, satisfied. "Sucks to be you then, because I've long suspected I'm a raging brat. Tell me everything."

"Fine, but you have to understand it was the full moon," Julian begins. "And full moons mean *chaos*."

"Did they teach you that at the Yale School of Medicine?"

"They did, you little smart ass, and I didn't believe it then, either, but it's a hundred percent true. Ask any hospital employee you know—if you're scheduled on a full moon, everything will go wrong. That night the ER was slammed, every room taken, and we were severely understaffed because a horrible stomach virus decimated our ranks. It was a terrible night. I hadn't had a bathroom break or a single cup of coffee since I'd clocked in six hours earlier."

"Yikes, *you*? No coffee?" I lean over and take a sip of water, emptying my bottle in the process. "The story could end here, honestly."

"Unfortunately, it doesn't." Julian takes my water bottle, heads to the kitchen, and begins to hand-wash it at the sink. I follow him meekly, mesmerized by the rightness of him in my space.

"A nurse that I don't care for interrupted me for the fifth time that night to demand that I come up to the cardiac unit, which wasn't even my floor, and I became extremely annoyed."

"Why don't you care for this nurse?" I take the clean, freshly filled water bottle that he offers me and take a long drink. Why is there nothing better than cold water that someone else has poured for you?

"He microwaves leftover fish."

My eyebrows rise. "So he's evil. I see."

Julian offers me his hand, and I take it, letting him lead me to my own bedroom. "Also, his name is Gilroy, and I resent having to make those two vowel sounds back-to-back."

"Ooh. Yeah." I wince. "Gilroy."

"So, Gilroy the Inconsiderate asks me to stop what I'm doing, *again*, to come pronounce this cardio patient dead." Julian takes my favorite sleep shirt off the hook on my bathroom door and lays it on the bed.

"Oh, *no*." I'd never considered Julian in that role. Standing over someone's bedside at the end of their life, confirming someone else's worst nightmare. "That's so sad."

"The worst part of the job, honestly. That, and making the call to their family afterward. May I?" His voice is low as his hands trail down my sides, tugging lightly at the hem of my hoodie.

I nod, not wanting my voice to crack, and raise my arms to let him lift it over my head. The soft cotton drags against the tender flesh of my stomach, ribs, and breasts. He sucks a short breath in as it comes off, my hair billowing down around my shoulders. Looking over my shoulder at us in the mirror, he meets my eyes there. But, with a look of serene discipline, Julian slips the large sleep shirt over my head.

"What happened next?"

"Bathroom first." He nudges me toward the door, and when I return, freshly washed up, brushed, flossed, and relieved, he's got the bedroom lighting down to the warm, honeyed glow of the bedside lamps, my covers pulled down, phone plugged in, and water bottle waiting. I slide into my waiting bed and sigh, audibly, as he pulls the covers over me.

"Will you get in, too? And finish the story?" I yawn and pat the other side of my bed.

He shucks off everything down to his boxer briefs and climbs into bed. "I didn't want to wear outside clothes in your fresh sheets," he explains, as though *that's* why I'm staring at him.

Facing each other on our sides, our hands tucked beneath our cheeks, he continues. "I follow Gilroy up and pronounce this poor patient dead, so the next step was calling his family. And the whole time I'm searching for the patient's information, Gilroy was yapping in my ear nonstop about all the things he needed me to do. I found the number, called, and the patient's wife answered."

Julian swallows.

"She couldn't believe it. '*I was just there two hours ago, and he was fine! You all told me he'd be released tomorrow!*' " Julian blows out a breath. "I felt bad for her, but I wasn't this man's doctor, and I couldn't really answer her questions. Based on his file, there's no way that man could've been released the next day—he'd been fighting for his life all week—but denial is powerful when facing the death of a loved one. So, I told her again I was sorry, her husband was deceased, and she needed to come to the hospital to make arrangements."

"God." I whisper. "How awful."

"The woman arrived extremely upset, and they let her in the room with her husband to say her goodbyes. She had this long, tearful conversation with him, and apparently, she'd been having an affair and needed to get it off her chest."

"Oh, shit."

"Yeah. With their chiropractor. And one of his fraternity brothers. Also, their dog-sitter."

"Jesus."

"Yeah, she was pretty unhappy. Told him that, too. And then, when he sat up in bed and started screaming at her, she was even unhappier."

"Julian!" My eyes nearly bug out of my head as I, too, launch upright in bed. "What? *How?*"

"When Gilroy was pestering me while I was trying to find the deceased man's information, I inadvertently typed this other man's name into the system—one that Gilroy was asking me to check on after a fairly minor stent procedure—instead. My brain just... misfired. Daniel Van Dyke was decidedly *not* dead, and yet, I told his wife otherwise. He was rightfully furious. With me. Philly Gen. The Board of Trustees. And particularly his wife, Lillian Corrington Van Dyke."

"Corrington... *your fellowship patrons*?!"

"Yes." Julian frowns miserably. "The hospital's biggest donor family thrown into an uproar when the prominent son-in-law set to take over the family business was wrongfully pronounced dead only to wake up and find out that his wife came out as polyamorous to him when she thought he was dead."

"Oh, Julian." I press my hand to my mouth, muffling a single, shocked laugh. "Oh, no."

Julian tugs me back down to the bed, his own smile reluctantly pulling at the corners of his mouth. "It's not funny."

"I mean, wasn't the husband visibly... alive? What about all the machines that beep because you're alive?"

Julian sighs. "According to Dr. Riveras, Ms. Van Dyke was '*overcome with grief*,' and this was '*my fault*' because I '*never listen*' and have my '*head stuck up my condescending ass.*' But also, Mr. Van Dyke complained about the beeping and lights keeping him awake earlier that evening, and because he's outrageously rich and important, the attending physician capitulated and let them turn off the monitoring equipment."

I whistle. "The perfect storm."

"The Corringtons want me fired, but Dr. Riveras convinced them it'd look bad if the Corrington fellow was suddenly fired in connection to their son-in-law's treatment. If the press found out, Lillian Corrington's secrets would be exposed, the family would pull their endowments as retribution, and millions of dollars would be lost. But it'd end my career, too. Donor-killer? No respectable hospital would have me after earning that reputation. So, I'm lying low until the Corringtons cool off and sign the check for the new hospital wing."

"Wow," I yawn, then blink appreciatively. "That was a wild ride. I'm glad I coerced it out of you."

He smiles. "Should I go now, Nomi? Let you sleep?"

"Let me sleep, yes. But stay, if you want."

"Do you *want* me to stay?"

I let my eyes close, the answer frothing along the entire surface of my being.

"Yes."

As bad as I've felt, I'm almost content now beneath the cool press of Julian's palm against my cheek. The care he's shown me tonight, the simple, un-fussy way he met my needs without me asking, feels like a gift. Maybe I don't get to have a future without Crohn's disease, but maybe I could have *this* future, where it doesn't get to have all of *me*.

CHAPTER TWENTY-EIGHT

JULIAN

It's been three hours, and I've already downloaded *Candy Clobber*, become addicted, bargained with God, emerged on the other side, and deleted it from my phone, and I'm *still* stuck in this waiting room that smells like glossy brochures and stale potpourri, hoping that every time the nurse appears, it'll be my name she calls to bring me to Nomi.

My thumb's quivering over *Candy Clobber* in the App Store when, finally, my name is called.

"Julian D'Angelo?" The nurse is wearing magenta scrubs and a skeptical frown as I scramble to my feet, as if she can see inside my soul and it's nothing but exploding lollipops. "Follow me."

"How did she do?" I struggle to keep up with the nurse's quick strides.

"Oh, she lay on that table like a champ. Real A-plus performance." The nurse rolls her eyes, like I'm the biggest idiot she's ever met.

I instantly like her.

"So... she's okay?"

The nurse's eyes cut to mine with a hint of an amused smile. "She's fine, sir."

The recovery area is a long hallway with beds parked diagonally, each separated by curtains. The pleasantly hostile nurse stops, pushes aside the curtain, and there she is. Even the bluish-white hospital gown can't dim the warm glow Nomi radiates. Her eyes flutter open, and she smiles loosely.

"Hey, Jolene." Nomi pauses, a divot appearing between her brows. "Josephine?"

The nurse snorts.

Nomi's eyes brighten. "Junior!"

"Is this normal?" I turn to the nurse. "This amount of... *inebriation*?" I whisper the last word. I've never done an exploratory procedure like a colonoscopy; the anesthesia used on ER patients is far more heavy duty, and I have zero idea what to expect.

"She's on propofol, the drug that killed Michael Jackson." The nurse lifts an eyebrow. "Yes, this is normal."

Nomi holds both hands out to me. "*Julian*."

My worries melt into relief. "That's it, baby."

"She's gonna be loopy for a while," Mean Nurse says, handing me Nomi's clothes. "Help her with the buttons, Junior."

The nurse pulls the curtain closed around us, and the fact that the heart is a muscle has never been so clear to me. Sitting in the waiting room, unable to see Nomi, unable to help or protect her, my heart clenched in worry, every beat an effort without knowing she was okay. But now, as she leans forward on her bed to wrap her arms around my neck, my heart unclenches in degrees, like a fist prepared to fight for her finally allowed to relax.

"Oh, Nomi," I whisper into her hair, almost drunk with relief that I have her in my arms, safe. It gives me new perspective for all the patients' families I had so little time and sympathy for. *"It's just a procedure,"* I can remember saying. *"The risk is less than two percent."* Two percent! As if two times out of a hundred aren't terrifying odds when faced with losing the person you love the most in this world. The person who makes it all make sense for you. Who makes *you* make sense to you. As if that wouldn't be the most profound loss a person could experience.

God, I was such an idiot before I fell in love.

"How are you feeling?" I pull back enough to scan her beautiful face.

"Like I had the best nap of my life," Nomi says dreamily. "And like I want to—" She leans toward my ear, as if she means to whisper, but says, quite loudly, "*—fuck*."

She slides her parted lips over my earlobe, skating down the planes of my neck.

"Nomi, you *have* to stop giving me erections in medical environments." I groan, running my hands gently down her back to the ties of her gown to undo them.

"Never!" She shimmies out of the gown, presenting herself topless like *ta-da*!

"I've got to get you dressed, now *stop* that." I try to avert my eyes as Nomi runs her palms lightly over her breasts. I encase her quickly in her pajama shirt, and she wriggles suggestively. I give her my sternest tone. "*Stop it*."

Her eyes dilate, excited.

Dammit, she *likes* my stern tone!

She looks down at the pajama prison I've wrapped her in, and her flirty face transforms into a giant *awww!* "You brought my lucky pajamas! How did you know?"

"They're covered in Snoop Dogg and Martha Stewart faces." I sniff, willing my erection to back off and read the goddamn room. "They're objectively auspicious."

"So smart." She smiles, preening for me as she lets me button her up. "You're *my* valedictorian, Julian D'Angelo."

And fuck if I don't swoon.

After I get Nomi dressed, we chat briefly with Dr. Rashad, Nomi's new GI specialist who came highly recommended from my peers at Philly Gen. She's open-minded, focused on the latest research, and versed in many different approaches to treating IBD, not just the biologics route.

Dr. Rashad has been great so far and got Nomi in for a comprehensive combination colonoscopy and endoscopy within a week of Nomi's call. Seeing her sit attentively at Nomi's side as she patiently reviews her preliminary findings with a clearly intoxicated woman makes me feel hopeful that Nomi will finally get the care she needs.

And if she doesn't, I'll be there to help her find the doctor who will.

"I'm surprised and impressed at the state of your colon," Dr. Rashad says, which has to be the weirdest compliment I've ever heard. "While there is inflammation suggesting that you're in an active flare, for you to have had Crohn's for so long and with so little long-term damage to the tissue is really miraculous." She smiles kindly at Nomi. "You've done a great job taking care of yourself, Nomi."

To Dr. Rashad's credit, she only *slightly* flinches when Nomi throws her arms around her neck and tells her she loves her.

"I'll follow up tomorrow with a full report after you sleep this off, okay?" Dr. Rashad turns to me. "Nomi may be uncomfortable as the anesthesia wears off. She should drink lots of fluids and rest. No major *activities* tonight."

I blush furiously.

"There will be lots of gas," Mean Nurse says as she reappears within our curtain. She smiles at me. "*Lots.*"

"Excuse me, but how far do you live from Sparrow Nook, New Jersey?" I rub my chin. "And would you be interested in a family clinic position?"

Mean Nurse scoffs. "You couldn't afford me." Then she leans in and says under her breath, "But my name's Tonya Jones, and you can find me on NursePros. Be prepared to negotiate." She claps me on the shoulder. "Get her home safely, Junior."

In the car, Nomi leans her seat all the way back, then thrusts her bare feet onto my dashboard, letting them slide back and forth with every turn. I let her, which is how I know I've truly evolved. She uses the car's voice command to call Eve, Graham, and then Eric, to his, frankly infuriating, delight.

"Nomi?" Eric's voice echoes throughout my car, more pleased than he ever sounds to talk to *me*. "So, you *are* real!"

I hang up on him.

Before Nomi can call my mother, a call comes in from Veronica. Nomi hits the answer button on the console with her big toe. "Yessssss?"

"Babe!" Veronica sings, her Jersey accent filling the car. "How was the procedure?"

"Great!" Nomi announces happily, then places her hands on her belly and pushes experimentally. "I've got the farts."

"Let 'em rip, girl. Julie won't mind. Right, Julie?"

I clear my throat. "Is there a reason you called?"

"I just had a great meeting with the city manager. She feels terrible about the zoning snafu and has agreed to cancel the lease, no penalties, and return all your deposits. She'll even prorate the September rent, so you only need to pay for however many weeks it takes to move out." Veronica's voice has taken on the chipper tone of someone delivering best-case-scenario news when *all* the scenarios are heartbreaking. "We can start looking for a new spot for the dispensary as soon as you're done with the farts, babe."

Nomi's pleasant smile flickers in and out, then disappears. "Great. Um. Any leads?"

I put my hand, palm up, on her leg. She takes it and squeezes.

"There's an old vacant tire shop on the highway. Zoning is anything goes out there, and it gets great light. Weed covers up rubber smell, right?"

Nomi swallows. "Let's see it. Monday, maybe?"

"You've got it, babe."

The call disconnects, and Nomi turns to me, giving me a small, brave smile. "It's going to be okay," she says, though it feels more for her benefit than mine. All traces of the goofy, loopy Nomi are gone, and I hate that reality's what sobered her up.

"It's going to be great, because you'll make it great." I bring our joined hands to my mouth and kiss hers softly. "I can take half-days this week and help you pack up. You'll be out in time for Labor Day."

"*After* Labor Day." Nomi's real smile returns. "I wouldn't give up my front-row seats for the Labor Day parade for anything."

I cut my eyes back to her. "You're not going to do anything embarrassing to me, are you?"

"Julian. You're voluntarily driving a tiny red clown car while wearing a fez. I don't have to *do* anything to embarrass you."

"It's in honor of Aunt Edna." I sniff. "It's the first Labor Day parade she's ever missed driving for the Shriners. This way, she won't have to."

"It's the best tribute imaginable. Super loose butthole of you, honestly."

"*Thank* you." Weird that that made me tear up, but in the year 2026, we feel our feelings.

"It's really cool that the Shriners are letting you drive, and you're not even a member."

"So cool," I lie. I haven't told Nomi that in a fit of intense Edna nostalgia, I *joined* the Shriners chapter of Sparrow Nook, so that fez is mine. Just like I haven't told her that I've officially accepted Dr. Appa's offer, informed Philly Gen of my plans not to return, adopted BonBon, and asked Veronica to find me a house. She probably called to update me on *my* potential leads, which means I'll have to secretly call her back later.

It's not that I'm afraid Nomi doesn't want me here. She's working on opening up and trusting me as much I'm working on not yelling at Carl, which shows just how invested she is in this relationship. It's more that I want to show her, and maybe also myself, that I'm listening to *my* heart for once, and this is what my heart wants. I *want* to play beer pong with my cousins. I *want* to be Nico's cool uncle. I even want to smoke joints on the porch with my mother and feed my dog ham chunks. I want to be there for Mr. Gutierrez for the long haul, and I want to love my job because of how it makes me feel instead of enduring it for validation I could never give myself. I'm making the decision to stay for me.

I will tell Nomi, though. Soon. And then, I'll ask her a question of my *own*.

CHAPTER TWENTY-NINE

NOMI

It's Labor Day and the last dregs of summer, the sky as blue as the water ice they're hawking across the street before the parade begins. Stranger Drugs sits behind me, all packed up except for a few things in my office. My laptop, those misdelivered packages I *still* need to return, the shattered remnants of my dreams, et cetera. After today, I'll lock up for the last time and try to make peace with leasing a spot in the industrial *anything goes* zone on the highway. My top contender shares a wall with a dildo store, so it isn't all bad, I guess.

I ease into the plasticky plaid retro lawn chair, feeling mellow and smiley. An emotionally loaded day calls for Unicorn Piss, a citrus-forward, high-THC hybrid that promises giggly bliss for experienced users. So far, it hasn't let me down. Even after all the drama, stress, and heartache of the last few months, I feel better than I have in a long time. My flare has begun to subside, my body feels like my own again, and having Julian there beside me, listening to me and loving me through it all, is a relief I've never known.

Plus, I *love* my bidet.

I hadn't realized I'd given up on finding my person until I found him. Now that I have, the shrill whine of loneliness that pervaded my life grows quieter every day, replaced by *his* voice loudly berating TV medical dramas, musing over the latest Parkinson's research while his glasses slip down his nose, whispering incoherent praise in my ear as he fills me with his heat, his longing, his love.

Life has never sounded better.

While it's sad spending Labor Day sitting in front of my failed labors, it's beautiful out, and I'm here with my best friends, snacks, and front-row seats for the parade, waiting for my giant boyfriend to drive by in a tiny car. I laugh at the sky, remembering how I helped Julian bobby-pin Edna's old fez into his waves this morning, and my body thrums with delight.

Ahh, horny pot.

Eve nudges me with a platter of cheesecake brownies which, sadly, I must decline.

"No dairy, remember?" I swat the platter halfheartedly away. "Dr. Rashad has ELIMINATED dairy from my diet. It is ELIMINATED."

"DELETED." Graham snatches the platter over me. "FORSWORN."

"*Ugh.*" Eve scowls. "I have to make I Can't Believe It's Not Butter Budder now."

"*What?* You canna bis-leaf it's not—" Graham yelps midsentence as Eve squirts him with a water gun, straight in the face. "Aww. You got my brownie wet."

The dairy elimination diet is the first of many measures I'm trying with Dr. Rashad to address the underlying sources of my chronic gut inflammation. It's a frankly rude way to begin a relationship, but I love the way she sends me research articles to support her cruel interventions. I'll give up cheese for science. For *now.*

"Look, it's starting!" Eve sits up as the high school color guard appears, the marching band's colonial drumbeat and piccolo morphing unexpectedly into a Sabrina Carpenter song. "God, I love parades."

Graham's eyes widen. "Maybe *we* should build a float next year for the dispensary."

"Ooh, I'll make a reminder to do the parade registration!" Eve starts dictating the reminder on her phone, which is nowhere to be seen. Because Unicorn Piss.

"The registration . . ." I yank my wrist to my eyes, but I haven't worn a watch in twenty years. "*Fuck!* It's due today!"

Eve frowns. "For next year's parade? That's intense."

"No, the LLC's quarterly report!" I groan, running my hands down my face. "There's a late fee if you miss it."

"They're making you *labor*?" Graham asks, indignant. "On *Labor Day*?!"

I lurch out of my chair. "I've gotta submit it now. Grab me when the weird honking starts—I don't want to miss Julian!"

I stumble inside to my office. It takes a full five minutes to remember how to access the NJ Secretary of State's corporate filings portal.

Because again, Unicorn Piss.

Bleary-eyed, I don't feel so blissful now as I try, and fail, to find my corporate ID number. Finally, I search by my building's address instead.

Two entries appear. There's Stranger Drugs, but weirdly, our Main Street address pulls up a second LLC, too.

I squint at the screen. Am I doing this right?

Yes, there's definitely a second business registered to this address. *JM Enterprises, LLC.* I sit back in my office chair. JM Enterprises. The stack of packages I need to return stares at me from the corner. Are those . . . I scramble up and check, and *yes—they're* addressed to JM Enterprises!

But who would claim this address, and why? A weird, nervy feeling coils in my belly as I click on *JM Enterprises, LLC*. It leads me to their registration page, which shows their status as inactive for failure to file. Was JM Enterprises the other business vying for the lease? My heart pounds as I click on the documents tab and bring up the Certificate of Formation. It's short and bare bones, but there at the end, it lists the directors. Each name lands like a punch.

Wilson Phillips.

Jacqueline Lombardi.

And . . . and . . . *Michelangelo DiFiore?*

After Wilson and Lombardi, I was *sure* that last name would be Tonuto. I frown at the screen, trying hard to understand. Unless . . . is Mike Tonuto's real last name DiFiore, like Sammy's? They *are* half brothers, and didn't Sammy say his dad adopted Mike?

And *Jesus*, does that mean his first name is *Michelangelo*?

I launch myself at the top box in the stack. It's a legit felony to open mail addressed to someone else.

"Unless it's an accident," I say in my most innocent voice. It sounds like an anime character, *God help me,* I'm stoned. I rip open the box, uttering *oops!* in case I'm being filmed, which I'm not.

A letter sits on top.

Dear Mr. DiFiore,

Welcome to the Jersey Mike's family! Enclosed you'll find our franchisee welcome package . . .

A Jersey Mike's? A chain cheesesteak shop *directly* across from Sammy's with the name *MIKE* in the title? I laugh incredulously.

"Ho-lee shit. Holy *SHIT*!" The impact of this finding hits me like an avalanche.

I take a picture of the Certificate of Formation on my phone and run, clutching the letter, out the front door where I collide with Eve to the sound of wild, manic honking.

"I was coming to get you." Eve catches me before I fall to the pavement. "You okay?"

"I've got it, Eve! I've got the proof!" I wave the letter in the air.

"Proof? Of what?"

"Proof tying Tonuto *and* Jackie Lombardi to the dispensary's sabotage!" I shake the letter again. "I...I *think*." The Unicorn Piss is making it hard to process the difference between colors, let alone government corruption. "I need to talk to Sammy DiFiore *right now*." I start to cut across the street, but Graham grabs my arm before I walk into oncoming float traffic.

"Sammy's not at the shop—his food truck's at the parade's end at the big picnic area."

"At the bandstand?"

"Yeah, I saw him setting up earlier."

I launch up the sidewalk, but there's no getting through this maze of chairs and tents and blue-mouthed children high on water ice. I moan at the sky and turn back to Eve and Graham, helpless. "What am I supposed to do?!"

Beep-beepity-beep-beeeeeep!

In a sea of big men in tiny cars, Julian appears in a little red convertible, the hottest one of all. On the car's hood is a picture of Edna laughing, her face lifted to the sky in a joy you can feel, an expression perfectly reflected on Julian now as he zips his beloved aunt's glorified Power Wheels down Main Street. Coupled with the maroon fez perched jauntily on his head, Julian looks completely unhinged.

Good. Because that's exactly the energy this plan's gonna require.

I race out in front of his car, and he slams on the brakes.

"What're you doing?!" His head whips around as I hoist myself onto the back of the tiny car.

"Get me to the bandstand right now!" I wrap my legs around a squirming, outraged Julian like a lap belt from behind. "It's a matter of grave importance!"

"What?! I don't—" Julian struggles helplessly between my thighs, a hot, pink flush rising high on his cheekbones.

Poor thing, he's *definitely* getting a boner.

"Listen to me, Julian." I take him by the cheeks. "I have proof tying Tonuto *and* Lombardi to sabotaging the dispensary!"

"You do?!" He squints. "Wait. Are you stoned?"

"Yes. Extremely. But I'm sure of this. Do you trust me?"

"More than anything." He smiles at me so tenderly that I give him a passionate kiss before pulling away and thumping his fez.

"Okay. I need to get to the front of this parade *now.* Will you drive me?"

"But all these people . . ." He's still dazed, staring at my lips.

"It's time to be D'Asshole, Julian." I tug at his shirt collar to bring him back. "Now, are you my *real ruff bitch* or not?"

His jaw tightens, and he nods once. We jolt forward, me wrapped around Julian's back, his fez's tassel slapping me obscenely in the face. The tiny car is now noticeably back heavy, but my extra weight doesn't stop us from zipping beneath the VFW banner and scaring the ever-loving Jesus out of Carl as Julian lays on the maniacal horn. *Beep-beepity-beep-beeeeeep!*

Sparrow Nook gasps as their new doctor rips through the Girl Scout troops, shouting obscenities as Thin Mints rain upon us. I try to grab one—they're dairy-free—and nearly fall off. In a stunning lack of conscience, Julian cuts off the Sparrow Nook High School Band, causing a ripple of discordant notes in Bruce Springsteen's "Dancing in the Dark" as we jolt to the parade's front and veer toward the bandstand.

The Council-friends have already taken their seats on stage, the city manager chatting with Tonuto a few feet from the mic. This is how all parades in Sparrow Nook end—in the park with a bandstand for civic speeches and wholesome entertainment, surrounded by food trucks shilling pierogis and cheesesteaks and all other manner of gut bombs. After the last float, the town joins the parade, walking down Main Street together, pulling beach wagons filled to the brim with zero-gravity chairs, kids, and Yeti coolers. Small Town America at its most tricked out.

Sammy's food truck is parked directly next to the bandstand—a prime location he must've camped out overnight to get. When the tiny car comes to a wheezing stop, I unclench my legs and hobble to the food truck window. "Sammy!" I screech over the sound of sizzling meat.

A bandana'ed head appears from the side, wielding a metal spatula. "Nomi? What's up, hun?"

"What is Mike Tonuto's last name?"

"Huh?" Sammy frowns.

"What's his full name, Sammy? Say it!" I slap the counter. It's at my face's level, which makes me feel like a toddler.

Sammy's face hardens, fingers gripping the spatula. "Michelangelo Shawn Tonuto DiFiore. Why?"

"We got him, Sammy!" The grin explodes on my face. "*Look!*"

Sammy reviews the welcome letter from Jersey Mike's, his face reddening in rage. "*Jersey Mike's?!* He's trying to destroy Mom's legacy with *corporate bread*!" His eyes are big and desperate. "They don't use Sarcone's, Nomi! They don't!"

"No." I grimace in agreement. Even I, a Georgia transplant, understand the sanctity of Sarcone's rolls. "They do not."

"This is low, *this is LOW*! Even for Mikey!"

The last float arrives, the town tailing behind. The audio tech's doing a last-minute sound check, tapping the microphone while Tonuto stands by, preparing to give the opening remarks.

I whip back around. "We've got to expose him, Sammy! Today, now, before it's too late!"

"Let's take 'im down," Sammy growls.

Julian jogs back to my side, having "parked" the tiny car in a nearby ditch. "I'm here! What's the plan?"

"Um, plan. Right." I wince, wishing I'd vaped literally any other strain. Julian and Sammy are looking to me to lead this rally against injustice, but I keep getting distracted by the siren smell of funnel cake. "I'm thinking."

"Welcome to Sparrow Nook's Annual Labor Day Big Day Off Celebration!" Tonuto's amplified voice bounces suddenly around the park. Families are still setting up their picnic blankets and chairs, battling tent poles and rolling out grills too big to be portable, but Tonuto's impatient as always. He clears his throat into the microphone, peeved already.

I form a tight huddle with Julian and Sammy. "We need to get Councilfriend Min's attention, lure her off the stage somehow. If we tell her what's going on, she'll know what to do. Sammy, you try from over here. Offer her—I don't know. A free cheesesteak or something. Julian, see if you can creep around backstage. I'll take the other side." As we break apart, my comrades look less than impressed with my plan, but I don't know what else to do.

"But there are security guards back there," Julian says.

"Seduce who you must. You have my permission." I slap his confused face lightly on the cheek, then sprint off for the other side of the stage, closest to where Min's sitting.

Tonuto rails over the general hubbub. "Our musical entertainment will begin shortly, but before that, it is time to appoint this year's slate of new officers for your city council!"

I trip over a family's blanket. They're appointing the new officers *today*? Shit. Is that why Tonuto's leading the ceremony? Is *he* up for chair? If he gets it, he'll control the agenda for the next year!

This might be our only chance to expose him for the fraud he is.

I take my position at the side stage, as close as I can get. "*Min!*" I hiss through cupped hands. "*Min!*"

She doesn't hear me. I try again. When that doesn't work, I take a deep breath and run up to the security guard posted at the side stage entrance.

"Listen, I *have* to talk to Min Lee—it's a council emergency! Can you get her attention for me?"

The security guard looks me up and down. Really regretting wearing this cropped wife-pleaser that states "Bong Hits for Jesus" right now.

"You can wait," the guard says from behind her black sunglasses, like I'm some weird council groupie here to get my bra signed. I groan, then stomp back to signal the others. Sammy's busy waving a long, foil-wrapped steak at Min, but he's having no more luck than I am. I can't see Julian anywhere, so either the seduction has failed or is still in progress.

"Council-friends, without further ado, the floor is open for motions to appoint the city council chair." Tonuto straightens his lapels and grins as Vlad the Tiler promptly stands and states: "I move to appoint Council-friend Mike Tonuto to Chair."

Fuck!

Mike places a hand on his chest, simpering. "I'm honored, Council-friend Vlad. Truly. Do I have a second?"

My eyes widen as Chester clears his throat. I don't have time for Min, or intelligent plans, or anything other than *action*. I hurry over and tap the security guard's shoulder. "That man has a free steak for you." I point to Sammy.

While the guard's head is turned, I race up the wobbly steps, boots thundering across the stage, then *snatch* the microphone from Tonuto's shocked hand.

"Assassin!" Council-chair Chester shrieks, then throws himself flat on the stage.

Really? I know Chester's paranoid, but he went straight to *assassin*?

"No, no, no." I wave my hands in the universal sign of *there's been a mistake, please don't shoot*! Lil Dom's already approaching the stage at a clip but slows when he sees it's me. "I'm not here to assassinate anyone, but I *am* here to expose Tonuto for corruption before you appoint him Chair!"

"Guards!" Tonuto bellows.

"Wait one second, Tonuto! Or should I say, *Michelangelo* uh... *Shawn*? Yes, *Shawn Tonuto DiFiore*!"

Tonuto's face blanches as the crowd gasps. It *is* a terrible name.

"Let Ms. Wyeth speak." Council-friend Shar raises her hands to stop the guards bustling onto the stage. Reluctantly, they halt, and she smiles at me grimly. "Nomi, this better be good."

"Sammy DiFiore's been claiming his half brother, the so-called Mike Tonuto, uses his city council position to unfairly target Sammy's Steaks for years. Well, I have proof!" I shake my phone in one hand, the welcome letter in the other. "Mike Tonuto used his real name, *Michelangelo DiFiore,* to start a secret LLC with Zoning Commissioner Jacqueline Lombardi and Tonuto's long-time lackey Wilson Phillips. Their LLC registered their business to *my* dispensary's address, which they planned to lease to deliver the ultimate slap in the face to Sammy—by opening a Jersey Mike's directly across the street!"

The crowd burbles in shock. "*Hell yeah!*" one guy yells. "*I love Jersey Mike's!*"

"But my dispensary beat Tonuto's LLC to leasing the space, and since then, he's done everything in his power to shut me down. Here's the proof." The Council-friends pass my phone and the letter down the line, shock painting their faces.

"Corporate bread, Mikey!" Sammy roars from below. "How could you?!"

Tonuto's eyes ground into mine, his face dimpled with a deep, furious scowl. "This woman is a complete loser, a stoner, don't listen to her—she's high right now! Do you deny it?"

A thousand pairs of eyes swing toward me, collectively fixating on my tank top.

"No," I assert, standing as tall as I can. I look hot in this tank top, and I know it. "I don't deny it, Tonuto. Today is supposed to be my big day off, but because of you, *I'm* up here *working* to take out the *trash*!"

Unaccountably, the entire sanitation workers union goes up in cheers.

I . . . think I'm a labor hero? I saunter over to Tonuto, high on rowdy union applause and the piss of a unicorn.

"You can try to vilify cannabis and the people who use it all you want, but I know who I am, I know my worth, and I deserve every good thing in this life whether I fit into *your* idea of a good capitalist achiever or not." I drive my finger into Tonuto's chest, hard, and take a deep breath in, swallowing as I turn to face my town. Mom's words come back to me in a rush, and I realize now that she's right. If there ever was a time to show both sides of the cannabis debate—how it could help the town *and* change people's lives at an individual level—it's now. It's here, with me, owning my illness and all the vulnerability I've fought so hard to hide. If I don't give this moment everything that I've got, if I hold back and Tonuto gets away with all his bullshit, I'll regret it for the rest of my life. I'm tired of living in shame, and maybe it's time that I expect more from myself and my town—acceptance and love for me, all of me, even the parts that, occasionally, shit fire. I take a deep breath.

"I didn't always believe happiness is possible. I—have Crohn's disease, and at times I get very, very sick."

I glance down and find Eve and Graham, still panting from their run up Main Street. Eve forms a heart with her hands, her eyes big and proud.

"But when I was hurting and too ill to eat, cannabis gave me my life back. When I was down because of how isolated my illness made me feel, cannabis helped me find joy. Maybe you're hurting, too. Maybe you're sad. Maybe you have loved ones facing these problems, and you're trying your very best to be there for them in the ways you know how. I can't promise that my dispensary will solve all your problems, but I can promise that you'll find people who care there. Who'll help you the best way we know how. And isn't that what we all really need? People who care? People who'll help so we don't have to face everything on our own?"

The emotions boom through my chest, each heartbeat sending a pulsating wave of love to my town. God, this is good pot.

"Right now, I need *your* help, Sparrow Nook. To stop Mike Tonuto's petty vendetta against his little brother, and to give my dispensary the chance to serve this town with love, and hope, and laughter. But I need to hear your voices—this city council needs to hear your voices, right now, demanding that these wrongs are righted." I swallow, my throat tight. "What do you say? Will you help me?"

For a second, all is quiet. Somewhere a port-a-potty door slams shut. I feel almost woozy with adrenaline, with how exposed and vulnerable I feel, all the Nomis on display, asking for help.

Ever since the *Jersey Shore* reality show went off the air, Jerseyans have sorely missed sitting in judgment of their own.

Until now.

"*Get Tonuto outta here!*" a woman yells, cracking the silence, and that's all it takes. The crowd goes *wild.*

"Tonuto's a crook! He's not even Irish!"

"Corporate motherfuckin' breaaaaad!"

"Let the nice girl sell her pot!" and *"I have Crohn's, too!"*

Just then, Julian bursts onstage, fez askew and shirt half-unbuttoned. I can't tell if he's been fighting or making out. My eyebrows rise higher as he drags Jackie Lombardi with him. "I found this one trying to get away!"

A fight then . . . I think?

Lombardi doesn't even look mad about being forced onstage. Her cheeks are flushed, eyes sparkling with excitement at the hundreds of angry picnickers demanding justice. She really *does* love violence.

Council-friend Shar stands, eyeing Tonuto and Lombardi warily, and reaches for the mic. I hand it to her, hoping beyond hope for a miracle, that the town's support and my evidence is enough.

She clears her throat, authority dripping from her steely gaze. "Under the Council's Code of Ethics, Mike Tonuto's involvement in the targeted attacks against Ms. Wyeth's dispensary and Sammy DiFiore's shop presents an inexcusable conflict of interest. Furthermore, Zoning Commissioner Lombardi's personal stake in JM Enterprises LLC renders the zoning decision against Ms. Wyeth's dispensary illegitimate. Council-friends, I move to overturn the zoning commission's ruling and put Mike Tonuto and Jackie Lombardi on immediate suspension pending the outcome of a *thorough* investigation."

"I second!" Min jumps to her feet.

"All those in favor, say aye!" Shar calls.

And to my great astonishment, every Council-friend does. Everyone except Tonuto, who's shouting "Nay! Nay!" as Lil Dom drags him offstage like a very belligerent horse.

"Congratulations, Ms. Wyeth," Chair-friend Chester says, reaching for a gavel to slam that isn't there. "You're officially in business." He air-gavels, anyway.

Wild cheering erupts across the lawn, interrupted only when Julian bellows, "Permission to approach the bench!"

"That's not how that works," Council-friend Shar says, then turns to Chester. "Does he know that's not how this works?"

"I have one last piece of information that everyone in Sparrow Nook needs to hear." Julian strides over to me, grabbing both of my hands. I am utterly speechless.

"Nomi Wyeth, I love you with my whole heart. And because of you, I've learned that I love this town, my batshit family, being a doctor, and oddly enough, civic service, too. I'm coming for that seat, District Five!" He points at Tonuto's empty spot and turns back to me. "Most of all, I've learned that I don't want any other future than you."

"But... what about Philly Gen?" I search his eyes.

"I turned them down weeks ago. I'm a family man now. A family practice man, at least, and more, if you'll have me." Julian drops to one knee, and my eyes flare wide. "Nomi Wyeth, will you marry me?"

The crowd gasps.

"Julian!" An incredulous laugh bursts out of me. "God, no! It's been, like, a month and a half."

Julian's beatific smile turns naughty, and my blood heats in response as he stands, looming over me, then sweeps me off my feet and into his arms, princess-style.

"Fine. I'll ask again next week."

CHAPTER THIRTY

Two months later…

NOMI

I've always loved the sounds of a busy, bustling café. People chatting, soft trills of laughter, chairs squeaking across floors as friends joining late take their seats, happy to be there at last, asking to hit that joint because their mom's *really* been on their ass lately.

"You can smoke that on the partaking patio out back," I call as I wipe down the bar, sliding crumbs of Eve's delectable edibles off my counter and into my waiting palm. "Only treats and beverages inside."

Stranger Drugs is *popping.* It's the Wednesday before Thanksgiving, also known as Green Wednesday, and I've already done enough business by two p.m. to pay all our salaries through the end of December. Luckily, I'm no stranger to Green Wednesday, having run Damon's dispensary for so many years, and I've ordered plenty of product to service the entire Sparrow Nook population through the year's biggest food holiday. The local Acme ought to pay me tribute for how many turkeys they've sold. Eve hasn't been able to sit down yet—when she's not selling her giant sugar cookies decorated as turkeys with red, bloodshot eyes, she's my best budtender, thoughtfully helping customers find the experience they're looking for. Graham's stationed by the door, checking IDs and managing the store's capacity as our sweet, docile security guard with a penchant for trivia.

It's not just Stranger Drugs, either. Sammy's Steaks is currently boasting a line down the block.

"I'll be right with you," I tell a woman with shy eyes and a Taylor Swift cardigan as she nervously peruses the flower listings. I love helping cute women find pot.

The door chimes as it opens, and a soft, winsome smile blooms on my face as Julian's white-coated shoulders fill the doorway.

"Welcome to Stranger Drugs, how may I help you?"

Julian saunters across the dispensary, eyeing the full booths, packed tables, and dwindling bakery case with open pride. I lean my elbows on the counter, looking up at him with lips pouting and ready for a kiss. When his hand cradles my cheek, I *mmm* happily, letting his warm, lush lips kiss me tenderly in front of the whole damned dispensary.

"I'll have my usual," he says against my cheek, placing another soft kiss there.

"One nasty black coffee with almond milk, coming right up."

"Make it extra nasty, please." He slides over a fifty-dollar bill, and we share a smile. "I'd also like to marry you and officially make you part of the D'Angelo clan of Sparrow Nook, New Jersey. If you'll have me."

I smile even bigger, responding as I do every week when he asks. "God, no."

Though a part of me thinks more and more, *Maybe...*

"I'll be working at the clinic tonight. Dr. Appa says Sparrow Nook always suffers a lot of eating-related injuries this week." Julian adjusts his gold-framed glasses higher onto his long, straight nose, his eyes flashing mischievously. "You can come and visit later, if you want."

"Maybe." I say the word aloud this time, smiling coyly, answering more questions than Julian realizes.

It's late by the time I close up and kick all the happy stoners off my patio. As I lock the doors and set the alarm, I notice the clinic's bright lights and feel a pull to them, or rather, to Julian within.

The reception desk is unmanned this time of night, though Julian's working on staffing up the clinic when he officially takes control January first. Dr. Appa could get away with a skeleton crew, but Julian prefers to outsource the customer service roles to those who are . . . more suited for such interaction. His first hire was that cool nurse from my colonoscopy.

"Excuse me," I call out. "Doctor? I have an emergency!"

Julian's quick strides bring him through the double doors and into the reception area where his serious face breaks into a happy, adoring grin. "You came."

"Because I'm having an *awful* emergency," I drawl, tugging the ties to my coat slowly open, then letting it drop to the floor. "Can you help me, doctor?"

Julian's eyes go wide, drinking in my half-nude body. I'm wearing my THC Colonel Sanders shirt and nothing else, of course. For old times' sake. "*Jesus*, Nomi—the windows!"

I throw my head back and laugh as he races over, removing his doctor's coat and quickly draping it around my shoulders. He pulls me to him by the lapels, his cheekbones streaked with heat.

"So," he swallows roughly. "What uh, seems to be the problem, ma'am?"

"It's my *area*," I whisper dramatically, then point down. "You should check it out."

Julian's eyes go dark as he lifts me effortlessly into his arms, then takes me back to Patient Room #2.

"Folds town or bust," I tease.

"No," Julian says archly, and I *just know* he's about to correct me, the punk.

"Folds town *and* bust."

The End

ACKNOWLEDGMENTS

I have always, always loved stoner comedy, and it's been a joy reinventing this classic comedic subgenre in a modern-day, legalized setting with a story that centers on women and women's pleasure. Thank you to my literary agent, Carrie Pestritto, for first encouraging me to try my hand at adult romantic comedies and then promptly letting me go bonkers in the genre. Thank you to my editors, Mika Kasuga and Stefanie Chin, for delighting in this crazy story and giving it such a loving home at Union Square & Co. Thank you to my production editor, Alison Skrabek, who helped deliver this book on an intense schedule, and to Vi-An Nguyen, Sandy Noman, Jared Oriel, and Patrick Sullivan, who all helped it look its best. Thanks to Alexandra Serrano and Chris Vaccari, who get the word out about my books to media and libraries, to Susan Moon for the work on the fantastic audiobook, and to all the other folks at Union Square and Hachette who have had a hand in bringing *Pot Shot* to life.

This is an intensely personal story, as I have Crohn's disease, and like Nomi, I have struggled with it for most of my life. Thank you to Dr. Souza, who was the first doctor who listened and correctly diagnosed my condition, and thank you to Dr. Rashid and Dr. Monahan, who handle my care now. I told Dr. Rashid and her nursing team about *Pot Shot* as I drifted off into a medicated sleep right before my last colonoscopy. I'll never forget how their whooping was the last thing I heard after I said it was a love story between a woman with Crohn's and a doctor, and how the first thing I had to do when I came to was to clarify that Julian was not Nomi's doctor, just *a* doctor. Awkward, especially considering our morning's intimate activities together.

Thank you to my writing friends who have expanded my heart and life so much. Leigh Mar, Ellie Palmer, Alexandra Vasti, Jill Tew, Danica Nava, Naina Kumar, Rosie Danan, Victoria Lavine, Cameron Kellogg, Melissa Kendall, Chloe Liese, Lyssa Kay Adams, and Betty Corrello, thank you so much for your help with *Pot Shot*, your friendship, and just, like, everything. To the amazing folks at Kiss & Tale Bookshop, but especially Katie, Jamie, and Sarah, you are the best cheerleaders imaginable! Thank you for all the joy you bring to our little corner of the world. Thanks to all the Bookstagrammers, librarians, and booksellers that have helped spread the word about my books, but especially Jennyfioreads, Dreamboat, Chelseareads_, and all the lovely folks in LPL Friends & Lovers! Thank you to my family, but especially my ultra-supportive siblings Amy, Christy, Adam, Guy, and Eric; to Leo, who teaches me just how much love there is in my heart every day; and most of all to Mark, who has loved me through sickness and health, good times and bad, and puts the H in my own personal HEA.

Lastly, thank you, readers, for spending a few hours with me and making my dreams come true. Please spread the word if you loved this book, and pop by my Instagram to say hello sometime. You make it all worth it.

ABOUT THE AUTHOR

LAURA PIPER LEE has wanted to be an author since she was a kid. She enjoys making people laugh, flirting, and avoiding exercise, so writing romantic comedies like *Zoe Brennan, First Crush* and *Hannah Tate, Beyond Repair* is pretty much a perfect career choice. She lives with her partner and their son in Philadelphia.

RAISING READERS

Books Build Bright Futures

Thank you for reading this book and for being a reader of books in general. We are so grateful to share being part of a community of readers with you, and we hope you will join us in passing our love of books on to the next generation of readers.

Did you know that reading for enjoyment is the single biggest predictor of a child's future happiness and success?

More than family circumstances, parents' educational background, or income, reading impacts a child's future academic performance, emotional well-being, communication skills, economic security, ambition, and happiness.

Studies show that kids reading for enjoyment in the US is in rapid decline:

- In 2012, 53% of 9-year-olds read almost every day. Just 10 years later, in 2022, the number had fallen to 39%.
- In 2012, 27% of 13-year-olds read for fun daily. By 2023, that number was just 14%.

Together, we can commit to **Raising Readers** and change this trend. How?

- Read to children in your life daily.
- Model reading as a fun activity.
- Reduce screen time.
- Start a family, school, or community book club.
- Visit bookstores and libraries regularly.
- Listen to audiobooks.
- Read the book before you see the movie.
- Encourage your child to read aloud to a pet or stuffed animal.
- Give books as gifts.
- Donate books to families and communities in need.

BOB1217

Books build bright futures, and **Raising Readers** is our shared responsibility.

For more information, visit **JoinRaisingReaders.com**

Sources: National Endowment for the Arts, National Assessment of Educational Progress, WorldBookDay.com, Nielsen BookData's 2023 "Understanding the Children's Book Consumer"